Penny Jordan, one of Harlequin's most popular authors, unfortunately passed away on December 31, 2011. She leaves an outstanding legacy, having sold over 100 million books around the world. Penny wrote a total of 187 novels for Harlequin, including the phenomenally successful *A Perfect Family, To Love, Honor and Betray, The Perfect Sinner* and *Power Play,* which hit the *New York Times* bestseller list. Loved for her distinctive voice, she was successful in part because she continually broke boundaries and evolved her writing to keep up with readers' changing tastes. *Publishers Weekly* said about Jordan, "Women everywhere will find pieces of themselves in Jordan's characters." It is perhaps this gift for sympathetic characterization that helps to explain her enduring appeal.

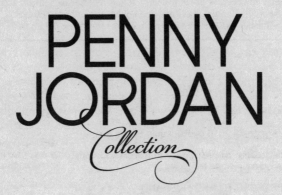

PENNY JORDAN
Collection

LEGALLY HIS

HARLEQUIN® READERS' CHOICE

ISBN-13: 978-0-373-24985-5

LEGALLY HIS

Copyright © 2013 by Harlequin Books S.A.

The publisher acknowledges the copyright holder of the individual works as follows:

MISTRESS TO HER HUSBAND
Copyright © 2004 by Penny Jordan

THE BLACKMAIL BABY
Copyright © 2002 by Penny Jordan

Recycling programs for this product may not exist in your area.

Printed in U.S.A.

www.Harlequin.com

CONTENTS

MISTRESS TO
HER HUSBAND

CHAPTER ONE

'KATE YOU'LL NEVER guess what! John told us this morning, whilst you were at the dentist. The business has been taken over. And the new boss is coming in tomorrow to interview everyone!'

Kate Vincent digested her co-worker's excited comments in silence. Dropping enviably thick, dark lashes reflectively over topaz eyes, she considered what she had been told. She had only been with the company for six months, as before that she'd only been able to manage a part-time job whilst she was completing her Master's. With the qualification nicely enhancing her CV she had felt confident enough to apply for this post, which previously she would have considered out of her range.

'So who's taking us over?' Kate questioned Laura, absently flipping the smooth length of her chestnut-brown hair over her shoulder as she did so. It had been hot outside in the street, and the coolness of the office's air-conditioning was very welcome.

'Well, John wouldn't say,' Laura responded, suppressing a small envious sigh as she studied Kate's elegantly slender body, clad in a neat white T-shirt teamed with a chocolate-brown linen skirt.

Laura had been with her when Kate had bought the skirt, an end-of-line sale buy which she herself would have deemed dull. But on Kate it looked not just good, but also somehow discreetly expensive.

'Apparently everything has to be kept hush-hush until tomorrow.' She gave Kate a rueful look.

'I suppose we should have seen it coming. After all, John has been hinting for ages that he'd like to take early retirement—but I never thought he was contemplating selling out. Mind you, he and Sheila don't have any children, do they? So I don't suppose there's much point in hanging on when they could be spending their time in that condo of theirs in Miami.'

Kate listened intently to Laura as she booted up her computer. The business John Loames had set up to supply specialist facilities and equipment to the building trade had been very successful, but Kate had seen for herself since she had started to work for the small private company as its accounts executive that John was growing less and less inclined to seek out new contracts. Which was a pity, because she knew that the business had a great deal of potential, and she was not entirely surprised that someone had bought John out.

'Everyone's worried about what might happen,' Laura confided to her. 'None of us want to lose our jobs.'

'Someone new taking over might not necessarily be a bad thing,' Kate pointed out to her calmly. 'There's ample room for the business to be expanded, and then there would be more than enough work for all of us—provided, of course, the new owner doesn't already own a similar business and just wants to amalgamate John's with his own.'

'Oh, don't say that!' Laura begged worriedly, giving a small shudder. 'Roy and I have only just increased our mortgage so that we can extend the house.' Her face became slightly pink. 'We're trying for a family, and a baby will mean that we definitely need extra space. The last thing I need right now is to lose my job! Which reminds me—John told us that he wants us all here especially early tomorrow. Apparently the new owner has said specifically that he will be here at eight.'

'Eight?' Kate switched her attention from her e-mails to Laura, her forehead crinkling in a worried frown. 'Are you telling me John wants us here at *eight*?'

'Yes.'

Kate's porcelain-clear skin paled slightly. It was impossible for her to make it to the office for eight o'clock in the morning. Pre-school didn't start until eight, and she would have to leave Ollie at seven-thirty at the very latest if she was to make it here for eight. She could feel the tension cramping her stomach.

It was hard enough for any mother to work full time—a constant finely-judged balancing act—but when one added into that delicate balance the fact that the mother in question was a single parent, fighting desperately hard to give as much emotional security as two loving parents would, plus the fact that she had not told her employers that she had child, then that balancing act became dangerously unstable.

Just thinking about Ollie was enough to have her stomach twisting in knots of maternal protective anxiety.

'What's wrong?' Laura asked curiously, sensing her tension.

'Er...nothing.'

Kate hadn't told anyone at work about Ollie. All too sensitive to the attitude of colleagues and employers to the difficulties that came hand in hand with a worker who was a mother—especially a single mother—Kate had made no mention of her son during her interview with John. It had only been after she had started to work for the company that she had learned that John had a somewhat old-fashioned attitude about employing women with very young children.

By then she had realised how well suited she was to her job, and it to her, and although it had caused her some sleepless nights and many qualms, she had decided to keep Ollie's existence a secret. Since she was fiercely honest by nature, this decision had pricked her conscience on more than one occasion, but she had told herself that it was a necessary omission if she was to succeed with her career plans.

She was well qualified now, and she was determined to provide her son with at least some of the material benefits he would have enjoyed had his father not abandoned her.

His father! Kate could feel the cold sickness and despair laced with anger spewing up inside her—it was a mixture as dangerous and toxic as arsenic, but she was the one it threatened to poison and destroy, not the man who had broken her heart and deserted her.

Now she considered that she and Oliver were better off without him—even though what she was earning only just covered the mortgage she was paying on the tiny cottage she had bought in a pretty village several miles away from the town and Oliver's out-of-school childcare, leaving just enough for food and other essentials.

Childcare! Her lips, normally soft and sweetly curved, hardened and thinned. *She* was the best person to be providing her son with childcare, but she was not in a financial position to be able to do so.

Her current job was the first rung on the career ladder she was going to have to climb in order to support them both properly. The head of her department was due to retire in two years' time, and Kate had secretly been hoping that if she did her job well enough John might promote her into the vacancy.

Her twenty-fifth birthday wasn't that far away, and neither was Ollie's fifth. His fifth birthday and her fifth year of being alone, of being without— Swiftly Kate buried the potentially damaging thoughts. She didn't need them, she didn't want them, and she damn well wasn't going to let them disturb her hard-won peace of mind.

It was her future she needed to focus on, and not her past! This takeover could destroy any chance she might have had of such a promotion, but it might also give her increased opportunities, she reflected, as she studied some comparison charts she had set up on her own initiative, to see which customers could be approached to increase their orders.

As she stood in the open doorway of the small village nursery and watched her son run towards her, his face lighting up as he saw her, Kate felt her heart contract with love. When she bent to scoop him up into her arms, and buried her face into the warm flesh of his neck to breathe in his delicious little-boy smell, she knew that no matter what sacrifices she had to make, or how hard she had to work, she would do it for Ollie's sake.

A small frown pleated her forehead as she looked round the classroom, empty now of the other children. She had chosen to live in the village because she had wanted to provide Ollie with a sense of belonging and community, to provide him with the kind of childhood she herself had been denied. But living here meant she had to travel to the city to work, which in turn meant that Ollie had to wait for her long after the others had been collected.

She had never intended that her child should grow up like this—an only child with no family other than her. She had wanted things to be so different for her child, her children, than they had been for her.

Two loving parents, siblings, the sure knowledge of being loved and wanted. *The sure knowledge of being loved and wanted!*

Pain gripped her. It had been five years—surely only a

woman with no sense of self-worth or self-respect would allow herself to think about a man who had betrayed her love and rejected her? A man who had sworn love for ever, who had sworn that he shared her dreams and goals, who had taught her to trust and love him, and who had whispered against her lips as he took her virginal body that he wanted to give her his child, that he wanted to surround that child with love and security.

A man who had lied to her and left her broken-hearted, disillusioned, and completely alone.

To be with him she had gone against the wishes of the aunt and uncle who had brought her up, and because of that they had disowned her.

Not that Kate would have wanted her aunt and uncle involved in the life of her precious son. They might have given her a home when she had been orphaned, but they had done so out of duty and not love. And she had craved love so badly, so very badly.

'Ollie was beginning to worry.'

The faint hint of reproach in the nursery teacher's voice made Kate wince inwardly.

'I know I'm a bit late,' she apologised. 'There was an accident on the bypass.'

The nursery teacher was comfortably round and in late middle age. She had grandchildren herself, and her small charges loved and respected her. Kate had lost count of the number of time she had heard Ollie insisting, 'But Mary says…'

Ten minutes later Kate was unlocking the door to their small cottage. It was right in the centre of the village, its front windows overlooking the green, with its duck pond, and at the back of the house a long narrow garden.

Ollie was a sturdily built child, with firm solid muscles

and a head of thick black curls. An inheritance from his father, although Ollie himself did not know it.

So far as Kate was concerned the man who had fathered her son no longer existed, and she refused to allow him any place in their lives. Ollie's placid nature meant that until recently he had accepted that he did not have a father, without asking Kate very many questions about him. However, the fact that his new best friend *did* have a father had led to Ollie starting to want to know more.

Kate frowned. So far Ollie had been content with her responses, but it made her heart ache to see the way he watched longingly whilst Tom Lawson played with his son.

Sean unfurled his long body from the seat of his Mercedes and stood still whilst he looked at the building in front of him.

His handmade Savile Row suit sat elegantly on his lean-limbed body, the jacket subtly masking the powerful breadth of his shoulders and the muscles he had built up in the years when he had earned his living hiring himself out to whichever builder would take him on.

His sweat had gone into the making of more than one motorway, as well as several housing estates, but even in those days as an ill-educated teenager he had promised himself that one day things would be different, that one day he would be the man giving the orders and not taking them.

As a young child he'd literally had to fight for his food until, aged five, he'd been abandoned by his hippie mother and been taken into care. In his twenties he had spent his days building extensions, and anything else he would get paid for, and his nights studying for a Business Studies degree. He had celebrated his thirty-first birthday by selling the building company he had built up from nothing for twenty million. Had he wanted to do so, he could have retired. But that was not his way. He had seen the potential of companies such as John's and had seized the opportunities with both hands. He was now thirty-five.

He had big expansion plans for the business he had just acquired, but for his plans to succeed he needed the right kind of workforce. A dedicated, energetic, enthusiastic and ambitious workforce. This morning he was going to meet his new employees, and he was going to assess them in the same way he had assessed those who had worked for him when he had first set up in business—by meeting them face to face. Then—and only then—would he read their personnel files.

He was an arrestingly good-looking man, but the early-morning sunlight picked out the harsh lines that slashed from his nose to his mouth and revealed a man of gritty determination who rarely smiled. He wore his obvious sexuality with open cynicism, and it glittered in the dense Celtic blue of his eyes now, as a young woman stopped walking to give him an appreciative and appraising look.

In the years since he had made his millions he had been pursued by some extraordinarily beautiful women, but Sean knew that they would have turned away in disgust and contempt from the young man he had once been.

Something—part bitterness and part pain—took the warmth from his gaze and dulled its blueness.

He had come a long way from what he had once been. A long way—and yet still not far enough?

Locking his car, he started to stride towards the building.

Kate could feel perspiration beginning to dew her forehead as she willed the traffic lights to change. Her stomach was so tight with nervous anxiety that it hurt.

She had swallowed her normal pride last night and asked Carol, Ollie's best friend's mother, if she could leave Ollie with her at seven-thirty for her to take him on to school with her son George. The pain in her stomach intensified. She hated treating her precious son as though he was a...a bundle of washing!

Why on earth had the new owner insisted on them arriving so early? Was he just unthinking, or uncaring? Whichever it was, it did not bode well for her future with the company, she decided fretfully.

As she reached the traffic lights she saw the broken-down car which had been the cause of the delay. It was already ten past eight, and it would take her at least another ten minutes to get to work.

Half past eight! Kate gritted her teeth as she hurried into the building. She was already walking fast, and she broke into an anxious run as she covered the last few yards. But the hope she had had that she might be able to slide discreetly into John's office whilst the meeting was still in progress was destroyed as the door opened and her colleagues came out into the corridor.

'You're late!' Laura whispered as she saw Kate. 'What happened?'

It was difficult to talk with so many people in the corridor.

'I'll tell you later—' she began, and then froze as two men came through the door.

One of them was John, and the other...the other...

The other was her ex-husband!

'Perhaps you'd like to tell *me*—now?'

How well she remembered that smooth chocolate voice, with its underlying ice.

People were staring at her, Kate realised, and she fought off her sick shock.

John was looking anguished and uncomfortable. 'Sean, I think perhaps... I am sure that...'

Arrogantly ignoring John, Sean demanded, 'In here!' He was holding the door open, waiting for her to walk past him and into John's office.

For a moment their gazes met and clashed, battled, topaz fighting dense blue for supremacy.

Her ex-husband was their new boss!

How could fate have dealt her such a low blow?

When Sean had walked out of her life to be with the woman he was leaving her for she had prayed that she would never, ever have to see him again. She had given him everything she had had to give—defying her aunt and uncle to be with him, helping and encouraging him, loving him—but that had not been enough for him. She had not been enough for him. The success she had helped him to achieve had meant that he no longer considered her good enough for him.

She was holding her breath and badly needed to exhale, but she was terrified that if she did she was going to start shaking—and there was so way she was going to allow Sean to witness that kind of vulnerability.

How well she remembered that challenging hard-edged blue gaze. He had looked at her like that the first time they had met, defying her to ignore him. No one would dare to ignore him now.

'Kate is a very—' She could hear John about to defend her.

'Thank you, John. I shall deal with this myself,' Sean announced curtly as she walked past him into the room, and he closed the door, excluding John from his own office.

'Kate?' he demanded grimly. 'What happened to Kathy?'

Just hearing him say that name resurrected far too many painful memories. She had been Kathy when he had taunted her the first time they had met, for being too posh to dance with a man like him. And she had been Kathy too when he had taken her in his arms and shown her— Fiercely she pushed away the tormenting memories.

Tilting her chin, she said coldly, 'Kathy?' She gave a mirthless laugh. 'She doesn't exist any longer, Sean. You destroyed her when you destroyed our marriage.'

'And your surname is?' Sean wondered whether she could hear or understand the cause of the anger that was making his throat raw and his voice terse as he grappled with his own shock.

'Kate Vincent,' Kate answered him coldly.

'Vincent?' he questioned savagely.

'Yes, Vincent. You didn't think I would want to keep your name, did you? And I certainly didn't want my aunt and uncle's—after all, like you, they didn't want me.'

'So you remarried just to change your name?'

Anger darkened Kate's eyes as she heard the contempt in his voice.

'Why were you late?' Sean demanded abruptly. 'Didn't he want to let you out of his bed?'

Furious colour scorched Kate's face.

'Just because you—' she began, and then stopped, swallowing hard as out of nowhere the memories started to fill her head. Sean waking her up in the morning with the gentlest of kisses…that was until she was fully awake…and then…

She could feel the tension building up inside her body, a tension activated by memories crowding out the reality she was trying desperately hard to cling on to, to use as a bulwark.

A bulwark? Against what? The love she had once felt for Sean had been completely destroyed, and by Sean himself. Cruelly and deliberately. Her body stiffened with pride. She was glad that he thought she had found someone else. Married someone else.

Had he married the woman he had left her for?

Sean's mobile rang, and he answered it, frowning briefly as he told Kate that she could go.

As she turned to leave Kate heard a female voice saying, quite clearly, 'Sean, darling...'

Kate was halfway through clearing out her desk when Laura came in.

'What on earth are you doing?' she demanded.

'Clearing my desk. What does it look like?' Kate responded tersely.

'You're leaving?'

Kate could see how shocked and dismayed Laura was.

'You mean he's sacked you just for being late?'

Kate permitted herself a thin and slightly bitter smile. 'No, he hasn't sacked me, but let's just say I'm leaving ahead of having him do so.'

'Oh, Kate, no!' Laura protested, obviously upset. 'I can see that things have got off to bad start for you—!' She stopped, biting her lip and looking uncomfortable.

Laura would never make a politician, Kate reflected wryly, witnessing her colleague's discomfort.

'Laura?' she prodded firmly.

'Well, I'm sure he didn't mean anything—to be critical...or unkind. But I did hear Sean asking John where you were,' Laura admitted reluctantly, adding quickly, 'I'm sure he'll be understanding, Kate. He seems such a sweetie, and so gorgeous.'

A sweetie! Sean! Kate suppressed a bitter laugh.

Sean might be many things, but he had never been a sweetie—not even when she had first known him.

A tough, streetwise, untamed rogue male, who could make a girl go weak at the knees and hot in places she hadn't previously known existed with just one taunting look, that was what he had been. And she...

Her face started to burn as she recognised where her unwanted thoughts were leading. She switched on her computer and started to type.

'Oh, thank goodness you've changed your mind,' Laura began, with relief, but Kate shook her head.

'No, I haven't. I'm just typing out my notice,' Kate informed her crisply.

'Your notice! Oh, Kate.' Laura looked aghast, and immediately tried to dissuade her, but Kate refused to let herself be swayed.

Finishing her typing, she checked and then printed off her letter, placing it neatly in an envelope, which she put in the internal post tray.

Her task completed, she headed for the door.

'Where are you going?' Laura demanded anxiously.

'I'm leaving,' Kate answered patiently. 'I've written my resignation letter. As of now, I no longer work here!'

'But, Kate, you can't leave just like that—without telling anyone!' Laura protested.

'Watch me!' Kate answered succinctly, walking calmly towards the door.

But inwardly she was feeling far from calm. Frantically she clamped down on her treacherous thoughts.

Kathy was working here! Sean paced the floor of his office, having terminated the call from the wife of his financial adviser. She had called to invite him to a dinner party she was planning, but Sean did not do dinner parties. His mouth twisted bitterly. Until he had met Kathy he hadn't even known the correct cutlery to use. She had been the one who had gently taught him. Gently rubbed off his rough edges. And he...

He strode angrily over to the office window and stared out of it. He had deliberately not kept track of Kathy after their divorce. There hadn't been any point. The marriage had been over and he had made her a generous financial settlement, even if she had returned it to his solicitor intact. Who had she married? When had she married him?

He went back to the desk and picked up the personnel files he had not yet read.

CHAPTER TWO

As SHE CLIMBED out of her car Kate acknowledged that really there was no way she should have been driving. She was shaking from head to foot, and she had no real idea of how she had driven home. The entire journey had been a pain-fuelled blur of fighting back unwanted memories whilst surge after surge of panic and anger had washed through her.

'Kate!'

Kate tried to looked relaxed and smile as Carol, her friend and neighbour, came hurrying towards her.

'What are you doing back so early?' Carol asked, adding teasingly, 'Did the interview go so well that the new boss gave you the rest of the day off?'

Kate opened her mouth to make a suitably light-hearted response, but to her chagrin she could feel her lips starting to tremble as emotions overwhelmed her.

'I've handed in my notice,' she told Carol shakily. 'I… I had to… My…the new boss is my ex-husband!' Tears filled her eyes. She was shaking so violently she could have been in shock, Kate recognised distantly.

'Come on, let's get you inside,' she heard Carol announcing in a motherly voice. 'And then you can tell me all about it.'

Ten minutes later, after she had made them both a cup of coffee and chatted calmly about their sons, Carol turned to

Kate and said gently, 'I'm not going to pry, Kate, but if you want to get it off your chest I'm a good listener, and I promise it won't go any further.' When Kate made no response, but simply continued to sit huddled in her chair, her hands gripping her coffee mug, Carol added quietly, 'Not even to Tom, if that's what you want.'

Kate turned her head to look at her, her gaze blank and withdrawn, then forced herself to focus on her friend.

Taking a deep breath, she began to speak, slowly and painfully. 'I met Sean when I was eighteen. He was building an extension for my aunt and uncle's neighbours. We'd had a very hot summer, and he worked bare-chested in a pair of old tight-fitting jeans—'

'Mmm, sexy. I can picture the scene.' Carol smiled encouragingly, relieved to see just the merest twitch of humour lifting Kate's mouth.

'I used to walk the long way round just so that I could see him,' Kate admitted. 'I hadn't thought he'd notice me, but then one night at a local club he was there and he asked me to dance. Fantasising over him when I walked past the building site was one thing. Being confronted with him there in front of me in the flesh was another! I felt intimidated by him.' Kate gave small shrug and looked at Carol.

'I was a naïve eighteen-year-old virgin, and all that fierce, potent hot male sexuality was a bit overwhelming. Unfortunately he thought I was rejecting him, and...' She shook her head. 'I didn't know it then, but like me he'd had a very unhappy and lonely childhood, which had left him with a bit of a chip on his shoulder and a determination to succeed. I can see now that I was a bit of a challenge to him, because I was a girl from a different background. A trophy girlfriend, I suppose the press would call it nowadays, and for a while I was good enough for him as just that. Good enough to marry, in fact. But once he'd become very successful I think he began to realise that I wasn't much of a trophy after all, and that with his money he could afford a much, much better one than me.'

Carol could hear the pain in Kate's voice. 'You obviously loved him,' she said softly.

'Loved him?' Kate looked at her starkly, her emotions darkening her eyes. 'Yes, I loved him—totally and completely, blindly and foolishly I realise now. Because I believed then that he felt the same way about me!'

'Oh, Kate!' Carol sympathised, her own eyes prickling with emotion as she covered Kate's cold folded hands with her own.

Kate swallowed and then continued. 'My aunt and uncle were furious when it came out that I was seeing him—especially my aunt. There was a dreadful row, and it came out that she had never liked my mother, had been appalled when she had married her brother. She told me that if I didn't agree to stop seeing Sean they would wash their hands of me and disown me. But I couldn't give Sean up. I loved him too much. He had become my whole world! And when I told him what my aunt had said he told me that he wasn't going to let me go back to them, to be hurt and bullied, that from now on he would look after me.'

Kate exhaled in a deep sigh.

'We were married six weeks later. Sean had finished the extension by then, and was ready to move on to his next job.'

Carol could see the events of the day were beginning to catch up with Kate and, surveying her friend's exhausted hollow-cheeked face, she stood up and told her firmly, 'Look, you're all in. Why don't you have a rest? I'll collect Oliver from nursery, if you like, and give him his tea.'

Kate was tempted to refuse. But while a part of her was longing desperately to have the warm, solid feel of Oliver's sturdy body in her arms, so that she could hold him and take comfort from his presence, another part of her said that this was not fair to her son and that she must not get into the habit of leaning on him emotionally. And anyway, she had things to do, she reminded herself grimly. Like finding a new job for a start!

'You're very kind,' she told Carol wanly.

'Nonsense. I know you'd do the same for me.'

She would, of course, but it was hardly likely that she would ever be asked to do so, Kate acknowledged wearily after Carol had gone. Carol had a loving husband, and George had two sets of adoring grandparents only too willing to spend as much time as they could with their grandson.

And Oliver only had her. No grandparents. Just her. Just her? What about Sean? He was Oliver's father, after all, Kate reminded herself angrily.

Sean!

Her whole body felt heavy with misery and despair. She had struggled so hard, and it seemed so unfair that she should have her precious financial security snatched from her because her ex-husband had taken over the company.

For the first time since Sean had announced that their marriage was over Kate felt angry with herself for not accepting the generous pay-off he had offered her. Two million pounds and she had turned it down! She had turned it down not knowing that she was already pregnant with Oliver. And then, when she had realised… Well, she had sworn that she would never ask for anything from the man who had cold-bloodedly told her that he had changed his mind about wanting to be a father and that he had no desire to tie himself to a wife he no longer loved.

The pain was just as sharp as she remembered it being, and she stiffened against it. It should not exist any more. It should have been destroyed, just like Sean had destroyed their marriage.

All those things he had said to her and she had believed in; like how he, too, longed for children. All those promises he had made her—that those children, their children, would have the parental love neither of them had ever known. They had all been lies.

Against her will Kate could feel herself being drawn back into the past and its painful memories.

There had been no warning of what was to come, or of how vulnerable her happiness was. In fact only the previous month Sean had taken her away on an idyllic and very romantic break to an exclusive country house hotel—to make up, he had told her lovingly, for the fact that the negotiations he had been involved in to secure a very valuable contract had gone on so long that they had not been able to have a summer holiday.

They had arrived late in the afternoon and had enjoyed a leisurely and very romantic walk through the grounds. And then they had gone back to their room and Sean had undressed her and made love to her.

They had been late for dinner, she remembered—very late. And during it Sean had handed her a large brown envelope, telling her to open it. When she had done so she had found inside the sale details of a pretty Georgian rectory she and Sean had driven past early in the year.

'You said it was the kind of place you had always wanted to live in,' he had reminded her simply. 'It's coming up for sale.'

She'd spent the rest of the evening in a daze, already excitedly planning how she would decorate the house, and insisting that Sean listen to her as she went through the house room by room.

They had made love again that night, and in the morning. And afterwards she had lain in Sean's arms, her eyes closed, whilst she luxuriated in breathing in the sexually replete scent of him and wondered what on earth she had done to merit such happiness.

Less than a month later she had been wondering what on earth she had done to merit such intense pain.

One minute—or so she had thought—Sean had been negotiating for the purchase of the rectory; the next he had been telling her that he no longer loved her and that he intended to divorce her.

Kate closed her eyes and lay back in her chair. She felt both physically and emotionally exhausted. What she should be doing right now, she told herself grimly, was worrying about how she was going to get another job, instead of wallowing in self-pity about the past.

She would have to enrol with an employment agency, and then probably take on as much work as she could get until she found a permanent position. She had some savings— her rainy day money—but that would not last for very long.

Why, why, *why* had Sean had to come back into her life like this? Hadn't he hurt her enough?

Tiredly Kate stopped trying to fight her exhaustion and allowed herself to drift off to sleep.

The dream was one she had had before. She tried to pull herself awake and out of it, as she had taught herself to do, but it was too late. It was rushing down on her, swamping her, and she was already lost in it.

She was with Sean, in the sitting room of their house. It was mid-afternoon and he had come home early from work. She ran to greet him, but he pushed her away, his expression not that of the husband she knew but that of the angry, aggressive man he had been when she had first met him.

'Sean, what's wrong?' she asked him, reaching out a hand to him and flinching as he ignored her loving gesture. He turned away from her and walked over to the window, blocking out its light. Uncomprehendingly she watched him, and the first tendrils of fear began to curl around her heart.

'I want a divorce.'

'A divorce! No… What…? Sean, what are you saying?' she demanded, panic, shock and disbelief gripping hold of her throat and giving her voice a hoarse, choked sound that seemed to echo round the room.

'I'm saying that our marriage is over and I want a divorce.'

'No! No! You don't mean that. You can't mean that!' Was that piteous little voice really her own? 'You love me.'

'I thought I did,' Sean agreed coldly. 'But I've realised that I don't. You and I want different things out of life, Kathy. You want children. I'm sick of having to listen to you boring on about it. I don't want children!'

'That's not true. How can you say that, Sean?' She stared at him in disbelief, unable to understand what he was saying. 'You've always said how much you want children,' she reminded him shakily. 'We said we wanted a big family because our own childhoods—'

If he heard the pain in her voice and was affected by it he certainly didn't show it.

'For God's sake,' he ground out. 'Grow up, will you, Kathy? When I said that I'd have said anything to get into your knickers.'

The contemptuous biting words flayed her sensitive emotions.

'Look, I don't intend to argue about this. Our marriage is over and that's that. I've already spoken to my solicitor. You'll be okay financially…'

'Is there someone else?'

Silently they looked at one another whilst Kathy prayed that he would say no, but instead he taunted her. 'What do you think?'

Her whole body was shaking, and even though she didn't want to she started to cry, sobbing out Sean's name in frantic pleading disbelief...

Why the hell was he doing this? Sean's hands clenched on the wheel as he drove. What was the point in risking resurrecting the past? She was easily replaceable. But Sean knew that he was being unfair. She was, according to John and from what he had been able to recognise himself, an extremely intelligent and diligent employee—the kind of employee, in fact, that he wanted. No way was he going to allow her to walk out of her job without working her statutory notice period.

She was his ex-wife, damn it, Sean reminded himself grimly. But this was nothing to do with her being his ex-wife, and nothing to do either with the fact that he had discovered from her records, contrary to his assumptions, she was not married.

He was in the village now, and his mouth hardened slightly. Oh, yes, this was exactly the kind of environment she liked. Small, cosy, homely—everything that her life with her appalling aunt and uncle had not been.

He swung the car into a parking space he had spotted, stopped the engine and got out.

He hadn't told anyone as yet about the fact that she had handed in her notice. Officially she was still in the company's employ...in his employ.

He skirted the duck pond, his eyes bleak as he headed for Kate's front door.

He was just about to knock when an elderly woman who had been watching him from her own front gate called out to him.

'You'll have to go round the back, young man.'

Young man! Sean grimaced. He didn't think he had ever

been young—he had never been *allowed* to be young! And as for being a man... Something dark and dangerous hardened his whole face as he obeyed the elderly woman's instructions.

It took him several minutes to find the path which ran behind the back gardens of the cottages. The gate to Kate's wouldn't open at first, and then he realised that it was bolted on the inside and he had to reach over to unbolt it. Hardly a good anti-thief device, he reflected, giving it a frowning and derisory look as he unfastened it and walked up the path.

He frowned even more when he realised that the back door was slightly open. If Kate had had his upbringing she would have been a damn sight more safety conscious!

His hand was on the door when he heard her cry out his name.

He reacted immediately, thrusting open the door and striding into the kitchen, then coming to an abrupt halt when he saw her lying in the chair asleep. He felt as though all the air had been knocked out of his lungs, his chest tightening whilst he tried to draw in a ragged breath of air.

He had always loved watching her as she slept, absorbing the sight of her with a greedy secret pleasure—her long dark lashes, lying silkily against her delicate skin, her lips slightly parted, her face turned to one side so that the whole of one pretty ear was visible. The very fact that she was asleep made her so vulnerable, showed how much she trusted him, showed how much she was in need of his protection...

Without thinking Sean stepped forward, his hand lifting to push the heavy swathe of hair off her face, and then abruptly he realised that this was the present, not the past, and he stopped.

But it was too late. Somehow, as though she had sensed he was there, Kate cried out his name in great distress. For a second he hesitated, and then, taking a deep breath, he put his hand on her shoulder and gave her a small squeeze.

Immediately Kate woke up, and as she opened her eyes he demanded brusquely, 'Sean, what?'

Kate stared up at him. Her dream was still fogging her brain, and it took her several valuable seconds to wake up fully, incomprehension clouding her eyes.

'You were crying out my name,' Sean prompted softly.

Kate felt a prickle of awareness run over her. And then the reality of what she had been dreaming hit her. Her face started to burn. All at once there was a dangerous tension in the small room.

'I was dreaming, that's all,' she defended herself sharply.

'Do you often dream about me?'

The danger was increasing by the heartbeat.

She could feel her skin tightening in reaction to his taunt. 'It was more of a nightmare,' she retaliated quickly.

'You haven't remarried.' He said it flatly, like an accusation, in an abrupt change of tack.

Clumsily Kate got to her feet. Even standing up she was still a long way short of his height. She cursed the fact that she was not wearing her heels, and felt the old bitterness mobilising inside her.

'Remarry? Do you really think I would want to risk marrying again after what you did to me?' she demanded hotly. 'No, I haven't remarried, and I never will.'

And there was also a very good reason why she wouldn't, but she had no intention of telling him so. It was her son. Her precious Ollie was not going to be given a stepfather who might not love him. Kate had firsthand knowledge of what that felt like, and she was not going to subject her son to the same misery she had known whilst she was growing up.

'Why did you change your name?'

So he still had that same skill at slipping in those dangerous questions like a knife between the ribs. She wanted to shiver, but she folded her arms instead, not wanting him to see her body's betrayal of her anxiety.

'Why shouldn't I? I certainly didn't want your name, and I didn't want my aunt and uncle's either, so I changed my name by deed poll to my mother's maiden name. What are you doing here anyway?' she demanded angrily. 'You have no right—'

'I've come round here because of this,' Sean said curtly, stopping her protests as he removed her letter of resignation from his jacket pocket, and with it another fat white envelope.

'This is your contract of employment,' he announced. 'It binds you to working a statutory notice period of four weeks. You can't just walk out on your job, Kate.'

Kate's mouth had gone dry, and she knew that her eyes were betraying her shock and her chagrin.

'You…you can't hold me to that,' she began valiantly. 'You—'

'Oh, yes, I can.' Sean stopped her swiftly. 'And I fully intend to do so.'

'But why?' Kate demanded wildly, stiffening as she heard in her own voice how close she was to the edge of her self-control. 'I should have thought you'd want me gone as much as I want to go, given the speed with which you ended our marriage! You can't want me working for you. Your ex-wife, the woman you rejected? The woman you—'

'Rules are rules—you are legally obliged to work your notice and I want you back at your desk so that you can hand over your responsibilities to your replacement.'

'You can't make me!' Kate protested. Her voice might sound strong and determined, but inside she was panicking, she recognised. She did, after all, have a legal obligation to work her notice period, and if she didn't it could cause other employers to think twice about taking her on. With Oliver to bring up she just could not afford to be out of work.

'Yes, I can,' Sean corrected her. 'You may have walked out on our marriage, but no way are you walking out of your job!'

Kate's shock deepened with every word he threw at her.

'I left because you were having an affair—you know that. You were the one who ended our marriage, Sean.'

'I'm not interested in discussing the past, only the present.'

His response left her floundering and vulnerable. It had been a mistake to refer to their marriage, and even more of a mistake to mention his affair. The last thing she wanted was to have him taunt her with still suffering because of it.

'I like value for my money, Kate. Surely you can remember that?'

His comment gave her a much needed opportunity to hit back at him, and she took it.

'I don't allow myself to remember anything about you.' The angry, contemptuous words were out before she could stop herself from saying them. She could feel the tightening of the tension between them, and with it came dangerous memories of a very different kind of tension they had once shared.

'Anything?' Sean challenged her rawly, as though he had somehow read her thoughts. 'Not even this?'

The feel of his hands on her arms, dragging her against his body, the heat of his flesh, the feel of his body itself against her own, was so shockingly and immediately familiar and welcome that she couldn't move.

Somehow, of its own volition, her body angled itself into Sean's. Somehow her hands were sliding beneath his jacket and up over his back. Somehow her head was tilting back and her eyes were opening wide, so that she could look into the familiar hot, passionate blue of his.

Shockingly, it was as though a part of her had been waiting for this, for him, and not just waiting but wanting, longing, needing.

The steady tick of the kitchen clock was drowned out by the sound of their mingled breathing: Sean's harsh and heavy; her own much lighter, shallow and unsteady.

The touch of his hand on the nape of her neck as his thumb slowly caressed her skin sent a signal to her body which it immediately answered.

Now she had to close her eyes, in case Sean could read in them what she could feel—the small, telling lift of her breasts as they surged in longing for his touch, the tight ache of her nipples as they hungered for his mouth, the swift clench of her belly and, lower than that, the softening swelling moistness of her sex.

She felt the hard warmth of his mouth and her own clung to it, her lips obediently parting to the fierce thrust of his tongue—a feeling she remembered so well.

Her fingers clenched into his shoulders beneath his suit jacket as the familiar possessive pressure of his kiss silenced the moan of pleasure bubbling in her throat.

When his hands dropped to her hips, and his fingers curled round the slenderness of her bones, Kate went weak with longing. Soon he would be touching her breasts, tugging fiercely at her clothes in his hunger to touch her intimately. And she wanted him to. She wanted him to so much.

Fine shudders of eager longing were already surging rhythmically through her. If she slid her hand down from his back she could touch the hard readiness of him, stroke her fingers along it, tormenting him, tormenting them both until he picked her up and—

'Mummy…?'

The sound of Oliver's voice from the other side of the back door jolted her back to reality.

Immediately Kate pulled back from Sean, and equally immediately he released her, so that when the door opened and Oliver came in, followed by Carol, they were standing three feet apart, ignoring one another.

'Ollie wanted to come home, so—' Carol came to a halt as she saw Sean, and looked uncertainly at Kate.

'Thanks, Carol.' Kate bent down to receive the full weight of Oliver's compact sturdy little-boy body as he ran towards her, only too glad of an excuse to conceal her face. Picking up Oliver, she avoided looking at both her neighbour and Sean.

'Er...I'll be off, then,' she heard Carol saying hurriedly as she backed out of the door.

Sean stared at the child in Kate's arms in shocked disbelief. She had a child—it was her child; he knew that. She had a child, which meant... Which meant that some other man must have...

Oliver was wriggling in her arms and demanding to be put down. Reluctantly Kate gave in and did so. The moment his feet touched the floor he turned to look at Sean, and Kate felt as though her heart was being clenched in a hard, hurting fist when he demanded, 'Who are you?'

'Ollie, it's bedtime,' she told him firmly, and without looking at Sean she added, 'I would like you to leave.'

'I meant what I said about working for me, Kathy,' Sean responded grimly.

'Don't call me Kathy!'

Too late Kate realised that Oliver was reacting to the anger in her voice. His eyes rounded and he put his hand in hers and stared at Sean. But her distress at upsetting him was nothing compared to the rage she felt when Sean told her curtly, 'You're upsetting the boy!'

To her shock, and before she could voice her fury, Sean bent down and picked Ollie up in his arms.

Kate waited for her son to struggle, as he always did when anyone unfamiliar touched him, but to her chagrin, instead of pulling away from Sean he leaned into him, looking at him gravely in silence before heaving a huge sigh and then saying determinedly, 'Story, please, man!'

Kate felt as though her heart was going to break. Her ex-husband was holding their son, and Oliver was looking at his father as though he were all of his heroes rolled into one. The pain knifing into her was unbearable. She wanted to snatch Oliver out of Sean's arms and hold him protectively in her own. Her poor baby didn't know that his father had rejected the very idea of him even before he was born!

'Oliver's friend's father reads him a story when he comes home from work,' she told Sean in a stilted voice, in explanation of her son's demand.

Oliver! She had even called the child by the name he had... And yet as he looked into the little boy's solemn eyes Sean found it impossible to resent or hate him.

'Story?' he enquired, smiling at him and ignoring Kate.

Oliver nodded his head enthusiastically. 'Mummy— book,' he commanded imperiously, turning his head to look at Kate.

'Please use proper sentences, Oliver,' Kate reminded him automatically.

'Mummy, give me book for man to read, please.' Oliver smiled winningly and Kate could feel her whole body melting with love.

'Sean has to go,' she informed Oliver, automatically using Sean's name without thinking. 'I will read you a story later.'

'No. Sean read Oliver story!'

The frowning pout he was giving reinforced Kate's awareness that her son was overtired, and all too likely to have one of his rare tantrums if he was thwarted—the very last thing she wanted him to do in front of Sean, who would no doubt enjoy seeing her in such an embarrassing situation.

'Why don't you just give me the book?'

The quiet voice and its soft tone made Kate turn her head and stare at Sean in surprise. Oliver was already lying against Sean's shoulder.

'It isn't really his bedtime yet,' she said.

'Is there a law which says he can only have a story at bedtime?'

Mutely Kate shook her head, too caught up in the heart-wrenching sight of her son in his father's arms to protest any further as she went to get Oliver's favourite story book.

Half an hour later Sean nestled Oliver deeper into his arms and told Kate, 'By the looks of him he needs to be in bed.'

'Yes. I'll take him up.'

Automatically she moved to take Oliver from him, but Sean shook his head.

'I'll take him up. Just tell me which room.'

Weakly, she did so.

As he laid Oliver down on his small bed Sean felt the ache of an old and powerful emotion he had thought safely destroyed. Kathy's child. He could feel his eyes starting to blur and he blinked fiercely.

As he left the room he hesitated outside the other bedroom door, and then quickly opened it.

'Where are you going? That's my bedroom!'

He hadn't heard Kate come up the stairs, and they confronted one another on the small landing.

'And you sleep there alone?' He couldn't stop himself from asking the question he knew he had no right to ask.

'No. I don't!' Kate turned her head, not wanting him to see the expression in her eyes and therefore missing the one in his. 'Sometimes Oliver comes in and gets into bed with me,' she continued.

He had no valid reason to feel the way he did right now, Sean acknowledged, and no valid right either!

'How do you manage on your own? I know you work full-time.' He was frowning, looking as though he was genuinely concerned, and Kate turned away from him quickly and hurried towards the stairs. She wasn't going to make that mistake again—thinking that Sean had real feelings.

'I manage because I have to, for Oliver's sake. I'm all he's got—'

'You mean his father abandoned you?' His voice was harsh and almost condemning. 'He left you?'

Kate could hardly believe the censure she could hear in his voice. 'Yes, he did,' she agreed as calmly as she could, once they were both back downstairs. 'But personally I think that Ollie and I are better off without him.'

She walked purposefully to the front door and unlocked it, pulling it open and making it clear that she wanted Sean to leave.

'I want you back at your desk tomorrow morning,' Sean warned her curtly.

'Well, I'm afraid I'm not going to be there,' Kate responded, equally curtly.

'I warned you, Kate—' Sean began.

'Tomorrow is Saturday, Sean,' she reminded him dryly. 'We don't work weekends.'

There was a small, telling pause, during which Kate wondered what the woman who now shared his life thought about the fact that he obviously worked seven days a week, and then he said, 'Very well. Monday morning, then, Kate. Be there, or face the consequences.' He walked past her and out of the door.

CHAPTER THREE

'No!' ANGRILY KATE sat up in bed. It was three o'clock on Monday morning and she needed to be asleep, not lying there thinking about Sean, remembering how it had felt when he—

'No!' she protested again, groaning in anguish as she rolled over and buried her face in her pillow. But it was no use; neither her memories nor her feelings were going to be ignored.

Well, if she couldn't ignore them then at least she could use them to remind herself of how Sean had hurt her. To inoculate herself against him doing so again, because on Friday, when he had kissed her, she had nearly forgiven him...

She could feel the sharp quiver of sensation aching through her body. So her body remembered that Sean had been its lover, she acknowledged angrily—well, her heart had an equally good memory, if not an even better one, and what it remembered was the pain he had caused it.

But the love between them had been so...so wonderful. Sean had been a passionate and exciting lover who had taught her things about her own body, as well as his, and their mutual capacity for pleasure had been something she had never even dreamed could exist.

Why was she torturing herself like this? And if she was

doing it then why didn't she do it properly and remember just what it had felt like that first time he had made love to her?

After she had left her aunt and uncle's house—she had never thought of it as home—she had moved into Sean's small flat, but he had told her that he was not going to make love to her properly until they were married. Through the weeks and months when he had courted her he had steadfastly refused to take their passionately intense love-play to the conclusion she ached for, warning her thrillingly—for her—that he was afraid that if he did so she would become pregnant.

'There's no way my baby is going to be born a bastard like I was,' he had said grimly.

He had been reluctant to talk to her about his childhood at first, but she had slowly coaxed the painful truth out of him, and they had shared with one another their dream of creating for their own children the idyllic, love-filled childhood neither of them had known.

'But we could use some contraception,' she had suggested, pink-cheeked.

'We could, but we aren't going to,' Sean had replied with that dangerously exciting hunger in his voice. 'Because when we make love, when you give yourself to me, Kathy, I want it to be skin to skin, not with a damn piece of rubber between us,' he had told her earthily.

They had married in the small country town where her own long-dead mother had originally come from—a wonderfully romantic gesture on Sean's part, so far as Kate had been concerned. And in order to marry there they had had to live in the town for three weeks prior to the wedding. The completion of some work project had given Sean enough money to rent a small house for them.

Three weeks was an eternity when you were as passionately in love and as hungry for one other as they had been then, Kate acknowledged. But Sean had made sure that they did wait. He had had that kind of discipline and determination even then.

They had spent their wedding night completely alone in the small rented house. And it had been so perfect that even thinking about it now she could feel her eyes filling with tears of emotion.

'Mummy.'

The voice interrupted her wayward thoughts. Immediately Kate got out of her bed and hurried into Oliver's room.

'What is it, darling?' she asked him lovingly.

'My tummy hurts,' he complained.

Kate tried not to sigh. Oliver was prone to upset tummies. Having checked that he was okay, she sat with him and soothed him, tensing when unexpectedly he asked her, 'Mummy, when's Sean going to come and see us again?'

This was the first time Oliver had mentioned Sean, and she had managed to convince herself that her son had completely forgotten about him.

'I don't know, Oliver.' That was all she could find to say. She felt unable to tell Oliver that he would probably never see Sean again, even though she knew she ought to do so. She had always tried to answer his questions honestly, but this time she could not, and the reason for that was the look of shining anticipation in her little boy's eyes.

By the time Oliver had gone back to sleep she was wide awake herself, her heart jumping uncomfortably inside her chest.

It couldn't be possible for Oliver to somehow sense that Sean was his father, could it? Her little boy couldn't have taken so uncharacteristically well to Sean because he felt some kind of special bond between them?

'It's a wise child that knows its own father,' Kate muttered grimly to herself, clinging to the old saying to protect her from her own wild imaginings.

Apprehensively, Kate parked her car and walked across the car park. The last person she wanted to see was Sean. Why had fate been so unkind as to bring him back into her life? She hated knowing that she was going to be working for him, but, as Carol had pointed out to her when she had told her what had happened, she could not afford to risk him carrying out his threat of pursuing her through the courts.

She nibbled anxiously on her bottom lip as she hurried into her office. Oliver had assured her that his tummy was better when he had woken up this morning, but she had still warned the nursery school teacher that he hadn't felt well during the night when she had dropped him off that morning.

'Kate!' Laura gave her a beaming smile as she came into the office and saw her. 'You've changed your mind and you're going to stay after all!'

'You could say that! Our new boss made me an offer I couldn't refuse,' Kate answered lightly, and then realised what she had done when she saw the curiosity in Laura's eyes.

'He did?' Laura sighed enviously. 'Don't you think he's just the most gorgeously, dangerously sexy-looking man you have ever seen?' she added dreamily.

'No, I do not!' Kate responded, fighting to ignore the sudden backflip performed by her heart.

'Well, if that's true you are the only female working here who doesn't,' Laura told her forthrightly. 'And when you think that he's single and unattached...'

Now her heart was turning somersaults. 'Says who?' she challenged her friend and colleague.

'John,' Laura informed her smugly. 'Apparently Sean told him himself.'

Kate wondered what Laura would say if she were to tell her that, contrary to what Sean had told John, he had one very substantial attachment in the form of her son!

Sean was frowning as he ended his telephone conversation with his accountant. But it wasn't his business affairs that were causing him problems. He felt as though he was on an emotional see-saw—something more appropriate for a callow youth than a man of his own age. Moreover, a man who considered himself totally fireproof as far as his emotions and his control over them were concerned.

When he had ended his marriage to Kate he had closed himself off completely from everything that concerned or involved her. He had deliberately and clinically expunged everything about her from his life. From his life, maybe, but what about from his heart?

Nothing had changed, he reminded himself angrily. The same reasons why he had divorced her still existed today, and would continue to exist for ever. Sean knew that he could never alter them. Nor forget them!

Pushing back his chair with an unusually uncoordinated movement, he got up and strode to the office window.

Was that really true? And if it was then what the hell had he been doing this weekend? He did not normally spend his weekends in toy stores, did he? And he certainly did not spend them doing idiotic things like buying ridiculously expensive train sets.

Sean closed his eyes and pushed his hands into his pockets, balling his fists in angry tension.

Okay, so he hadn't deliberately set out to buy the train set. And he had had every excuse to be in the large department store as he had gone there in order to replace some household items. It had been mere coincidence that the toy department was on the same floor as the television set he had been looking at. He didn't really need to put himself through rigorous self-analysis just because he had bought a train set, did he? After all, he had only bought the damn thing because he had felt embarrassed not to do so when the sales assistant had mistakenly thought he was interested in it!

And then he had got rid of it at the first opportunity.

A gleam of reluctant amusement lit his eyes as he recalled the expression on the face of the young boy he had given his embarrassing purchase to. His tired-looking mother had protested at first, but Sean had insisted. He just hoped she didn't think he had had any kind of ulterior motive for doing what he had done. Not that she wouldn't have been right to be suspicious of his motives—they certainly would not withstand too much scrutiny! Dwelling on the past and buying toys just because… Just because what? Just because the warm weight of Kate's son in his arms had reactivated memories from a time in his life that…

A time in his life that was over, Sean tried to remind himself. But the stark truth was already confronting him, even if he did not want to recognise or acknowledge it.

'Fancy going to the pub for lunch?'

Kate shook her head without lifting her gaze from her computer screen. 'Can't, I'm afraid, Laura,' she responded. 'I want to get this finished, and anyway I've brought sandwiches.'

Lunch at the pub with her co-workers would have been fun and relaxing, but as a single parent Kate was always conscious of having to watch her budget.

After Laura had gone, Kate got up and collected her sandwiches. The company provided a small restroom, equipped with tea- and coffee-making facilities and a microwave, for the workforce to use during their lunch and tea breaks. She had just reached the end of the corridor and had started to descend the narrow flight of stairs when suddenly Sean came out of one of the lower level offices and started to hurry up the stairs towards her.

To Kate's dismay her reaction was immediate and intense, and unfortunately a relic from the days when they had been a couple. So much so, in fact, that she had taken the first of the few steps that would put her right in his path before she could stop herself.

Immediately she realised what she was doing and froze in pink-cheeked humiliation as a visual memory came vividly alive inside her head. A memory of Sean rushing up the stairs of their small house to grab her in his arms and swing her round in excitement before sliding her down the length of his body and beginning to kiss her with fierce sexual hunger.

Later they had gone on to celebrate the news he had brought her—that he had secured a new and lucrative contract—in bed, with the champagne he had brought home…

Red-faced, she pulled her thoughts back under control.

'Kathy!' Sean demanded grimly as he saw her shocked expression. 'What the hell's…? What's wrong?'

Alarmed, Kate tried to move away, but Sean stopped her, curling his fingers round her bare arm.

'It's not Kathy any more,' she reminded him sharply. 'It's Kate! And as for what's wrong—do you really need to ask me that?'

She might be Kate now, but Kathy was still there inside her, Kate was forced to acknowledge. Because in direct contradiction of her angry words her body responded to Sean's touch. Was it because no one had touched her since he had ended their marriage that her caress-starved flesh was quivering with such intense and voluptuous pleasure? Was it because it was Sean who was touching her? Or was it simply that when he had kissed her he had unleashed memories her body could not ignore? Kate wondered frantically.

Was it a past need her flesh was responding to, or was it a present one? She knew what she wanted the answer to be! But somehow she couldn't stop herself from stepping closer to him, exhaling on an unsteady sigh of pleasure. Sean was looking at her and she was looking back at him, with the mesmeric intensity of his blue gaze dizzying her.

She could feel his thumb caressing the inner curve of her elbow, just where he knew how vulnerable and responsive her flesh was to his touch—so vulnerable and responsive that when he had used to kiss her there her whole body had melted with wanton longing.

It would be so easy, so natural, to walk into his arms now and feel them close protectively around her. To look into his eyes and wait for the familiar look of hot eagerness darken them, whilst his mouth curled into that special smile he had...

A door opened noisily, bringing her back to reality. Abruptly she stepped back from Sean, her face burning. Maybe years ago she had not needed to hide her feelings from him—her lover, her husband, her best friend—nor her longing and sexual excitement when he looked at her and touched her. But things were different now, Kate reminded herself as she pulled away from him.

'What's that?' she heard him demanding as he released her and frowned at the box she was carrying.

'My lunch.'

'Lunch? In that?' he derided grimly as he looked at the small plastic container. 'I should have thought for your son's sake you would want to make sure you ate properly.'

As she listened to his ill-informed and critical words,

her passionate response to him a few minutes earlier was swamped by outrage and anger.

'For your information—not that you have any right to question anything I choose to do any more, Sean—it just so happens that it is for Ollie's sake that this is my lunch,' she told him, waving the plastic container defiantly. 'It costs money to bring up a child—not that you'd know or care anything about that, since you chose not to burden yourself with children,' she added sarcastically. 'And a packed lunch is a lot less expensive than going out to the pub. What's wrong, Sean?' she demanded when she saw his fixed expression. 'Or can I guess? You might come across to everyone else here as a caring, sharing employer, but I know different. And I also know, before you remind me, that you are rich enough to eat in the world's most expensive restaurants these days. But there was a time when even a sandwich was a luxury for you.'

As she saw his face tighten with anger Kate wondered if she had gone too far, but she wasn't going to back down, and she hoped that the determined tilt of her chin told him so.

'I imagine that your child has a father,' Sean said coldly. 'Why isn't he providing for his upbringing?'

Kate looked at him in silence for a few seconds, bitterly aware of how much he was hurting her and how little he cared, and then told him evenly, 'Oliver's father isn't providing for him financially—or in any other way—because he didn't want him.'

Unable to risk saying anything more without her fragile control being destroyed, Kate stepped past him and hurried down the stairs.

Sean watched her go. Packed lunches, a too-thin body, tension and worry that showed in her eyes. Even if she thought she had it well hidden, her life now was a world away from the luxuries he could have surrounded her with.

Had she thought of him at all when she was with the man who had fathered her son?

Grimly Sean shut down his thoughts, all too aware of not just how inappropriate they were but also how extremely dangerous.

All through her lunch hour, and the two hours following it, Kate couldn't concentrate on anything other than Sean. Her heart was racing at twice its normal rate and she was so on edge that her muscles were aching with the tension she was imposing on them. And the situation could only get worse. She knew that.

Only the knowledge that she had had to protect the life of the baby growing inside her had given her the strength to get through the pain-filled months after Sean had ended their marriage. What was more, she'd had to make the best of it for Oliver's sake. Her love was going to be the only parental love he was going to have.

She had discovered she was pregnant two months after Sean had announced that he wanted a divorce and walked out on her. She had fainted in a store, exhausted by the brutality of her grief.

Until then she hadn't cared if she lived or died. No, that was not true. Given the choice, she would have preferred death. She hadn't been able to imagine how she could go on living without Sean, whose callous words—'You'll soon get over me and meet someone else and start producing those bloody babies you want so much'—had cut her to the heart. The only man whose babies she had wanted was his. But he no longer loved her. The house they had shared was empty and she'd been living—existing—in rented accommodation, fiercely refusing to take any money from Sean. She had had no idea where he was living. And then she had found out that she was having his child. The child he had told her he did not want!

It was in that knowledge that she had made her decision not to let Sean know she was pregnant. He had rejected her and the pain had almost destroyed her. She wasn't going to inflict that kind of pain on her baby.

She had promised herself that she would find a way to stop loving Sean, and when Oliver had been born she had thought that she had. Until now.

She had to get away from Sean. She had believed that she had stopped loving him, but now she was desperately afraid that she had been wrong. A pain that was not all pure pain, but part helpless longing was unfurling slowly inside her. No matter what Sean might threaten to do she had to leave here, and she was going to tell him so…right now!

Agitatedly she got up and hurried to her office door, dragging it open and hurrying towards the office which had once been John's and which Sean was now using whilst he familiarised himself with the day-to-day running of the business.

There was no one in the outer office, and, too wrought-up for formalities, Kate rushed into the inner office, only to stare around it in dismay when she saw that it was empty.

Or at least she had thought it was empty. The door to a small private room which contained a changing room and shower facilities was half open, and she could hear someone moving about inside it. Someone? It could only be Sean.

Taking a deep breath, Kate walked purposefully towards it and then hesitated, her hand on the door handle. A part of her wasn't ready for another confrontation, but another part of her just wanted to get the whole thing over and done with.

Clearing her throat nervously, she took a deep breath and called out, 'Sean—are you in there? Only, there's something I need to speak to you about…'

In the empty silence that followed Kate began to lose

her courage. Perhaps she had been wrong. Perhaps Sean wasn't even here...

She started to turn away, stiffening with shock when the door was wrenched back and Sean was standing there naked, apart from the water running over his skin and the towel he was still wrapping around his hips.

For half a dozen seconds she couldn't move, couldn't speak, couldn't do anything other than stare at him whilst her eyes widened and her face burned.

'Oh. You were having a shower!' Was that really her voice—that soft, breathy, almost awed thread of sound?

'I *was*,' Sean agreed dryly, emphasising the past tense of his statement.

As she fought down the aching feeling that was spreading through her body Kate seized on anger as her main weapon of defence, telling herself fiercely that Sean should have done more to cover his nudity than simply drape—well, not even drape, really, simply hold, Kate decided, before hurriedly dragging her traitorous gaze away—the smallest of towels around his hips.

It was whilst she was doing battle with her suddenly rebellious sense of sight—and coming close to losing—that she heard Sean saying laconically, 'You'd better come in—and close the door.'

What?

She was just about to object, and in very strong terms, when he added dulcetly, 'That is unless you want to risk someone else coming into the office and finding you here with me like this.'

Kate knew there must be a hundred objections she could raise to what he was saying, but as she fought to find one of them Sean reached behind her and quietly closed the door. Closed it and locked it.

'Why…why have you locked the door?' Kate demanded, ashamed to hear the betraying quaver of anxiety in her voice.

'Because I don't want anyone else wandering in here,' he told her dryly. 'Why did you think I'd locked it? Or were you remembering…?'

'I wasn't remembering anything.' Kate stopped him in panic. 'I just wanted—'

He had moved slightly away from her and inadvertently she glanced at him, her gaze held in helpless thrall by the sight of his virtually naked body.

He had already been a fully adult male when they had met, and she had been thrilled at her first sight of his naked body, her gaze openly eager and hungry to see every single bit of him. She had thought then that it would be impossible for him to be more physically perfect—from the silken strength of his throat and neck to the powerful width of his shoulders, to the arms which had held her so close, the hands that had taken her to places of unimaginable pleasure, the chest so magnificently broad, tapering down to his belly, flat and tautly muscled, with its fascinatingly sensual line of male hair that her fingers had ached to explore.

But she had been wrong! Or had time just done her the favour of allowing her to forget the sexually erotic and perfect maleness of him, her own awareness of it and of him, to save her pain?

An ache at once both familiar and bewildering started to spread out from the pit of her stomach, overpowering her attempt to tense her body against it. A longing that tore at her emotions and her self-control grew with it.

Just above where the towel was knotted she could see the small white scar she remembered so well. The scar was the result of an accident he had had when he had first started working as a labourer, as a boy of fifteen who should have been at school. When he had told her how he had suffered with the pain of his wound, rather than risk being ridiculed by the other men on the gang and also lose a day's pay, she had wept and pressed her lips to the scar whilst Sean had buried his hands in her hair.

And then he had…

As she recognised the erotic path her thoughts were taking, and that it was not so much a memory from the past that was arousing her but a shocking need to experience it in the present, Kate started to panic. She had to get out of here, and now!

Quickly she turned towards the door.

'Kate!'

Caught off-guard by her sudden agitated movement, Sean reached out to stop her. The wrist within his grip felt far more fragile than he remembered. It angered him that she should have so little care for her own wellbeing, and it angered him even more that the man whose child she had conceived had hurt her and left her. The thought of anyone hurting her made him want to hold her and protect her.

Before he could stop himself Sean pulled her into his arms, ignoring her demands to be set free as he burrowed his hand into her hair, unwittingly bringing to life at least a part of Kate's own sensual memory.

'I'm glad you haven't cut your hair.'

The thick, raw words shocked Kate into stillness. She could feel the heat of Sean's hand against the back of her head. And against the front of her body she could feel the heat of…him.

Overwhelmed by her own feelings, she made a sound somewhere between a sigh and a moan, and as though it was the signal he had been waiting for suddenly Sean was kissing her, possessing her mouth with a fierce, driving need and a hunger that her own body instinctively recognised.

There was no past, no pain, only the here and now—
and Sean.

His free hand was cupping her face, his fingers caressing her skin, sliding down her throat and then tracing her
collarbone.

Hungrily Kate pressed herself closer to him, her fingers
automatically seeking the unwanted barrier between them
and tugging away the towel. Her actions were those of the
woman she had been and not the woman she now was. That
woman had had every right to lay claim to the intimacy of
Sean's body, to touch it and caress it however and wherever
she wished, just as Sean had had every right to do the same
with hers. Those rights had been bestowed on one another
with love and strengthened by marriage vows.

And though Kate tried to remind herself that they no longer shared those rights, her senses were refusing to listen.
They were too drugged by pleasure.

Sean groaned as he felt Kate's eager touch against his
naked flesh. It had been so long! Too long for his damned
self-control, he acknowledged, as his mouth found the tender hollow at the base of her throat and he buried the sound
of his need there, registering the pulse that had begun to
beat frantically in response.

Unable to stop himself, Sean allowed his hands to dispose
of the layers of clothing denying him access to Kate's body.

Was it Sean who was shaking with pleasure as his hands
cupped her naked breasts or was it her? Kate wondered achingly. She could feel the urgent peaking of her nipples and
she knew that Sean must be able to feel it as well. When he
rolled the tight, aching flesh between his thumb and finger the ferocity of the pleasure that shuddered through her
made Kate press herself pleadingly into Sean and grind her
hips against him.

'You know what happens when you do that, don't you?' Sean groaned thickly.

In response, Kate took hold of his hand and guided it down her body.

'Two can play at that game,' Sean warned her, but Kate didn't resist when he placed her hand against the hard, hot flesh of his erection.

She hadn't touched a man in all the years they had been apart. She hadn't so much as wanted to touch a man, never mind even think about it, and yet immediately and instinctively her fingers stroked lovingly over him in silent female acknowledgement of his potency before slowly caressing him.

'Kate...Kate.'

The anguished, tormented sound of her name only added to her arousal, and she stroked him again, moving her fingertips swiftly around the swollen head and down the underside of the thick shaft. The ache deep inside her mirrored the rhythmic movement of her fingers over him.

This was heaven—and it was hell. It was everything he had ever wanted and everything he could never have, Sean recognised as he submitted helplessly to Kate's power over him. But he was too much of an alpha male to allow Kate to take the lead for very long. Hungrily he pulled her into his arms and started to kiss her with fierce, possessive passion.

She wanted him so much, so very much. Eagerly, Kate clung to Sean, waiting...wanting... And then abruptly they both tensed as a phone rang shrilly in the outer room.

Mortified by what she had done, Kate straightened her clothes and fled, ignoring Sean's command to her to stay where she was.

CHAPTER FOUR

'AND NOW THERE'S this wretched virus going round...'

Kate pressed a hand to her temple, trying to ease the pounding of her headache and concentrate on what Carol was saying to her.

'It's a really nasty one!' Carol was continuing. 'I've been wondering whether or not I should keep George away from nursery for the time being.'

Through the pounding of her headache Kate tried not to feel envious of her friend for having the luxury of being able to make such a decision. Without childcare she could not work, and if she didn't work how were she and Oliver to live?

After Carol had gone, Kate looked a little worriedly at Oliver. Although he had been playing happily enough with George, he was somehow more subdued than usual.

'Have you still got that pain in your tummy, darling?' Kate asked him anxiously, but Oliver shocked her into silence.

'Will Sean come again?' he asked her.

There was a huge hard lump in Kate's throat, and a pain in her heart like none she had ever known. She wanted to take hold of her son and hold him tightly in her arms, so that no one and nothing could ever, ever hurt him. But there was no point in trying to hide the truth from herself any longer. This afternoon in Sean's arms she had known that she still loved him.

And it was that knowledge that had made her run away from him. He didn't love her any more. He had told her that five years ago. And once it had died love could never be resurrected, surely?

'No, Oliver. He won't be coming again,' she told him gently, her chest locking tightly as Oliver pouted.

'But I want him to,' he said truculently.

Kate could feel her self-control being ripped to pieces by her pain. As she stroked his hair Oliver looked back accusingly at her, and then to Kate's horror asked her the question she had dreaded.

'Why haven't I got a daddy, like George?'

Anguish and despair washed icily through her. How could she tell him that he did have, but that his father hadn't wanted him? He was too young to understand the truth, but she couldn't bring herself to lie to him.

'Not all daddies and mummies live together like George's mummy and daddy do,' she explained gently, watching as he silently digested her words.

'So where does my daddy live, then?'

It was the pounding in her head that was making her feel so sick, Kate tried to reassure herself. But the knowledge that one day Oliver would not be so easily sidetracked felt like a heavy weight dragging down her heart. 'It's bedtime, Oliver. What story would you like me to read tonight?'

For a moment she thought he was going to refuse to be sidetracked and then repeat his question, but to her relief he didn't.

Sean stared bleakly out of the window of the luxurious penthouse apartment he was renting whilst he assessed the future of his new acquisition. On the rare occasions when he had allowed himself to think about Kate ever since their divorce, he had visualised her living in contented rural bliss, with a doting husband and the houseful of children he had known she wanted to have. The reality of her life had shocked him. Yes, she had fulfilled her longing for motherhood—but where was the man who should be there with her, loving her and supporting her?

Sean hadn't forgotten the life he had had before he had become wealthy—how could he?—and he knew her current life must be a hard financial struggle for Kate.

Why the hell hadn't she made at least some kind of financial claim on the bastard who had deserted them both? In Sean's opinion any man who fathered a child should contribute financially to its upbringing. Sean thought of his own childhood—he knew how hard a child's life could be when growing up in poverty. Not that Oliver was growing up in poverty, but it was obvious that his mother was having to struggle to support him.

Angrily Sean pushed his hand into his hair. When he had met Kate—Kathy, as she had been then—he had been an uneducated, anti-social young man with a very large chip on his shoulder. Kathy hadn't only given him her love, she had given him a lot more as well. She had helped and encouraged him in every way she could, and it was because of her faith in him, her love for him, that he was the man he was today.

If only he could acknowledge that debt to her.

He turned away from the window. The penthouse looked like something out of an expensive magazine, and it was definitely not child-friendly. Not like the rectory he had once promised Kate he would buy for her.

Sean closed his eyes and took a deep breath. Had she loved the man who had fathered Oliver? And who the hell was he anyway?

His car keys were on the immaculate kitchen worktop. It would take him less than half an hour to drive to Kate's cottage.

Sean had made up his mind what he was going to do. He was going to insist that she give him the name of Oliver's father and then he was going to make sure that the man was made aware of his responsibilities to both his son and his son's mother, and that he fulfilled them.

Oliver was in bed and asleep, and her headache had finally dulled. The washing she had hung out to dry this morning before leaving for work was dry and ready to iron, filling the kitchen with its clean fresh-air smell.

Kate liked to do as many of her chores as possible in the evenings, when Oliver was asleep, so that she could keep her weekends free to be with him. The village possessed a small shop, and it was part of their weekend ritual to walk there every weekend to collect the papers and chat with their fellow villagers.

Kate was determined to do everything she could to provide Oliver with a sense of community and belonging, even if she wasn't able provide him with his father.

A shadow darkened the kitchen window, causing her look up from her ironing. She froze when she realised that the shadow belonged to Sean.

A tiny shudder ran through her, the hairs lifting on her skin as she fought against an illogical fear that somehow her own thoughts were responsible for his presence.

Her thoughts or Oliver's need?

She must not think like that, she told herself firmly as she unplugged the iron and then hurried to open the door before he could knock. She didn't want him waking Oliver.

What had he come for? To tell her that he had changed his mind and that he didn't want her working for him after all?

Irrationally, instead of bringing her pleasure, that thought only brought her more pain. Pain and a fear that her response to him earlier might have caused him to recognise, as she had, that she still loved him.

Whatever else he was, Sean was certainly not the kind of man whose vanity was so great that he would enjoy knowing a woman loved him when he could not and did not love her back. Judging from his determination to remove her from his life, he would be equally as brutal now as he'd been when he had divorced her.

As Sean strode into the kitchen she just about had time to reflect on how ironic it was that now she was fearing him sacking her when it wasn't long since she'd been determined to hand in her resignation from the company.

'Sean. What are you doing here? What do you want?' Kate demanded, but as she spoke she was achingly aware that what she wanted was for him to take her in his arms and then...

Already a familiar and dangerous weakness was slipping through her veins. He was standing far too close to her—close enough for her to see that he had shaved, and that there was the smallest of nicks on his throat.

Out of the past she could see herself standing opposite him on the sunny street where he had been working. He had been teasing her and she had tried to tease him back, commenting naïvely on his unshaven face. He had looked at her and then he had responded with deliberate sensuality to her comment, telling her that he preferred to shave before he went to bed. 'So I won't scratch your skin,' he had added, watching the bright colour burn her face as the meaning of his words sank in.

A sense of desolation and loss rolled over her.

'Who is Oliver's father, Kate?'

The way Sean was looking at her made Kate's heart turn over inside her chest.

What?

Weakly Kate clung to the edge of her kitchen table as she battled with her shock, wondering wildly how on earth— and, more importantly, *what* on earth she could answer. And then suddenly she knew there was only one way, and that was to tell him the truth.

Before she could lose her courage and change her mind, she took a deep breath and answered him quietly, 'You are, Sean.'

In the silence his face lost its entire colour, and then it burned with a dark tide that swept slowly over his skin until his cheekbones glowed with its heat.

'No.' He denied her words explosively.

His denial ricocheted around the room, burst apart and then bounded back off the walls at her like a deadly missile. Kate's hopes died under its onslaught.

'No!' Sean was repeating savagely, shaking his head. 'No! You're lying to me, Kate. I know I hurt you when I ended our marriage, and I can easily understand why you would have turned to someone else, but no way do I accept that I am Oliver's father.'

Someone else? Kate could taste the acid bitterness of her own anger as she listened to Sean rejecting his son. Beneath her anger, though, lay the bleakness of her own pain. What had she been expecting? Or could she answer her own question more easily if she asked herself what she had been hoping for?

She'd wanted Sean to take her in his arms and tell her that he had made a mistake, that he still loved her. That in fact he loved her all the more because she had given him a son.

'Yes, you did hurt me then, Sean,' she agreed evenly. 'But believe me that cruelty was nothing compared with what you've just done. You can hurt me as much as you like, but I will never, ever let you hurt Oliver.'

As she forced herself to look into his eyes, her own emotion, her own pain was pushed to one side by the strength of her maternal need to protect her child. For Oliver she would sacrifice anything and everything, and if necessary even herself. She could not ignore or deny the fact that her love for Sean had never really died, but for Oliver's sake she would control and banish that love. And somehow she would learn to live with the pain of having to do so.

Everything about Sean's reaction to her information that he was Oliver's father confirmed the wisdom of her decision not to tell him originally that she had conceived his child. But at the same time everything about it tore at her heart until she could scarcely endure the pain.

But it was her anger and contempt on behalf of her son that was glittering in her eyes now, motivating the scathing tone of her voice as she told him, 'That's right, Sean. Reject Oliver just like you rejected me. But that won't alter the fact that he is your son.'

It gave her a sense of almost anguished satisfaction, along with a feeling as if someone was turning a knife over inside her heart, to see the effect his efforts to rein in his temper were having on him. His face once more leached of colour, leaving it looking bone-white.

'He can't be mine,' he insisted harshly.

'Can't be? Why not? Because you were sleeping with the woman you left me for when he was conceived? What happened to her, by the way, Sean? Did you get bored with her, just like you did with me?' Too wrought up to wait for his reply, she threw at him furiously, 'You can deny it all you like, but it won't alter the truth. He is your child.'

Kate shook her head angrily. 'Don't you think I wish that he wasn't?' she demanded passionately when he didn't respond. 'Don't you think I wish that he had been fathered in love, with love, by a man who loved me? By a man who loved him? A man who wanted to share our lives and be there for both of us? You'll never know how much I wanted those things, Sean—for Oliver and for myself. But unlike you I've faced up to the truth.'

She was shaking from head to foot, Kate recognised, and she was humiliatingly close to tears.

For a minute Sean was too shocked by Kate's angry and contemptuous outburst to make any response. And then for a minute more he discovered that he actually wanted to be able to believe her. She was certainly doing a good job of believing herself, he recognised cynically. But all the cynicism in the world could not wipe away the strength of his immediate response to her emotional outburst. Pain, anger and unbelievably longing tore at him in equal proportions.

What had happened to the self-control he had been so proud of? And what had happened to the honesty that had been such a strong part of Kate's personality? Obviously it was something else for him to mourn, along with his other losses. It took him far too long to suppress his instinctive urge to go to her and take hold of her, but eventually he managed to do so, instead telling her brutally, 'You're wasting your breath. There's no point in any of this. Oliver is not my child.' He hesitated, deliberately turning away from Kate so that she would not see his expression. 'And nothing you can say will ever make me acknowledge him as such.'

Kate stared at him, angry colour burning her skin, her mouth compressing, but before she could say anything, Sean demanded harshly, 'For God's sake, Kate, don't make it even worse than it has to be. I can just accept that you gave yourself to someone else after our marriage was over. I can even accept that if you gave yourself to someone else as an act of retribution against me, and that I deserved such an action, but I damn well can't accept that you slept with someone else whilst we were still together.'

'You mean like you did?' Kate shot at him bitingly. 'What happened to her, Sean?'

'She isn't in my life any more. It was just a short-lived fling.'

He sounded more irritated than concerned, and his response added further fuel to Kate's anger.

'Clever her! She must have realised that ultimately you'd probably betray her, just like you did me.'

Sean gave her a bitter look. 'When it comes to betrayal, you outclass me, Kate. You've committed the worst betrayal of all in trying to pretend that another man's child is mine!'

Kate's face burned with anger. 'I would never stoop to that kind of deceit,' she stormed furiously. 'I can't bear to think of what you've done—not just to me but more importantly to Oliver! You've denied your child the right to know his father and—'

Angrily Sean reached out and took hold of her wrist. 'Oliver is not my child!'

The harsh words echoed round the small kitchen, causing Kate to try and pull away. 'I hate you, Sean,' she told him passionately. 'You don't know how much I wish I'd never met you, how much I hate myself for letting you—'

'Letting me what?' Sean stopped her.

Kate could feel the hard bite of his fingers in the soft flesh of her upper arms as he dragged her body against the hard tense length of him.

'Letting me make you feel like this?'

His mouth possessed hers, its pressure bending her head back and making her arch her spine. Anger and pride mingled turbulently inside her as longing streaked scarlet trails of danger through her veins. She could feel the fierce judder of reaction galvanise Sean's body, and somehow, shock-

ingly, immediately and against all logic, she was swept back
to another time and another kiss.

A time when they had virtually only just met, and a kiss
had been taken fiercely from her in the concealing darkness
when Sean had walked her home from their first real date.

Then her body had thrilled with shocked and excited
pleasure at its recognition of his predatory male passion. She
had been young; naïve, but oh, so very, very passionately in
love with Sean, and so very eager and aroused.

Now she was…

But where did then end and now begin? Kate wondered
with dizzy fatality as the years rolled back and her body,
her senses, her emotions were those of that young girl again.

Kate heard the small whimper escaping her lips. Instantly
the hot, hard pressure of Sean's mouth caught and answered
it. His hands moved from her arms to her back, no longer
constraining her but caressing her, as though something in
that sound she had made had been a plea and not a protest.

She trembled as his hands cinched her waist, his thumbs
caressing its narrow curve, before sliding lower to cup the
rounded flesh of her behind and then urge her even more
closely against his own body, holding her tight and hard
against the obvious thrust of his erection. Automatically
and instinctively Kate tilted her hips hungrily against him
and moaned his name.

As she sobbed her arousal and need against his lips Kate
felt his hand move to her breast.

She was lost to time and place, to everything but Sean
and her need for him. A sound, a high, hot, female-hungry-
for-her-mate sound of raw sexual hunger slit the thickness
of air, which was filled with the raggedness of breath exhaled in mutual passion.

And Sean responded to it as though a door had swung
open, admitting him to a lost and long-sought magic kingdom.

Kate trembled as the hand he had raised to her breast began to stroke and then massage it with familiar intimacy, arousing an equally familiar sensation which spread from his touch through her stomach to the soft warmth within her. A soft warmth that was rapidly turning into a tight, wet, aching heat.

Unable to stop herself from answering the clamouring need, Kate arched her whole body against his touch, moaning into his mouth as his hand cupped her breast and his thumb and finger started to pluck sensually at the hard peak of her nipple.

In a heartbeat of brief lucidity Kate was shockingly aware that just the feel of his erection straining against her was as erotically arousing as if she had still been a virginal teenager. But then Sean groaned, tugging fiercely at her top, and she watched him tense as the pale, soft nakedness of her breast, with the ripe swollen peak of her nipple, was revealed to his sight and his touch. Her lucidity became a thing of the past, to be overwhelmed, overturned by the flash-flood of her own response.

Would Sean remember how much she had liked to feel him stroke the hard flesh of her aroused nipples with his fingertip? How it had made her call out to him in shocked, excited arousal? Would he remember the way he had driven her beyond the boundaries of her self-control with the slow touch of his mouth?

She quivered as she felt his hand on her naked breast—waiting, yearning, needing.

'Kathy…'

The raw sound of her name seemed to have been dredged up from somewhere deep and hidden inside Sean, and Kate tensed immediately in response to it.

Kathy! But she wasn't Kathy any more. She was Kate. She was Kate—and Sean wasn't the man who loved her, he

was the man who had betrayed her! The man who refused
to accept that he had fathered her child. Sickness rolled
through her. How could she feel the way she had, behave
the way she had, when she knew…?

She froze as the kitchen door was pushed open and she
saw Oliver standing staring at them.

CHAPTER FIVE

SEAN'S REACTION HAD been quicker than hers, and to her shock Kate realised that she was looking at her son from behind Sean's sheltering body. Hot-faced with shock and guilt, she straightened her clothes and moved to go to Oliver, but he was oblivious to her, instead heading straight for Sean.

Frantically Kate tried to stop him, unable to bear the rejection her little boy was going to suffer, but to her disbelief Sean stepped past her, scooping Oliver up as her son held out his arms to him.

Holding Kate's child in his arms, Sean felt a pain like none other he had ever experienced—not even when his mother had left him, not even when he had heard that he could not father a child himself, not even when he had locked Kate out of his life, he acknowledged as he fought down his own anguish and torment.

The small head tilted back and solemn eyes looked into his. Sean felt as though someone had slid a knife into his ribs poisoned with longing, jealousy and despair. Longing for Oliver to be his; jealousy because Kate had given herself to another man; despair because of the situation he was now in.

Abruptly he thrust Oliver into Kate's waiting arms and turned towards the back door.

As he reached it he stopped and turned round, shadows

cloaking the pain in his eyes as he demanded, 'When was he born?'

Kate tightened her arms around Oliver, who had already fallen back to sleep, in the way that small children could in just a few seconds, and she told him the date.

After the smallest of pauses, Sean grated, 'So he was conceived two weeks after we separated, then?'

The air in the kitchen felt so heavy and sour with the weight of their combined emotions that Kate felt as though it might choke her.

'He was two weeks overdue.' She answered Sean's unspoken accusation despairingly. Shaking her head, she added huskily, 'They wanted to induce me but I asked them to wait. I…I wanted him to be born naturally.'

Kate closed her eyes and turned away, not wanting to be reminded that she had held out until the last possible minute, clinging desperately and stubbornly to her hope that there would be a miracle and that somehow Sean would be there with her to witness the birth of their child.

But he hadn't been, and in the end there had been no one other than the hospital staff to share her awed and exhausted delight at the birth of her son.

She came out of her reverie to hear the back door closing. Sean had left. But he had already left her life and Oliver's a long time ago, she reminded herself.

Somehow that reminder wasn't as comforting as it should have been. Her pain was too sharp and strong to be so easily soothed.

She could, of course, have challenged Sean to let her prove that Oliver was his son by demanding a DNA test. Kate dropped her cheek onto Oliver's soft springy curls. But proving that Sean was Oliver's father would mean nothing if Sean refused to be that father. No way was she going to expose Oliver to that kind of pain—not even to prove to

Sean that she had not, as he had accused, shared her body
with another man as he had shared his with another woman!

The pain hadn't changed at all. It was still as strong as it
had always been. Where was her pride? Why wasn't it res-
cuing her from her own vulnerability by reminding her of
what Sean had done? How dared he make accusations re-
garding her when he had told her openly that he had taken
another woman to bed?

Oliver was still asleep in her arms, which meant that she
did not have to hold back any longer the slow, painful tears
burning the back of her eyes. It hadn't just been her that
Sean had betrayed, he had betrayed Oliver as well!

Sean grimaced as he accidentally nicked his skin, and put
down his razor. 'It's your own damned fault,' he muttered to
his reflection as he stanched the small wound. But it wasn't
the cut he was talking about, and it wasn't his own face he
could see in the mirror—it was Oliver's.

Cursing, he tried to banish his thoughts—but it was too
late.

He had seen in Kate's eyes just how she felt about his refusal to accept that Oliver was his child. But no matter how
much she had managed to persuade herself that Oliver was
his, Sean knew that he could not be.

And he knew for a very good reason.

He closed his eyes and swallowed against the sick taste
of his own self-loathing and humiliation.

That reason was that it was medically impossible for him
to father a child.

He hadn't known that when he had married Kate, of
course. If he had done then he would never have married
her, knowing how important having children was to her.

He thought back to the medical appointment which had

been responsible for the destruction of his marriage and his life.

'There is one thing I do have to mention,' the doctor had begun. 'One of the tests we ran was a sperm count. I'm afraid I have to tell you that it's highly unlikely you will be able to father a child.'

Even now he still had bad dreams about those words and that meeting with his doctor at which the announcement had been made.

He hadn't been able to take it in at first. How could it not be possible for him to father a child? He was a fit, healthy man in the prime of life. He had protested that the doctor must be wrong, that there must be some mistake, and all the time he had been aware of the humiliating pity in the other man's eyes as he shook his head. The doctor might be twenty years his senior, small, balding, and with a paunch, but suddenly he had become the one who was the virile potent male whilst Sean had been reduced to a mere pathetic apology for a man, at least in his own eyes.

Real men, in the culture of the rough, fight-to-survive world in which Sean had grown up, were not unable to father children.

Inside his head Sean had heard a brief snatch of stored conversation, between his mother and one her friends. They had been talking about a man they both knew, and Sean could remember the mockery in his mother's laughter as she had told her friend, 'He's a poor thing, by all accounts. Hasn't fathered a child yet, nor likely to, and in my book that means he isn't a man at all.'

Not a man at all—just like him.

Another memory surfaced.

'Oh, Sean, I just can't wait for us to have children.'

Now it was Kate's voice haunting him, and he swore savagely beneath his breath.

'I'd hate to have the kind of marriage that didn't include a family, like my aunt and uncle's.'

He could still see the way she had shuddered, as though in revulsion.

'Don't worry, I'll give you as many as you want,' he had boasted, already aroused at the thought of how he would give her the children they both wanted so much.

And each and every time he had made love with her that feeling had been there, that surge of atavistic male pride in the knowledge that he had the power to create a new life within her.

Only he had not had that power. Not according to what his doctor had told him.

It hadn't been just his present and his future the doctor's words had destroyed; it had been his own belief and pride in himself as well. Suddenly he was not the man he had always thought himself to be. Suddenly he was not, in his own opinion, very much of a man at all.

Holding Oliver had brought back with savage intensity all that he could never have, and yet he couldn't hate the little boy—far from it, in fact. Instead of wanting to reject the child another man had given the woman he loved, he had actually felt drawn towards him.

If only Kate knew just how much he wished that Oliver *was* his child! And Kate herself still his wife?

After she had betrayed him by sleeping with another man? A bitter smile twisted Sean's lips.

Kate might have thought that hurling his infidelity at him was a powerful weapon, but instead it was just his own lie to her. His supposed affair had been a lie, made up to expedite the speedy ending of their marriage so that he could set Kate free.

And since the reason he'd been so grimly determined to set her free had been so that she could find another man to father the children he knew were so important to her, it was illogical for him to feel the way he did about the fact that she had done so.

Whoever the man was, he was a fool as well as a scoundrel for abandoning Kate and his son—and for throwing away Kate's love.

The savagery and immediacy of his own pain felt like a hammer-blow against his heart.

'Everyone's surprised that our new boss is spending so much time here,' Laura confided chattily to Kate on Thursday, as she came into her office shortly after lunch. 'I mean, he has two other companies. Do you suppose it means that we can all stop worrying about being made redundant?' she asked hopefully. 'I mean, if he wasn't planning on keeping this place going he wouldn't be spending so much time here, would he? Kate?' she prompted when Kate didn't make any response. 'Other things on your mind?' Laura guessed.

'Sorry—I didn't get much sleep last night,' Kate answered. It was the truth after all.

'You do look a bit peaky,' Laura acknowledged as she studied her.

Peaky! Kate grimaced to herself. She felt as though her emotions had been ripped apart and devoured by a pack of scavengers, and that now all that was left of them was the dead bones.

It was the dry grittiness of her eyes that made her want to blink, not something stupid like crying, she assured herself fiercely. After all, she had done enough of that during the night, hadn't she? With her face buried in her pillow so that she wouldn't wake Oliver.

She was still in shock, Kate admitted to herself, and the cause of that shock was her discovery of just how vulnerable she still was to Sean!

'Oh, no! Look at the time! I'd better go.' Kate hurried past Laura as she made her exit.

Behind her shock and pain lay a huge, deep dam of pent-up anger. How dared Sean refuse to believe that Oliver was his child? How dared he be such a hypocrite as to accuse her of sleeping with someone else?

Thinking of her son made her turn anxiously to her silent mobile. Oliver had complained that his tummy hurt again at breakfast time, but to her relief when she had taken his temperature it had been normal and so she had taken him to school.

Sean drummed his fingers irritably on his desk. Pushing back his chair, he stood up, raking his hair with one hand, and paced the floor as he mentally practised what he intended to say to Kate.

Halfway through the carefully chosen words he stopped abruptly and asked himself angrily what the hell was wrong with him. All he had to say to Kate was that he wanted her to have the money she had refused to accept when they had divorced. Hell, if need be he could tell her that his accountants were insisting it was handed over otherwise he would invoke some kind of tax penalty. His decision had nothing whatsoever to do with Oliver, other than the fact that he hated seeing Kate have to struggle—especially when she had a small child to support.

A small child who wasn't his.

Opening his office door, he instructed his secretary to tell Kate he wanted to see her.

'Jenny rang down to say that you wanted to see me?'

'Yes, I do,' Sean confirmed, turning away to look out of his office window. 'You must have found it hard to make time to study for your Master's?'

'Yes, in some ways I did,' Kate agreed warily, wondering why he had sent for her and what this was leading up to.

'I imagine that it would have been difficult with Oliver,' Sean pressed her.

'Yes, it was,' Kate confirmed.

'Why didn't you ask his father for financial support?'

When she didn't answer, Sean swung round. The light streaming in through the large window highlighted the tension in his face, and for a moment Kate almost weakened. He had been everything to her after all. As she was now everything to Oliver, she reminded herself immediately, before taking a deep breath and asking sharply, 'What are you trying to do? Trap me? You're wasting your time, Sean. *You* are Oliver's father. Nothing and no one—not even you— can alter that fact.'

Her stomach churned as she saw Sean's expression hardening with rejection.

'You are the one who is wasting your time, Kate. Oliver is not my son. He can't be—' Sean tensed and stopped speaking, taking a deep breath before he continued tersely, 'He can't be foisted off on me!'

His heart was hammering against his ribs. It was a sign of the effect Kate was having on him that he had come so close to blurting out the truth! Fortunately he had just managed to stop himself in time!

Kate clenched her hands as she caught the underlying and suppressed violence in Sean's voice, her dismay giving way to shock as she heard him adding grimly, 'What I wanted to talk to you about was—' He stopped speaking as the abrupt shrill of Kate's mobile cut across his words. Red-faced, she fished it out of her bag, her embarrassment forgotten as she saw that the call was from Oliver's nursery.

'He's been sick and he's asking for me?' Kate couldn't keep the anxiety out of her voice as she repeated what the other woman was telling her. 'He wasn't very well this morning,' she admitted. 'But he didn't have a temperature then...'

Even though Kate tried to turn away from Sean she knew that he could hear the conversation she was having with the nursery school teacher.

'I...I'll try to—' she began, only to find that Sean was spinning her round to face him.

His expression was grim as he took the mobile from her and said tersely into it, 'She's on her way.'

'You have no right—' Kate said angrily, but Sean had ended the call and his hand was on her arm, urging her towards the door.

'We'll go in my car,' he told her. 'For one thing we'll get there faster, and for another you'll be worrying too much to drive safely.'

Kate opened her mouth to protest, but they were already in the car park and heading for Sean's car. He held the passenger door open for her and reluctantly she got in.

'Did the nursery say exactly what's wrong with him? Have they called a doctor?' Sean asked as he slid into the driver's seat and started the engine.

Kate wanted to refuse to tell him anything—after all, he had just rejected Oliver—but her maternal anxiety overruled her pride, and apprehensively she began to repeat what she had been told. 'He's been sick, apparently. There's a bug going round. He said this morning that his tummy was hurting him.'

'You sent him to nursery, knowing that he wasn't well?'

Kate could hear the criticism and disbelief in Sean's voice.

'Why didn't you stay at home with him?'

Angrily Kate defended herself. 'I have to work, remember? Anyway, I can't just take time off like that.'

'Of course you can,' Sean contradicted her flatly. 'You're a mother. People would understand.'

'No one at work knows about Oliver,' Kate admitted abruptly, deliberately turning her head to face the window so that he couldn't see her expression.

'Ashamed of him?'

'No!' Kate denied furiously, and immediately turned to look at him. She realised too late that Sean had deliberately provoked her, knowing what her reaction would be.

'Then why?'

'For goodness' sake, Sean, surely I don't have to tell you the business facts of life?' Kate answered wryly. 'Not all firms will take on women who are mothers, especially if they are single mothers. I needed this job. I didn't mention Oliver at my first interview, and then after I had been offered the job I discovered that John had an unwritten rule about not employing mothers of young children.'

'A rule it would be unlawful for him to try to enforce,' Sean pointed out. 'And Oliver needs you! Hell, Kate, both you and I know what it's like to grow up without a mother.'

'Oliver has a mother.'

'But not a mother who can be there for him when he needs her.'

Kate couldn't maintain her barriers against the pain that swamped her. It invaded every nerve-ending and tore at her heart.

'Since you refuse to accept that Oliver is your child, you hardly have the right to tell me how to bring him up, do you?' she challenged him bitterly, only realising as she managed to blink away her angry tears that they had reached the village.

The moment Sean pulled up outside the nursery Kate was reaching for the car's door handle, throwing a stiff, 'Thank you for the lift,' to him over her shoulder.

But to her consternation Sean was already out of the car and opening her door, announcing curtly, 'I'm coming in with you.'

'I don't want you to,' Kate protested.

'Oliver might need to see a doctor,' Sean told her flatly. 'I can run you there.'

A doctor? Anxiously Kate hurried towards the nursery, her concern for her son far more important right now than arguing with Sean.

The moment Kate pushed open the door Oliver's nursery teacher came hurrying towards her.

'Where's Oliver? How is he?' Kate demanded frantically as she scanned the room anxiously, unable to see her son amongst the throng of children in the room.

'He's fine, but he's asleep.'

'Asleep? But—' Kate began, only to be interrupted.

'Has he seen a doctor?' Sean demanded sharply.

It irritated Kate a little to see the immediacy with which the older woman responded to Sean's calm authority.

'I'm a trained nurse,' she informed him, almost defensively. 'I don't think there's anything seriously wrong. Oliver felt poorly before lunch, and then he was sick afterwards, but he seems fine now—if rather tired.'

Turning to look at Kate, she added, slightly reprovingly, 'He seems upset about something, and I do rather think that might be the cause of the problem. Young children often react with physical symptoms to emotional stress.'

Kate flushed sensitively, sure that she could hear a note of criticism in the other woman's voice.

'I'll go through and get Ollie and take him home,' Kate told her quietly, unaware of the way Sean was watching her reaction to the older woman's remarks.

Oliver was asleep in one of the beds in a room off the playroom, and Kate felt the familiar pull on her emotions as she leaned over him. In so many ways he was Sean's son, even if Sean himself refused to accept Ollie as his child. Tiredly she bent to pick him up.

'I'll take him.'

Kate turned round. She hadn't realised that Sean had followed her into the small shadowy room.

'There's no need,' she told him in a small clipped voice, focusing her gaze not on Sean's face but on one dark-suited shoulder. A big mistake, she recognised achingly, when she had to suppress a longing to lean her head against its comforting strength and feel Sean's arms come round her, hear Sean's voice telling her that he believed her and that he loved her, that right now this very minute he was going to take both her and Oliver home with him.

As she stood there, staring fixatedly at his shoulder, Kate was suddenly overwhelmed by the searing knowledge of how alone and afraid she sometimes felt. Her throat ached and so did her head, shocked nausea was churning her stomach, and just the sight of Sean lifting his sleeping son into his arms was enough to make her feel as though her heart was breaking.

Get a grip, Kate advised herself sharply. This kind of emotion was a luxury she simply could not afford.

Once they were outside the nursery Kate stood in front of Sean and demanded, 'Give him to me now. I can carry him home from here.'

'You carry him? You look as though you can barely carry yourself,' Sean told her bluntly.

'I'll carry him!'

They had just reached the cottage when Oliver woke up, stirring sleepily in Sean's arms.

Opening the door, Kate stood just inside it and held out her arms for her son. But to her chagrin Oliver turned away from her, burrowing his head against Sean's chest and going back to sleep.

A huge splinter of ice was piercing her heart. This was the first time Oliver had rejected her in favour of someone else—and not just anyone else, but Sean, his father.

'You'd better give him to me,' she told Sean sharply. 'I'm sure the last thing you'll want is him being sick on your suit.'

As he handed Oliver to her and she put him down gently on the shabby sofa that took up one wall of the kitchen she heard him say quietly, 'No, actually the last thing I want is knowing that you went to another man's bed so quickly after leaving mine!'

Immediately Kate stiffened. 'You have no right to say that.'

'Do you think I don't know that?' Sean retaliated savagely. 'Don't you think I know that I have thrown away all my rights where you are concerned!'

'All your rights?' Horrified, Kate wondered what reckless surge of self-destruction had prompted such dangerous words, and spoken in such a soft, sexually challenging voice. And, as though that was not folly enough, she discovered that she had a sudden compulsion to let her gaze slide helplessly to Sean's mouth and then linger wantonly there, whilst her body reminded her hungrily of the pleasure he had once given it, how long it had been since…

'Kate, for God's sake, will you please stop looking at me like that?' Sean warned her harshly.

Mortified, she defended herself immediately, fibbing, 'I don't know what you mean!'

Instantly Sean took a step towards her, a look smouldering in the depths of his eyes that made a fierce thrill of dangerous excitement race through her.

'Liar! You know perfectly well what I mean.' Sean

checked her thickly. 'You were looking at my mouth as though you couldn't wait to feel it against your own.'

What the hell was he doing? Sean challenged himself inwardly. His sole reason for having anything at all to do with Kate was to give her some much needed financial help, and that was all. Nothing else. Absolutely nothing else.

And yet within seconds of telling himself that, Sean could hear himself asking softly, 'Is that what you want, Kate? Because if it is…'

Just the sound of his voice was having a disturbingly erotic effect on her body—and on her senses. Defensively she closed her eyes, and then realised she had made a bad move as immediately she was swamped with mental images from the past.

Sean leaning over her in their bed, the morning sun on his bronzed skin, his eyes gleaming with sensual intent and knowledge between his narrowed eyelids. How quickly that cool look had grown hot and urgent when she had reached out to touch him, tugging teasingly on the fine hair covering his chest, before giving in to the erotic pleasure of sliding her fingers down the silky pathway which led over the hard flat plane of his belly to where the soft hair thickened.

Before she even realised what she was doing, never mind being able to stop herself, Kate felt her fingers stretching and curling, as though they could actually feel the strong, hard pulse of Sean's erection within their grip.

As soon as she realised what she was doing—and what she was feeling—Kate thrust her hands behind her back, guilty heat scorching her skin.

Angry both with herself for feeling the way she had and with Sean for being responsible for that feeling, she told him fiercely, 'No, it isn't.' She lied. 'Why should I want someone who did what you did? Someone who broke his marriage vows and took someone else to his bed? How could I want you, Sean?'

'Snap—that's exactly how I feel about you!' Sean stopped her passionately. 'You do realise, don't you, that I can throw the same accusations at you? How do you think it feels to discover that you didn't even wait a full month before jumping into bed with someone else? Why did you do that, Kate? Was it loneliness, or just spite?'

'I didn't do any such thing,' Kate denied shakily. His words had touched a wound in her heart that she had thought completely healed. But, as she had recently discovered, the scar tissue over it had been vulnerably fragile, and now the pain was agonisingly raw again.

Kate's face went white, but before she could say anything Sean had turned on his heel and was heading for the door.

'Don't come in to work tomorrow, and if Oliver isn't better by Monday let me know. And that's an order,' Sean instructed her grimly. 'I'll make arrangements to have your car brought here for you.'

CHAPTER SIX

'WELL, OLIVER MIGHT have escaped going down with the dreaded bug, but it doesn't look as though you've been quite so lucky,' Carol commented forthrightly as she studied Kate's wan face.

'I've had a bad night,' Kate admitted reluctantly.

Kate had met her friend as she walked Oliver to school, and now the two boys were walking together, leaving Kate to fall into step with Carol.

'My daddy can do anything,' Kate heard George boasting.

'Boys!' Carol laughed, shaking her head and exchanging a rueful look with Kate.

'Well, Sean can do everything in the whole world!'

Kate bit her lip as Oliver's voice rang out, miserably aware of the comprehensive and sympathetic look Carol was giving her.

'Sounds as though Sean is a big hit with Oliver,' she commented lightly, but Kate could guess what she was thinking. The griping pain in her stomach bit harder and she winced, causing Carol to exclaim with concern, 'You really aren't well, Kate, are you? You should be in bed! Look, why don't you go home and go back to bed? I'll take Oliver to school and collect him for you.'

'I can't. I've got to go to work,' Kate told her. 'I didn't go in on Friday because of Oliver. I can't take more time off.'

'Kate, you can't possibly go to work. You look dreadful,' Carol protested, adding worriedly, 'Look at you! You're shivering, and it's nearly eighty degrees. This bug is really nasty if it gets a grip.'

'Thanks!' Kate said dryly, adding determinedly, 'Anyway, I'm fine.'

But she could see from her friend's face that Carol knew she was lying, and the truth was that she felt anything but fine.

Unlike Oliver, who had recovered from his upset tummy within a matter of hours, ever since she'd been sick the morning before she had steadily become more and more unwell. Her head felt as though it was being pounded with a sledgehammer, she had been sick on and off all night, and every bone in her body ached. She felt as if she was having flu and food poisoning all in one go.

Now the pain in her head increased, and when she closed her eyes against it a wave of nauseating dizziness hit her.

'No way are you going to work!' Carol's firm voice broke into her misery. 'How on earth are you planning to get there? You can't possibly drive. Go home, and as soon as I've dropped the boys off I'll call in and make sure you're okay.'

Another surge of nausea reinforced the truth of what Carol was saying, and, handing Oliver over to her, Kate hurriedly made her way back home. She was unable to tell which felt worse—the agonising pain in her head, which made her want to crawl into a dark place and with any luck die there, or the knowledge that unless she got home soon she was all too likely to be sick in public.

Half an hour later Carol returned from dropping the boys off. Kate was barely aware of her knocking and then entering through the back door.

'Thank goodness you've seen sense,' her friend exclaimed in relief, finding Kate safely tucked up in bed and adding with concern, 'I'd stay with you, but I promised I'd take my mother to hospital for her check-up today.'

'I'll be fine,' Kate assured her wanly. 'I just need to sleep off this headache, that's all.'

'Well, if you're sure...'

'I'm sure,' Kate insisted, only realising when Carol had gone that she ought to have asked her to telephone the office for her and explain what had happened.

Somehow just the thought of making the call herself was exhausting—and besides she needed to be sick again...

Sean frowned as his gaze flicked round Kate's empty office. Why hadn't she rung in? Was Oliver more seriously ill than anyone had realised?

It was the human resources department's responsibility to check up on why Kate hadn't reported in, not his, Sean reminded himself grimly. He was simply her employer now, and that was all.

A muscle twitched betrayingly in his jaw. Who the hell did he think he was deceiving?

He was supposed to be leaving here today, to return to headquarters for an important meeting, and he had not planned to come back until the following week.

If the woman in human resources was surprised that he should ask for Kate's home telephone number she was professional enough not to show it, Sean acknowledged.

In the privacy of his office Sean dialled the number, his frown deepening as it rang out unanswered.

Slipping in and out of a feverish half-sleep, Kate was vaguely aware of the telephone ringing, but she felt far too ill to get up and answer it.

* * *

Sean waited until he heard Kate's answering machine cut in before hanging up. Where on earth was she? Unwanted thoughts tormented his imagination. Kate sitting in a hospital waiting room whilst medical staff sped away with Oliver's vulnerable little-boy body… His feeling of anguish and anxiety, combined with a need to be there, surged through him and caught him off guard.

He would feel the same concern for any young child, Sean assured himself grittily. Just as he had been himself, Oliver was a fatherless child. He knew all too well how that felt. How it hurt.

A brief telephone call to Head Office was enough to cancel his meeting. How could he chair a meeting when Oliver might be ill?

He stuck it out for as long as he could, punctuating his anxiety with several more unsuccessful telephone calls, but midway through the afternoon he threw down the papers he was supposed to be studying and reached for his jacket.

When Sean reached Kate's house the open back door and the relief on two of the three anxious faces that turned towards him told its own story—or at least some of it.

'Sean!'

'Oh, thank goodness!'

As Oliver raced towards him Sean bent automatically to pick him up.

'My mummy is very sick,' Oliver said, causing Sean to grip Oliver tightly.

'Kate isn't at all well,' Carol explained quickly. 'In fact when I came round with Oliver after school I was so worried I sent for the doctor.'

Sean looked at the tired-looking middle-aged man who was the third member of the trio.

'Kate appears to have contracted a particularly virulent

strain of this current virus,' he explained wearily. 'She's de-
hydrated and very weak, and in no way able to look after
herself at the moment—never mind her child. She needs
someone here to make sure she drinks plenty of fluids and
generally look after her.'

He was looking meaningfully at Carol, who bit her lip
and told him uncomfortably, 'Normally I would have been
only too happy to have Oliver to stay, but—'

'That won't be necessary,' Sean announced firmly, breaking into the conversation. 'I'll stay with Kate and look after
her and Oliver. I'm her ex-husband,' he explained tersely,
when he saw the doctor beginning to frown.

'I should warn you that she's only semi-conscious,' the
doctor told him sharply, after Carol had left to go back to her
own family. 'And slightly delirious and confused in fact,' he
added. 'But that will pass. She's got a high fever, combined
with stomach cramps. I have given her some medication
which should start to make her feel better within the next
twelve hours, although it will be considerably longer than
that before she starts to recover properly and—'

'Why the hell aren't you admitting her to hospital?' Sean
demanded angrily.

'For several reasons,' the doctor answered. 'One, I doubt
very much that I could get her a bed. Two, she has a child,
who will no doubt be distressed by such an action. And
three, whilst she's very unwell, her condition isn't acute. I
appreciate that looking after her isn't going to be easy. If
you're having second thoughts then perhaps you could let
me know now, because I shall have to organise some kind
of temporary foster care for the child and a district nurse to
call round when she can to check on my patient.'

'Foster care! Oliver doesn't need foster care and Kate
doesn't need the district nurse—they've got me,' Sean announced protectively.

The doctor tried not to show his relief. This virus was stretching local medical resources beyond their limits.

'Very well. Now, this is what you will have to do…'

Sean listened grimly as the doctor gave him his instructions.

Oliver was still nestled sleepily in his arms, and after the doctor had gone Oliver looked up into Sean's face and demanded anxiously, 'When is my mummy going to get better?'

'Soon,' Sean assured him calmly, but inwardly he was feeling very far from calm.

Ten minutes later, as he stood beside the bed looking down into Kate's pale face whilst she lay frighteningly still, he felt even less so. Her left hand lay limply on top of the duvet, her fingers ringless and her nails free of polish. She had beautiful hands and fragile, delicate wrists, he reflected sombrely. They had been one the first things about her he had noticed. Now, if anything, her wrist looked even narrower than he remembered.

Suddenly she made a restless movement and turned her hand over. He could see the blueness of her veins through the fine skin. Beads of sweat burst out on her forehead and she moaned suddenly, shivering violently, her eyes opening and then widening in confusion and bewilderment as she saw him.

'It's all right, Kate,' Sean reassured her as she looked vaguely up at him. But even as he was trying to reassure her Sean knew that he could not reassure himself. He could feel the heavy, agonised thud of his heartbeat.

'My head hurts,' Kate told him plaintively.

'Why don't you sit up and drink some of this water, take these tablets the doctor has left for you?' Sean suggested gently. 'They should bring your temperature down and help you to feel better.'

Obediently she tried to do as he suggested, but Sean could see that even the small effort of trying to sit up was too much for her.

Without giving her the chance to protest, he sat down on the bed and put his arm round her, supporting her as he plumped up the pillows.

She was wearing some kind of cotton nightshirt, which was soaked with sweat and damp, and as he supported her she started to shiver so violently that her teeth chattered together.

It made Sean's own throat hurt to see the difficulty she had swallowing even a few sips of water.

'My throat hurts so much,' she whispered to him as she pushed the glass away. 'Everything hurts.'

Automatically Sean placed his hand against her forehead.

'That feels good,' she told him quietly. 'Cool.'

Sean had to swallow back the feelings both her words and the burning hot feel of her skin had aroused.

'I feel so hot,' she complained fretfully.

'You've got a bad virus,' Sean told her.

'I don't want to keep you away from work, Sean. Not with the Anderson contract to get finished.'

Her eyes were closing as he lowered her back against the pillows, and Sean watched her with a frown. The Anderson contract she had referred to was one he had worked on in the early days of their marriage.

'Slightly delirious.' The doctor had warned him. And she was wringing wet, burning up and shivering at the same time.

She had been his wife, his lover, and her body held no secrets from him. How could it when she had given herself so freely to him, when he had been the one to help her to explore and discover the power of its female sexuality? Even so he could feel his muscles clenching as he worked to remove her fever-sodden nightshirt, blessing the fact that it fastened down the front with buttons. Or was it a blessing? Instead of removing it quickly he was having to fight against the savage stab of arousal he felt when he exposed the pale curves of her breasts, to force himself to ignore the sensuality of her naked body and to focus on her illness instead.

Reluctant to search through her drawers for a clean nightshirt, after he had sponged down her fever-soaked body he wrapped her in a towel instead, answering the disjointed questions she asked when she woke up briefly.

By the time he was satisfied that she was both dry and warm, and was finally able to cover her with the duvet, his hands were shaking.

'Sean?'

He froze as he realised she had woken up again. 'Yes?' he replied.

'I love you so much,' she told him simply, smiling sweetly at him before she closed her eyes and drifted back to sleep.

There was, Sean discovered, a dangerous pain inside his chest, and the backs of his eyes were burning, as though they had been soaked with limewash.

It was two o'clock in the morning and Sean was exhausted. Kate's temperature seemed to have dropped a little, much to his relief. And Oliver was fast asleep in his own bed, unaware of the sharp pangs of emotion Sean had felt when Oliver had solemnly explained to him his bedtime routine.

Suppressing a yawn, Sean pushed his hand through his hair. Kate was asleep but he was reluctant to leave her.

He went into the bathroom and had a shower. It had been a long day. His eyes felt gritty and tired. He looked at the empty half of the bed. It wasn't going to hurt anyone if he just lay down and snatched a few minutes' sleep, was it?

* * *

Kate could feel the pain of her anguished despair. A bleak, searing sense of loss engulfed her, lacerated by panic and agonising disbelief. In her jumbled fever-induced dream she ran on leaden legs from room to room of a shadowed empty house, frantically searching for Sean whilst the icy-cold tentacles of her fear took hold of her heart.

Sean had left her and she couldn't bear the pain of losing him. She couldn't endure the thought of living without him. She felt bereft, abandoned, and totally alone.

The pain of her dream was unbearable, and she fought to escape from it, dragging herself frantically through the layers of sleep, crying out Sean's name as she did so.

The moment he heard Kate cry out, Sean was awake.

'Sean?'

He could hear the panic in her voice as she repeated his name, and even in the semi-darkness he could see how her body was shaking.

'Kate, it's all right,' he tried to reassure her, and he placed his hand on her arm and leaned over her.

Kate could feel herself shaking with the intensity of the emotions flooding through her, piercing her muddled confusion. When she managed to force her eyes open she exhaled in relief. She could see Sean's familiar outline in the bed! Sean was here. He had not left her! She had just been having a bad dream!

But, despite her relief, somewhere on the edge of her consciousness something was niggling at her—something she did not want to recognise. Defensively she pushed it away, escaping instead into the comforting security of Sean's presence. But she needed more than just his presence to banish the dark shadows of the dream, she recognised.

Instinctively she moved towards him, wanting, needing

to be closer to him. Although her brain felt muddled, and somehow not fully functioning, her senses were sharply acute and her whole body shuddered as she breathed in his warm, musky scent. She could feel the familiar arousal taking over her body.

She wanted Sean to hold her.

'Hold me close, Sean,' she begged huskily, shivering as she told him in a low, unsteady voice, 'I was dreaming that you weren't here... And everything seems so muddled. I can't seem to think straight...'

'You've had a bad virus and a high fever,' Sean told her quietly, deliberately using the past tense so that he didn't frighten her.

'I think I must have been suffering from delusions.' Kate tried to laugh, but her smile disappeared as her whole body shuddered violently. 'It was so frightening, Sean,' she whispered. 'I dreamt that I was in a house looking for you but you weren't there.'

Emotional tears filled her eyes and Sean listened helplessly. Fever burned in her face and glazed her eyes. She made a small movement towards him and Sean began to draw back. But it was too late. Kate was already nestling trustingly into him.

Sombrely Sean looked down at her. His throat felt tight and he was acutely conscious that this should not be happening. Right now his role was that of nurse and guardian— but how could he explain that to her in her present confused and feverish condition? Would she even understand what he was trying to say? Somehow Sean doubted it. And, as though to confirm his thoughts, he felt her move, saw that his slight hesitation had made her focus on him, her anxious gaze searching his face.

'Sean?' she questioned as she reached out and curled her fingers onto the polished skin of his shoulder.

And then, before he could stop her, she moved closer to him and pressed her face against his chest.

Eagerly Kate snuggled closer to the security of Sean's body. Just breathing in the familiar scent of him was immediately reassuring and calming. Calming? When had anything to do with being close to Sean had a calming effect on her? Kate smiled inwardly at herself. Calm was certainly not the way she was feeling right now, with her heart hammering and her body feeling so ridiculously weak. Weak, maybe, but also acutely and erotically aware of Sean. And her physical longing was heightened by the intensity of her aching, emotional need to be close to him.

It was as though her dream had left her with a vulnerability that only Sean's intimate closeness could repair, Kate acknowledged vaguely. Dismissing her thoughts, she nuzzled into the warmth of his chest, tasting it with absorbed delight. And then, whilst Sean was still grappling with his own shock, she moved her head and placed her lips against his flesh, openly luxuriating in the pleasure of slowly and languorously caressing him.

Sean could feel the shallow, rapid race of his heartbeat as he tensed his body against its immediate reaction to her. He had never for one minute imagined, and certainly not intended anything like this should happen.

But now that it had…

Now that it had he was having to battle against the reality of the situation, against the achingly sensual pleasure of Kate half lying over him. There was no way he could allow himself to even acknowledge what it did to him, having the softness of her lips delicately brushing his skin.

If he didn't put an end to what was happening, and soon, he would be in danger of racing out of control and down a road he had no right to travel. A road which Kate in full health would refuse to allow him to travel.

Determinedly Sean reached out and closed his hands around her upper arms, intending to lift her away from his body and place her back on her own half of the bed. But the minute he tried to move her she moaned and clung to him.

It was more than his self-control could bear. Sean swallowed hard. He had to put a stop to this.

'Kate—'

'Mmm…' Kate exhaled on an ecstatic sigh as she pressed a small kiss to the corner of Sean's mouth. Helplessly he returned it—with interest—whilst inside him a savagely bitter voice reminded him condemningly that Kate was sick, that she did not really know what was happening, and that just because she was kissing him back, and trying to touch him, it did not mean that he should let her.

It took all the strength he had to lift his mouth from the sweetness of her, and when he did she looked up at him in confused bewilderment.

He had to put a stop to this, and he had to do it now, Sean told himself fiercely.

But the look in Kate's eyes made him want to take her in his arms and hold her there until it disappeared.

The duvet had slipped away to reveal the curves of her breasts, palely silvered by the moonlight streaming in through the window, in contrast to the sensually darkened areolae from which her nipples rose in stiffly erect peaks.

Dizzily Kate watched with open sensual pleasure as she saw Sean's gaze fasten helplessly on her exposed breasts. But she knew that she wanted to feel more than his hot gaze touching her. A fierce shudder gripped her, making her gasp and exhale.

And as he watched her, and recognised what she was feeling, somehow, without him knowing how it had happened, Sean started to lower his mouth towards her lips.

Eagerly Kate offered herself up for Sean's possession,

her hands reaching out with surprising strength to draw him to her waiting body. A wild shudder contorted her as she parted her lips for the driving pressure of his tongue, her own mating with it.

Beneath his hands Sean could feel the familiarity of her—the longed-for and long-loved familiarity of her—and it was more than his self-control could stand. He hadn't meant for his hand to touch her breast, to slowly caress its fullness as it swelled sweetly into his hand, and he certainly hadn't intended to allow his fingers to stroke softly against her thigh as she trembled beneath his touch. Dear heaven, he should not be permitting this, Sean admitted helplessly. He should be putting in place the barriers between them that Kate could not. He should be stopping what was happening, not feeling that he would die if he did not hold her and love her.

His need was overruling his conscience and his self-control. The tight, swollen feel of the nipple pressing into his hand, the feel of Kate's mouth against his skin, the knowledge that he had only to move his hand and place it between her open thighs to feel the familiar pleasure of her sweet, wet warmth, was obliterating everything but his overpowering need for her.

He moved her body and cupped her face, kissing her until she was moaning longingly beneath his mouth, her hands seeking his hard arousal as hungrily as his were seeking the swollen wetness of hers.

He kissed her breasts, slowly and then far more fiercely, making her shudder with desire as she felt the rough sensual lapping of his tongue against the sensitivity of her nipples, then cry out in primitive female pleasure when his mouth closed over one swollen peak.

Her own hand pressed over the hand he had placed between her thighs, holding it there as his fingers caressed her receptive flesh.

Sean felt that his actions were not premeditated so much as preordained. What was happening between them just seemed so natural, so right—and so very, very much what their bodies wanted. So much so, in fact, that for a few seconds he allowed himself to suspend reality and give in to his love.

Almost as soon as he touched her intimately Sean heard Kate cry out as her body quickened to his touch. Her hands clamped around his arm as though seeking and needing reassurance—and the small, almost startled cry ended as the contractions of her orgasm began.

'Sean,' Kate whispered dreamily, with appreciative pleasure, lifting her hand to touch his face, but she was asleep before she could finish doing so.

Numbly Sean waited until he was sure that Kate was deeply asleep before moving away from her. He could not comprehend how he had allowed things to get so out of hand, why he had not somehow stopped. Not so much Kate, but more importantly himself. Why and how had he allowed his feelings to become so out of control that he had given in to them? A stab of revulsion against himself hit him like a sledgehammer-blow to his heart.

Deep down inside Sean, despite the trauma of his childhood, was a core of pure old-fashioned male protectiveness that was an essential part of how he regarded himself. As a man who would protect the woman he loved—from everything and everyone, even including himself, if and when necessary. Wasn't that, after all, why he had divorced Kate in the first place? So that she should be free to have with another man the children he knew he could not give her.

That element of his personality was of vital importance to him; it underpinned his sense of who he was and his pride

in himself. But how could he be proud of himself now?
As his anger against himself grew Sean paced the floor of
Kate's room, refusing to allow himself to escape from his
own contempt.

A sound from the bed—a whimper and then a small
burst of unintelligible words—caused him to freeze, and
then go to Kate's side.

It was obvious that the fever was mounting again, and
when he woke her to give her the medication the doctor had
left, and to make sure she drank some water, the blank, un-
seeing look she gave him made Sean suspect that she didn't
even realise who he was...

She would hate knowing that she had clung to him and
begged him to love her, he recognised grimly. Although he
doubted that in her feverish state she would remember what
had happened. She would certainly not *want* to remember
it; he knew that.

But when he laid her down again, and sponged her hot
skin, Sean acknowledged that he would remember it, that
he would store the memory deep inside himself, where he
had already stored so many memories of her.

Bleakly he looked away from her. The pain inside him
that never went away was tearing at his gut. Just being here
in this small house intensified it almost beyond bearing.
Within this house were the woman he loved, always would
love, and the child he would give his life to have been able
to give her. Kate had no idea what she did to him when
she tried to insist that Oliver was his son. Kate could feel
the warmth of sunlight on her closed eyelids. Weakly she
struggled to understand the feeling of panic that the warmth
engendered, her body stiffening as the knowledge hit her
that the sunlight only shone through her bedroom window
early in the afternoon.

As she opened her eyes she tried to sit up in her bed, only

to collapse against her pillows as her virus-weakened body refused to support her. Shock and panic spiked through her, multiplied by fear as she realised how quiet the house was.

Where was Oliver, and why was she here in bed? She had to get up and find her son. Shakily she pushed back the bedclothes, frowning in alarmed bewilderment as she looked down at the unfamiliar sea-green fine cotton night-gown she was wearing, its hem and bodice lavishly trimmed with expensive lace.

Instinctively she touched the fabric. Once, long ago, she had owned such things—not that she had ever worn them very much. Her expression changed. Sean had always pre-ferred them to sleep skin to skin, and so had she. A tiny shudder gripped her body as a vague, unsettling memory—confusing misty images of Sean and her as lovers—stirred inside her head like ripples on water. And just as elusive to grasp. But she had an urgent and anxious feeling that she had to grasp it.

Her heart was hammering against her ribs; she felt oddly disorientated—light-headed, almost. She put her feet on the floor and stood up, shocked to discover that her legs could barely support her and that she had to cling to the side of the bed.

Whilst she was struggling to keep her balance the bedroom door opened, but her initial relief was quickly swamped by angry panic when she saw Sean coming to-wards her. Immediately she backed up towards the bed. Sean stood still.

Shockingly surreal and unwanted mental flashbacks were tormenting her. Disjointed but frighteningly potent memo-ries of Sean and herself as lovers, of herself begging Sean to make love to her.

Nausea and pain tore at her in equal measures. She could

hardly bring herself to look at him. Her head was pounding, and with every second that passed she felt weaker.

'Where's Oliver?' she demanded anxiously. 'And what are you doing here?'

'Oliver's at nursery, and I'm here because both you and he needed someone here to look after you.'

'To look after me? You've been looking after me?' Try as she might, Kate couldn't keep the near hysterical anguish out of her voice. 'Why you?'

'Why not me? I was here, and I am your ex-husband.' He gave a small dismissive shrug.

'My ex-husband?'

'There was no one else, Kate.' Sean stopped her almost gently. 'Your friend Carol wanted to help, but she has a husband and a child of her own. I did wonder at one stage if perhaps hospital…'

'Hospital?' Kate could feel the terrifyingly heavy thud of her heart.

'The virus you've had hit you very hard,' Sean told her patiently, adding, 'Look, why don't you get back into bed—?' As he spoke he came towards her.

'No! Don't touch me,' Kate protested in panic when he looked as if he were about to pick her up.

The way he was looking at her made her flush painfully, her skin burning. Just having him stand so close to her was activating all kinds of disturbing memories. It wasn't just some feverish act of her imagination that was responsible, Kate acknowledged miserably. The memories were there because it had happened. She had said and done all those things she was being forced to remember.

Helplessly she waited for Sean to mock and taunt her with the words she could hear ringing so clearly inside her own head, to remind her that she had already begged him to do far more than merely touch her. Instead he said noth-

ing, simply bent down to pick her up and placed her firmly
back in the bed.

'You're still very weak—' he told her, and then broke off
as the doorbell rang. 'That will be the doctor. I'll go down
and let him in.'

As soon as he had gone Kate lifted her hand to her forehead and pressed her skin tightly as she tried to force herself to remember exactly what had happened. Humiliatingly,
all her body could and would remember was the pleasure
Sean had given it, whilst inside her head she could hear the
ringing echo of her own passionate pleas for his possession.

The bedroom door reopened and Sean ushered in the
doctor, whose face was full of concern.

'So, Kate, you are back with us. Good! Your husband
has obviously done an excellent job of looking after you.'

Her husband! Kate wanted to remind the doctor that Sean
was her ex-husband, but somehow it was too much of an effort. The frightening realisation of just how physically weak
she felt was just beginning to hit her.

'You are over the worst now, but that does not mean you
are better. You are very far from better,' the doctor told her
emphatically.

'So when will I be better?' Kate demanded, with a show
of energy she was far from feeling. A little uncomfortably
she saw that the doctor was looking at her as though he knew
perfectly well how she was really feeling.

'Well, if you do as you are told, and don't try to rush
things, I would say that you will be fully back to normal in
three weeks or so.'

'Three weeks!' Kate struggled to sit up as she stared at
him in shock. 'But, no! That's impossible!' she started to
tell him frantically. 'I need to find a new job! I have to go
back to work. I've just had a bit of a virus, that's all—it can't
possibly take three weeks for me to get better!'

'You've had a very serious strain of the virus, and without wanting to frighten you…' the doctor paused. 'It is fortunate that you have such a naturally strong constitution,' he told her. 'And as for you going back to work…' He shook his head. 'No, you cannot do that.'

'Nor will she be doing that, Doctor.' Sean joined the conversation grimly, giving Kate a warning look as he added smoothly, 'I know that no employer would allow her to work anyway, until she has been given a clean bill of health.'

Kate felt distraught, but she had to satisfy herself with giving Sean a seethingly furious look as he escorted the doctor to the door.

When he came back, she told him determinedly, 'I can't not work for three weeks! I would have found a new job by now if I hadn't been ill,' she added fretfully.

When Sean remained silent she reminded him angrily, 'I have to work. I have a child to support and a mortgage to pay.'

'We'll talk about this later,' Sean said in a clipped voice. 'It's time for me to go and collect Oliver from nursery.'

Kate wanted to argue, but her head was pounding and all she could do was watch him leave with helpless fury.

It just wasn't possible that it would take three weeks before she was back to normal! She was sure the doctor was exaggerating her weakness—no doubt prompted and aided by Sean, she decided, scowling. And she was going to prove it!

The moment she heard Sean leave she thrust back the bedcovers, refusing to acknowledge that even that action left her arms aching. She was in her twenties, for heaven's sake, not in her nineties, she reminded herself determinedly, and she ignored her dizziness.

Placing her feet firmly on the floor, she stood up, and immediately had to make a wild grab for the bed as her legs refused to support her properly. Okay, she was feeling a little bit weak—but that was because she hadn't been doing anything, because she had been lying in bed and not using her muscles.

Kate could feel her face starting to burn as she was forced to remember just what she had done in bed. And as she clung unsteadily to the bed other vague images wove themselves in and out of her memory: strong arms lifting and holding her, supporting her whilst she drank, careful hands soothing her hot and hurting skin, the presence of a shadowy but oh-so-comforting figure doing for her everything that needed to be done, even anticipating her every need.

Shakily Kate wondered for just how long the fever had consumed her. She touched her hair; it felt clean and soft. She had an immediate and shocking image of being held beneath the shower, whilst blissfully cleansing water cascaded over her sticky and uncomfortable body.

Sean had done all those things for her. Sean had cared for her as though…as though… As though they were still a couple—a pair bonded together by mutual love and commitment. As though he still loved her!

But he had abandoned her for someone else, she reminded herself fiercely as she forced her weak aching legs to move. He had given the love she had thought exclusively hers to another woman. No matter what her deepest and most secret feelings, she must not allow herself to forget that betrayal.

Her deepest and most secret feelings? A recognition she did not want to acknowledge tightened its hurting grasp around her heart. Gritting her teeth, she took three steps, and then gasped out loud with shock as her legs refused to support her any longer and she sank awkwardly to the floor.

Ten minutes later she was safely back in bed—her bones, never mind her flesh, feeling as though they had been pummelled and bruised, every bit of her filled with an aching, nagging pain she couldn't ignore.

Kate had never really been physically ill, and the only real physical pain she had had to endure was when she had given birth to Oliver—and anyway, that had been different.

This unfamiliar aching weakness was alien to her, and very frightening. She loathed the thought of being dependent on anyone, no matter who it might be, and that it should be Sean brought a whole raft of emotional complications she just did not feel able to cope with. But she was going to have to cope with them. Because, as she had just proved to herself, the doctor had been quite correct—she was far too weak to even look after herself, never mind care properly for Oliver, or find a new job!

Angry tears burned the backs of her eyes, followed by a feeling of panicky fear. How was she going to manage? How would she support them both? It seemed so unfair that after all the hard work she had done this should happen—now when she had finally begun to allow herself to hope that her plans for their financial security would be successful. Hastily she blinked the tears away as she heard the door open, followed by the sound of Oliver's excited voice.

The sight of him bursting into her room and running towards her, followed by Sean, immediately lifted her spirits—although she frowned a little to see that he was wearing obviously new clothes she didn't recognise.

As though he could guess what she was thinking, Sean explained carelessly, 'I couldn't get the washing dry because of the rain, so I bought some new stuff.'

Oliver had reached the bed and was scrambling onto it. As she reached down to help him Kate saw the labels on the new clothes and her mouth compressed, her panic returning. Expensive designer labels! How on earth was she going to repay Sean for them? She had only ever been able to afford to buy Oliver good second-hand clothes, and sometimes new things from chain stores.

'Mummy, you're properly awake at last!' Oliver beamed as he kissed her enthusiastically. 'Look what I painted for you!' he said, triumphantly showing her the brightly painted paper he was holding.

'It's me and you and Sean, and Sean's house where we're all going to live.' Immediately Kate went still, keeping her arm around her son whilst she looked accusingly at Sean. Her heart was pounding so heavily that it hurt.

'What—?' she began fiercely, but Sean was already lifting Oliver off the bed.

'Come on,' he was saying to Oliver. 'Let's go downstairs and make Mummy some tea. We'll talk later,' he added quietly to Kate.

'Yes, and then I'll read you a story, Mummy,' Oliver told her happily. 'We've read you a story every night—haven't we, Sean? But you weren't properly awake. Having lots of sleep made you get better, though,' he informed Kate importantly. With a graveness that tore at her heart, Oliver continued, 'You have to have lots of water to drink, doesn't she, Sean?'

'Lots of water, and now some proper food,' Sean agreed calmly.

Kate could feel her eyes smarting with emotional tears as Sean disappeared with Oliver.

She had been miserably worried about her illness affecting Oliver emotionally, but now it was plain to her that she had worried unnecessarily. Because Oliver had had Sean. Because Oliver had had his father.

A huge groundswell of emotional pain began deep down inside her. How could Sean behave as he was doing with Oliver and yet at the same time so completely reject the fact that Oliver was his son? And as for Oliver's innocent remark about them going to live with Sean!

Tiredness began to swamp her, overwhelming her angry attempts to fight it off and remain awake.

When Sean walked into the bedroom five minutes later she was fast asleep. Putting down the tray holding the pot of tea he had brewed for her, and the light omelette he had just made, Sean went over to look at her, frowning deeply as he did so. The previous day the doctor had told him that he believed she was over the worst, and today, with her return to full consciousness, Sean had seen that for himself.

He was reluctant to wake her up, but he knew that she needed to start eating again in order to build up her strength.

Going over to her, he reached out to touch her, and then hesitated. The strap of the nightdress he had bought her when he had been forced to go out and buy food and extra clothes for Oliver had slipped down over her exposed shoulder.

Without thinking, his actions still on the automatic pilot of having looked after her, he curled his fingers around the strap and started to tug it back up.

Kate woke up immediately, her whole body tensing as she saw Sean leaning over her.

The sight of the afternoon sunshine falling against his skin made her stifle a small sound deep in her throat. She had never admitted it to him, but she could still remember how all those years ago, when they had first met, she had deliberately walked past the building site where he was working, unable to stop her avid gaze feeding hungrily on the sight of his naked torso, pinpricks of dangerous excitement prickling all over her body. Just as they were doing now, Kate realised, as the emotions she was fighting to hold in check swept through her.

She must not allow herself to react to him like this, she

told herself fiercely. She must not weaken and let him touch her emotions. She must not forget now much he had hurt her and, much more importantly, how much he could still hurt Oliver.

Thinking of her son gave her the strength to drag her gaze from Sean's and look pointedly at where his hand still rested on her shoulder.

'You must let me know how much you have spent on mine and Oliver's behalf,' she told him stiffly. She knew just from the feel of the fabric against her skin that the night-dress would have cost far more than she would ever have paid—and far more than she could possibly afford. But no way was she going to be beholden to him, even though she felt sick at the thought of having to waste her small precious savings on such unnecessary luxuries.

'There are several things we need to discuss,' Sean told her equably. 'But first you must have something to eat.'

Rebelliously Kate looked at him, the words 'I'm not hungry' dying on her lips as he added gently, 'Doctor's orders, Kate, and if necessary I can assure you I am perfectly willing to feed you myself.'

'That won't be necessary.'

'Good.'

Unable to contain herself any longer, she burst out, 'I can't be off work for three weeks.'

'You can't *not* be,' he corrected her curtly. 'And personally I don't think that your doctor is going to change his mind and allow you to return to work sooner. I take it that you haven't found another job as yet?'

Kate's mouth compressed whilst she contemplated lying to him, but then she was forced to admit that she was unlikely to get away with doing so. 'No,' she answered tersely. 'But I intend to spend the time I have to have off work looking for one.'

'On the contrary,' Sean told her firmly. 'What you are going to be spending the next three weeks doing is recuperating, as I am sure your doctor will inform you. But if you don't believe me you can check with him yourself. He'll be coming back to see you tomorrow, to make sure you're well enough to travel to...' He paused, and then continued coolly, 'To my home.'

'What?' Kate went hot and then cold with shock and disbelief. 'Oh, no. No way!' Kate shook her head violently. 'No way am I ever, *ever* going to live with you again, Sean...'

'Oliver is already looking forward to it,' he said blandly.

Kate felt as though she had been kicked in the stomach. 'You had no right to say anything to Oliver. Nor to use him to—'

'To what?' Sean challenged her. 'Right now you need someone to look after you—someone to look after you both. Physically and financially,' he emphasised unkindly.

'You don't know anything about my financial situation,' Kate denied hotly. 'And you have no right—'

'I know that on the salary you are being paid, given the outgoings you must have, you will have to budget carefully.' He gave a small shrug to conceal from her what he was really feeling. 'Logically it seems unlikely that you have a financial cushion to fall back on if, for instance, you are unable to work. As is the case now!'

Kate could feel a dangerous prickle in her throat as her emotions reacted to his extremely accurate assessment of her situation.

'I may not have your wealth, Sean, but I don't need your charity, or—' she began, only to be cut short as Sean interrupted her.

'Not for yourself, maybe, Kate. But you do need it for Oliver's sake—and don't bother trying to deny it!' He gave another dismissive shrug and turned slightly away from her so that she couldn't read his expression.

Helplessly Kate acknowledged that what Sean had said to her was true. For Oliver's sake she had no option other than to give in and agree to what Sean was suggesting.

Besides, wasn't there somewhere deep inside her still a foolish little shoot of hope that, given time and the opportunity to be with Oliver, Sean would somehow recognise and accept that Ollie was his child? And a part of her wanted that desperately—not for her own sake, but for their son's.

'The only person you have is me!' Sean told her abruptly. 'Unless, of course, you want to get in touch with Oliver's father,' he added harshly, shattering her fragile fantasy.

Kate felt sick with rage and pain. She wanted to scream at him that she did not need anyone, and that if she did need someone she would die before she let that someone be him.

'Carol will help me,' she began sharply, but Sean immediately shook his head.

'She has her own family to look after; you know that! And besides—'

'Besides what?' she demanded angrily.

'Besides, I don't think it would be in Oliver's best interests.'

For a few seconds Kate was rendered speechless with disbelief. When she did find her voice she could hear it trembling with the intensity of her rage.

'You don't think—! Since when have you concerned yourself with Oliver's best interests? Or don't you think it would be in Oliver's "best interests",' she mimicked, 'to be acknowledged and loved by his father?'

'Oh, for God's sake.'

Kate flinched as she heard the savagery in his voice.

'Regardless of who Oliver's father is, you are his mother and Oliver should be near you. If Carol were to look after you both that would necessitate her having Oliver spending a great deal of time at her house, away from you. I'm not denying that she would do her best for both of you, but…'

Kate closed her eyes. She knew exactly what Sean was saying, and what he was not saying—and, even worse, she knew that he was right.

'So who are you proposing will look after us?' she asked defeatedly.

'Me.'

Kate lifted her head and stared at him. 'You? No… That's not possible!'

'On the contrary, as I think I have proved these last few days, it is perfectly possible.'

'But you have to work. You've got your business to run,' Kate reminded him wildly.

'I can run my business from home,' Sean answered laconically. 'And it seems to me that I can look after you and Oliver and work much more easily in a house with more than two bedrooms. At least that way I'll have my own bed to sleep in.'

His own bed!

Kate could feel her anger giving way to panic. This was definitely not a line of conversation she wanted to pursue.

'So where is this house with more than two bedrooms?' she forced herself to demand. 'Oliver is very happy at nursery, and I don't want him upset.'

'Oliver won't be upset. It's only for a short while, and he needs to get used to change as he'll soon be leaving nursery anyway, to start school.' He started to frown. 'Your nearest infant school is nearly ten miles away…'

'I know that,' Kate snapped at him. Of course she knew it! Hadn't she been worrying herself sick for the last year about the fact that the village was too small to have its own school?

'Oliver has got used to having me around,' Sean said abruptly as he walked away from the bed and stood with his back to her, looking out of the window. 'It seems unfair and definitely not in his best interests to subject him to further changes. He's naturally been very upset by your illness, but he's looking forward to the three of us being together.'

The three of us!

A fierce pang of sharp pain stabbed at Kate's heart. How could she deny her son the opportunity to be with his father?

CHAPTER SEVEN

'Now, DON'T WORRY about the cottage. I'll keep an eye on it whilst you're away, and it will be here waiting for you when you come back,' Carol assured Kate comfortingly as she bustled around Kate's bedroom, packing her clothes in the suitcases Sean had provided. 'That is if you are coming back,' she added slyly, giving Kate a questioning look. 'Sean's made no bones about telling everyone that the two of you were married.'

Carol's teasing expression changed to one of anxious concern as she saw the tears filling Kate's eyes. 'Oh, Kate, I'm so sorry,' she apologised.

'It's all right,' Kate assured her. 'I suppose feeling emotionally weak is just another manifestation of this wretched virus. Why has this had to happen to me? All I want is for the next three weeks to be over and for me to be back on my feet,' she told her friend fiercely.

'Mmm. Well, Oliver is certainly enjoying having Sean in his life,' Carol said with gentle warning. 'On the way to school this morning I overheard him trying to convince Sean that a puppy was an essential addition to his life.'

Kate groaned. 'He's been on about having a dog ever since he saw the puppies at the farm last year. I'd love to get him one, but it's just not possible with me working.'

'Heavens, I think Sean's bought you and Oliver enough

clothes to last twelve months, never mind three weeks.'
Carol laughed, ruefully. 'He'll be back soon, and I know
he wants to get off as soon as he can. Where is this house
you're going to be staying, by the way?' she asked Kate
conversationally, and she ruthlessly squashed the last of
the new clothes Sean had insisted on buying for Kate and
Oliver into the new cases, whilst Kate looked on unhappily.

'I don't know,' she admitted, for the moment more concerned about her irritation with Sean for bringing yet more
new clothes that morning than the location of his home.

'Oliver and I aren't charity cases, you know,' she had
thrown bitingly at him when he had arrived back from his
shopping spree. 'We don't need you to buy clothes for us,
Sean.'

'Oliver is outgrowing virtually everything he has,' Sean
had replied quietly. 'And, so far as I can tell, your own
clothes—'

'Are my own concern,' Kate had snapped viciously.

Sean hadn't made any further response, but Kate had
seen the warning grimness of his mouth as he listened to
her churlish outburst.

'Okay, that's the car packed.'

Kate forced a smile for Carol and her husband, Tom,
who had come round to see them off. Her smile turned to
an anxious frown as Oliver and George came rushing towards them, and Oliver missed a step and fell.

Tom was standing closest to him and automatically bent
down to pick him up, smiling reassuringly at him as Oliver's bottom lip thrust out and began to wobble.

'I'll take him!'

Kate's head swivelled round in Sean's direction when she
heard the curtness in his voice, and she saw the immediate
and determined way in which he went to take Oliver from

the other man. When he held Oliver there was a look in his eyes that made Kate's heart turn over. Sean had resented the fact that Tom had gone to Oliver's rescue!

The scuffed knee and bruised pride attended to, Sean put Oliver down whilst he helped Kate to the car. She could walk a few yards now, but she had to admit that it was easier to lean on Sean than to insist on walking by herself. There was surely no real need, though, for Sean to fasten her seat belt for her?

In the enclosed space of the car she was acutely conscious of the scent of his skin, and of the way the dark bristles of his beard were already roughening his jaw. If she leaned forward only just a little she would be able to press her lips to his skin. Her heart turned over and she gazed at him whilst he was absorbed in his task of making her comfortable. The dark thick fans of his eyelashes cast shadows over his skin, making him look unfairly vulnerable. His concentration on his task reminded her poignantly of Oliver whenever he was engrossed in something.

A small sound bubbled in her throat and Sean turned to look at her. At her and into her. His gaze fastened on her eyes and then dropped with merciless swiftness to her mouth. Kate felt her lips parting as though he had willed them to do so. A small, fine shudder ran through her, and she knew exactly why Sean was no longer looking at her or through her, but at her breasts. She could feel the tight betraying stiffness of her nipples as they responded to her sudden arousal.

'When are we going?'

Oliver's impatient demand brought Kate swiftly back to reality.

'We are going right now,' Sean answered him, standing up and closing the passenger door.

* * *

Not even the comfort of Sean's luxurious saloon could completely prevent her body from aching, and by the time they had been travelling for three hours all Kate wanted to do was to be able to lie down and go to sleep, but when Sean asked her if she was all right she nodded, refusing to admit how very uncomfortable and exhausted she felt.

'I'm fine,' she insisted doggedly, refusing to look at him even though she knew he had turned his head to look at her.

'There's bound to be a hotel somewhere round here,' was Sean's undeceived and clipped response. 'We can stop there and you can rest.'

'No,' Kate protested. Hotels, like the new clothes Sean had bought for them, cost money—and she was determined that somehow she was going to repay him every penny he had spent on them.

She hadn't realised that Sean's house was going to be so far away, but her pride would not allow her to ask him exactly where it was or how long it would take them to get there.

Oliver, though, had no such inhibitions, and demanded, 'Are we nearly there yet?'

'Almost,' Sean assured him, without turning his head, and Kate knew that he was smiling because she could hear the smile in his voice.

A wave of tiredness swamped her and she started to slip in her seat, unaware of the anxious look Sean was giving her.

'Not much further now,' she heard him saying quietly. 'Just another couple of junctions on the motorway and then we'll be turning off. We can stop then, and—'

'I've already told you that I don't want to stop,' Kate burst out irritably. 'I never even wanted to go to this wretched house of yours in the first place!' she reminded him bitterly.

As she struggled to make herself comfortable she intercepted the wholly male look her son and his father were

exchanging. Anger and anguish tore at her in equal measures—because these two males who shared one another's
blood had bonded against her. Her anguish grew to fear that
she might not be able to prevent her son from ultimately
being hurt by his father.

She should never have agreed to allowing Sean to do
this, she berated herself inwardly, as she tried to keep awake
and failed.

'Mummy's sleeping.'

Sean gave Oliver a reassuring glance as he pulled off the
motorway. 'She's still not properly well.' Inside, he was more
anxious than he wanted Oliver to know—and not only because of his concern that the journey might have been too
much for Kate.

Perhaps it was just as well that she was asleep, he acknowledged as he drove down the familiar lanes, slowing
for the small villages they passed through until finally they
came to the one that was their destination.

The slowing movement of the car woke Kate, and she stared
out of the passenger window, blinking away her tiredness
and then freezing as she recognised her surroundings.

Accusingly she turned towards Sean, but he was concentrating on his driving as they went through the pretty little
village she had sighed so ecstatically over the first time
they had come here. Nothing had changed, she acknowledged numbly. Everything was still the same, right down
to the small river and the main street of huddled soft stone
houses with their mullioned windows.

They had reached the end of the village now, and Sean
had turned, as she knew he would, up past the ancient church
and along a narrow lane. A high stone wall guarded the
house from her sight, but already she could see it in her
memory. She felt sick, shocked, betrayed as Sean turned

in through the familiar gates and the car crunched over the
gravel drive.

This was the house he had promised he would buy for her;
the house she had fallen so deeply in love with; the house
she had talked so excitedly to him about as being the home
where they would bring up their children. The house she
had never lived in because he had told her that their marriage was over before she had had the opportunity to do so.

The savagery of her pain gnawed at her stomach and
anger boiled up inside her. If Oliver hadn't been with them
Kate knew that, however unwell she felt, she would have
insisted that Sean turn the car round and take her back to
her own home.

Instead she had to content herself with an acid whisper.
'I can't believe you would do something like this.'

Without replying Sean opened the car door and got out.
The early-evening sun was already warming the soft cream
stone of the house, and the scent of the lavender and roses
filled Kate's nostrils the moment Sean opened the passenger door for her.

'I've told Mrs Hargreaves to prepare rooms for you and
Oliver,' he informed Kate distantly, as he moved to help
her out of her seat.

'Don't touch me,' Kate almost spat at him, hurt eyes
glowing with the heat of her rage.

How could he do this to her? How could he bring her
here, to the home she had thought they would be sharing?
She had to swallow against the nausea in her throat.

Oliver got out of the car and danced up and down on the
gravel, announcing excitedly, 'Sean, I think a puppy would
like it very much here.'

'I'm sure it would,' Sean agreed gravely, but Kate could
see that he was grinning, and a wave of fury swept her,
making her tremble from head to foot.

'Don't you dare—' she began again, and then had to stop as the door to the house opened and a pin-neat middle-aged woman came hurrying towards them.

'I've done everything you asked me to do, Sean,' Annie Hargreaves told her employer, glancing discreetly at Kate and Oliver as she did so.

'Thanks, Annie,' Sean responded easily. 'We won't keep you any longer. I know that Bill will be waiting for his supper.'

'I'll get off, then, shall I?' she answered, turning and starting to walk away from the house.

'Annie and Bill Hargreaves look after the place for me,' Sean told Kate quietly. 'They don't live in, though—they prefer the staff quarters above the garage. I'll take you up to your room and get you settled, and then Oliver and I will bring everything in—right, Oliver?' Sean asked the little boy.

'Right!' Oliver agreed, with a worshipping smile.

Numbly Kate let Sean take her arm and start to guide her towards the house. She wanted to cry very badly but she was not going to allow herself to do so. Not now. Not ever whilst Sean was around.

The large double doors opened up onto the pretty oval hallway she remembered, with its fairy-tale return stairway, but Kate almost faltered and missed a step as she stared around the room. She remembered it as being painted a depressing muddy beige. Now the walls glowed softly in warm butter-yellow—the same yellow she had excitedly told Sean she wanted to have it painted.

The linoleum floor had been replaced with black and white tiles, and an oval pedestal table stood in the middle of the room. As she looked round the hallway Kate started to tremble. Everything in it was just as she had told Sean she wanted to decorate it, but instead of giving her pleasure the

realisation that he had opted for her choice of decor made
her feel acutely sick.

As Sean studied Kate's colourless face and blank eyes,
she started to sway. Cursing under his breath, he swept her
up into his arms. She had always been delicate and slender,
but now she felt frightening frail, he acknowledged as he
ignored her husky rejection of his help and carried her up
the stairs, taking them two at a time.

The rooms he had asked Annie to prepare for her and
Oliver connected with one another. Kate herself had told
him laughingly when they had first viewed the house that
the larger of the two would make an ideal master bedroom,
with the smaller one perfect for a nursery.

'The nurseries are upstairs,' Sean had told her, tongue
in cheek.

Immediately she had turned her face up towards his, and,
laughing, told him, 'You can't fool me, Sean. You're going
to want to have our babies close to us.'

'Our babies,' he had murmured huskily. 'You know, just
hearing you say that makes me want to start making them
right here and now...'

'We haven't bought the house yet—and anyway there
isn't a bed,' Kate had reproved him, mock primly.

'Since when have we needed a bed?' Sean had asked.

Even so she had refused to make love in the house, saying
firmly that it wasn't proper since it didn't belong to them.

'I suppose that's another of those "good manners" rules,
is it?' he had teased her. But in reality he had been very
grateful for the tactful and loving way she had helped him
acquire some necessary social polish.

When they had got home, though, it had been a different story. He had wrapped his arms around her the moment
they were inside their front door, and the only sound she
had made had been one of eager approval...

'Put me down—I can walk!'

Kate's fiercely independent demand told Sean that she was certainly not sharing the bitter sweetness of his sensual memories.

'Maybe you can walk,' he countered grimly. 'But on the evidence of what just happened I doubt that you could have made it all the way up these stairs unaided.'

Kate wanted to argue with him, but she was too conscious of the frantic beat of her heart. She could still remember how she had teased Sean when they had first started dating about the way he loved picking her up, accusing him of wanting to show off his superior male muscle power. But secretly inside a part of her had been thrilled by such evidence of his strength.

Now, though, it was resentment that was responsible for the rapid flip-flopping of her heartbeat, she told herself firmly, determinedly ignoring the small, conscientious inner voice that cautioned her that her resentment was desperately self-defensive.

Why should she need to feel self-defensive, after all? she asked herself in silent bitterness. There might be a very small rebellious and unheeding part of her that was still physically responsive to Sean, but that was all. How could she, a loving and responsible mother, ever forget Sean's refusal to accept that Oliver was his son?

It was just the realisation that he had brought her here to this house—the house she had fallen in love with, had believed she would bring their family up in—that was making her feel so vulnerable, making her long to pillow her head against his shoulder and let her body relax into the comfort and security of his.

'Here we are.'

Sean used his foot to nudge open the heavy door and Kate swivelled her head to look into the room beyond it.

Sunlight warmed the soft cream walls, and wonderfully heavy curtains made of terracotta and cream toile de Jouy fabric hung from the windows, draped the antique half-tester bed. A cream carpet covered the floor, and the whole colour scheme set off the pretty late-Georgian mahogany furniture.

When Sean placed her on the bed Kate had to struggle not to give way to her emotions. The room was exactly as she had excitedly planned to decorate it, right down to the elegant cream blind at the window.

'I've had a bed put in the nursery for Oliver,' Sean was telling her practically, clearly oblivious to the emotional impact the room had on her. Had Sean converted the room next to the nursery into a bathroom, as she had wanted?

She didn't feel she could trust herself to ask, and was glad that she hadn't when Oliver came rushing in, his face alight with excitement.

'Annie says that I can go and see her dog if you say yes, Mummy,' he announced importantly.

'Annie?' Kate checked him swiftly. Sean might refer to his housekeeper and her husband by their Christian names, but Kate wasn't going to have Oliver copy his father unless he had been given permission to do so.

'Annie prefers to be addressed by her first name.' Sean stepped in immediately, reading her mind so easily and so quickly that for a moment Kate couldn't reply. 'And Oliver will be perfectly safe with her dog,' Sean continued. 'I'll take him down to meet her myself.'

Ignoring Kate, Oliver threw his arms around Sean's legs and hugged him tightly, looking up at him with an expression of beatific adoration.

Looking on, Kate could feel her heart turning over slowly and painfully inside her chest, its cavity tight with pain and love and fear.

'Can we go now?' Oliver was pleading, but Sean shook his head.

'No, not now. We'll go tomorrow morning.'

Kate held her breath warily, half anticipating that Oliver might refuse to accept what Sean had told him. Certainly he scowled, and looked as though he was about to object, but, as if he had prepared himself for Oliver's reaction, Sean simply ignored his behaviour.

'Come and have a look at your bedroom, Ollie,' Sean said instead. 'It's right here, next to Mummy's.'

Sean's use of that familiar sweet 'Ollie' made Kate clench her hands into small fists—as did the automatic way in which Sean put his hand down so that Oliver could put his much smaller one into it. Hand in hand, father and son went to inspect the room, leaving her to stare anxiously after their departing backs.

From inside the room she heard Oliver saying, 'There's plenty of room on the floor in here for your sleeping bag, Sean. You'll be able to sleep in my room, and not Mummy's.'

'Well, I'd like to do that, Oliver,' Kate could hear Sean responding seriously. 'But, you see, I have my own bedroom here—like you do at your house.'

'But I want you to sleep here with me and my mummy,' Oliver was insisting, and somehow, without knowing how she knew, Kate sensed that Sean had bent down and picked Oliver up.

'Well, when we were at your house your mummy wasn't very well, was she? And I had to be there in case she needed me. But she's much better now.'

'Well, you could sleep in the same bed, like George's mummy and daddy do,' Oliver offered, with almost-five-year-old logic that made Kate's eyes burn with dry pain.

In the room where a small child's bed had been set up for Oliver, Sean turned towards the window, the boy still in his

arms. He could still feel the gut-wrenching kick of longing
that Oliver's innocent suggestion had prompted.

Kate—the Kate who was no longer his gentle, loving
Kathy—would never willingly welcome him into her bed.
Sean knew that. Yes, on one fever-racked night when she
had not known the difference between their past and their
present she might have been his Kathy once again, but not
in reality.

It was growing dusk and Oliver was leaning heavily
against him. Reluctantly Sean remembered the emotions
that had struck him when he had seen Tom go to Oliver's
rescue, when he had felt irrationally that the other man was
usurping his rightful role. His arms tightened around Oliver. Was the emotional bond he was beginning to develop
with Oliver caused by the fact that Oliver was Kate's child?
Or was it because somehow he had begun to love Oliver for
himself, to feel a fatherly love towards him?

'Why don't I put a video on for you, Ollie?' he suggested
gently now. 'And then you can sit and watch it for a while
before bed.'

'And then will we read Mummy a story?'

Sean ruffled the thick hair ruefully. Determined not to
be accused by Kate of using the television as a baby-minder
for her son, Sean had instituted a bedtime ritual, aided by
Oliver, of them reading a story together. Quite why he had
decided that this should be done in Kate's bedroom he had
no real idea, other than that he'd known how important it
would be to her that she shared in her son's life in every
way she could.

A small sound by the door made him turn round, and
the tightening of his mouth concealed his anguished concern as he saw Kate standing there, holding onto the door
itself for support.

'You're supposed to be resting,' he said curtly.

'Only when I need to, and right now I don't need to,' Kate answered evenly, refusing to look at him and holding out her arms to Oliver instead.

'Why don't I read you a story tonight, Ollie?' she suggested. 'I'm sure that Sean has lots to do.'

To Kate's shock, instead of wriggling to be set free by Sean, Oliver leaned even further into him as Sean set him on his feet.

Kate looked out through the French windows of the pretty sitting room to where Oliver was playing excitedly on the lawn with the Hargreaveses' good-natured collie dog. Child and dog were indulging in what was obviously a mutually blissful game of chase, and when Oliver stumbled and fell on the lawn the dog was immediately all canine concern, standing anxiously over him as the little boy got to his feet undamaged.

They had been living in Sean's house for just over two weeks, and Kate was convinced that she was now fully recovered. Which meant…which meant that it was time for her and Oliver to return to their own home and their own lives.

Kate couldn't deceive herself that Oliver would want to leave. He adored Sean. Kate tensed as she saw Sean strolling across the lawn towards their son. He had left the house shortly after breakfast to attend a business meeting. The moment Oliver saw him he ran towards him, laughing happily when Sean picked him up and swung him round.

As she watched them, inside her head Kate could see another picture. In this one she was standing at Sean's side as Oliver ran towards them both, and Sean's arm was holding her close to his side whilst her head rested on his shoulder.

Her legs felt weak and her whole body was trembling—but not because she had been ill. No, she had to face up to the truth that was responsible for her physical malaise.

It seemed that nothing, not even his rejection of his son, could totally destroy her love for Sean. It was too deeply embedded within her.

Panic, anger and fear fought frantically inside her. She had to tell Sean that she wanted to leave and she had to tell him now!

Taking a deep breath, Kate went out to join them.

As he saw her approaching Sean put Oliver down.

'I'm going to take Nell home for her tea now,' Oliver announced importantly to Kate, manfully taking a firm hold of the obliging dog's collar.

At any other time Kate knew she would have been tenderly amused, ruefully suspecting that it was the dog who was in charge of her son rather than the other away around as the two of them headed to where the housekeeper was waiting for them. But as she watched them Kate was acutely conscious of Sean coming to stand by her side. Immediately she moved slightly away from him. Letting him get too close to her was dangerous!

Bending his head, he told her quietly, 'I've been thinking there's no real reason why Oliver shouldn't have a dog of his own. In fact I called in to see a litter of Labrador pups on my way back this afternoon. They aren't quite old enough to leave their mother yet, but if you feel up to it we could drive over there tomorrow and Ollie could choose his own—'

'No! Oliver is not having a dog!' Kate stopped him sharply and Sean started to frown.

'Kate, he's desperate for one.'

'Do you think I don't know that?' Kate challenged. 'You might have been "thinking", Sean, but you obviously haven't thought enough,' she told him passionately. 'Surely you must realise how impossible it would be for him to have a dog at home? You know that I have to work.' Angrily she turned away from him.

'Kate—' Sean protested, putting his hand on her arm.

Immediately Kate tried to snatch her arm away, demanding furiously, 'Let go of me. I hate you touching me.'

'What?'

When she saw the expression darkening Sean's eyes Kate knew that she had gone too far. But it was too late to retract her reckless words, because he was pulling her into his hold, his arms pinioning her to his body as he looked down into her face.

'No!' Kate protested, but her denial was already being crushed beneath the pressure of Sean's angry kiss. His lips ground down on hers and his fingers tightened into the soft flesh of her arms.

Anger boiled through her veins, making her return the savage intensity of Sean's kiss. But it was an anger bred from longing and need, Kate recognised helplessly, as her own body turned traitor against her and she heard herself moaning softly with liquid pleasure beneath the demanding pressure of Sean's mouth.

Somehow the past and his betrayal of her slipped away. Without her realising it, her hands had lifted to hold Sean's face, and her heart leapt with shatteringly intense emotion. Just the slightly rough feel of his morning-shaved skin was enough to take her arousal levels dangerously higher.

Whilst her hands held Sean's face, his were moulding her body with familiar caresses, kneading her shoulders, then stroking down her spine, spanning the back of her waist and then moving lower. Kate could feel herself starting to tremble as his hands slid past her hips. His thumbs grazed her hipbones themselves, and were then withdrawn as he pulled her fiercely against his own body.

It should have been impossible for her to feel the same shockingly intense thrill of sensual arousal now, as she felt the hard fullness of Sean's erection, as she had done that very first time he had held her like this—but she did. If anything her awareness and the reaction of her body now, as a woman and not as a girl, was far more immediate and fiercely erotic than it had been then.

Perhaps it was because then she'd had no experience by which to measure the pleasure his arousal could lead to, whereas now she most certainly did. Already her imagination had broken free of her control and was filling her head with wanton images, bombarding her senses with messages and promises that totally destroyed her defences.

Within the space of a few seconds her own body was as eager for his as it had been when she was eighteen.

The movement of his hand from her bottom to her breast evoked a low sound of delirious pleasure from her throat and she angled her body so that her breast filled his hand.

'No, Sean. No... Mmm, like that...' Kate could hear herself whispering incoherent urgent words of praise and pleasure between the frantic hungry kisses with which she was caressing his mouth. She no longer cared about what she might be revealing, only what she was feeling! 'Sean.' As she moaned his name she covered the hand he had placed over her breast with her own and whispered achingly, 'Touch me properly, Sean.'

'Properly?'

She could hear the thick male arousal roughening his voice and her skin prickled in female response to it.

'You know what I mean,' she urged him hotly. 'You know what I like.'

'You mean this?'

He was caressing the tender flesh surrounding the tormented nub of her nipple and Kate trembled violently in reaction.

'Mmm, yes. That,' Kate agreed huskily. 'And more,

Sean—but without my clothes. No clothes. Just you,' she continued. 'Just you and me.'

'No clothes? Not even like this?' Pushing down her bra, Sean used his thumb and finger to delicately rub the silk fabric of her top against the stiff thrust of her nipple.

Immediately Kate cried out in agonised pleasure.

'Good…? That was good?' Sean's voice was so thick and low Kate could barely hear it, but she didn't care. He had pushed her clothes completely aside now, and she could see the creamy swell of her breast filling the darkness of his hand as he slowly caressed her eager nipple.

Standing silently in his hold, she gave in to the violent shudders of pleasure ripping through her.

'And with your mouth…' she begged him. The words were jerked from her lips as her body suddenly convulsed against him.

'Kate! Kate!'

Just the way he was saying her name touched every one of her senses. He took hold of her hand and dragged it against his own body. Her fingers curled eagerly around the erection straining against his clothes, making a feverish exploration of their remembered territory. But she wanted to feel him without anything in the way.

She was stretching her hand towards his zip when his mobile rang shrilly, the sound jerking Kate back into reality.

What was she doing? Pulling away from Sean, she started to run towards the house, wanting to escape not just from him but also from her own self-imposed humiliation.

'Kate!'

Sean cursed under his breath when she refused to listen. The mobile was still ringing. Impatiently he switched it off, then started to follow her.

As soon as she reached her room Kate opened the wardrobe and pulled out the suitcases Sean had bought for them.

Opening one of them, she started to drag clothes off the rail and throw them into it.

'What are you doing?'

The sound of Sean's voice made her swing round. 'What does it look like?' she snapped. 'I'm packing. Oliver and I are leaving! We should never have come here in the first place. I knew—'

'You knew what?' Sean stopped her.

He was looking at her with a glint in his eyes that made her heart thump and apprehension feather chillingly down her spine, but angrily Kate refused to bend.

'I know that I just don't want to be here with you, Sean,' Kate answered angrily. 'Look, I don't want to talk about it,' she threw at him when he didn't answer her.

'Less than five minutes ago you were in my arms and—'

'I've just told you I don't want to talk about it!' Kate stormed. 'That…what just happened…meant nothing. It was just…'

'Just what?' Sean challenged her with a softness that was far more dangerous than anger would have been.

He was trying to make her look at him, Kate recognised, but if she did she knew he would see in her eyes how vulnerable she was. Keeping her face averted from him, she insisted stubbornly, 'Nothing!'

Something in his voice had warned her of what was to come. Panicking, Kate dropped the clothes she was holding and started to run, only realising when it was too late that—idiotically—she had run towards the bed instead of the door. Now she was backed up against it, with Sean standing in front her and no option but to turn round and try to scramble over it.

'Nice move,' she heard him say with soft amusement from behind her, and his fingers curled round her ankle as he kneeled on the bed looking down at her.

'I always did think that you've got the sexiest backside I've ever seen: nicely curved and temptingly peachy. And I can remember...'

Kate did not want to hear what he could remember, and for a very good reason. She feared that listening to what Sean could remember might make her feel even more dangerously vulnerable.

Surely there was no good reason why she should feel almost the exact same mix of nervousness and excitement lying here on a bed now, with Sean leaning over her, as she had done that very first time they had been together like this? They had been lovers; they had been married and they had been divorced—his body was almost as familiar to her as her own.

But she did feel the same, and she did feel... Stubbornly Kate tried to deny her feelings, to ignore as well the sensual caress of the bracelet of Sean's fingers round her ankle. She stiffened her body against it, just as she refused to look away from Sean when he turned his head to smile into her eyes.

'Now, about this "nothing",' he murmured, almost affably. 'Let's go through it all again, shall we? Starting right here...'

Somehow he was down on the bed beside her, the upper half of his body pinning hers to the bed, and shamingly Kate knew that a part of her was already greedily soaking up the pleasure of having him so close.

One look at his eyes told her what was going to happen. He was looking directly and deliberately at her mouth, and somehow that look was making her part her lips and wet their nervousness with the tip of her tongue.

'Nothing?' His fingertip traced the curve of her jaw and then the shape of her lips, slowly and heart-stoppingly, whilst he continued to look down at her.

'You know that I'm going to kiss you now don't you?' he whispered.

She tried to say no. She tried to mean no. But Sean was using unfair weapons against her. He knew how very vulnerable she had always been to that slow, sensual, oh-so-seductively-sweet way he had of kissing her, that made her insides melt and her lips cling to him, and the reason he knew was because she herself had told him so, over and over again, in their shared past. And maybe more recently in the heat of that fevered night? Right now all she seemed capable of doing was focusing on his mouth, whilst her heart-rate accelerated.

It had been a bad mistake to close her eyes, Kate acknowledged helplessly, a flurry of heartbeats later, because closing her eyes had somehow transformed her back into the girl she had been the first time Sean had kissed her like this.

Now, as then, her lips parted willingly and eagerly, her senses tensely aroused by the passionate intimacy of his tongue against her own, primed by the kisses they had already shared. Shockingly Kate recognised that her body was rebelliously impatient of any gentle preliminaries, that she was being consumed by a fierce, hungry surging need.

She lifted her hands to Sean's shoulders and held onto them, needing the security of their strength as her own longing smashed down on her, carrying her bodily in its fast-paced flow.

Beneath Sean's, her mouth clung and hungered, and her hands left his shoulders to press his body down harder into her own. She felt Sean tense and lift his mouth from hers to look down into her face.

Surely the hand lifted to his face, the fingers dragged sensuously against his jaw and then raised to trace the shape of his lips and run over and over his mouth could not be hers?

Surely that liquid aching heat spreading through her body could be controlled if she really tried?

Surely this wasn't her, lifting her head off the bed and cupping Sean's face so that she could press impassioned kisses into his skin whilst she moaned her need softly into his mouth?

'Touch me, Sean.' *Love me,* Kate whispered silently inside herself as she stroked a trembling finger over the mouth she had just kissed. 'Make it like it used to be for us...'

Had she really said that?

'Like it used to be?' she heard Sean repeat softly. 'You mean when we were so hungry for one another that not being together was a physical pain? Is that what you mean, Kate? That you want me like that? Like this?'

As he spoke his hands were shaping her body, and Kate could feel the small flames of desire inside her, feeding on his words and growing stronger. Soon there would be a conflagration which would threaten to destroy her, and yet somehow she no longer cared about her danger—all she cared about was this, and now, and Sean's hands on her flesh, Sean's mouth on her mouth, Sean's body covering her body. The wild, untrammelled flood-force of her own dammed-up love and need crashed through the barricade, taking every single last bit of her resistance with it.

Willingly, eagerly and passionately she savoured the hot, urgent strength of Sean's kiss, meeting it and matching it just as she had done when their love was new and her faith and trust in him whole and unbroken. With her eyes closed she could even almost smell the scent of their shared past—the hot dusty air in the small suburban street mingling erotically with the fresh male heat of Sean's skin and her own excited arousal.

But the hand she lifted to curl round Sean's neck, to hold him whilst she prolonged their kiss, was the hand of the woman she was today—and today she wanted Sean as the woman she was, Kate recognised emotionally. And how she wanted him! So much, so very, very much. Her body hungered for him like parched earth crying out in silent agony for the caress of rain.

Only her need wasn't silent any more. It poured from her lips in a soft litany of longing, word on word, plea on plea, as she begged him, 'Sean—my clothes... I don't want them. I want you—your hands, your skin. You.' Kate could feel herself shuddering with the intensity of her own feelings as she twined her arms around him and her body moved restlessly against his. 'I want you, Sean,' she told him. 'The whole essence of you...all of you...'

It had always amazed her that those big, strong hands could be so delicately gentle and assured when removing her clothes, but now their unexpected impatience as Sean pulled and tugged at fabric and fastenings sent a fierce thrill of pleasure through her.

'Kate. Kate. Oh, God, how I've missed you—and this—us...'

The words tumbled thickly from Sean's tongue and were breathed against her skin as he kissed the flesh he was revealing. The sensual drift of his hands had become an urgent, compelling possession that demanded her body give itself over to him completely. The hard need of his mouth on hers spoke of a hunger so long denied that it might easily devour them both. But Kate only gloried in the realisation. How could she not when it so exactly mirrored her own feelings? The fierce thrust of Sean's tongue against her own; the heavy weight of his hand cupping the curve of her hip so possessively; the grinding heat of his body against her own—she welcomed them all.

'Take off your own clothes, Sean,' she begged him huskily. 'I need to feel you against me.' As she spoke she shuddered slightly, remembering how it had felt to have the hot satin of his skin next to her own.

'You do it,' Sean answered.

When she hesitated, he took her hand and lifted it to his body.

'Did I ever tell you how much it turned me on when you undressed me?'

When Kate just looked at him, in passion-soaked silence, he added thickly, 'Do you want me to tell you how much you are turning me on now? Do you want me to show you how much you are turning me on now, Kate?'

She was trembling so violently that she couldn't even unfasten the buttons on his shirt.

'You do it like this,' Sean said huskily, covering her hand with his own. 'And then you do this—' He guided her hand to push his shirt off his body. 'And I do this…'

Kate's whole body arched as he cupped her breast with his hand and then bent his head to cover her tight nipple with his mouth. Kate heard her own raw moan of fierce arousal as his tongue stroked the hard nub of flesh, teasing it, tormenting it. Sean seemed to know exactly when she reached the point where she couldn't bear the torment any longer, because suddenly he took the hard, wanton ache of her nipple into his mouth and drew rhythmically on it, until Kate felt as though that same rhythm was pulsing through-out her whole body, gathering deep inside her, making her want to open her legs and wrap them tightly around him.

Fiercely she tugged at his clothes and Sean helped her.

'Kate!'

The explosive denial Sean made as he virtually pushed her away made Kate stare uncomprehendingly at him.

'If I let you touch me like that I'll come too soon,' he told her rawly. 'And I don't want to do that until I've given you more pleasure than you've ever known. Until I've given you that pleasure and watched you take it from me. Until I'm inside you, where I've ached to be every single night since I've been without you. Until I've done this…'

Long, long before the leisurely journey his hands and his mouth were making over her body had reached the small swell of her belly, Kate was trembling visibly with desire.

As she felt the brush of his mouth against the soft skin of her inner thigh she closed her eyes in aching mute anticipation. His hand covered her sex, making the demanding, hungry pulse deep inside her beat faster. When his fingers parted the arousal-swollen lips of her sex she cried out loud eagerly, almost unable to bear the searing pleasure of his touch.

Her body ached and pulsed, and just the touch of his fingers against her wetness made her rake her fingers against his skin. But the eager sensual movement of her body stilled when Sean exposed the swollen, secret nub of pleasure those lips had concealed to the hungry caress of his tongue.

Kate was helpless to stop the feeling that ran through, over her, filling her and taking her over, making her cry out and lift her body to Sean's mouth as he brought her to that place she had not known for so very long.

And then, when Sean moved and positioned himself in between her legs, taking her in his arms, Kate welcomed him with fierce pleasure. This was what she ached for—this total possession of him and by him, this hard, purposeful thrusting of him within her, that fulfilled and completed her. This climbing together towards that shimmering, shining place where for a brief heartbeat of time they were almost immortal.

Kate reached it first, crying out, her body tensing round Sean to take him with her. And as she felt the familiar pulse of his satisfaction within her Kate's eyes filled with tears.

That this act, so very, very intense and erotically a pleasure beyond all pleasures for those who loved one another, could also be the creation of life, had always given it an extra special intensity for her.

Once she had believed that Sean shared that feeling with her—he had even said that to her the first time she had shyly confided to him her deep, almost spiritual feelings about making love.

And yet now he was denying his own child!

Bitter self-loathing filled her. Where was her pride and her self-respect?

She could feel Sean withdrawing from her, not just physically but emotionally as well, and suddenly a black wave of misery and exhaustion swamped over her.

Sean looked down at the bed where Kate lay fast asleep. He had left her to go to the bathroom, and when he had come back she had been asleep. Anguish shadowed his eyes and hollowed his face as he watched her.

Whilst making love with her he had forgotten there had been another man in her life—someone man enough to give her a child. Bitterness carved his mouth into hard anger.

In his arms she had responded to him as though no other man had ever touched her, as though she had never wanted any other man to touch her... And God alone knew how much he ached and needed to believe that she hadn't. The sweet taste of her still clung to his lips, and the scent of her filled the air around him.

He couldn't endure to live without her any longer, Sean recognised bleakly. Even knowing all that he knew about her!

CHAPTER EIGHT

KATE WOKE UP slowly and languorously, her mouth curling into a smile of remembered bliss. Still half asleep, she stretched her body. Its telltale ache made her smile deepen. There was nothing like waking up in the morning filled with feel-good hormones, she acknowledged happily, reaching out her hand to Sean.

Sean! The speed with which she was catapulted from her warm security to stark reality physically hurt.

She sat up in the bed, her mind an agitated jumble of anxious, angry thoughts. The clothes she had been intending to pack had gone, and so too had the suitcases! The realisation that it was nine o'clock in the morning increased her agitation. It had been late afternoon when she had come up here, and…

Frantically she reined in her speeding thoughts. She couldn't believe she had slept so long and so deeply—although Sean had always teased her about it, claiming that he took it as a compliment that his lovemaking fulfilled her to such an extent.

The very words 'Sean' and 'lovemaking' linked together were making her heart thud erratically—with fury, she told herself crossly, not because of any other reason.

The sudden opening of her bedroom door brought an abrupt halt to her thoughts.

'Mummy!'

Kate's heart turned over as she looked at her son. He was wearing some of the new clothes Sean had insisted on buying for him: a pair of workman-like denim dungarees that made him look heartbreakingly grown up and yet endearingly little-boyish at the same time.

'We've brought you your breakfast,' he said excitedly.

Kate's heart plummeted at his 'we', and she prayed it was the housekeeper he was referring to, not Sean. But the tension in her stomach told her that it was Sean even before he followed Oliver into her room, carrying a heavily laden tray.

'You've been asleep for a very long time,' Oliver reproached her, and then beamed from ear to ear. 'Mummy, I made your toast—and my daddy helped me...'

All three of them froze, and above and beyond her own anguish Kate was seared by the look in Oliver's eyes, his face scarlet as he ran to her and clambered onto the bed, burying his hot, embarrassed face against her body. Automatically she wrapped her arms protectively around him. Unlike Kate, he was too young to recognise why he had called Sean his daddy, but he was not too young to know that he should not have done.

Over Oliver's downbent head Sean looked at Kate, and he put down the tray in silence before turning to leave.

It couldn't be put off any longer, Kate told herself fiercely. Her heart had bled drops of pure concentrated emotion for her son, his betrayal of his feelings and his need, but Oliver's innocent indication of the role he longed to have Sean play in his life had hardened her resolve to leave.

It filled her with a pain like no other she had ever known to recognise her son's vulnerability. How much unintentional damage had she already done by letting him know Sean?

She was well aware of the old cynical saying that it was

a wise child that knew its own father. But what if some-how, somewhere, unknown to modern scientists, there was a primitive, instinctive bond between father and child that had been activated by Sean's appearance in Oliver's life?

The feelings she had experienced at Oliver's realisation of his *faux pas* in calling Sean his 'daddy' went way beyond tears. Of course she had pretended not to be aware of the cause of Oliver's crimson face and discomfort, had coaxed him to share her toast and to tell her about the previous afternoon's activities, when the housekeeper had let him play with the dog and then given him his tea.

But even that had been a mistake, Kate reflected unhappily. Because Oliver had gone on to tell her that Sean had collected him from the housekeeper's quarters, brought him back, given him his bath and read his story to him.

'D— Sean said that you were very tired and needed to sleep.' Oliver's innocent comment had torn at her heart as Kate had acknowledged just why she had 'needed to sleep'.

But even worse than that had been the longingly hopeful look in Oliver's eyes when he had looked up at her and told her, 'I want to stay here for ever, with Nell… and with Sean…'

Kate's heart had sunk when he had suddenly avoided looking at her.

'Well, it has been very nice here,' she had agreed, trying to sound calm. 'But what about George? He's your friend and—'

Oliver had stopped her stubbornly. 'Sean is my friend, and so is Nell. A dog can be a friend, and Nell is mine!' And had completely defeated her when he had added, 'I wish that Sean was my daddy.'

Now, from the sitting room window, she could see Oliver industriously helping the gardener to 'weed'. Helplessly she closed her eyes against her own pain.

When she opened them again she could see Sean's reflection in the glass beside her own. Immediately she turned round.

'We need to talk,' Sean told her flatly.

'There's nothing to talk about.' Kate stopped him bitterly. 'I've almost finished packing, and—' Unable to stop herself, she said quickly, 'I know you must think that I primed Oliver to...to say what he said. But I didn't. He sees George with Tom and... He...he's had this bee in his bonnet for a while, about not having a father...'

Sean recognised that the new name she had chosen for herself suited her. She was Kate now, a woman. Not Kathy, a girl. And he knew that there was something about Kate that he responded to as a man. Kathy the girl had gone, and it grieved him to know that this maturing process had taken place without him being there to share in it. And if that grieved him how the hell was he going to feel if she spent the rest of her life apart from him?

'I've got a proposition to put to you,' he said curtly. 'Or perhaps I should more properly say a proposal,' he amended heavily into the silence that followed his initial words.

'A proposal?' Kate tasted the word cautiously, her stomach churning. What was he going to do? Offer her money to take Oliver away and deny that he was his father? 'What kind of proposal?' she challenged him suspiciously. The look he was giving her was decidedly ironic.

'I thought you knew, Kate, that in my world there is only one kind of proposal a man makes to a woman the morning after they have spent the night together. Anything else *would* be a proposition.' When she went rigid and simply stared at him, he elucidated tiredly, 'I am asking you to marry me, Kate.'

The shock ran through her like lightning, a vivid flash of disbelief followed by an unbelievably intense and coruscating pain, out of which she could only demand sharply, 'Why?'

'Why? Because I want you back as my wife, and—' Sean turned his head and looked out across the lawn, his face averted so that Kate could not see his expression as he added emotionlessly, 'And because I want Oliver as my son.'

It was, Kate decided, almost as though she was hearing Sean speak from very far away, through an impenetrable glass wall.

The angry and rejecting words, *But Oliver* is *your son* rolled like thunder through her heart, but somehow she managed to hold them back. And she held them back because inside her head she had a painfully clear image of a small boy who desperately wanted a father. If she knew anything about Sean she knew that he was a man who committed himself totally and completely to everything he decided to do—almost single-mindedly so at times.

She had seen for herself the rapport he was developing with Oliver, and she knew that to pretend such a bond was simply not in Sean's nature. But she could not and would not take risks with her son's emotional future!

'Your son?' she questioned coldly 'But, Sean, you have already refused to accept that Oliver is your son. You have told me that you believe another man fathered him, and, believing that—'

'That isn't a road I'm prepared to go down.' Sean stopped her sharply. When he saw her face he demanded savagely, 'Don't you realise how it feels for me to know that there's been another man in your life? In your bed? Didn't last night tell you anything about how much I still want you? The only way I can deal with this is to draw a line under it, Kate, to box it up and bury it somewhere so deep that it can never be disinterred.'

'Do you think it's any different for me? You were unfaithful to me, Sean.'

'You can forget all about her, Kate. She never really—'

'Meant anything to you?' Kate stopped him bitingly.

Sean looked away from her. He had almost fallen into the trap of saying that the other woman had never really existed!

What would Kate think if she knew the pitiful, pathetic truth about him? How would she react? Would she pity him? Reject him? Would knowing the truth enable her to understand how deeply and completely he loved Oliver and wanted to be a father to him?

A part of him yearned to share his knowledge and his pain with her, but his pride held him back.

'Oliver needs a father,' he said heavily instead. 'And I—'

'You want to take pity on us?' Kate suggested angrily, reluctant to admit even to herself just how strongly his impassioned words had touched her emotions.

'No,' Sean denied, the glimmer of ironic self-mockery glinting in his eyes, concealing his pain. 'I want you and Oliver to take pity on me.'

It was as close as he could bring himself to telling her the truth.

When she didn't answer he told her bleakly, 'Both of us know how it feels to grow up without the love of a parent. Oliver wants a father.'

Kate couldn't stand any more. The words *Oliver has a father* burned on her lips, but in the garden she could see her son, and already she knew how much it would mean to him if she agreed to what Sean was suggesting. 'I—I…' As she tried to squeeze out her denial all she could hear was Oliver calling Sean his daddy.

She might be able to resist all the emotional pressure that Sean could possibly put on her, but no way could she resist that special sound she had heard in her son's voice.

She took a deep breath. 'Very well. I accept. But if you ever, *ever* do anything to hurt Oliver I shall leave you there and then,' she warned him passionately.

She had already turned away from him when she heard him coming after her. As she stopped moving he took hold of her, imprisoning her in his arms whilst he kissed her with fierce passion.

Helplessly Kate felt her mouth softening beneath his, and her traitorous body, still flooded with sensual memories of his lovemaking, simply softened into his until she was moulded against him so closely that she might have been a part of him. He might have started the kiss, but she was the one who prolonged it, Kate recognised hazily as her mouth clung to his, and she gave in to her need to trace the shape of his mouth with her tongue-tip and to slide her fingers into the thick darkness of his hair.

Against her body she could feel the hard pulse of his erection. Mindlessly she pressed closer to it, waiting for Sean to cup her breast with his hand and discover the hard eagerness of her nipple. But instead he pushed her way from him, breaking the kiss.

Humiliated, she was about to walk away from him when she heard him saying in quiet explanation and warning, 'Oliver!'

It shocked her to realise that Sean had been more aware of their son's approach than her, but her hope that Oliver had not witnessed their intimacy foundered as he stepped through the open French window and immediately demanded, 'Why were you kissing Sean, Mummy?'

Before Kate could think of anything to say, Sean answered for her, telling him calmly, 'We were kissing because we are going to get married, and that's what married people do.'

As he finished speaking Sean kneeled down and held

out his arms to Oliver. 'I've asked your mummy to marry me, Oliver. And now there's something I want to ask you.' Kate couldn't help it; emotion welled up inside her. But it was nothing to what she felt when Sean continued, 'Will you let me be your daddy, Oliver?'

The look on Oliver's face as it lit up with delight was all the answer he needed to give—that and the fact that he threw himself bodily into Sean's arms!

As Sean stood up, hoisting Oliver onto his shoulder, the little boy was chanting, 'Daddy—Daddy. I can call you Daddy now, can't I, Sean?'

As Sean nodded his head Kate was sure she could see the glint of moisture in his eyes.

CHAPTER NINE

SEAN HAD INSISTED on a church ceremony, much to Kate's surprise, and even more surprising was just how very much like a new bride she actually felt, standing in the doorway of the small church ready to walk down the aisle to where Sean was waiting for her.

The graceful dress she was wearing was cream, the heavy satin fabric rustling expensively as she turned to look down at Oliver. 'Ready, Ollie?' she asked him tenderly.

He had been so excited about today, but now that it was here he looked round-eyed and slightly over-awed.

John was going to give her away, but it was Oliver who was going to walk down the aisle with her. That had been her decision, and one that Sean had listened to in shuttered-eyed silence.

Inside the church, with the heat of the sun shut away, the timelessness of this place where people had worshipped century upon century cast its own special grace over them as Oliver reached up and slipped his hand into hers.

Together, as the sound of the organ music surged and swelled, mother and son walked towards the man waiting for them, and into whose care they were giving themselves.

They had almost reached him when Oliver tugged

on Kate's hand and announced in a loud stage whisper, 'Mummy, I'm really glad that Sean is going to marry us.'

Kate completed the last few steps in a blur of tears, totally overwhelmed by her emotions.

The artfully simple bouquet of lilies and greenery she carried were removed from her by Carol, but when her friend went to take Oliver's hand, to lead him away, Sean shook his head and took it himself.

Then, with Oliver standing between them and both of them holding one of his hands, the vicar began the service that would reunite them, bind them not just as husband and wife, but this time as parents as well.

'Okay?'

As the bells pealed in celebration of their marriage and the sun shone down Kate nodded mutely. Surely she wasn't still brooding on the perfunctory kiss with which Sean had acknowledged his new commitment to her, was she?

She had remarried him because he was Oliver's father, and not for any other reason, she told herself fiercely.

Their wedding breakfast was being held in a private dining room at a very exclusive local hotel, and from there they were flying to Italy for a few days. Initially she had tried to protest, but Sean had overruled her, announcing that the three of them needed time together alone, away from their normal environment, to start establishing their new roles in one another's lives.

Of the three of them, Oliver had certainly had no difficulties whatsoever in adapting. The word 'daddy' seemed to leave his lips with increasing regularity. In fact she could hear him saying it now, as he beamed up at Sean and told him importantly that he was now his little boy.

A small shadow touched Kate's face.

   'I want to adopt Oliver legally,' Sean had told her abruptly
the previous week.

   Kate had refused to respond. How could he adopt his
own son?

Kate opened her eyes reluctantly, unwilling to abandon the
dream she had just been having in which she had been lying
in Sean's arms, their naked bodies entwined. The huge bed
in their hotel suite was empty of her husband, though. Last
night, following their arrival, when she had seen the suite,
she had unwisely exclaimed, 'Are we all in the same room?'

   'I thought you'd prefer it that way,' Sean had responded.

   'Yes. I do,' Kate had agreed, but she knew that a tiny part
of her couldn't help comparing the circumstances of this,
their second honeymoon, to the first one they had shared.
Their surroundings might not have been anything like as
luxurious, but even the air in the small room had been so
drenched with the scent of their love and hunger for one another that it had been an aphrodisiac all on its own.

   That had been then, though, and this was now!

   And where was Oliver? The small bed Sean had insisted
on having set up in their room was also empty.

   Anxiously she pushed back the bedclothes and reached
for her robe. They'd arrived so late in the evening that she
had done no more than nod in acceptance of Sean's description of their suite and its facilities, but now, as she pushed
opened the door onto their private patio, she caught her
breath in delight.

   The hotel had originally been a small palace, and their
suite was at ground level for Oliver's benefit. From the patio
Kate could see the still blue water of the hotel's breathtak-
ingly effective infinity pool. The sound of splashing water
to the side of her caught her attention, and she froze as she
realised that it was Oliver who was causing it, and Sean

stood at his side in what was obviously a children's swimming area, encouraging him to swim.

Encouraging him to swim! But Ollie couldn't swim. She had done everything she could to get him to swim, right from him being a baby, but he had steadfastly clung on to his terror of the water. Until now... Until Sean...

Out of nowhere a feeling she just did not want to analyse struck her. She felt excluded, unwanted. She felt jealous, Kate recognised, angry with herself for having such feelings.

Sean had told her that he wanted to remarry her because of Oliver, but suddenly it was striking her exactly what that meant.

Sean had always wanted a son, and now, as a very successful businessman, no doubt he wanted one even more. Given his own childhood, Kate could see that creating his own dynasty would appeal to Sean. But that did not mean that he loved Oliver—and it certainly didn't mean that he loved her.

Had she done the right thing in marrying Sean? Or had she given in to her emotions? Hadn't there been somewhere deeply buried inside her a small, desperate hope that somehow Sean would come to recognise that Oliver was his son and that in doing so he would...?

He would what?

She could hear Oliver and Sean making their way back. Quickly she pushed her anxiety to one side.

The moment they walked onto the patio Oliver ran towards her, shouting excitedly, 'Mummy—Mummy, I was swimming.'

As he launched himself at her Kate caught him up in her arms, closing her eyes as she savoured the echoes of his babyhood in the smell of his skin and its softness.

'I can't believe you haven't taught him to swim,' she

heard Sean commenting grimly, and he reached out and took Oliver from her arms with the automatic action of a man who knew it was his right to hold his child.

Kate held her breath, telling herself fiercely that it wasn't disappointment that filled her when Oliver went happily to Sean.

'I tried.' She answered Sean's criticism defensively. 'But right from being a baby Ollie has been frightened of water...'

'Well, he isn't frightened now,' Sean announced. 'Shower now, Ollie, and then breakfast,' Kate heard him saying firmly as he put Ollie down.

Once he was out of earshot Sean said, 'Perhaps he could sense that you were afraid for him? Children need to feel that they are safe.'

'Thanks for the child guidance lecture,' Kate snapped furiously. 'But I'd just like to remind you, Sean, that I've been Oliver's mother from the moment he was conceived.'

'And I am now his father,' Sean replied fiercely.

They were words which were constantly inside her thoughts and her heart over the following few days of their brief 'honeymoon', as Sean and Oliver formed a close male bond from which she felt totally excluded.

And now, with their holiday over, Kate couldn't help observing as they walked towards Sean's parked car that Oliver was even beginning to talk like his father.

Mrs Hargreaves was waiting to welcome them when they arrived home, and although Kate was vaguely aware of the conspiratorial look the housekeeper exchanged with Sean, she didn't pay very much regard to it, or to the few private words she hurried to have with Sean.

Upstairs, she was turning to head for her bedroom when Sean stopped her.

'I've asked Mrs Hargreaves to move your things into the master bedroom.'

Kate's stomach muscles quivered. Angry with herself for the fierce stab of pleasure the thought of sleeping with Sean again caused her, she forced herself to object. 'But that's your bedroom.'

'It was my bedroom,' Sean agreed coolly. 'But it's now our bedroom.'

Their bedroom. The unwanted feeling intensified and spread. Kate knew that she was perilously close to giving in to her renewed love for Sean. He might want her sexually, but he had told her himself that he had remarried her for Oliver's sake.

She wasn't going to humiliate herself by offering him a love he didn't want!

How long, though, would she be able to keep her feelings to herself if she was sleeping with him every night and all night?

'I don't—' she began.

'Not in front of Oliver,' Sean checked her firmly, leaving her to wait to resume their conversation once Oliver had been introduced to and safely established in his own new bedroom.

'That was ridiculously extravagant, Sean, buying him a computer games console,' Kate protested when Sean had finished showing Oliver how to operate his new toy and they were back on the landing outside his room.

'It will be good for his spatial dexterity,' Sean told her without a glimmer of contrition. 'Come and see how the master bedroom looks,' he added, guiding her to the door.

The first thing Kate saw when he opened it was the huge new bed. And her concentration remained stuck on it.

'It's a double bed!' she pronounced foolishly.

'King-size, actually,' Sean corrected her dryly.

Panic filled her. Double or king-size, it didn't really matter. What mattered was that she would be sharing it with Sean and she knew, just knew, it would be impossible for her to stop herself from snuggling up to him and allowing herself the luxury of behaving as though they still were the loving couple they had once been.

Blindly she swung round, and then found that her exit from the room was blocked by Sean's arm, Sean's hand holding the door—a door which he promptly closed and leaned against, folding his arms as he watched her furious agitation.

'I can't sleep in that bed with you!' Kate burst out.

'Why not? We shared a room when we were away!'

'That was different!' Kate insisted, wishing he wouldn't give her that look of slow, deliberate scrutiny that made her feel he could see right into her head.

'We are married, after all,' Sean reminded her. 'And besides, the bed's plenty big enough for us to keep our distance from one another, if that's what you want!'

'Of course that's what I want,' Kate lied quickly. He couldn't have guessed how much it affected her to think of sleeping in the same bed with him, could he?

'We've got to think of Oliver,' Sean told her firmly. 'What kind of impression is it going to give him if we have separate rooms?'

She had been outmanoeuvred, Kate recognised, unable to do anything other than retaliate furiously, 'I saw the look Mrs Hargreaves gave you when we arrived, and now I realise why,' she accused him wildly.

To her surprise her comment seemed to have a more powerful effect on Sean than she had anticipated, because he suddenly started to frown, and a look she couldn't translate shadowed his eyes.

* * *

'I've told Mrs Hargreaves that from tomorrow we'll both have a light tea with Oliver at five o'clock, and then our own dinner later on, when he's in bed. I think it's important that we share his mealtimes with him. And I thought I'd take him over to the farm tomorrow—the pups are almost ready to leave their mother, and Mrs Hargreaves has told them we're going to have one. Ollie can choose his own.'

It was nine o'clock at night. Oliver was already tucked up and fast asleep in his new bed, and she and Sean were eating the delicious meal Mrs Hargreaves had left ready for them before going home. Suddenly the last thing Kate felt like was eating.

'Since when did you and Mrs Hargreaves make arrangements concerning Oliver without me being informed?' Kate demanded ominously. As she spoke she stood up, throwing down her linen napkin and gripping the table in her fury.

'He's desperate to have a dog of his own,' Sean told her. 'You know that!'

'I also know that I said I didn't want him to have a puppy yet.'

'Because he would be at nursery and you would be working. That doesn't apply any longer,' Sean pointed out firmly.

Kate was shaking with a mixture of anger and misery without really knowing why—other than that it had something to do with that large master bedroom and its huge bed, in which she and Sean were going to sleep—with most the bed between them…

'I'm not listening to any more of this,' she told Sean angrily, pushing back her chair and almost running out of the room, ignoring his pleas to return.

'Kate! Come back!'

Idiotically, it was the master bedroom she headed to for

refuge, swinging round white-faced as Sean followed her into it, shutting the door.

'What's got into you?' he demanded.

'I've managed to spend five years bringing Oliver up without your assistance and without your interference, Sean. I am his mother…and I—'

'And you what?' Sean challenged her savagely. 'And you shared another man's bed in order to conceive him?'

The raw emotion in his voice shocked through her. She had never seen him so out of control, and the intensity of his unexpected outburst paralysed her.

'Do you think I don't think about that every single day, every damned hour? Hell, Kate, do you think that because I can't father a child, because I'm not man enough to father a child, I'm not man enough to think about you and him and this?' Silently they stared at one another.

Kate drew a ragged breath and demanded shakily, 'What do you mean, you can't father a child?'

Her mouth had gone dry and her heart was thudding in heavy, erratic hammer-blows. Even through her own shock she was aware of the look of sick, anguished despair in Sean's eyes, and she could feel the intensity of his pent-up emotions.

When he started to turn away from her she reached out and took hold of his arm.

'You are Oliver's father, Sean,' she said quietly.

'No, I'm not. I can't be,' Sean denied bitterly. 'I can't father a child. It isn't medically possible.'

'I don't understand,' Kate said in a dry whisper as she struggled to take in what he was telling her.

It was too late for him to backtrack now; Sean knew that. Behind the shock he could see in Kate's eyes he could also see a growing determination. He knew she would insist on being told the truth—and what point was there in hiding it now, after what he had just said?

He took a deep breath.

'At a routine annual check-up for my private medical insurance the doctor suggested that I might as well have the full works.' He gave a small bitter shrug. 'It was just a formality, or so I thought—just a means of putting on paper what I believed I already knew. That I was a healthy, fully functioning man. When the results came back there was a problem...'

He paused and Kate waited, aching with compassion for him, but with the sure knowledge that, no matter what he had been told, the experts had got it wrong. He had fathered Oliver.

'It seemed—he said... He told me that my sperm count was so low it would be impossible for me to father children,' he said bleakly. 'I refused to believe him at first. In fact I was so convinced he must be wrong that I demanded that they run the tests again. They weren't wrong!' He closed his eyes. 'Shall I try to explain to you, Kate, how savagely humiliating I found it to have to stand there and listen to the doctor telling me that I wasn't capable of giving you a child? How I wished I hadn't heaped fresh humiliation on myself by demanding they re-run the tests?'

'Why didn't you tell me...say something?' Kate demanded in a dry whisper.

'I couldn't,' Sean said bleakly. 'I couldn't bear to see your face when I told you that I couldn't give you the children I knew you wanted so much.'

So much, Kate wanted to tell him. *But never, ever more than I wanted you, Sean.* She knew what he was like, though. She knew how deeply such news would have cut into him, into everything he'd believed about himself.

'I had a right to know, Sean,' she told him quietly.

'And I had a right to protect you from knowing,' he countered.

'To protect *me*?'

Sean's mouth compressed. 'I knew if I told you you would insist on…on accepting that there could never be any children for us and…and sacrificing your own chance to be a mother because of that. I decided there and then that I wasn't going to let you do that, and that I…I had to set you free to find another man to…to give you what I could not.'

'To set me free?' Now that she was over her initial shock Kate was beginning to get angry. 'You were unfaithful to me, Sean, and—'

'No!'

'No?'

'There wasn't anyone else. I…I just made it up because…because I knew how you would feel and how you would react. I didn't want to keep you trapped in our marriage, sacrificing yourself to it for my sake, pitying me and eventually hating me for what you were being denied. I must say, though, that I didn't expect you to find someone else quite so quickly. Was that why it didn't last?'

A lump had lodged in her throat and she could only shake her head in helpless denial. She didn't know what was hurting her the most—her pain for Sean or her pain for herself.

'Sean, I don't care what the medical reports said. Oliver is your child,' she told him passionately. 'Sometimes such things are possible and—'

'No!' His harsh, haunted cry made her flinch.

'Don't offer me that kind of temptation, Kate. You are worthy of so much more than deception, and so is Oliver.'

Kate went white, but before she could defend herself he was continuing rawly.

'Can't you understand how I feel? How much I wish that Oliver could be mine? How much it hurts me that he isn't?

I only have to look at him, never mind hold him, to feel my lo—something here inside me that… Having children with you, giving you our children, was so deeply rooted in me, so instinctive, that I thought I could never endure knowing that another man had given you what I couldn't. I thought it would drive me quite literally mad to see you with another man's child. But—'

'Oliver *is* your child,' Kate protested emotionally. 'He is yours, Sean—ours…'

'Don't do this to me, please, Kate. I can't bear it! What do I have to do to stop you lying to me? This?'

Kate couldn't move when he took hold of her, the fierce pressure of his mouth on hers bending her head backwards against the hard strength of his arm. The heat of their emotions, anger on anger, welded them together, and sent a shaft of pure molten reaction speeding through Kate.

How could it be that such a fierce primeval desire could be born out of anger? Her whole body shook in recognition of her vulnerable naïveté. She hadn't recognised her danger and tried to evade it. It was too late now.

She was held in thrall, emotionally and sexually, as much to the intensity of her own surging need as she was physically to Sean's iron-armed imprisonment of her.

When he broke the kiss, lifting his mouth from hers, his chest rising and falling quickly, Kate tried to pull away from him. But Sean refused to let her go.

'Perhaps the only way I can stop thinking about it is to put my own sexual imprint on you, for ever.'

'You were the one who divorced me, Sean,' Kate reminded him, trying to free her senses from the effect his hot, turbulent gaze was having on them, and at the same time fighting frantically to stem the excited surge of liquid sexual longing that was pulsing through her.

'I may have divorced you but I didn't replace you in my

bed, Kate,' he answered her bitterly. 'How much did you want him?' he demanded rawly.

'Sean! No!' Kate protested, torn between shock and pain—shock that he could actually believe she had given herself to someone else when he knew how much she had loved him, and pain for him, for herself, because he did.

'No? You didn't say no to him, did you?' he challenged her thickly. 'I'm going to make you forget that you ever knew him, Kate. I'm going to make you want me so much that you'll forget he ever existed.'

Sean was already caressing the side of her neck with his lips, deliberately seeking the special place where, she had once confessed shyly to him, feeling his mouth made her melt with longing for him.

'Did he do this?'

The words muffled against her skin made her throat ache with agonised suppressed tears, her only response a mute shake of her head.

'You didn't tell him how much it turns you on?'

There was an ugly note in Sean's voice that spiked her heart with angry pain. To her own shock, despite her anger, she ached to be able to reassure him, to convince him that no man ever had or ever could take his place in her life. In either her life, her heart, or her body. But the words wouldn't come, despite Sean's angry assault on her senses.

'Did he touch you like this, Kate? And like this?'

The angry, destructive words hammered into her like blows, numbing her body and freezing her emotions. A cold emptiness was spreading inside her, squeezing the life out of her love with icy binding tentacles of rage that stiffened her body into furious rejection.

'Oh, God, Kate.'

The groaned, anguished words were expelled with so much force that she could feel their pressure against her skin.

Releasing her, Sean went over to the bed and sat down on it, his elbows on his knees as he dropped his head into his hands.

'What the hell am I doing?'

The suffocating anguish of his pain filled the space between them.

With his head bent over his hands, she could see how exactly like Oliver's his hair grew, Kate noticed. For some reason that knowledge made her take a tentative step towards him.

'What the hell's happening to me? I know I've always been a jealous bastard where you're concerned, but—'

The muffled words bled shocked despair.

Kate lifted her hand and placed it on his head.

Immediately his whole body froze.

'For God's sake, Kate, don't touch me. How can you touch me?' he demanded savagely.

As his hand moved Kate saw the telltale moisture on his face and her heart turned over with love and compassion. An extraordinary feeling of strength and understanding filled her. Reaching out, she placed her hand over his.

Immediately Sean pushed her hand away and stood up, in rejection of her touch.

'I'll sleep in one of the other rooms tonight,' he said stiffly.

As he started to walk away from her Kate saw the way the light falling against his thigh revealed the swell of his arousal, and something inside her, something elemental and untamed, reacted to it.

Quickly she stepped in front of him, looked up into his face.

'No more, Kate,' Sean told her wearily. 'I don't want—'

'This?' She stopped him, placing her lips against his and caressing them slowly and sweetly, letting her senses and her heart revel in self-indulgent pleasure as she did so. She felt the involuntary movement of his body as he tensed it against her, but she wasn't going to give in.

'Or this?' she whispered against his mouth, sealing it with her own as she let her hand drop to his body so that her fingers could stroke possessively against him.

He didn't respond for so long that she was almost on the point of giving up, and then suddenly and explosively the power was taken from her and he was returning her kiss—not angrily, but passionately, hungrily, as though he was starving for her.

Just as she was starving for him?

Somehow, some way, somewhere, the anger between them had taken another direction, had pushed through the barrier of her self-protection and found that place deep within herself where she was still the girl who loved Sean and responded to his lovemaking with eager, open passion.

She could feel that passion flooding through her now, taking her to a place she had thought lost to her for ever.

Clothes tugged and pulled by impatient fingers left a trail to the bed, where they stood body to naked body. Kate's arms wrapped around Sean's neck as she continued to kiss him with fierce female hunger.

'Kate!'

She felt his hands on her breasts, holding and shaping them, and she shuddered, racked by fierce tremors of pleasure at his open appreciation of their soft weight in his hands. A wild wantonness had entered her blood and taken her over. As she was now taking him over! It manifested itself in the hot sensuality of the way she kissed him, touched him, the way she subtly and deliberately encouraged and invited him, winding her arms around him, pressing her naked body against him, driven by a force she could neither control nor deny.

A force she didn't want to control or deny, Kate recognised with feverish arousal, and she slid her hands down Sean's torso and through the soft thickness of his body hair, stroking over the hardness of his erection and then curling her fingers around the hot swollen shaft, caressing it slowly and then more urgently whilst the tension seated deep inside her own body tightened and ached until she knew it could not be contained any longer.

Sean! As she held out her arms to him Kate let the top half of her body drop onto the bed.

The last of the light was fading across the bedroom, but there was still enough left for her to see Sean's expression, to watch the way his glittering gaze was drawn to her body, over the firm swell of her breasts, over her nipples, dark rosy peaks of open arousal. The last glow warmed her belly and highlighted the soft little curls decorating the swollen mound that signposted her sex.

Deliberately she opened her legs, and watched the shudder that racked Sean's body.

Briefly she gave in to the temptation to stroke the wetness of her own sex, watching the way Sean's gaze followed her small erotic movement, and then blazed with heat. A fierce spiral of female excitement ran through her.

'You do it,' she told him boldly.

And, as though he knew what she was feeling, Sean groaned and reached for her.

Possessively Kate wrapped her legs around him, moaning her pleasure as he touched her just as she had wanted him to do, replacing his fingers with his body when he realised how close she was to her orgasm.

Within seconds it was over, her climax so immediate and so intense that her womb actually ached with its aftermath.

Her womb!

Bright tears glittered in her eyes and she turned her head

away so that Sean couldn't see them. Once she would have taken that fierce clenching of its muscles as a sign that it was claiming the seed of life Sean had planted there, but Sean refused to believe that he could give her a child.

CHAPTER TEN

'READY, THEN?' SEAN asked curtly, not looking directly at Kate herself as he strode into the sitting room, but crouching down instead to hold out his arms to Oliver, who immediately ran into them.

He had been like this with her—cold, distant and rejecting—ever since the night they had made love. If he had written them out in ten-feet-high letters he could not have made his feelings plainer, Kate admitted unhappily.

He might share the large bed in the master bedroom with her, but he slept with his back to her, and the cold space between them might as well have been impassable snow-capped mountains. His whole body language told her he didn't want her anywhere near him.

And why should he? In his eyes he had got what he wanted out of their marriage, after all, Kate acknowledged bleakly, as she looked down at her son and her husband.

'You don't have to take us to the hospital, Sean,' Kate told him now. 'This check-up is only a formality. The doctor said that himself, and I already know that I'm fully recovered.'

'I thought you said you wanted to check on your house?'

'Yes, I do,' Kate admitted. 'I know that the letting agent says he's found someone who wants to rent it right away—'

'You'd be better off selling it,' Sean interrupted her grimly.

Now it was Kate's turn to look away from him. How could she explain to a man in Sean's enviable financial position how she felt about the small home she had worked so hard to buy? And how could she tell him there was a part of her that was afraid that somehow history might repeat itself, that she might find herself on her own and in need of the security her little cottage could provide?

'I prefer to keep it,' she answered him.

'I spoke to my solicitor yesterday,' Sean announced, standing up. 'About the adoption.'

Oliver was running towards the door, but even so Kate gave Sean a warning look—which he obviously misinterpreted. As Oliver hurried out to the car Sean's face hardened.

'In your eyes I might be Oliver's father, Kate, but in my own eyes I am not—so I want to make sure that I am in the eyes of the law, for Oliver's sake as much as my own.'

Too heartsore to make any response, Kate followed him out to the car.

They had stopped off on their way to have some lunch, and now Sean was parking his car outside the doctor's surgery.

'There's no need for you and Oliver to come in with me, Sean,' Kate said as she opened the car door, but she might as well have saved her breath.

Not only did Sean insist on waiting with her to see the doctor, he also insisted on going into the room with her.

'I can understand your husband's concern,' the doctor further infuriated her by saying placatingly. 'You were very poorly.' He shook his head. 'Yours was certainly the worst case of this virus I have seen.'

'Perhaps she should have a full medical—with heart and lung checks?' Sean suggested.

'Sean, there is nothing wrong with me,' Kate told him angrily.

'Mummy was sick after breakfast!'

In the silence that followed Oliver's innocent but reveal-ing piece of information all three adults turned to look at him.

'I...it was the red wine I had with dinner,' Kate explained uncomfortably.

Immediately the doctor's expression relaxed, although he did tell Kate warningly, 'Red wine can sometimes prove too strong for a delicate stomach.'

'You barely touched your wine last night,' Sean pointed out as they left the surgery.

'Because I wasn't enjoying it,' Kate returned quickly.

To her relief he didn't pursue the matter. Instead he said, 'We might as well leave the car here and walk to your house. It isn't very far.'

Automatically Kate fell into step beside him, with Oli-ver in between them.

Perhaps the walk was too familiar to her, or perhaps her mind was on other things—Kate didn't know which, but obviously her concentration wasn't what it should have been, because when Oliver pulled his hand free from hers and shouted out the name of his friend she didn't react as quickly as she could have done. Oliver had run into the road before she had realised what was happening.

She did see the huge lorry bearing down on him, though, and she did hear her own voice screaming out his name in anguished terror as she started to run towards him, even though she knew she would be too late.

There was a blur of movement at her side as Sean ran past her and into the road, grabbing hold of his son in a rugby tackle movement, covering Oliver's body with his own.

Kate heard Oliver's screams and the hiss of air brakes. She could smell the odour of burning rubber, taste her own fear in her mouth. The lorry had slewed to a stop and people were running into the road to stand over the still, crumpled figure lying there.

But Kate got there first.

Sean lay motionless on the tarmac, blood oozing from a cut on his head, one of his legs splayed out at a sickeningly unnatural angle. And, lying safely next to Sean's unconscious body, Kate could see Oliver, his eyes wide with shock as he whimpered, 'Daddy…'

There were people everywhere—the doctor…sirens… an ambulance…

Hugging Oliver tightly to her, Kate got in it—after the paramedics had carefully lifted Sean onto a stretcher and placed him inside.

His face was drained of colour and Kate had to fight back the sickly sensation of wanting to faint as one of the paramedics expertly set up a drip and started to check his vital signs.

'His body's in shock, love,' one of them said, trying to comfort Kate as she stared at him in anguish. Unable to stop herself she took hold of one of his hands. It felt icy cold—as though…

Her heart lurched against her ribcage, her gaze going fearfully to the heart monitor.

'Hospital's coming up now. And we've got one of the best A&E departments in the country here,' the friendly medic told her proudly. 'Good timing, too. We've still got over half the golden hour left.'

'The golden hour?' Kate questioned numbly.

'That's what we call the window we get after an accident—leave it too long and—' As he saw Kate shudder he checked himself and looked uncomfortable, realising he had said too much.

In Accident and Emergency a nurse took Oliver from

Kate's numb arms whilst Sean was rushed past them on a trolley.

'I want to go with him—' Kate began, but the nurse stopped her firmly.

'We've got to get him ready for the duty surgeon to see him. You wouldn't want to watch us cutting off those good clothes he's wearing, would you? Now, let's have a little look at this young man, shall we?'

Distractedly, Kate tried to focus on what she was saying.

Miraculously Oliver had sustained little more than some grazes and bruises—no, not miraculously, Kate recognised. Because Sean had risked his life to save him.

A huge lump rose in her throat. Sean was right. It did take more than fathering a child to be a father, and he had proved that today. And he had proved, too, just how much he loved Oliver.

The medical staff were kind, but nothing could really alleviate the anguish and fear Kate experienced as she waited to hear how Sean was.

To her horror, a neurologist had to be called in to examine Sean and check for brain damage.

An hour passed, and then another. Oliver fell asleep in her arms and Kate's eyes prickled dryly with the weight of her unshed tears. After what felt like a lifetime, a consultant strode into the waiting area and came across to her.

Numbly Kate focused on the spotted bow tie he was wearing. 'My husband?' she begged anxiously.

'He's sustained a broken leg, and some cuts and bruises, and for a while we were concerned that the bump on his head might turn out to be rather nasty.' When he saw Kate's expression he gave her a kind look. 'Fortunately it's nothing more than a bad bump, but we had to make sure. I'm sorry that you've had to wait so long, but you'll understand that we had to be certain…'

Tears of overwrought emotional relief were pouring down Kate's face.

'We've had to mess him around rather a lot, and we've had to operate on his leg. We've still got a few samples to take, but he's fully conscious now. He won't accept that his son—Oliver, is it?—is all right until he has seen him. Susie will take you through,' he told Kate kindly, waving a hand towards a nurse waiting next to him.

But Kate didn't move. She couldn't. An idea…a hope… was burning on her tongue.

'The samples you have to take,' she began in a fierce rush. 'Would you—could you…?' Taking a deep breath, she told him helplessly, 'Sean won't believe that Oliver is his son, but he is. If you could do a DNA test—'

The consultant was frowning. 'That would be most irregular.'

'Sean already loves Oliver,' Kate told him desperately. 'He risked his own life to save him.'

'How sure are you that the child is his?' the consultant asked bluntly.

'Totally sure,' Kate answered him.

'I'm afraid that I can't do as you ask without the patient's permission,' the consultant told her, adding quietly as her face fell, 'However, I believe it is possible to have such tests conducted via certain Internet websites, should a person deem it necessary to do so.'

'But how—?' Kate began helplessly.

'All that is required is a small sample—a snippet of hair, for instance.'

Kate swallowed hard. 'You think I should…?'

'What I think is that anyone doing such a thing should

be guided by their own conscience,' the consultant told her seriously.

Biting her lip, Kate turned to follow the nurse down the corridor.

Sean was in a small private room, surrounded by a heart-stoppingly serious-looking battery of medical equipment, and when Kate saw the 'bump' on his head the consultant had referred to she almost cried out loud.

It looked as though the side of his head had been dragged along the road—which it most probably had, she acknowledged shakily.

'Look, Sean, we've brought Oliver to see you, like we promised,' said the nurse.

As Sean turned his head Kate had to fight the compulsion to hand Oliver to the nurse and run to his side, to take Sean in her arms.

How could such a big man look so frail? Her heart turned over as she whispered his name—but Sean wasn't looking at her. His whole attention was concentrated on Oliver.

'Daddy!' Oliver exclaimed, suddenly waking up and holding out his arms to him.

'Give him to me,' Sean demanded in a hoarse croak.

Uncertainly Kate looked at the nurse, who nodded her head briefly. Gently Kate carried Oliver over to the bed, but instead of handing him to Sean she sat down on the bed next to Sean, keeping hold of Oliver, afraid that her son might inadvertently hurt his father.

'He's all right?' Sean asked Kate as he lifted his hand and touched his son.

'He's perfectly all right—thanks to you,' Kate replied, her voice trembling.

It wasn't Oliver she wanted to hold and protect right now, she recognised achingly, it was Sean himself. But she knew that he wanted neither her comfort nor her love.

'Gently, Oliver,' she protested automatically as Oliver leaned forward to give his father a big smacking kiss.

'There's no need for you to keep visiting me twice a day like this, Kate,' Sean announced curtly as Kate opened the door to his private room.

Suppressing her hurt, Kate forced herself to smile. 'Mr Meadows says that you'll be coming home tomorrow.'

Sean frowned.

'Oliver can't wait,' Kate told him.

Immediately the frown disappeared.

'He's been pining for you, Sean.'

Ruefully Kate decided that she wasn't going to tell him what she had done to try to alleviate her son's longing for his father—he would discover the new addition to their household for himself soon enough. Kate had to admit that she had been pleasantly surprised at how quickly Rusty, as Oliver had decided to call his new puppy, had become housetrained.

'Did you get the neurologist to check that absolutely no damage had been done when he…?'

Every time she visited him Sean demanded to know how Oliver was, and even though she kept telling him that he was fine he still persisted in worrying. Kate suspected that he wouldn't be reassured until he was home and could observe Oliver's excellent and boisterous good health for himself.

'I spoke to my solicitor this morning,' he announced abruptly. 'He says you're refusing to sign the adoption papers.'

Kate poured herself a glass of water from the jug at Sean's bedside in an attempt to quell the feeling of nausea the hospital smell was giving her.

'I'm not refusing, Sean, I…' Crossing her fingers behind her back, she said quickly, 'Your adoption of Oliver is such an important and…and special thing, I didn't want it to be purely businesslike and clinical. I thought if we waited until you came home we could have a little celebration.'

'So it isn't because you're having second thoughts, then?' Sean cut across her hesitant excuse.

The temptation to tell him emotionally that the only time she could have had second thoughts about his role as Oliver's father had been nine months before Oliver's birth was something she had to stifle before she could give it voice.

Deep down inside she still felt guilty about that little snippet of hair she had cut from his head whilst he had been sleeping. As the consultant had hinted, she had found a website offering the kind of service she had needed and Sean's hair, together with a lock of Oliver's, had been sent to it. She had no doubts, of course, as to the result she would receive back.

Automatically her hand dropped to her stomach and rested there.

So far as Sean's accident was concerned, the consultant had told her cheerfully that she was worrying for nothing, that Sean was a fit, healthy man with a skull thick enough to protect him from its contact with the road and a broken leg that was healing extremely well. But Kate knew that as long as Sean was here in this hospital she would continue to feel that he was vulnerable and needed to be treated with care.

Dry-eyed, Sean watched Kate leave. He had had time and more to spare during these last few days to think. And he'd had plenty to think about. The past and the future.

The present situation was a warning to him of how the people who mattered most to him were precious and yet so vulnerable. *All* that mattered to him, Sean acknowledged fiercely, was Oliver, the child he had come to love with a true father's love, and Kate, the girl he had loved, the woman

he still loved, beyond and above anything and everything
that had happened or might happen.

Oliver and Kate. He couldn't bear the thought of losing
either of them. Even in that half-second as he'd recognised
Oliver's danger he had known that it didn't really matter that
he hadn't fathered him, or even that there had been another
man for Kate. That was the past. He had their present, and
he wanted their future.

'So, no playing football with that leg, and come back for
your check-up in six weeks,' the consultant told Sean breez-
ily as he gave him his final examination before discharg-
ing him. 'You'll be looking forward to getting home to your
wife and son,' he added easily, but he was watching Sean
as he spoke.

Following Kate's request, he had sent for and checked all
Sean's medical records. One of them recorded a specialist's
opinion that it would be a miracle if Sean ever managed to
father a child.

'You were damn lucky not to be much more seriously
injured, you know,' he commented. 'But then, as we in the
medical profession are often forced to accept, miracles do
happen!'

Sean closed his eyes. He wasn't going to dispute what
the consultant was saying; after all, he had his own private,
secret miracle to rejoice in.

Five years ago, if someone had told him that there would
come a day when he would not only accept another man's
child as his son but he would love that child more deeply
than he had ever imagined he could or would love anyone,
apart from Kate, he would have denied it fiercely and immediately. But that was how he felt about Oliver.

When he had seen the little boy standing in the path of
the lorry he had known that he loved Oliver as fiercely and

protectively, as deeply and instinctively as though he were his biological father. Oliver was his son, and he loved him as his son. But legally Oliver was *not* his son, and if for any reason she chose to do so Kate could simply take Oliver and walk out of Sean's life with him.

Any reason? Sean's mouth compressed. Kate had a very good reason to want to leave him, and he had given her that reason that night they'd made love…

It made no difference to Sean's contempt and disgust for himself that ultimately mutual passion had flared between them. His only excuse was that his pent-up jealousy had overwhelmed him, and that was no real excuse at all. He loathed himself for what he had done, and he knew that Kate must loathe him as well—for all that she was concealing it.

The door to his room was opening. A smiling nurse came in, and behind her were Kate and Oliver.

When Oliver broke free of Kate's hold and ran towards him Sean bent his head over Oliver's to conceal his emotions.

'He refused to wait at home for you,' Kate explained as Sean picked up the crutches he would need to use.

Immediately Kate was at his side, but Sean refused to let her help, turning away from her.

White-faced, Kate watched as the nurse went to Sean's aid…Sean's side…taking the role which should have been hers. Sean might have remarried her, but he didn't want her as his wife, Kate acknowledged bleakly.

'I've asked Mrs Hargreaves to move my things into one of the other bedrooms.'

Kate was glad she had her back to Sean, so that he couldn't see her reaction to his words, although she couldn't stop herself from demanding, 'But what about Oliver? You said—'

'I've told him that it's because of my leg,' Sean answered her curtly.

But of course that was just an excuse, and Kate knew it! He didn't want to share a room with her, a bed with her, any longer—because he didn't want her!

They were standing in the hallway, Sean leaning on his crutches whilst Oliver chased his puppy around the room, trying to catch him so that he could show him to his father.

'I see you changed your mind,' Sean commented sardonically as he looked at her.

'I'm a woman. I'm entitled to,' Kate replied as lightly as she could. There was, though, another reason she had decided that this was the optimum time to allow Oliver to have his puppy.

Had Sean recognised the pup as being the one he himself had picked for Oliver? she wondered. If he had he didn't make any mention of it, and ridiculously, after everything else that told her how he felt about her, she felt absurdly disappointed and hurt.

'I'll help you upstairs,' she offered, going to his side. But immediately Sean stepped back from her in such an obvious gesture of repudiation that Kate froze, then turned round so that Sean wouldn't see the humiliating tears burning her eyes.

CHAPTER ELEVEN

NAUSEOUSLY KATE PUT her head back on the pillow and closed her eyes. Perhaps it was just as well that Sean was not sharing the room with her.

Sean!

It was Sean's birthday today. She reached for the packet of dry biscuits she had bought herself earlier in the week, when she had bought his birthday card.

She took her time getting up, waiting for the nausea to subside before going in to Oliver.

He was as excited as though it was his own birthday, Kate acknowledged ruefully as he collected the present they had wrapped together so carefully the previous day.

Sean was already sitting in the breakfast room when they went in, and immediately Oliver ran over to his father and scrambled onto his knee, shouting, 'Happy birthday, Daddy!'

Bending her head to hide her own emotion, Kate picked up the card Oliver had dropped in his excitement, reflecting that it was just as well she had carried the present for him.

'Happy birthday, Sean,' Kate echoed more sedately, adding, 'and it's a double celebration now that your plaster cast is off!'

He had had the plaster cast removed the previous day,

and the consultant had expressed himself totally satisfied
with the way the leg had healed.

'I've got you a card and a present!' Oliver exclaimed importantly, still sitting on Sean's lap.

Obediently Kate handed over the card and the present.

'You've got to open this one first—it's my card,' Oliver
instructed. 'Mummy has a card for you, too, and so does
Rusty. He's put his own paw mark on it,' Oliver told him
excitedly. 'Mummy made some special mud, and we put his
paw in it, and then we put it on the card!'

'Some special mud? That sounds clever!'

Was that really a gleam of amusement she could see in
Sean's eyes as he looked at her? Kate's heart somersaulted
inside her chest.

'That explains the odd marks on Mummy's jeans yesterday, then, does it?' he added dulcetly.

'We did have a couple of aborted attempts.' Kate laughed,
but when she looked at him Sean wasn't sharing her laughter. Instead he was looking at Oliver's card. And he continued to look at it for a several seconds, before lifting his
head and looking at Kate.

'Do you like it, Daddy?' Oliver demanded, tugging on
his arm.

'I love it, Ollie!' Sean assured him gruffly. 'But I love
you even more.'

As he hugged him he put the card down and Kate reached
for it, standing it up on the table. Oliver's writing wasn't
very good as yet, but his message to his father was: 'I love
you lots, Daddy.'

'And you've got to open my present now,' Oliver insisted.

Kate watched as Sean unwrapped the photograph she had
taken of the two of them and had framed. As Sean studied
it she held her breath. Could he see, as she had, the like-
ness between them?

If he could he obviously wasn't going to say so.

The rest of the cards were opened, including the one from Rusty. Then Sean assured Oliver gravely that he was indeed looking forward to his birthday tea, and eating the cake Oliver and Kate had made for him.

Kate said nothing.

'Mummy, you haven't got a present for Daddy,' Oliver piped up suddenly.

'Yes, she has, Ollie,' Sean told him, before Kate could say anything. 'Your mummy has given me a very, very special present—the best present in the world.'

'Where is it?' Oliver asked him, bewildered.

Over his head, Sean looked at Kate. 'You are it,' he answered. 'Your mummy has given me you.'

Kate knew that she should have been thrilled to hear Sean's words of love for Oliver, and of course she was, but a part of her ached with pain because she knew that they confirmed what she didn't want to hear: that Sean only wanted her because he wanted Oliver.

That was not the kind of relationship she wanted with the man she loved, the man who—

Abruptly, she got up.

She had left her gift for Sean in the room he used as an office. When he found it he would realise that in order to have Oliver he did not need to have her as well.

'Kate, where are you going? You haven't eaten any breakfast.'

She didn't turn round.

'I'm not hungry,' she answered, and instinctively her hand went to her stomach.

Not hungry? Sean wondered bitterly as she walked away. Or not able to endure his company?

As soon as they had finished their breakfast, Sean took

Oliver out into the garden, along with the puppy. Did Kate even realise she had picked the same pup he had chosen?

As they walked side by side Oliver chattered happily to him, and when he looked down at him Sean felt a stab of pain for the years of his life he had missed, for not being there at his birth. His large hand tightened around Oliver's smaller one. Oliver was his son, but he had not been entirely truthful when he had said that Oliver was the most precious gift he could have been given.

He was precious, very precious, but Kate's love was just as precious. There hadn't been a night since it had happened when he had not lain awake, hating himself for the way he had treated Kate. No wonder she couldn't bear to be in the same room as him.

It was lunchtime before he went into his office and saw the large white envelope lying on his desk.

Frowning, he picked it up, recognising Kate's handwriting on it,

'For you,' she had written, 'and for Oliver.'

Still frowning, Sean opened it. Removing the contents, he read them, and then read them again. And then again, trying to focus through the blur of his own shocked emotions.

He had fathered Oliver. It was here in black and white. The incontrovertible proof in their DNA records.

He read them again, and then again, over and over, until finally it sank in that there was no mistake.

Miracles do happen, the consultant had told him, and now Sean knew that it was true! But his miracle had come at a dreadful price, he recognised as the reality of what the results meant sank in.

He had refused to believe that Kate had not slept with another man. He had done so much more than refuse to believe her…

He heard the office door open.

Kate walked in and closed the door. She looked at the desk, and then at him.

'So you've opened it?'

'Yes. But I wish to hell that I hadn't!'

Kate felt sick. What was he trying to say? 'But it proves that Oliver is your son!' she protested.

'Oliver was already my son!' Sean told her harshly. 'Here in my heart was all the proof that I needed or wanted— even if it took a near tragedy to make me realise that. Kate! This—' he told her, furiously picking up the results, 'means nothing!'

Kate was too shocked to speak.

'I want Oliver to grow up knowing that my love for him comes from here,' he told her, as he touched his own heart, 'and not from this!' Angrily he threw down the piece of paper. 'I had a lot of time on my hands to think whilst I was in hospital, Kate, and what I thought, what I learned, and what I finally accepted was that love—real love—should and can transcend all our weaker human emotions. Jealousy, doubt, fear. I love you as I have always loved you,' he continued thickly. 'As the only woman for me. My other half, who I need to complete me…my soul mate. Nothing can change that. Nothing and no one. And I love Oliver as the child of my heart.

'This…' he gestured towards the test results '…underlines the fact that I haven't just abused you and your trust once, but twice. That I have created yet another barrier between us with my own selfishness and stupidity.'

Dizzily Kate looked at him. 'You love me?'

Sean frowned, caught off guard not just by her question but by the exultant pleasure that lightened her voice.

'You want me to?' he demanded.

'Oh, Sean!' Tears blurred her vision as she took a step

towards him, and then another, until she was close enough
to wrap her arms around him. 'Always and for ever. You
and your love.' Emotion choked her voice and she shook
her head. 'If you love me, why have you been rejecting me?
Why have you—?'

A tide of colour began to creep up under Sean's tan.

'I thought—I felt… That night when we made love…
God, Kate, do I have to spell it out for you? I lost control
and I—'

Gently Kate placed her fingers against his lips to silence him.

'We both lost control, Sean, and as a result of that…'
She paused. 'Do you really mean this, Sean? Do you really love me?'

'How could you even ask?' Sean groaned as he pulled
her closer and kissed her downbent head.

'Well, it isn't just for myself that I have to ask,' Kate answered slowly, trying to pick her words as carefully as she
could.

It was obvious to her when he put his hand under her
chin and tilted her face up towards his own so that he could
look into her eyes that he hadn't grasped what she was trying to say.

'You mean because of Oliver?' he asked her, puzzled.
'You know I love him.'

'No, not because of Oliver,' she told him. 'But you're on
the right track.'

Encouragingly she looked at him, until he made a smoth-
ered sound and bent his head to take the softness of the half-
parted lips she was offering to him.

Their kiss lasted a long time and said a great deal, promising love and commitment and sharing sadness and regret,
but eventually it ended, and Sean demanded rawly, 'You
can't mean that you're pregnant?'

Kate gave him a quizzical look. 'Who says I can't?' she teased flippantly, before giving a small shrug that didn't quite manage to conceal her excitement.

'Apparently modern research has shown that a woman's body has the capability to fight hard to receive and cherish the sperm of the man she loves—and after all, Sean, it only takes one!'

Tenderly Sean drew his fingertip down the curve of her cheek. 'Well, this is certainly not a birthday I'm going to forget.'

'Mmm, and it isn't over yet,' Kate reminded him softly, adding naughtily, 'You know how women get cravings for things when they're pregnant...?'

Dutifully, Sean nodded his head.

'Well, my craving is for you, Sean,' she told him gently. 'And besides, you don't want your baby to think you don't love her mother, do you?'

'*Her* mother?' Sean questioned softly, several hours later, as he propped his head on his hand and looked down into Kate's face.

Her mouth was curved in a smile of warm, sensual satisfaction whilst her eyes glowed with love and happiness.

'Well, I think she's a girl,' she answered him lovingly, before adding, 'it's because of the pregnancy that I got Ollie his puppy now. One baby at a time is enough for any household!'

'Oh, God, when I think of what I could have lost. What I did lose in those hellish years without you,' Sean said, drawing her back into his arms and nestling her against his body. 'Thank you for forgiving me for what I did, for making it possible to have you and Oliver in my life.'

'Once I understood why you had done what you did, it changed everything—especially when I saw the way you were bonding with Ollie. Of course I hated the fact that you were refusing to accept that Oliver was your child, but from a logical point of view I understood why you'd refused to believe it. And I never stopped loving you, even if I didn't like admitting it!'

'Well, from now you aren't going to be allowed to stop loving me,' Sean told her softly. 'And I am certainly never going to stop loving you.'

EPILOGUE

'I THOUGHT YOU SAID that one baby at a time was enough?'

Kate gave Sean a rueful look and they both looked at the two perfect and identical babies sharing the same hospital cot.

Their daughters had been born within ten minutes of one another earlier in the day, and after bringing Oliver to see his new sisters Sean had taken him home and put him in the care of Mrs Hargreaves before returning to the hospital to be with Kate.

'I thought you said it was impossible for this to happen!' Kate responded, and then felt her eyes moisten with ridiculous emotional tears as she saw the male pride in Sean's eyes battling with the awareness that Kate had done the hard work of carrying and giving birth to them.

From the moment they had known Kate's pregnancy was twins Sean had worried anxiously over her, but now...

Gently Sean reached for her hand and carried it to his lips. 'Without you this wouldn't have been possible,' he told her emotionally. 'You could have fallen in love and had your children with another man, Kate. But somehow I know that my problem would have made it impossible for me to father children with anyone but you.'

Of course she ought to tell him that he was being silly, but she wasn't going to, Kate decided. No, what she was going to do was to cherish this moment for the rest of her life.

'I see Rusty has managed to send one of his unique paw-print cards,' she murmured teasingly. 'Three paw-prints, too, and two of them pink!'

Sean laughed. 'I've got a confession to make,' he warned her. 'The creation of that card involved the destruction of several items of clothing and Annie Hargreaves threatening to leave! But Oliver was insistent! Fortunately the lure of the twins was enough to make her change her mind!'

The babies were waking up and would soon be demanding a feed, Kate knew. But there was still time for her to lean forward and show their father how much she loved him, and she placed her lips to his.

* * * * *

THE BLACKMAIL
BABY

PROLOGUE

'SO YOU'RE GOING to go through with it? You're going to go ahead and marry Dracco, even though he doesn't love you?'

Imogen flinched as the full venom of her stepmother Lisa's words hit her. They were in Imogen's bedroom, or at least the bedroom that had been Imogen's until after her father's death. Since then Lisa had declared her intention to sell the pretty country house where Imogen had grown up and to buy herself a modern apartment in the small market town where they lived.

'Dracco has asked me to be on hand to help him entertain the clients,' Lisa had said at the time of her shock announcement about the house. 'He says he can see how much more business the company has been attracting since I became your father's hostess. Unfortunately your mother never seemed to realise just how vitally important being a good hostess was.'

She had given the openly dismissive, almost contemptuous shrug with which Imogen had become teeth-grittingly familiar whenever Lisa spoke about her late mother. Instinctively Imogen had wanted to leap to her mother's defence, but she had sufficient experience of Lisa to know better than to do so. Even so, she had not been able to stop herself from pointing out quietly, 'Mummy was ill. Otherwise, I know she would have wanted to entertain Daddy's clients for him.'

'Oh, yes, we all know that you think your precious mother was a saint.' Imogen had seen the furious look of hostility in Lisa's hard blue eyes. 'And Dracco agrees with me that you made life very difficult for your father all these years by constantly harping on about your mother, trying to make him feel guilty because he fell in love with me.'

Lisa had preened herself openly, making Imogen's stomach churn with sickening misery and anguish. Then her stepmother had continued triumphantly, 'Dracco considers that your father was very fortunate to be married to me. In fact…' She had stopped, giving Imogen a small, secret little smile that had made her heart thump heavily against her ribs. It hurt, unbearably, to hear Lisa speaking about Dracco as though a special closeness existed between them, especially when Imogen was so desperately in love with him herself!

Imogen had never truly been able to understand how her beloved father had fallen in love with a woman as cold and manipulative as Lisa. Granted, she was stunningly attractive: tall, blonde-haired, with a perfect and lushly curved body, totally unlike Imogen's own. Imogen took after her mother, who had been petite and fine-boned with the same thick dark mop of untameable blackberry curls and amazingly coloured dark violet eyes. And, where Imogen remembered her mother's eyes shining with warmth and love, Lisa's pale blue eyes were always cold.

Imogen had loved her father far too much, though, to say anything to him. Her mother had died when she was seven, and when he'd decided to remarry when she was fourteen Imogen had made up her mind to accept her new stepmother for his sake. She had adored her father and been fiercely protective of him, in her little-girl way, after her mother's death, but she had been ready to welcome into their lives anyone who could make him happy.

Lisa, though, had quickly made it plain that she was not prepared to be equally generous. She had been thirty-two when she married Imogen's father, with no particular fondness for children and even less for other members of her own sex. Right from the start of their relationship she had treated the young girl as an adversary, a rival for Imogen's father's affections and loyalty.

Lisa had been in their lives less than three months when she had told Imogen coolly that she considered it would be far better for her to go to boarding school than live at home and attend the local private school her mother had chosen before succumbing to the degenerative illness which had ultimately killed her. It had been Dracco who had stepped in then, reminding Imogen's father that his first wife had hand-picked her daughter's secondary school even when she knew she would not be alive to see Imogen attend it. It had been Dracco too who had come to that same school to break the news of her father's fatal accident to Imogen, tears sheening the normally composed and unreadable jade depths of his eyes.

That had been nearly twelve months ago. Imogen had been seventeen then, now she was eighteen, and in less than an hour's time she would be Dracco's wife.

The car that was to take her to the same small church where her parents had been married and her mother was buried was waiting outside. Inside it was her father's elderly solicitor, who was to give her away. It was to be a quiet wedding. She had pleaded fervently with Dracco for that.

So you're going to go through with it? You're going to go ahead and marry Dracco, even though he doesn't love you? Imogen's mind returned to her stepmother's deliberately painful question.

'Dracco says it's…it's for my own good…and that it's what my father would have wanted,' she answered.

'"Dracco says,"' Lisa Atkins mimicked cruelly. 'You are such a fool, Imogen. There is only one reason Dracco is marrying you and that's because of who you are. Because he wants to gain full control of the business.'

'No, that isn't true!' Imogen protested frantically. 'Dracco already runs the business,' she reminded her stepmother. 'He knows I would never try to change that.'

'*You* might not,' Lisa agreed coolly. 'But what about the man you may one day marry if Dracco doesn't step in? He may have other plans. Your father's will leaves your share in trust for you until you are thirty unless you marry before then. Oh, come on, Imogen. Surely you don't actually think that Dracco wants you?' One elegant eyebrow arched mockingly before Lisa went on, 'Dracco is a man! To him you are just a child, less than that, in fact… Dracco wants what you can give him. He has told me himself that if it wasn't for the business there is no way he'd be marrying you.'

Although she tried to stop herself, Imogen could not quite prevent the sharp gasp of pain escaping. She could see Lisa's triumphant smile, and hated herself for letting the older woman break through her defences.

In an effort to recover the ground she had lost, she began unsteadily, 'Dracco wouldn't—'

But she wasn't allowed to go any further; Lisa stopped her, saying softly, 'Dracco wouldn't what, Imogen? Dracco wouldn't confide in me? Oh, my dear, I'm afraid you are way behind the times. Dracco and I…' She paused and examined her perfectly manicured fingernails. 'Well, it should be for Dracco to tell you this and not me, but let us just say that Dracco and I have a relationship which is very special—to both of us.'

Imogen could hardly take in what she was being told. She felt sick with a numbing disbelief that this could be happening on her wedding day; the day that should have been one of the happiest of her life, but which now, thanks to Lisa's shocking revelations, was fast turning into one of the worst.

So far she had not given very much thought to the complexities of her father's will. She had been too grief-stricken by his loss to consider how his death would affect her financially. She knew, though, of course, that he had been an extremely successful and wealthy man. As an acclaimed financial adviser, John Atkins had been held in high esteem by both his clients and those he did business with. Imogen could still remember how enthusiastic and pleased he had been when he had first taken Dracco under his wing as a raw university graduate.

They had met when her father went to debate an issue at Dracco's university. Dracco had been on the opposing side and her father had been impressed not just by his debating skills but by his grasp of the whole subject, and what he had described as Dracco's raw energy and hunger to succeed.

Dracco had had a stormy childhood, abandoned by his own father and brought up by a succession of relatives after his mother had remarried and her second husband had refused to take him on. He had worked to pay his own way through university, and when he had first come to work for Imogen's father he had for a time lived with them.

It had been Dracco who had chauffeured her to school when her father was away on business; Dracco who had taught her to ride her new bike; Dracco the Dragon, as she had nicknamed him teasingly. And when her father had made him a junior partner in his business it had been Imogen Dracco had taken out to celebrate his promotion—to an ice-cream parlour in the local town.

Quite when her acceptance of him as Dracco, her father's partner and her own friend had changed, and she had begun to see him as Dracco, the man, Imogen wasn't sure.

She could remember coming out of school one day to

find him waiting for her in the little scarlet sports car he had bought for himself. It had been a hot, sunny afternoon, the hood had been down, the sunlight glinting on the thick night-darkness of his hair. He had turned his head to look at her, as though sensing her presence even before she had reached him, and studied her with the intense dark greenness of his gaze.

Suddenly it had been as though she was seeing him for the first time. As though she had been struck by a thunderbolt. Her heart had started to race and then thud heavily.

She had felt sick, excited, filled with a dangerous, heady exuberance and a shocked self-consciousness. Without knowing why, she had found that she wanted to look at his mouth. Somewhere deep inside her body an unfamiliar sensation had begun to uncurl itself; a sensation that had made her face blush bright red and her legs turn to jelly. She had felt as though she couldn't bear to be near him in case he guessed how she felt, but at the same time she couldn't bear him not to be there.

'Only a child as naïve and inexperienced as you could possibly think that Dracco wants you. A woman, a real woman, would know immediately that there was already someone else in his life. He hasn't even tried to take you to bed, has he?' Lisa challenged, before adding cruelly, 'And don't bother trying to pretend that you haven't wanted him to. That crush you have on him is painfully obvious.'

The sharp interruption of Lisa's goading voice broke into Imogen's thoughts. Instinctively she turned away from her stepmother to guard her expression, catching sight of her own reflection in the mirror as she did so. It had been Dracco who had insisted that she should wear a traditional wedding dress.

'Your father would have wanted you to,' had been his winning argument.

If there was one thing she and Dracco did share it was their mutual love for her father.

'Dracco doesn't love you. Not as a man loves a woman.'

Once again Imogen couldn't prevent a small sound of anguish escaping her lips.

Narrowing her eyes, Lisa dropped her voice to a soft, sensual purr. 'Surely even someone as sexless as you must have thought it odd that he hasn't taken you to bed? Any normal woman would guess immediately what that meant. Especially where an obviously red-blooded man like Dracco is concerned.' Lisa smiled unkindly at her. 'If you're determined to be an unwanted wife you will have to learn to conceal your feelings a little better. Surely you couldn't have imagined that there haven't been women in Dracco's life? He is, after all, a very potent man.'

Imogen prayed that she wouldn't be sick and that she wouldn't give in to her desire to run out of the room and away from Lisa's hateful, mocking voice. Of course she knew there had been other women in Dracco's life and she knew too what it felt like to be agonisingly jealous of them— after all, she had had enough practice.

Dracco with other girls; girls that he found attractive and desirable in all the ways he obviously did not view her; girls that he wanted in all the ways he did not want her, in his arms, in his bed, beneath the fierce male hardness of his body, naked, skin to skin, whilst he...

To Dracco she was nothing more than a baby, the daughter of his partner and closest friend, someone to be treated with amusement and paternalism as though twenty-odd years separated them and not a mere ten... Ten...a full decade... But soon they would be equals; soon now she would be Dracco's wife. Imogen gave a small shiver. All through her teenage years she had dreamed of her private fantasy coming true and of Dracco returning her love, telling her that he could not live without her, demanding passionately that she give herself to him and become his wife.

Of course, a tiny part of her, a voice she had refused out of fear and anguish to listen to, urged her to be cautious, to wonder why in all the things that Dracco had said to her since her father's death there had been no mention of love.

And somehow until now she had managed to ignore what that omission could mean. Until now.

There was, Imogen recognised through her shocked pain, an odd air of almost driven determination in her stepmother's manner, an air that bordered on furious desperation, but Imogen felt too weakened by her own anguish to consider why that might be.

Drawing herself up to her full height, she told Lisa with quiet dignity, 'Dracco is marrying me—'

'No,' Lisa told her furiously, 'Dracco is marrying your inheritance. Have you no pride, you little fool? Any woman worthy of the name would walk away now before it's too late, find herself a man who really wants her instead of crawling after one who doesn't; one who already has in his life the woman he really wants!'

Imogen felt as though she was inhabiting a nightmare. What further cruelty was Lisa trying to inflict on her? Whatever it was, she didn't want to hear it. She did not want to allow herself to hear it.

It was time for her to leave. Imogen started to walk past her stepmother but Lisa grabbed hold of her arm, stopping her, hissing viciously to her, 'I know what you're hoping but you're wasting your time; Dracco will never love you. He loves someone else. If you don't believe me, ask him! Ask him today, now, before he marries you, if there is someone; a woman in his life whom he loves. And ask him, if you dare, just who she is.'

* * *

A woman in Dracco's life whom he loved. Imogen's head
was swimming with pain and fear as she started to walk
down the aisle. She could see the back of Dracco's dark
head as he waited for her to reach him. The scent of the lilies filling the church was so heady that it was making Imogen feel slightly sick and faint. How could that be true? How
could he possibly even consider marrying her if he loved
someone else?

Lisa had been lying… Lying, as she had done so often
in the past, trying to cause trouble for Imogen; to hurt and
upset her.

And as for her final comment, it had to be impossible,
surely, as Lisa had been implying that she herself was the
woman Dracco loved.

Totally, completely, unbearably impossible, at least so
far as Imogen was concerned.

'Dearly beloved…'

Imogen felt herself start to sway. Immediately Dracco's
fingers curled supportively around her arm.

Pain and longing filled her in equal measures. This
should have been the happiest day of her life. She was, after
all, marrying the man she loved. The man she had loved
since she had first realised what love was.

'Imogen. Are you all right? For a moment in there I thought
you were going to faint.'

Imogen tried to force a smile as she met the frowning
concern in Dracco's gaze. Her husband's gaze. She could
feel her knees threatening to buckle. She felt so odd. So…
so alone and afraid.

'Dracco, there's something I want to ask you.'

They were standing outside the church whilst the bells pealed and their wedding guests chattered happily.

'Mmmm…'

Dracco was barely even looking at her, Imogen recognised miserably. They didn't seem like a newly married couple at all…like husband and wife, a pair of lovers. A sharp pain seemed to pierce her to her heart. Before she could lose her courage she demanded unevenly, 'Have you…? Is there…is there someone…a woman you love?'

He was looking at her now, Imogen recognised bitterly, concentrating all his attention on her, but not in the way she had longed for. He was frowning forbiddingly in the tense silence her nervous question had created.

Imogen could hardly bear to continue looking at him. She saw the flash of emotion glitter in the jade depths of his eyes; heard the furious anger in his voice as he demanded curtly, 'Who told you about that?'

Her heart felt as though it was breaking. It was true.

In numb despair she watched as he cursed grimly under his breath and then said more gently, 'Yes. Yes, there is. But…'

Dracco loved another woman. He loved another woman but he had still married her.

Imogen felt as though her whole world had come crashing down around her. Where was the man she had put on a pedestal; adored, trusted, loved? He didn't exist…

With a low cry of torment she turned on her heel and started to run, desperate to escape from her pain, from her stepmother's knowing triumph, but most of all from Dracco himself, who had betrayed her and everything she had believed about him. Behind her she could hear Dracco calling her name, but that only made her run even faster. In the street beyond the church a taxi was pulling up to disgorge its passenger, and without stopping to think what she was doing Imogen ran up to it and jumped in. At any other time the way the taxi driver was goggling at her would have made her giggle, but laughing was the last thing she felt like doing right now...

'Quick,' she instructed the driver, her voice trembling. 'Please hurry.'

As she spoke she darted a quick backward glance towards the church, half expecting to see Dracco coming in pursuit of her, but the street behind her was empty.

'Don't tell me,' the taxi driver quipped jovially as he took in both his passenger's bridal array and her breathless anxiety, 'you're in a hurry to get to a wedding—right?' Laughing at his own joke, he started to negotiate the traffic.

'Wrong,' Imogen corrected him fiercely. 'I'm actually in a hurry to get away from one.'

As he swung round to stare at her, ignoring the busy traffic, Imogen could see the bemusement in his eyes.

'What?' he protested. 'A runaway bride? I never thought.'

Quickly Imogen gave him her home address, adding tersely, 'And please hurry.'

So far there was no evidence of any pursuit—no sign of either Dracco's sleek Daimler or her stepmother's Rolls-Royce.

Never had a drive seemed to last so long, nor caused her to sit on the edge of her seat, her fingers clenched into the upholstery in anxiety as she checked constantly to see if they were being followed. But at last the taxi driver was setting her down outside her home, waiting whilst she hurried inside to get the money to pay him—as a bride, there had been no need for her to have any cash with her.

Once she had paid him and soothed his unexpectedly paternal concern for her, she ran back upstairs to her room, dragging off her wedding dress with such force that the fragile fabric ripped. Just as her stepmother and Dracco between them had ripped apart her foolish dreams.

Feverishly she pulled on jeans and a top, hastily emptying the suitcase packed for the honeymoon she and Dracco were to have been taking and refilling it with clothes wrenched blindly off hangers and out of drawers.

She still hadn't really taken in what she had done; all she knew was that she had to get as far away from Dracco as she could and as fast as she could. If, as her stepmother had warned her, he had only been marrying her to gain control of the business then he would not be satisfied until he had that control. She knew how determined he could be. How focused and… A small shudder shook her body. Dracco! Dracco! How could he have done this to her? How could he have humiliated and hurt her so? Tears burning her eyes, Imogen picked up her new cream leather handbag—bought especially for her honeymoon. Inside it was her passport, and the wallet of traveller's cheques Dracco had given her earlier in the week.

'Spending-money,' he had told her with a small smile. The same smile that always made her heart lift and then beat frantically fast, whilst her insides melted and her body longed…

She had counted them after he had gone, her eyes widening as she realised just how much he had given her.

Well, that money would be put to good use now, she reflected bitterly as she allowed herself to enjoy the irony of her using the money Dracco had given her to spend on their honeymoon on funding her escape from him.

She would use it to buy herself a ticket to fly just as far away from him as she could!

* * *

'Well, there are seats left on the flight due to leave for Rio de Janeiro in half an hour,' the clerk responded in answer to Imogen's anxious enquiry.

Even whilst she listened to the clerk she couldn't stop herself from glancing nervously over her shoulder, still half expecting to see Dracco's familiar figure bearing down on her, and was chagrined to discover that there was a part of her that was almost desperately hoping that he would be.

But now it was too late. Now she was booked on to the flight for Rio. Shakily she walked over to the check-in desk and handed over her case.

Goodbye, home; goodbye, everything she knew; goodbye, love she had hoped so very very much to have.

Goodbye, Dracco!

CHAPTER ONE

Four years later

THROUGHOUT THE FLIGHT from Rio Imogen had been rehearsing exactly what she was going to say, and the manner in which she was going to say it. She reminded herself as she did so that she wasn't a naïve girl of just eighteen any more, who knew virtually nothing of the real world or the shadowed, darker side of life, a girl who had been sheltered and protected by her father's love and concern. No; she was a woman now, a woman of twenty-two, who knew exactly what the real world encompassed, exactly how much pain, poverty and degradation it could hold, as well as how much love, compassion and sheer generosity of spirit.

Looking back over the last four years, it seemed almost impossible that she had anything left in common with the girl she had once been. Imogen closed her eyes and lay back in her seat, an economy-class seat, even though she could technically at least have flown home first class. You didn't do things like that when you had spent the last few years working to help destitute orphans who lived in a world where children under five would fight to the death over a scrap of bread. Now, thanks to the small private charitable organisation she worked for, some of those orphans at least were being given a roof over their heads, food, education and, most important of all in Imogen's eyes, love.

Imogen couldn't pin-point exactly when she had first started to regret turning her back on her inheritance—not in any way for her own sake, but for what it could mean to the charity she worked for and the children she so much wanted to help.

Perhaps it had begun when she had stood and watched the happiness light up the face of Sister Maria the day she had announced to them all, in a voice that trembled with thrilled gratitude, that the fund-raising they had all worked so hard on that year had raised a sum of money that was only a tithe of the income Imogen knew she could have expected from her inheritance—never mind its saleable value.

All she did know was that increasingly over recent months she had begun to question the wisdom of what she had done and just how right she was to allow pride to stand in the way of all that she could do to benefit the charity.

And, as if that weren't enough, she had begun, too, to wonder how her friends and fellow workers would view her if they knew how wilfully and indeed selfishly she was refusing to use her own assets where they could do so much good. Pride was all very well but who exactly was paying for her to have the luxury of indulging in it? These and other equally painful questions had been causing Imogen to battle within herself for far too long. And now finally she had come to a decision she felt ashamed to have taken so long in reaching.

The nuns were so kind, so gentle, so humbly grateful for every scrap of help they received. They would never blame or criticise her, Imogen knew, but she was beginning to blame and criticise herself.

During her years in Rio Imogen had learned to protect and value her privacy, to guard herself from any unwanted questions, however kindly meant. Her trust was not something she gave lightly to others any more. Her past was a taboo subject and one she discussed with no one.

She had made friends in Rio, it was true, but her past was something she had kept to herself, and the friends she had made had all been kept at something of a distance—especially the men. Falling in love, being in love—these were things that hurt too much for her to even think about, never mind risk doing. Not after Dracco. *Dracco.* Even now she still sometimes dreamed about him. Dreams that drained her so much emotionally that for days afterwards she ached with pain.

There was no one to whom she wanted to confide just how searing her sense of loss and aloneness had been when she had first arrived in the city, or just how often she had been tempted to change her mind and return home. Only her pride had stopped her—that and the letter she had sent to her father's solicitor a week after her arrival in Rio, informing him that she was disassociating herself completely from her past life. She had said that she wanted nothing to do with the inheritance her father had left her and that henceforward she wanted to be allowed to lead her own life, on her own. She had made her letter as formal as possible, stating that under no circumstances did she want any kind of contact with either her stepmother or Dracco.

She had, of course, omitted to put any address on the letter, and as an added precaution she had used the last of the money Dracco had given her to fly to America, where she had posted her letter before returning to Rio.

In order to support herself she had found work both as an interpreter and a teacher, and it had been through that work that she had become involved with the sisters and their children's charity.

It had taken her what was now a guilt-inducing amount

of time to bring herself to take the action she was now taking, and she still felt acutely ashamed to remember the look of bemused disbelief on Sister Maria's face when she had haltingly explained to her that she was not the penniless young woman she had allowed everyone to believe she was.

Sister Maria's total lack of any attempt to question or criticise her had reinforced Imogen's determination to put matters right as speedily as she could.

Initially she had believed that it would be enough simply for her to write to her father's solicitor, explaining that she had changed her mind about the income she could receive under her father's will. She had explained in the simplest possible terms how she wished to use it to benefit Rio's pitifully needy street children. It had distressed her to receive a letter back not from Henry Fairburn but from an unknown David Bryant. He had introduced himself in the letter as Henry's successor and nephew, explaining that his uncle had died and that he had taken over the business.

As to Imogen's income from the inheritance left to her by her father, the letter had continued, he considered that because of the complications of the situation it would be necessary for her to return to England to put her wishes into action, and he had advised her to lose no time in doing so.

Of course, she had baulked at the idea of returning home. But, after all, what was there really for her to fear other than her own fear?

There was certainly no need for her to fear her long-dead love for Dracco. How could there be?

There had been no contact between them whatsoever, and for all that she knew he and Lisa could now be living together in blissful happiness. They certainly deserved one another. She had never met two people who matched one another so exactly in terms of cold-bloodedness.

It was a great pity that her father had seen fit to make

Dracco one of her trustees and an even greater one that Henry, her other trustee, was no longer alive. Imogen wasn't quite sure just what the full legal position with regard to her inheritance and her rights was, but no doubt this David Bryant would be able to advise her on that.

And on the other crumple in the otherwise smooth surface of her life that she really ought to get ironed out?

That small and impossible-to-blank-out fact that she and Dracco were still legally, so far as she was aware, married?

Disconcertingly the only gently chiding comment Sister Maria had made when Imogen had been explaining her situation had been a soft reminder that the vows of marriage were supposed to be for life!

Foolishly she had never bothered to get their marriage annulled. She had been far too terrified in those early days that Dracco might somehow persuade her to return home and to their marriage.

Now, of course, she had no such fear, and no need for the status of a single woman either, other than as a salve to her own pride, a final step into a Dracco-free future.

She was also looking forward to, as she had promised she would, writing to Sister Maria to tell her that everything was going smoothly and that she would soon be returning to Rio.

Her stomach muscles tensed with a nervous apprehension that she told herself firmly was entirely natural as the plane began its descent into Heathrow Airport.

The Imogen who had left Heathrow four years earlier had been pretty in a soft, still-girlish way, but the woman she had become could never in a thousand years have been described as wishy-washily pretty. The hardship of a life that was lived without any kind of luxury, a life that was spent giving one hundred and fifty per cent physical commitment and two hundred and fifty per cent emotional love, had stripped Imogen's body of its late-teenage layer of protective flesh and honed her face to a delicately boned translucency. This revealed not just her stunningly perfect features and the deep, intense amethyst of her amazing eyes, but also gave her a luminosity that was almost spiritual and that made people turn to look at her not just once but a second and then a third time.

She was dressed simply in soft chinos and a white cotton shirt, but no woman could possibly live in Rio without absorbing something of the sensuality of its people, of a culture that flagrantly and unselfconsciously worshipped the female form. Brazilian clothes were cut in a way that was unique, and not even the loose fit of what she was wearing could conceal the narrowness of Imogen's waist, the high curve of her breasts, the unexpected length of her legs, but most of all the rounded curve of her bottom.

Her dark hair meant that her skin had adapted well to the South American sun, which had given her a warm, ripe, peachy glow. As she raised her hand to shield her eyes from the shaft of sunlight breaking through the grey cloud the gold watch her father had given her shortly before his death glinted in the light, emphasising the fragility of her wrist. A group of stewardesses walking past her looked enviously at the careless way she had tied the tangled thickness of her curls back off her face with an old white silk scarf.

Taking a deep breath, Imogen summoned a taxi. Once inside it, she studied the piece of paper she had removed from her purse, and gave the address written on it to the driver.

As he repeated it he commented, 'Bute Wharf. That'll be one of them new developments down by the river.'

Imogen smiled dutifully in acknowledgement of his comment but said nothing. She had asked the advice of her solicitor on where to stay, specifying that it had to be reasonably close to his office, and cheap.

To her astonishment, not only had he replied with a terse note that explained that he had made arrangements for her to stay 'at the enclosed address' but which had also enclosed a cheque to cover her air fare. A first-class fare—although she had chosen not to make use of it.

This particular Docklands area of London was unfamiliar to her and Imogen's eyes widened a little as she studied it through the taxi window: streets filled with expensive cars, young men and women dressed in designer clothing, an air about the whole area of affluence and prestige. Was this really the kind of place where she was going to find cheap accommodation? She began to panic a little, wondering if the solicitor had misunderstood her request.

The taxi was pulling up outside an impressive apartment block. Getting out, Imogen glanced up uncertainly at her surroundings, paying off the taxi and then picking up her one small case before squaring her shoulders and heading determinedly towards the entrance.

As she did so she was vaguely aware of the dark shadow of a large car gliding into the space left by the taxi, but she paid no attention to it, too busy making sure that she had the right address to concern herself with it.

Yes, the address was the same one the solicitor had given her.

A little warily Imogen walked into the luxurious atrium that was the apartment block's lobby and then stopped, drawn by some compelling force she couldn't resist to turn round and stare, and then stare again. Her breath froze in shock in her lungs as she recognised the man casually slamming the door of the car she had been so vaguely aware of before turning to stride determinedly through the entrance towards her, exclaiming coolly as he did so, 'Imo! I had hoped to meet you at the airport, but somehow I missed you.'

'Dracco!'

How weak her voice sounded, shaky and thin, the voice of a child, a girl… Fiercely she tried to clear her throat, reminding herself that she was twenty-two and an adult, but her senses had shut down. They were concentrating exclusively on Dracco.

Four years hadn't changed him as much as she believed they had changed her, but then, he had already been an adult when she had left.

He still possessed that same aura of taut male sexual power she remembered so vividly, only now, as a woman, she was instantly, intensely aware of just how strong it was. It was like suddenly seeing something which had previously only been a hazy image brought sharply into focus, and she almost recoiled physically from the raw reality of it.

Had she forgotten just how magnetically sexy he was or had she simply never known, been too naïve to know? Well, if so, she wasn't now.

His hair was still as dark as she remembered, but cut shorter, giving him a somewhat harder edge. His eyes were harder than she remembered too. Harder and scrutinising her with a coldness that made her shiver.

'You didn't travel first class.'

'You knew that I was coming?' Try as she might, Imogen couldn't keep her appalled shock to herself.

'Of course. I'm your trustee, remember, and since the purpose of your visit is to discuss your inheritance…'

Her trustee! Well, of course she knew that, but somehow she had assumed, believed, that it would be David Bryant she would be talking to and that he would act as a negotiator between herself and Dracco. The last thing she wanted or needed was to be confronted by him like this when she was already feeling nervous and on edge. Not to mention jet-lagged.

Determined to grab back at least some small measure of control, she threw at him acidly, 'I'm surprised that Lisa isn't with you.'

'Lisa?'

She could see from his sharply incisive tone and the look he was giving her that he didn't like her pointed comment.

'This was nothing to do with Lisa,' he told her coldly.

Of course, he would want to protect his lover, Imogen acknowledged angrily.

The shocking realisation of how much she wanted to hurl at him all the accusations she had thought safely disarmed and vanquished years ago hit her nerve-endings like the kick of a mule. The old Imogen might well have given in and done so, but there had been something in the way he had looked at her when he had reminded her that he was her trustee that was warning her to tread very carefully.

Surely it was only a matter of formality for her to be able to reclaim the income she had previously rejected? It was, after all, legally hers, wasn't it?

Surely David Bryant would have told her, warned her, if this wasn't the case or if he had foreseen problems, rather than encouraging her to come all this way?

When it came to disposing of her share of the business, Imogen felt that she was on firmer ground. Since Dracco had been willing to marry her to secure it, surely it made sense that he would be delighted to be given legal control of her share of it in return for guaranteeing its income would be given to the charity?

After all, if she wished she could always sell it on the open market! Knowing that she held that power, that threat over him, helped to rally her courage.

Dracco had reached her now, and Imogen discovered that one thing hadn't changed. She still had to tilt her head right back to look up into his eyes when he stood next to her.

Too late to regret now the comfortable low-heeled pumps she was wearing.

'Come on.' As he spoke Dracco was propelling her forward, the fear of experiencing the sensation of that powerful long-fingered hand of his, placed firmly in the small of her back, causing her to hurry in the direction he was indicating.

What was the matter with her? Why on earth should she fear Dracco touching her now? Once she had feared it because then she had known that even the briefest and most non-sexual contact with him was enough to make her aching body feel as though it might explode with longing, but those days were over! All around her on the streets of Rio she had seen the living, suffering evidence of what happened when two human beings indulged in their sexual desires. She would never abandon her child—never in a million years—but then, she was not a girl, a child herself, penniless and without any means of support. No, that wasn't the point. The point was…the point was…

Dizzily, dangerously Imogen realised that she was having a hard time focusing on anything logical or sensible; that she was, in fact, finding it virtually impossible to concentrate on anything other than Dracco himself.

'It's this way.'

Automatically she followed him towards the glass-walled lift, numbly aware of the brief nod of the hovering uniformed commissionaire as he greeted Dracco with a respectful, 'Good afternoon, Mr Barrington.'

'Afternoon, Bates,' Dracco responded calmly. 'Family OK?'

'Yes, they're fine, and young Robert's over the moon about that job you got for him.'

The smile Dracco gave the doorman suddenly made him look far less formidable and reminded Imogen of the smiles he once used to give her. An almost unbearably tight pain filled her chest, which she firmly put down to the speed with which the lift was surging upwards.

'Still scared of heights? Don't look down,' Dracco told her coolly. 'Heaven knows why, but for some reason every architect in the city seems to have decided that glass-walled lifts are the in thing.'

Where once he would have made such a comment in a voice that was ruefully amused, now he sounded terse and cold. Well, there was no reason why he should show her any warmth, was there?

But why shouldn't he? She had, after all, spared him the trouble of having to pretend that he had wanted to marry her or that he cared about her, and she had given him what he really wanted at the same time. In the letter she had sent to Henry renouncing her inheritance she had given Dracco complete and total authority to use the power that came with her share of the business as he saw fit.

In doing so, she had known beyond any kind of doubt that Dracco would uphold her father's business ideals and aims. In that regard at least she had known she could trust him totally.

She had closed her eyes when the lift started to move, but unexpectedly the images, the memories suddenly torment-ing her were even worse in their own way than the heights she feared. She would, she knew, never forgive Dracco for what he had tried to do; for the way he had tried to manipu-late her; for the way he had abused the trust her father had placed in him.

The lift shivered to a silent stop.

'You can open your eyes now,' she heard Dracco tell-ing her wryly.

As she edged out of the lift Imogen saw that they had stopped at the floor marked 'Penthouse Suite'.

Penthouse suite. Her solicitor had roomed her in a penthouse suite? Discomfort flickered down her spine. She just knew that this was going to be expensive.

It had taken her a long time to get used to the shared dormitory she had slept in when she had first arrived in Rio, but when she finally found her own small apartment for the first few weeks she had actually missed the presence of the other girls. Now, though, she had to admit to relishing the privacy and the luxury of having her own bathroom.

'I asked David Bryant to find me somewhere cheap and convenient for his office,' she murmured as Dracco produced a key and unlocked the apartment's door.

Imogen could see his eyebrows rise as he listened to her.

'Well, he's complied with both those instructions,' he informed her. 'His office isn't that far away, and you're staying here as my guest.'

'Your guest?'

Imogen froze on the spot, staring at him with wide eyes, whilst Dracco pushed the door to, enclosing them both in the intimacy of the empty hallway.

'Your guest?' Imogen repeated starkly. 'This is your apartment?'

'Yes,' Dracco confirmed. 'When David told me that you'd specified you wanted to stay somewhere close to his office I told him that you might as well stay here with me. After all, there's a great deal we need to discuss…and not just about your inheritance.'

He was, Imogen recognised, looking pointedly at her left hand, the hand from which she had removed the wedding ring he had placed on it, throwing it as far as she could through the open taxi window on her way to Heathrow, too blinded by tears to see where it landed, and too sick at heart to care.

'You mean…' She paused and flicked her tongue tip over

her suddenly dry lips, nervously aware of Dracco's iron gaze following her every movement.

'You mean our marriage?' she guessed shakily.

'I mean our marriage,' Dracco confirmed.

'You know,' he told her conversationally as he bent to pick up her lightweight case, 'for a woman who is still a virgin, you look…decidedly unvirginal.'

Imogen tried to convince herself that the rushing sensation of faintness engulfing her was caused by the airlessness of the hallway rather than by what Dracco had said, but still she heard herself demanding huskily, 'How…how do you know?'

'That you are still a virgin?' Dracco completed for her. 'I know everything there is to know about you, Imo… After all, you are my wife…'

His wife!

Imogen felt sick; filled with a cold, shaky disbelief and an even colder fear. This was not what she had expected; what she had steeled herself to deal with.

During the long flight from Rio she had forced herself to confront the fear that had raised its threatening head in her nightmares in the days leading up to her journey. She had been terrified that somehow, totally against her will and all logic, if she were to see Dracco again she might discover a dangerous residue of her teenage love for him had somehow survived; that it was waiting, ready to explode like a time bomb, to destroy her new life and the peace of mind she had fought so hard for. But now! Now it wasn't love that Dracco was arousing inside her but a furious mixture of anger and hostility.

So she was still a virgin—was that a crime?

'You have no right to pry into my life, to spy on me,' she began furiously, but Dracco refused to allow her to continue.

'We are still married. I am still your husband; you are still my wife,' he pointed out coldly.

Imogen turned away to conceal her expression from him. Married in the eyes of the church, perhaps, but surely not in the eyes of the law, since their marriage had never been consummated. And that certainly didn't give Dracco the right to claim her as his wife in a voice that suggested... Wearily Imogen shook her head. Now she was letting her imagination run away with her. Thinking she had heard possessiveness in Dracco's voice.

His words had given her a shock. Why on earth hadn't Dracco had the marriage set aside? He, after all, loved another woman—her stepmother!

Even after all these years it still filled her with acute nausea and disgust to think of Dracco with Lisa. Her father's wife and the man her father had loved and valued so very much. Had Dracco slept with Lisa whilst her father was still alive? Had they...? Had he...? Unstoppably all the questions she had fiercely forbidden herself to even think before suddenly stormed through her. The images they were conjuring up sickened her, causing a red-hot boiling pain in her middle.

All those years ago, Dracco had implied to her that he was marrying her to protect her, when all he had really wanted to protect had been his own interests!

Tiredly Imogen closed her eyes. She had come to England for one purpose and one purpose only and that was to claim whatever money might be owing to her. And to persuade Dracco to transfer her interest in the business into the name of the charity so that in future it could benefit direct from her inheritance. Anything else...

'I haven't come back to discuss our marriage, Dracco.' Firmly Imogen took a deep breath, determined to take control of the situation. 'I've already written to David Bryant, explaining what I want, and that is—'

'To give away your inheritance to some charity,' Dracco interrupted her grimly. 'No, Imo,' he told her curtly. 'As your trustee, there's no way I would be fulfilling my moral obligation towards you if I agreed, and as your husband...'

She ached to be able to challenge him, to throw caution to the wind and demand furiously to know just when moral obligations had become important to him. But some inner instinct warned her against going too far. This wasn't how their interview was supposed to go. She was an adult now, on an equal footing with Dracco, and not a child whom he could dictate to.

'Legally the money is mine,' she reminded him, having mentally counted to ten and calmed herself down a little.

'Was yours,' Dracco corrected her harshly. 'You insisted that you wanted nothing to do with your inheritance—and you put that insistence in writing—remember.'

Imogen took another deep breath. The situation was proving even more fraught with difficulties than she had expected.

'I did write to Uncle Henry saying that,' she agreed, pausing to ask him quietly, 'When did he die? I had no idea.'

Dracco had turned away from her, and for a moment Imogen thought that he had either not heard her question or that he did not intend to answer it, but then without turning back to her he said coldly, 'He had a heart attack shortly after... on the day of our wedding.'

Horrified, Imogen could only make a soft, anguished sound of distress.

'Apparently he hadn't been feeling well before the ceremony,' Dracco continued as though he hadn't heard her. 'When he collapsed outside the church...' He stopped whilst Imogen battled against her shock. 'I went with him to the hospital. They hoped then... But he had a second attack whilst he was in Intensive Care which proved fatal.'

'Was it…?' Too shocked to guard her thoughts, Imogen blurted out shakily, 'Was it because of me? Because I…?'

'He had been under a tremendous amount of pressure,' Dracco told her without answering her anguished plea for reassurance. 'Your father's death had caused him an immense amount of work, and it seems that there had been certain warning signs of a heart problem which he had ignored. He wasn't a young man—he was ten years older than your father.' He paused and then said abruptly, 'He asked me to tell you how proud he had been to give you away.'

Tears blurred Imogen's eyes. She had a mental image of her father's solicitor on the morning of her wedding, dressed in his morning suit, his silver-grey hair immaculately groomed. In the car on the way to the church he had taken hold of her hand and patted it a little awkwardly. He had been a widower, like her father, with no children of his own, and Imogen had always sensed a certain shyness in his manner towards her. Her father had been a very loving man and she had desperately missed the father-daughter warmth of their relationship. She had known from the look in his eyes that, like her, Henry Fairburn had been thinking about her father on that day.

She had been sad to learn of his death from his nephew, but she had never imagined…

'If you're going to throw yourself into a self-indulgent bout of emotional guilt, I shouldn't bother,' Dracco was warning her hardly. 'His heart attack was a situation waiting to happen and would have happened whether or not you had been there.'

Somehow, instead of comforting and reassuring her, Dracco's blunt words were only making her feel worse, Imogen acknowledged.

'I don't want to argue with you, Dracco,' she said quietly.

'You are a wealthy man in your own right. If you could just see the plight of these children…'

'It is a good cause, yes, involvement with the shelter. My sources inform me that—'

'Your sources?' Imogen checked him angrily. 'You have no right—'

'Surely you didn't think I would allow you to simply disappear without any trace, Imo? For your father's sake, if nothing else; I owed it to him to—'

'I can't believe that even someone like you could stoop so low. To have me watched, spied on,' Imogen breathed bitterly.

'You're overreacting,' Dracco told her laconically. 'Yes, I made enquiries to ascertain where you were and what you were doing and with whom,' he agreed. 'Anyone would have done the same in the circumstances. You were a young, naïve girl of eighteen. Anything could have happened to you.'

He was frowning broodingly and Imogen had to shake herself free of the foolish feeling that he had been genuinely concerned about her.

'It doesn't matter what you say, Dracco, I'm not going to give up,' she warned him determinedly. 'The shelter needs money so desperately, and I warn you now that I'm prepared to do whatever it takes to make sure it gets mine.'

The silence that followed her passionate outburst caused a tiny sliver of apprehension to needle its way into Imogen's nervous system. Dracco was looking at her as though…as though…

Why had she never realised as a girl how very hawkish and predatory he could look, almost demonically so? She shivered and instantly blamed her reaction on the change of continent.

'Well, you're a woman now, Imo, and not a girl and, as

you must have surely come to realise, nothing in this life comes without a price. You handed your inheritance over to me of your own accord. Now you wish me to hand it back to you, and not only the income which your share of the business has earned these last four years, but the future income of that share as well.'

'It belongs to me,' Imogen insisted. 'The terms of my father's will stated that it would become mine either on my thirtieth birthday or when I married, whichever happened first.'

'Mmm…' Dracco gave her a look she could not identify. 'You have told me what it is you want me to give you, Imo, but what are you prepared to give me in exchange for my agreement—supposing, of course, that I am prepared to give it?'

Imogen started to frown. What could she give him?

'We are still married,' Dracco was reminding her yet again. 'Our marriage was never annulled.'

Imogen's face cleared. 'You want an annulment,' she guessed, ignoring the sharp, unwanted stab of pain biting into her heart and concentrating instead on clinging determinedly to the relief she wanted to feel. 'Well, of course I will agree, and—'

'No, I do not want an annulment,' Dracco cut across her hurried assent. 'Far from it.'

CHAPTER TWO

'YOU DON'T WANT an annulment?' Imogen stared at Dracco as though she couldn't believe what she had heard. 'What… what do you mean?' she demanded.

She could hear the nervous stammer in her voice and despised herself for it. Dracco couldn't mean that he wanted to remain married to her. That was impossible. And just as impossible to accept was that sharp, shocking thrill of excitement his words had given her.

Dracco watched her carefully. As Imogen's trustee, it was his moral duty to safeguard her inheritance for her, to be worthy of the trust her father had placed in him, and that was something he fully intended to do. And if in helping her he was able to progress his own personal agenda, then so much the better! And as for him telling her just why… but, no…that was totally out of the question. Fate had generously dealt some very powerful cards into his hand, and now it was up to him to play them successfully. And he intended to play them and to win!

Imogen felt a nervous tremor run through her body as she waited for Dracco's response. His expression was hard and unreadable, his eyes cold and distant.

'I hope that you don't need me to remind you of just how much your father meant to me,' he began abruptly.

'I know that you married me because of his will,' Imogen responded ambiguously. She had wanted to give Dracco a subtle warning that she was not the naïve girl who had trusted him so implicitly any longer, but even she was shocked by the swiftness with which he decoded her message. Shocked and, if she was honest, just a little bit apprehensive when she saw the immediate and fearsome blaze of anger in the look he gave her.

'And what exactly is that supposed to mean?' Dracco challenged her softly.

Imogen took a deep breath. There was no way she was going to allow him to face her down! There was too much at stake. She had a responsibility to those who were dependent on her for her help.

'I was very young when I married you, Dracco,' she told him as calmly as she could. 'My father's will, as we both know, stipulated that I should have control of my share of the business upon my marriage. Naturally, since I was so young, I would have deferred to you where matters of business were concerned, so that in effect you would have had full control of the business—and the income it generated. Of course, had you chosen to sell the business and utilise the profits from that sale on your own behalf...'

'What?'

For a moment Dracco looked almost as though she had shocked him.

'If you are trying to imply that I married you for financial gain then let me tell you you're way off the mark. In fact, I am wealthier now than your father ever was—thanks, I have to admit, to everything he taught me.'

He was speaking to her as though he were admonishing a child, Imogen decided angrily.

'So why exactly did you marry me, then?' she asked him sharply.

'You know why.' He started to turn away from her so that she couldn't see his face, his voice becoming curt.

Imogen could sense that her question had made him uneasy in some way. Because he felt guilty? Well he might!

'Yes, I do, don't I?' Imogen agreed acerbically. 'My father—'

'Your father was a man I admired more than any other man I have ever met.' Dracco cut across what she had been about to say, his tone warning her against questioning the truth of his words. 'In fact, in the early years of our friendship, I often wished that he had been *my* father. I have never met a man I have respected or loved as much as I did John Atkins, Imogen. I felt proud to have his friendship and his trust. He was everything I myself most wanted to be. He was everything that my own father was not.'

He paused, whilst Imogen silently swallowed the huge lump of emotion in her throat.

Dracco's father had left his mother whilst Dracco had still been a baby; a gambler and a womaniser, he had been killed in a drunken brawl when Dracco had been in his early teens.

'I have never lost either my admiration or my love for your father, Imo, nor the wish that he and I might share a closer, more personal tie.' He paused meaningfully whilst Imogen fidgeted with anxiety. Whatever conditions Dracco imposed on his agreement to hand over her inheritance, Imogen knew that somehow she would have to meet them. There was no way she wanted to disappoint the nuns now, nor did she intend to do anything that would prevent her being able to improve the lot of those who were dependent on the shelter.

'Your father could never be my father, Imo, but he could be the grandfather of my son—our son,' Dracco told her meaningfully.

His son…their son. Stupefied, Imogen gaped at him. She couldn't possibly have heard him correctly.

'No!' she protested frantically. 'You can't mean it.' But she could see from his expression that he did, and her heart somersaulted inside her ribcage and then banged dizzyingly against her ribs themselves.

'No,' she whispered painfully. 'I can't. I won't! This is blackmail, Dracco,' she accused him. 'If you want a child so much—'

'I don't want "a" child, Imo,' he cut across her coolly. 'Haven't you been listening to what I said? What I want is your father's grandchild. My blood linked to his, and only you can provide me with that.'

'You're mad,' Imogen gasped. 'This is like something out of the Dark Ages…it's…I won't do it!' she told him fiercely.

'Then I won't give you your money,' Dracco informed her in a voice that was dangerously soft.

'You'll have to… I'll take you to court. I'll…' Imogen began wildly, but once again Dracco stopped her, shaking his head as he told her unkindly,

'Somehow I don't think a court would agree to you giving away your birthright. Especially if it was to be implied that part of the reason your father set up his will as he did was because he feared that you were not financially astute enough to protect your own interests.'

Imogen glared furiously at him. 'You wouldn't dare,' she began, but Dracco was smiling at her, a mocking smile that didn't touch his eyes as he told her softly, 'Try me!'

Imogen shook her head in angry disbelief. This was emotional manipulation at its worst. How on earth could she ever have loved Dracco? Right now she positively hated him.

'You can't do this,' she protested, her face raw with emotion as she told him shakily, 'If you could see these children—they have nothing, Dracco. Less than nothing. They need help so badly!'

'And they can have it, Imo,' Dracco told her calmly, 'but not from your inheritance. As your trustee, I cannot allow that, but—' he paused and looked at her, his penetrating gaze holding her own and refusing to let her look away '—but,' he repeated coolly, 'as your husband,' Dracco continued with a pseudo-gentleness that made her tense her stomach muscles against whatever it was he was going to say, 'as your husband,' he stressed with deliberate emphasis, 'I would be quite prepared to promise to pay one million pounds to the shelter now, and another one million when you give birth to our child.'

If Imogen hadn't already decided she hated Dracco she knew she would have done so now. How could he be so cynical, so cruel, so corrupt? Two million pounds! He must be rich indeed if he could afford to part with so much money so easily and just so that… He had loved and revered her father, she knew that, and she could even see too why he might want to have a child who carried her father's blood. But to go about it in such a way, when he knew that he would be forcing her to have sex with him and when he knew too that he didn't love her… Imogen couldn't stop herself from shuddering with angry loathing.

'I…I need time to think,' she told him defiantly.

'To think, or to run away again? I thought this charity was all-important to you, Imo, but it seems…'

'Stop it.' Covering her ears with her hands, Imogen turned away from him.

His cruelty appalled her but she couldn't stop herself from acknowledging the truth of what he was saying. When she thought about the difference his money would make to Rio's homeless street children Imogen knew that she could not possibly put her own needs before theirs.

'So do we have a deal—two million for your charity, a wife and, hopefully, your father's grandchild for me?'

Somehow Imogen managed not to show how desperately tempted she was to refuse. Summoning all her courage, she took a deep breath and agreed huskily, 'Yes.'

Bleakly Imogen stared out of the window of Dracco's car—a sleek silver BMW now and not the Daimler she remembered him driving—as they sped through the uniquely green English countryside. She had not asked Dracco where they were going, had not addressed any questions or conversation to him at all, in fact, since she had woken up in his city apartment earlier on in the day. His apartment but thankfully not his bed; no, she had been spared that at least for now, having slept alone in his guest room.

She had no idea where they were going and had no intention of asking. All Dracco had told her once he had ascertained that she was prepared to accede to the terms he had proposed to her—an agreement she had thrown at him with flashing eyes and an angrily set mouth as she tried to remind herself that his proposition surely demeaned him far more than it demeaned her—was that he was taking her to the house that was going to be her home.

'Stop behaving like a tragedy queen, Imo,' she heard him saying drily to her. 'It doesn't suit you and, besides, there's no need.'

'No need? After what you've done,' Imogen exploded.

'After what I've done?' Dracco checked her. 'I haven't done anything other than offer you a deal.'

'A deal!' Indignation flashed from Imogen's eyes. 'You're blackmailing me into having a child with you.' Quickly she turned away from him before he could sense the emotions she was struggling to overcome. 'What's going to happen once you have your child, Dracco?'

'What do you think is going to happen?' he challenged her sharply. 'No child of mine is going to be abandoned by either of its parents, Imogen.'

'You expect me to stay married to you?'

Surely that wasn't actually relief she could feel spreading through her tensed muscles?

'What I expect is that you and I will stay married to one another for just as long as our child needs us to be. What were you expecting?' he demanded as he skilfully negotiated a tight bend.

Imogen shook her head, not wanting him to see how relieved she was that he wasn't going to try to separate her from her child, to send her away whilst he brought it up alone. Because she knew that, no matter what she might think about Dracco himself, no matter how much she might loathe and hate him for what he was doing, she would never be able to walk away from her baby.

She frowned as she suddenly recognised the countryside they were driving through, her heart starting to beat increasingly heavily as the road dropped down into the village where she had grown up. At the end of the village street Dracco turned left. The lane started to climb steeply and, even though it had been four years since she had last travelled down it, Imogen remembered every inch of it. It had been down this road that Dracco had driven her to school; down this road that he had driven her when he had come to fetch her the day her father had died; down this road she had travelled on her way to her wedding.

'You've bought our old house.' She said it as a statement rather than a question, her voice flat as she fought to control her emotions.

'I was already negotiating for it before our wedding,' Dracco answered her unemotionally. 'It was supposed to be a surprise wedding present for you. I knew how much you hated the idea of Lisa selling it. By the time it became obvious that you weren't going to be around to collect any wedding presents from me or anyone else, it was too late to pull out of the deal.' He gave a small dismissive shrug. 'I suppose I could have put it back on the market, but…'

Dracco had turned into the house's familiar drive and for a moment, as the car crunched over the gravel and came to a halt outside the front door, Imogen almost felt that if she closed her eyes and then opened them again she would see her father come hurrying towards her.

But her father was dead, and something inside her had died now as well.

'It still looks just the same,' she told Dracco distantly as they both got out of the car. He was a stranger to her, a man she loathed, and yet tonight he would…

Whilst she fought to control the shudders of fear that rocked her Dracco was unlocking the front door.

'Well, you'll find there have been some changes,' he warned her casually. 'I left your father's room as it was, but…' He paused and turned away from her, his voice suddenly shadowed and edged with an emotion she couldn't analyse. 'I haven't really used the house much myself. However, I have made some changes to some of the other rooms.'

When she looked questioningly at him he turned to face her fully and told her bluntly, 'I didn't think that either of us would want to use the rooms that had been your parents', so I had a new master-bedroom suite built on—and the conservatory your father once told me your mother had always wanted. He didn't have the heart to add it after her death, but I thought…' He stopped, his mouth compressing, pushing open the front door without enlightening her as to what his thoughts had been.

Imogen discovered that she was shaking as she followed him inside. It had been down these stairs that she had semi-stumbled on the way to her wedding, her whole world destroyed by Lisa's cruelty, and down them too that she had run in her haste to escape from Dracco and her marriage to him.

Her tastes had changed and matured in the last few years, and she recognised with a sharp pang of pain just how old-fashioned and, yes, shabby the dark red stair carpet her mother had chosen looked. She could almost feel how unloved and desolate the whole house was. Dust motes danced in the sunshine and she could see a film of it lying on the table beneath the ornate Venetian wall mirror that her parents had bought on their honeymoon.

Her mother had been a wonderful homemaker before her illness had struck her down and suddenly Imogen discovered that her own inner eye was itching to bring the house back to life, to turn it back to the love-filled home she could remember. Irritated by her own vulnerability, she demanded sharply of Dracco, 'Why exactly have you brought me here? Apart from the obvious reason, of course.' She added acerbically, 'I have to admit that I'm surprised you don't actually want to conceive this child in my father's bed.'

She stopped in mid-sentence, shocked into silence by the look in his eyes. It was far more dangerous than any verbal warning could have been.

'I have brought you here because this will be your home from now on,' Dracco told her levelly, once he had forced her to drop her gaze from his.

'But you don't live here?' Imogen guessed, thinking about the dust she had seen.

'I haven't been doing,' Dracco agreed. 'There wasn't any point. But now... A city apartment isn't, in my opinion, the right place to bring up a child.'

'But you will still be spending some time in the city?' Imogen pressed him. Please God, let him say that he would;

let him say too that his visits here to the house, to her, and to the bed he was forcing her to share with him, would be infrequent and of short duration.

But instead of answering her directly he surprised her by asking softly, 'What exactly is it about sex that you find so threatening, Imo?'

'Nothing! I don't,' she denied quickly, knowing that her face was burning hotly with a self-consciousness that he had to have seen before she turned defensively away from him. 'It isn't the sex,' she denied doggedly, 'it's you…and the way…'

'I don't believe you,' Dracco told her. 'For a woman of your age still to be a virgin suggests…'

'Suggests what?' Imogen immediately challenged him. 'That I'm choosy about who I give my…' My love, she had been about to say, but she quickly corrected herself and said instead, 'Myself to.'

'Suggests that you're afraid of something,' Dracco continued smoothly, as though she hadn't interrupted him. 'Are you, Imo? Are you afraid?'

'No,' she denied vehemently. But she knew that she was lying. She was afraid. She was very afraid. To her the physical act of sex was inextricably linked with the emotion of love, and she was desperately, mortally afraid that…

That what? That being forced to have sex with Dracco to produce the child he wanted would somehow force her to love him again? How could it?

Last night, lying awake in Dracco's guest room, she had told herself that what she was sacrificing was nothing weighed against what the charity would be gaining and that she was too old to have any right to start feeling sorry for herself. But no amount of trying to be logical about what had happened had helped to ease the sharp, stark pain in her heart—or the fear that accompanied it.

As she moved away from Dracco and walked down the hallway, instinctively heading for her father's study, she could hear him saying wryly, 'A team of cleaners from the village comes in once a month to go over the whole place and I asked them to stock up the fridge and freezer. If their shopping is of the same calibre as their cleaning it might be as well to check the fridge. I have booked a table for dinner at Emporio's for tonight. I trust you do still like Italian food?'

'You're taking me out for dinner?' Imogen couldn't keep the cynicism out of her voice. 'Why not just take me straight to bed? Why waste time—and money? After all, you've already committed yourself to paying two million for it.'

'Stop that at once.'

Imogen gasped as Dracco crossed the distance that separated them with startling speed, taking hold of her forearms, his lean fingers biting hard into her vulnerable flesh as he gave her a small shake.

'You're my wife, Imogen, not some paid harlot. And if I choose to woo you—'

'Woo me!' Imogen could feel the hysterical laughter bubbling up inside her. 'Why on earth would you want to do that?' she challenged him acidly. 'All you really want is a child, my father's grandchild! You can achieve that without going to the expense of buying me dinner. After all, you don't care whether I'm willing or not!'

Dracco released her so quickly that Imogen felt the unwanted shock of his withdrawal from her right through her body. The shaming knowledge that a tiny part of her was actually daring to miss the warm male touch of Dracco's hands on her arms infuriated and frightened her. She told herself that it was just her memory playing tricks, reminding her of a time when she had welcomed and wanted his touch. Welcomed and wanted it! Craved it, ached for it, hungered for it and for him—that was a far more accurate description. Abruptly Imogen dragged her mind back to the present, wincing a little as she saw the furious look Dracco was giving her.

He shook his head, his mouth compressing. 'What I want, and what I intend for this child—*our* child—is that it is born if not out of mutual love then at least out of mutual pleasure.'

His words shocked her, almost thrilled her in some atavistic and explosively dangerous way.

Recklessly Imogen flung back her head and demanded, 'And how is that going to happen when there is no way I could ever want you?'

She could almost hear the seconds ticking by as Dracco looked at her. What could he see…what was he looking for? Her tongue snaked out and touched her suddenly dry lips. Dracco's diamond-hard gaze fastened on her small betraying gesture, seizing on it even more fiercely than his hands had grasped her only minutes earlier. Imogen could almost feel the physical effect of his gaze on her; on her mouth; her body; her senses!

'There is nothing you could ever do that could make me want you, Dracco. Do you hear me?' The excited fury in her own reiteration frightened her but she refused to allow herself to acknowledge either her fear or her folly.

'Are you challenging me, Imogen?' Dracco asked her softly. 'Because if you want me to prove you wrong I can promise you that I am more than willing to do so. Very much more than willing,' he emphasised with meaningful deliberation.

Imogen's heightened senses relayed to her every aspect of what was happening: the scent of the dust in the air, the limpid warmth of the sun streaming in through the window, which in no way could match the white heat of the fury she could see burning in Dracco's eyes. She shivered, but not with cold, as feelings she had thought long dead sprang to life inside her.

'No!' she whispered painfully beneath her breath. No! It was over. Dead, done… She did not love Dracco any more and she wasn't going to allow herself to do so ever again.

Drawing a shaky breath, she met the look he was giving her.

'You couldn't,' she denied, making herself believe it.

'No? Watch me!' Dracco breathed. 'Just watch me, Imogen. And when you're lying in my bed, my arms, beneath my body, crying out for my possession, wanting me, I shall remind you of this moment.'

CHAPTER THREE

IMOGEN TURNED AWAY from the window of her childhood bedroom and glanced at her watch.

Seven-thirty; soon she would have to go downstairs and join Dracco, who had warned her that unless she was ready to go out for dinner with him by eight o'clock he would personally 'escort' her downstairs.

'Why are you doing this?' she had demanded in furious frustration.

'Why are you?' he had countered with a coolness that had made her grind her teeth in impotent rage.

'You know why I'm doing it. I don't have any choice.'

'Of course you do,' he had returned promptly. 'You could choose to simply walk away if you wished to do so.'

'The shelter needs money—you know that,' Imogen had argued bitterly.

That was true, and what was also true was that she didn't think she could live with herself if she didn't do everything she could to help. Perhaps a part of her determination to do so had its roots in the fact that she felt guilty because she had withheld her financial help for so long, she acknowledged. But it had taken her a long time to stop being afraid of the power the past had over her; to stop being afraid of the love she had had for Dracco. Now she had overcome that fear!

But to allow Dracco to consummate their marriage; to

have his child! Unwillingly Imogen's gaze was drawn back
to her bedroom window. Did she really have the resolve, the
courage to do that?

It had been from this window that she had watched so
many times for her father to come home. She had knelt on
the window seat, her elbows on the sill propping up her head
as she strained her ears and her eyes for the familiar sound
and sight of her father's car. The moment she could hear it
she had dashed downstairs, ready to fling herself into his
arms just as soon as she could.

Even during the dark days of her mother's final illness
her father had never failed to give her the loving reassurance of his time and attention.

And then had come the darker days of his marriage to
Lisa, when it had so often been Dracco she had turned to for
comfort. Dracco she had waited impatiently to see arriving
at the house from the sanctuary of her bedroom.

Her father had loved this house. He had once told her
that to him it epitomised everything that a family home
should be.

'One day you will bring your children here to see me,
Imo,' he had often told her as she grew up.

He had been looking forward to becoming a grandfather.

The scene in front of Imogen's eyes began to blur.

A child. A child that was both a part of him and of herself and Dracco. Her father would have loved that so much,
cherished that child so much.

A child. Dracco's child. How often had she sat at this
very window and fantasised about that happening; about
Dracco loving her; about that love resulting in the birth of
their baby?

Dracco loving her! Angrily Imogen shook away her
threatening emotional tears. Dracco did not love her. He

simply wanted to share a blood tie with her father. He had
told her so.

And yet as she turned away from the bedroom window
she could still see so vividly in her mind's eye the three of
them walking together up the drive, Dracco, herself and,
between them, the dark-haired green-eyed boy-child who
shared his father's strong bone-structure and his grandfather's loving smile.

'I must be mad,' Imogen whispered reprovingly to herself as she snatched up her jacket and her bag and headed
for her bedroom door.

There was no way she could ever willingly do what
Dracco was forcing on her. And surely no way either that
she could ever deny that fierce tug of maternal love she had
felt so very sharply for the child her own treacherous imagination had conjured up.

When she opened her door she saw Dracco advancing
along the landing towards her.

Unlike her, he had changed his clothes, removing the
city suit he had been wearing and putting on in its place a
more casual pair of cotton chinos and a short-sleeved shirt.

England must have been having a good summer, Imogen
acknowledged absently as her gaze slid helplessly along the
length of Dracco's bare bronzed arms. There had always
been something about his arms that fascinated her, something that had sent a shower of excited girlish sensuality
shivering over her skin. In those days, just the thought of
Dracco's arms closing round her, holding her in the tender
and protective embrace which had been all her innocent
mind had then been able to conjure up, had been enough
to set off that hot, aching, melting feeling in the pit of her
stomach.

Later, as she grew older, it hadn't been so much Dracco's arms holding her she had fantasised about as his hands,

touching her, caressing her, stroking and arousing her will-ing flesh with the kind of intimate and wildly dangerous touch that even in the privacy of her own bed had made her face burn with hot, guilty, excited desire.

He had, Imogen guessed, not only changed his clothes but showered as well, which made her feel uncomfortably aware of the fact that she was still wearing the clothes she had flown into Heathrow in. She had refused to allow herself to change out of a stubborn determination to show him just how unimportant either his opinion of her or his company was. Right now, however, it wasn't a sense of satisfaction in her own stubbornness she was experiencing but rather a very unwanted feeling of gritty discomfort, and general grubbiness, which caused her to reach up defensively to rake her fingers through her tangled curls.

'Too busy to have time to get changed? Never mind, I'm sure Luigi will understand,' Dracco commented.

'You've told Luigi that you…we're…'

'I've told him that you're going to be my dinner guest, yes,' Dracco confirmed. 'I just hope you still like pear and almond tart and honey ice cream.'

Ignoring his dry reference to her teenage love of her fa-vourite local Italian restaurant's pudding, Imogen demanded wildly, 'What else have you told him?'

Dracco gave a small shrug. 'Nothing,' he denied.

As she absorbed his response Imogen struggled to under-stand why instead of feeling relief that Dracco hadn't made any kind of public statement about their marriage what she actually felt was a kind of anger.

'But you are going to have to say something?' she per-sisted. 'We can't just suddenly start living together as a married couple.'

Dracco gave another dismissive shrug. 'As to that, I shall tell people what they will want to hear.'

'Which is?' Imogen challenged him.

'Which is that there has been a rapprochement between us, a mutual agreement with the benefit of hindsight and maturity that we wish to give our marriage a second chance.'

'A second chance?' Imogen couldn't help querying, and then wished that she had not when she saw the look Dracco was giving her.

'Most of them will assume, no doubt, that we were lovers before our marriage, and somehow I doubt that you will want people to know that you are still a virgin.'

Imogen could feel her face reddening.

'Don't flatter yourself that my virginity has anything to do with you!' She threw the words recklessly at him, unaware of just how they might be interpreted or what they might reveal. 'The fact that I haven't…that I'm… Well, that's my business and has nothing to do with anyone else.'

Dracco was already heading for the stairs and automatically Imogen walked with him.

'Just a minute,' he demanded as they reached the hallway.

Warily, Imogen waited as he reached into his pocket and withdrew a small box.

'You're going to need this,' he told her coolly. 'I notice that you aren't wearing the original. This one doesn't have the benefit of a clerical blessing, and I had to guess at the size. You're more slender than you were…'

Without giving her the opportunity to take the box from him, he flipped open the lid, revealing a gold wedding band so similar to the first one he had given her that Imogen had to suppress a superstitious feeling that it was the same ring.

And with it was something she had desperately wished she had not had to leave behind when she had run away—the engagement ring she had not been wearing on the day of her marriage that Dracco had had made for her. It incorporated in an elegant modern setting the three diamonds

that had originally been in her mother's engagement ring.
Those stones meant so much to her that now as she stared
at it, tears stung Imogen's eyes.

'My ring,' she whispered.

'It might be a little bit too big now,' Dracco warned her
as she reached for it. He forestalled her and took hold of
her hand.

Imogen could feel herself starting to tremble. Against
her will she went back in time; she was in church, waiting
for Dracco to place his ring on her finger.

Now, as he slid the cold metal over her knuckle, she
could remember exactly how she had felt, how much she
had wanted to believe that their marriage was more to him
than simply a business arrangement.

He was right—the engagement ring was slightly loose,
she reflected shakily as he placed it on her finger. Suddenly she was finding it extraordinarily difficult to breathe
properly. Her chest felt tightly constricted, her heart was
hammering ferociously against her ribs. As though it was
happening in slow motion, she was aware of Dracco watching her, waiting, and then lifting her hand towards his mouth.

'No.'

Imogen pulled frantically away from him as the denial
was torn from her tense throat. In church he had kissed her
hand, the warmth of his lips brushing her cold fingers, making her tremble violently, her whole body ablaze with the
intensity of her longing for him as her lover. Yet despite that
feeling she had not been able to stop herself from asking
him the question that had destroyed her foolish illusions.
What would have happened if she had said nothing? But no,
she must not even think of asking herself that. Would she
really have wanted to live in ignorance of the truth? No, of
course she wouldn't!

Unable to bring herself to look at Dracco, she hurried

towards the front door. The warm evening sun dazzled her for a moment as they walked outside. She could smell the scent of the roses from the rose bed close to the front door. They had been her mother's favourite flowers and for a moment a wave of nostalgia and pain pierced her. This house held so many memories, so much of her past. The thought of her own child growing up here was unbearably poignant.

Locked into her thoughts, she stood stiffly, staring unseeingly into the distance. The future, with all the hideous complications and emotional pain it now threatened, lay darkly ahead of her. Marriage in these modern times was not necessarily for life, but a child, the bond between parent and child, mother and child, that most certainly was. For her, at least.

'If you're having second thoughts, I shouldn't,' she heard Dracco telling her caustically.

Imogen frowned as the sound of Dracco's voice pierced the bubble surrounding her. For a moment it had almost seemed as though Dracco was actually afraid that she *might* change her mind. He must want this child very badly. Was that the reason he and Lisa had not married, because he had not wanted his child to be her child? Imogen didn't like herself very much for the sharp thrill of pleasure the thought gave her.

'Ah, but you have not changed at all; you are even more beautiful, even more bella, than ever!' Luigi was telling Imogen in a voice vibrant with emotion as he showed them to their table.

'If she has not changed then how can she be more *bella*, Luigi?' Dracco was demanding drily.

'Then she was a beautiful girl,' Luigi responded with aplomb. 'Now...' His dark eyes glowed with appreciation and approval as he surveyed Imogen in the kind of way that only an Italian male could get away with. 'Now she is a beautiful woman! And what a woman! *Mamma mia!* Ah, but you are one lucky man, my friend, to have such a beautiful wife.'

So Luigi had remembered that they were married!

'Well, it is just as well that one of us can remember what she looked like after one of your lessons in how to eat spaghetti.' Dracco grinned, the dryness of his voice so at odds with the genuine amusement in his eyes that Imogen found somehow she was unable to drag her own gaze away from his face. A face that suddenly, dangerously, looked so much like the face she remembered from her teens, his eyes warm and teasing, his mouth curved into that sizzlingly sexy smile that had made her toes curl up in delight. Luigi's had always been her favourite restaurant, a place she had associated with the happy times in her life.

'I have saved you a special table.' Luigi was beaming as he led them through the busy restaurant to the table that had always been her father's favourite.

A huge lump rose in Imogen's throat. Impulsively she threw her arms around Luigi's rotund frame and gave him a swift hug.

Luigi was hugging her back enthusiastically, then he let her go with unexpected suddenness, stepping back from her whilst apologising to Dracco.

Frowning, Imogen looked from Dracco's now set face to Luigi's apologetic one, unable to fathom out quite what was happening.

'I was forgetting for a moment that you are no longer a little girl but a married woman,' Luigi told her, but it was Dracco he was looking at as he spoke.

As they sat down and Luigi hurried off to get them menus Dracco told her quietly, 'I would prefer it if you didn't flirt with other men.'

'Flirt.' Imogen repeated in disbelief. 'I wasn't flirting. I was just…' She stopped. Why was she bothering to defend herself? She had done nothing wrong. All she had done was to hug Luigi, and for Dracco to accuse her of flirting was totally ridiculous!

'You may still be a virgin, Imo,' Dracco told her, leaning across the table so that no one else could hear what he was saying, 'but that does not make you totally naïve. You're a married woman…my wife.'

'I can't believe I'm hearing this,' Imogen cut in stormily. 'I was just hugging Luigi, that's all. It was nothing at all.'

'It may be nothing to you,' Dracco stopped her grimly. 'But it's a hell of a lot more than I've ever had from you.'

'You're different,' Imogen returned smartly, and then wished she hadn't as she saw his expression. Her stomach writhed nervously.

'Yes. I am different,' Dracco agreed. 'I'm your husband.' He broke off as a young waiter brought them their menus, waiting until he had gone before telling her coldly, 'Before tomorrow night I expect you to move your things into the master bedroom.'

Imogen wondered if he knew just what effect his words had had on her, how shocked and, yes, terrified they had made her. In an effort to conceal those feelings she picked up her menu and, hiding behind it, told him flippantly, 'So much for the threatened seduction.'

When there was no immediate response she carefully lowered her menu, reflecting gleefully that she had at least scored one hit against that impenetrable, tough armour that had both repelled and attracted her for as long as she had known him. But then she saw his face, and the hand holding her menu shook betrayingly.

'Oh, that wasn't a threat, Imo. It was a promise. A promise that I shall do such things to you and for you as to make you scream my name with longing in the darkness of the night; make you ache with your need for my possession; make you—'

'No!'

The denial was strangled in Imogen's throat as the young waiter suddenly appeared and nervously asked if they were ready to order. She knew that her face was burning scarlet with colour, her thoughts a wild, chaotic stampede of disbelief and fury.

How could Dracco say such things to her one minute and the next be calmly discussing with their waiter what exactly the 'specials' were, and whether or not they had a particular wine he wanted?

'You will like this wine, Imo,' he told her calmly once they were alone. 'Your father introduced me to it. It was produced in the same year as you. And, like you…' he continued, his voice dropping to a slow, sensual rasp that licked against Imogen's raw nerve endings in the same way her tormented, traitorous imagination was telling her that his tongue might rasp against the intimate sensitivity of her skin. 'But no!' he told her softly. 'I shall not tell you now what characteristics it shares with you!'

Imogen had ordered mussels as her first course, and her mouth watered when they arrived, cooked in Luigi's special sauce. They had eaten simply and cheaply in Rio, and she was unaware of the way Dracco was watching her as she ate her food with almost childlike enjoyment.

He wondered how she would react if she knew what he was really thinking; feeling; wanting! He took a deep swallow of his wine; like Imogen herself, it had an allure that drew one back almost compulsively to it. His mouth twisted bitterly. It was probably just as well that she didn't know just what was going on inside his head, or inside his body.

If she did she would probably run a mile, or rather six thousand miles or so, back to Rio.

Dracco's eyes grew bleak when they rested on Imogen's downbent head as she mopped up the last of her sauce with a piece of bread. If she hadn't come back of her own accord he had had plans in hand for bringing her home. And now that she was home it was up to him to make sure that she stayed there.

As Imogen lifted her head, as if somehow conscious that he was watching her, Dracco dropped his. Observing Dracco's hooded gaze fixed on his plate, Imogen frowned, wondering why on earth she had thought he was looking at her.

'Good; you enjoy that?' Luigi was demanding, beaming as he removed her empty plate.

'Scrumptious,' Imogen assured him, reverting to her favourite childhood word as she started to smile at him and then stopped, the smile which had begun to dimple her mouth fading as she glanced warily at Dracco. Was a married woman allowed to smile at another man? And why should she care anyway whether Dracco approved of her behaviour or not? She didn't, and there was certainly no way she was ever going to allow him to dictate to her what she did!

'Dracco, and Imogen, isn't it? I thought I recognised you. My goodness, what a surprise!'

The angry turbulence of Imogen's thoughts came to an abrupt halt as she stared into the familiar face of one of her stepmother's closest friends.

Her stepmother and Miranda Walker had been tennis partners and had both had membership at an exclusive local health club. Imogen had liked Miranda only marginally less than she had liked her stepmother. Miranda's husband, she remembered, had spent a lot of time working abroad, but he was obviously back at home now.

It was a shock to see someone so closely and so unpleasantly connected with the past so soon after her return, although she admitted she should perhaps have expected it, as Emporio's had always been the town's most favoured restaurant.

She could almost feel the speculation emanating from Miranda as she continued to stand at their table, ignoring her husband's obvious desire to move away.

'Are we to take it that the two of you are back together?' Miranda was asking with a suggestive coyness that nauseated Imogen. 'I always did think it was rather impetuous of you to run away from him like that, darling.' She laughed as she gave Imogen a fake smile accompanied by a sharply assessing look. 'Wait until I see Lisa. Fancy her not telling me.'

When neither Imogen nor Dracco said anything Miranda demanded excitedly, 'She doesn't know, does she?' There was a pause. 'Oh, dear! She isn't going to be very pleased. She's still in the Caribbean and won't be back for another week yet, will she?' She directed this question at Dracco.

'Excuse me.' Without waiting to hear what Dracco's response was, Imogen got up and headed for the ladies' cloakroom.

It was stupid of her to feel shocked, and as for that daunting, aching pain that was draining her, well, there was no way that could be betrayal. She already knew what the score was; knew how cynically determined Dracco could be to have his cake and eat it.

As she reached the sanctuary of the rest room, and started to run restoring cool water over her wrists, she told herself that she didn't care what his relationship with Lisa was any more. After all, there was only one reason she was here with him tonight and it had nothing to do with any personal desire to be with him. It was because of the children, the shelter, that was all! Just as he was here with her not because he wanted her, but because he wanted her child.

She ought, she told herself judicially, to feel sorry for Lisa.

So far as Imogen was concerned, the whole tone of Miranda's conversation had given away the relationship between Dracco and her stepmother. Had he told Lisa what he was planning to do? Somehow Imogen rather suspected that he had not.

Carefully drying her hands, she took a deep breath. It was time for her to go back.

There was no sign of Miranda or her husband when Imogen returned to the table. Without saying anything, she sat down. Her head had started to ache badly. She felt almost as though she was about to come down with a bad case of flu; her throat felt tight and sore, she felt slightly sick, and—

Imogen gave a small gasp as the whole room spun round.

'Imogen. Are you all right?'

Somehow Dracco was standing next to her.

'No,' she told him muzzily. 'I feel sick.'

Frowning, Dracco glanced from Imogen's barely touched glass of wine to her white face.

'Let's get you outside. You might feel better in the fresh air.'

As Imogen felt him moving closer to her she instinctively shrank away from him. Listening to Miranda had underlined for her all the most unpalatable aspects of her situation that she least wanted to think about. The hands that Dracco was reaching out to her had touched Lisa, her enemy; the voice expressing distant concern for her had no doubt whispered soft, passionate words of desire and wanting to her stepmother. The act of procreation he would share with her would be a cold, mechanical, loveless thing, very different from his physical intimacy with Lisa... Imogen shuddered, unable to control her revulsion. No wonder she felt so sick.

Imogen saw in Dracco's eyes his reaction to her instinctive rejection of him. Bending his head, he muttered angrily to her, 'We're supposed to be giving our marriage a second chance. Remember?'

'You don't want to give our marriage a second chance,' Imogen managed to hiss swiftly. 'You just want...'

Somehow Dracco had shepherded her to the door, and was opening it. Greedily Imogen gulped in the fresh evening air. Her dizziness was beginning to clear, her nausea retreating.

'Want to tell me what all that was about?'

Warily she looked at Dracco. 'I felt sick, that's all. Surely it's hardly surprising in the circumstances. Nothing's changed, has it, Dracco?' she challenged him bitterly.

'Did you expect it to have done? Don't you think that's rather naïve?'

The hard expression she could see in his eyes made her muscles clench. He wasn't even remotely ashamed of what he was doing.

'You didn't tell me that Lisa was still living locally,' she told him bitterly. He was shrugging dismissively as though he found her anger an irrelevance, and his attitude goaded her into a fiercely hostile reaction.

'Lisa was married to my father. She's—'

He interrupted her. 'I know what Lisa is, Imo.'

'You know but you don't care, do you?' Imogen couldn't stop herself from saying the words, even though she could already see the truth in his eyes.

Just as she could hear the anguish shaking through her own voice.

She heard Dracco mutter something under his breath before telling her grimly, 'You always were too damned sensitive for your own good. And too damned...' Whatever he had been about to say was lost as the restaurant door opened and another couple emerged, pausing to give them a briefly curious look, no doubt able to sense the hostility and tension crackling between them. Taking hold of Imogen's arm, Dracco informed her curtly, 'This isn't the place for a discussion of this nature,' as he propelled her to where he had parked his car.

'Let go of me,' Imogen demanded through gritted teeth as they reached it. 'I can't bear to have you touching me, Dracco. Not now. Not after…' She stopped as she saw the intensity of the fury darkening his eyes as he opened the car door for her.

Logic told her that he wasn't responsible for Miranda's appearance at the restaurant, but he was responsible for the fact that he had betrayed her father's trust and was now callously using her. How she hated him, loathed him, despised him!

She took a deep breath as she tried to close her mind against the unwelcome knowledge of just how much she herself hurt, how raw and painful her emotions felt. It was humiliating to know that he could still affect her like this, even now, as an adult.

Wrapped up in her thoughts, Imogen didn't realise that they had reached the house until Dracco leaned across her to open the car door. This close she could see the fine, soft hairs on his arm, see the taut structure of the sinew and muscle beneath his skin, smell the soap he used, clean and cool—and something else. Something that made her flesh come out in a rash of goosebumps, whilst her nostrils quivered with delicate female recognition of the potent maleness of his personal body scent, hot, musky and dangerous. Her eyes widened as she made an involuntary movement that somehow brought her body into immediate physical contact with his bare arm, her breasts pressing against it as though… Hot-faced, Imogen refused to acknowledge just what the insolent peaking of her nipples might be trying to proclaim as she pulled quickly back from him.

Ignoring him, she climbed out of the car, heading for the house. Behind her she could hear Dracco's footsteps crunching across the gravel. A sudden tremor of panic flared through her and she started to walk faster, only to realise that she couldn't get into the house without him, since she didn't possess a key.

Standing to one side, she waited for him to open the door. For the rest of her life she would hate him for what he was doing to her! Imogen could feel her hands balling into angry fists.

'Imo.'

Imogen felt Dracco's hands resting on her shoulders.

'Don't you dare touch me!' she spat furiously at him. But as she tried to pull away he refused to let her go, following the movement she made, so that she was backed up against the door.

'Imo, listen.'

'No.'

There was just time for Imogen to see the furious brilliant glitter of his eyes before his head blotted out the light as he grated angrily against her ear, 'Well, if you won't listen then perhaps this is the only way of communicating with you.'

She gasped once in outraged protest that he should dare to ignore her wishes, and then a second time, in shocked disbelief, as she felt the heat of his breath searing across her lips. And then she was not capable of gasping at all, as her breath was snatched away and with it her ability to think, and reason, and reject, because every fibre of her being, every single cell she possessed, was fully occupied in dealing with the nuclear fall-out caused by Dracco's kiss.

Its effect on her anger was like hot chocolate being poured on ice cream, she reflected dizzily, like every feeling, every pleasure, every delicious taste she had ever experienced magnified a million times over. It was like nothing she had ever dreamed of experiencing and at the same time it was exactly…exactly what she had always dreamed it might be, only more so…much more so.

Somehow the original furious anger of Dracco's kiss had turned to a sensuous, coaxing, lingering caress that involved not just their lips but their tongues as well. And their hands too, Imogen was discovering as her body melted beneath Dracco's touch, then burned, flamed and hungered…

'You kiss me like you've been aching for me for half a lifetime. Starving for me.' She could hear Dracco groaning as his hands ran fierce hot shudders of delight over her skin. He drew her body into his own, fitting her against him, fitting himself against her, into the cupped eagerness of her parted thighs.

As the full meaning of his words penetrated the sensual daze of her feelings Imogen suddenly realised what she was doing, and with a sharp cry she pulled away from him.

'I'm not starving—for anything, and certainly not for you,' she told him in passionate denial. 'But the street children of Rio are starving, Dracco, and that's why I'm here, because of them and only because of them.'

White-faced, she confronted him across the small space that now divided them.

His face was in the shadows, so that she could not see his expression, only sense his hunting immobility and know that he was watching her, making her feel vulnerable and exposed. She waited for him to voice some cutting put-down, but instead of retaliating in any way he simply turned from her and went to unlock the front door.

All the way up the stairs Imogen expected to hear him if not following her then at least commanding her to stop, but there was only silence. She didn't turn round to see why, though. She did not dare.

CHAPTER FOUR

IMOGEN WAS DEEPLY asleep, lost in the most wonderful dream.

'Mmm.' Languorously she reached up to curl her hand against the firm, smooth skin at the nape of Dracco's neck. She could feel the silky thickness of his hair as she burrowed her fingertips into it, firmly drawing his head closer to her own.

'You know this is very dangerous, don't you?' Dracco was warning her in a sensually raw whisper, the sound caressing her skin with deliciously rough male warmth.

'I like danger,' Imogen responded provocatively as she looked up into the deep sea-green depths of his eyes. 'And I like it even more when that danger is you,' she added.

A small bubble of laughter gurgled in her throat as she saw the way Dracco was looking at her. It felt so good to be so at ease with him, so intimately aware of the special relationship they shared. At ease, and yet at the same time... A tiny thrill of wanton excitement shivered across her skin as she watched his eyes darken. Her own closed, her lips parting in eager anticipation of his kiss.

When it came the hot sweetness of it melted right through her body, touching every single nerve-ending, reaching into the deepest core of her, so that suddenly what they were doing was no longer a teasing game that she controlled, but a fierce, elemental need that controlled them both.

'Dracco!' Hungrily she reached out to drag him down against her naked body, driven to feel him against her, skin to skin, lips to lips, breath to breath! Helplessly her nails raked the firm flesh of his back as her body arched up against his, drawn into a tight, aching bow of longing.

As Dracco responded to her body's hungry demands he groaned her name against her lips. Imogen opened her eyes. Sunlight streamed in through her bedroom window, glinting on the gold of her wedding ring.

Dracco was holding her tightly now, his hands roving wantonly over her naked body with the powerful touch of a hungry sensualist, dipping lingeringly into her most secret places of delight, drawing from her a need to arouse him in the same way. Each kiss, each touch was taking her closer and closer to the shatteringly climactic culmination she knew was waiting for her, but as they did so somehow her joy was being overtaken by a fear that her happiness was about to be snatched away from her. A fear that made her cry out in anguish as she clung frantically to Dracco, desperately afraid that somehow she might lose him, lose his love.

'No!'

The sound of her own sharp moan of panic brought Imogen immediately out of her dream. For a few seconds she was still so wrapped up in it that it took her several deep breaths to realise just where she was. When she did she sat up in bed, reaching for her bedside light, illuminating the bedroom in a soft peachy glow. But nothing could warm the cold tentacles of dread reaching out to wrap themselves around her heart. She had been dreaming about Dracco, dreaming that he…that she…that they… Closing her eyes, Imogen hugged her arms around her body in an instinctive gesture of protection.

'Imogen, what's wrong? I heard you cry out.'

The sound of Dracco's voice as he thrust open her bedroom door and strode into her room made Imogen open her eyes immediately.

'Nothing. Nothing's wrong,' she denied tensely.

There was no way she could disclose to Dracco the content of her dream, nor exactly why she had given that anguished moan of distress.

'I heard you cry out,' Dracco persisted.

He was walking towards her bed as he spoke, and he was still fully dressed, although he had unbuttoned the top few buttons of his shirt and on the flesh they exposed Imogen could see the tangled criss-crossed darkness of his body hair.

Unable to drag her gaze away from it, she felt her stomach lurch. In her dream he had been totally naked. In her dream she had touched his skin, drawn her fingertips through that silky male covering of fine dark hair whilst her whole body quivered in thrilled sensual pleasure... Imogen shuddered.

What was happening to her? It had been years since she had fantasised about touching Dracco like that. She had been a mere girl then, sleeping in this very same bedroom. Was that it? Was it because she was sleeping in the room that had been hers as a girl that she had dreamed so inappropriately of the kind of intimacy with Dracco she most certainly no longer wanted? She was just beginning to relax into the security of finding a logical explanation for what had happened when she suddenly remembered how in her dream she had seen sunlight shining on her wedding ring.

A second shudder, even more apparent than her first, galvanised her body, bringing Dracco to the side of her bed, where he frowned down at her.

'Perhaps we should get Dr Armstrong to take a look at you,' he told her. 'You felt sick earlier on; now you're shivering.'

Imogen could feel her self-control starting to slip.

'There's nothing wrong with me. Apart from the fact that I'm being blackmailed into having sex with a man I don't want so that he can have the son he does want. But,' she added with angry sarcasm, 'I'm sure you aren't going to tell Dr Armstrong that. You're very good at not telling people things they ought to know, aren't you, Dracco?'

'And just what the hell do you mean?' he demanded.

'Work it out for yourself,' Imogen challenged him. When he continued to frown at her she flung at him bitterly, 'Somehow I don't imagine you've told Lisa about your plans for me. For the child you want me—*us*—to have,' she emphasised savagely. 'And...'

She took a deep breath, intending to remind him that he had also neglected to tell her, when he had originally proposed marriage to her, that he was already in love with her stepmother, but before she could do so he was interrupting her, exclaiming, 'No, I haven't. Why should I?'

How could he stand there and say that? Furiously Imogen confronted him.

'Why?' Imogen repeated in disbelief. Shaking her head, she changed tack slightly, unable to trust herself to say what she was really feeling and settling instead for a quietly contemptuous, 'She's bound to find out, you know. Miranda will tell her.'

To her own shock she discovered that she was holding her breath, waiting, almost as though she was hoping that he would tell her Lisa was nothing to him now, that it was over between them. Was she really so frighteningly stupid, so crazily vulnerable?

'Our marriage, our relationship and the plans we make within it have nothing whatsoever to do with Lisa.'

'And you don't care what she thinks or feels about the situation?' Imogen challenged.

'My desire to have a child with your father's genes doesn't impact in any way at all on Lisa's life.'

'Nor on your relationship with her?' Imogen couldn't stop herself from persisting. There was a brief pause before Dracco answered.

'I know how you feel about Lisa, Imo, but you're an adult now. My relationship with her, as you term it, is what it is and cannot be changed. My feelings towards her haven't changed either, you know,' he told her as gently as he could.

Dracco frowned as he watched the look of anguished disbelief darkening Imogen's eyes. He knew how bitterly unhappy her stepmother had made her, and, as he had just told her, he liked Lisa as little now as he had done when John had first married her. In Dracco's eyes she was a shallow, selfish, greedy woman, but that did not alter the fact that, just as he had a responsibility towards Imogen, he also had a responsibility as one of the executors of Imogen's late father's will to ensure that Lisa received the biannual allowance she was entitled to. It was obvious, though, that Imogen was in no mood to listen to such logic.

Imogen felt as though someone was squeezing her lungs in a frighteningly painful grasp, making it almost impossible for her to breathe, but not impossible for her to feel. Oh, no, she could still do that! But why could she, when for the last four years she had believed that she no longer cared, that Dracco no longer had the power to hurt her, that her love for him had died along with her trust and respect?

'I think I hate you, Dracco,' she whispered savagely, correcting herself to tell him, 'No, I know I hate you.'

He was turning away from her and going to stand in front of her bedroom window, looking out into the darkness beyond it.

'Fine, you can hate me all you like,' he told her coolly, 'but you will still give me my son, Imo.'

Without giving her the opportunity to retaliate, he strode through her still open bedroom door, pulling it shut behind him.

As she glared at it, Imogen was not surprised to discover that she was shaking from head to foot—with burning hot rage. How could he; how dared he stand there and tell her he expected her to bear his child when he had just admitted that there was another woman in his life? And not just any 'other' woman, but her stepmother Lisa!

Of course, it was impossible for her to go back to sleep. A glance at her watch told her that it was only just gone midnight and she realised that Dracco must have heard her cry out on his own way to bed. How could she have allowed herself to dream about him like that? What part of her subconscious had produced those treacherous images? And why was the discovery that Dracco still loved Lisa making her feel not just that she wanted to hurl her furious contempt at him for his betrayal of her own youthful adoration, but also so filled with pain and despair?

Anyone would think that she still loved him, she derided herself warningly. And of course she did not!

If only she were back in Rio. There she had been safe; there she had been far too busy to think about Dracco. She made a small restless movement in her bed as her conscience prodded her for the lie she was telling herself. 'All right, then,' she muttered beneath her breath, 'so I did think about him occasionally.'

You thought about him and you dreamed about him, that same voice reminded her relentlessly. You know you did.

'Yes, yes, all right,' she conceded, 'but those were not dreams, they were nightmares, and I had quite definitely stopped loving him. Quite definitely!

* * *

'You've got half an hour to have breakfast and then we're leaving for London.'

As she heard what Dracco was saying to her for a moment Imogen's hopes rose. Had he changed his mind after what she had said to him last night? Was he taking her back to London in order to put her on a plane to Rio?

Oh, please…please! she begged fate fervently as she told Dracco automatically, 'I don't eat breakfast. I'll go up and pack.'

'Pack?' Dracco's eyebrows lifted as he drawled the single word laconically, shaking his head as he did so. 'We're going to see our solicitor, Imo, and it won't involve an overnight stay, although I dare say you might want to wear something a little more formal,' he added as he flicked a disparaging glance at her well-worn outfit.

Immediately Imogen was on the defensive. 'If you don't like my clothes, Dracco—' she began, and then was forced to stop, as without allowing her to finish Dracco cut in smoothly,

'I can buy you some new ones? My feelings exactly, Imo, and that's what I intend to do, once our business with David is concluded. I don't doubt that you trust me, just as I do you, but I thought it might give you some degree of reassurance if I committed myself legally to our…agreement. I intend to take your adherence to your part on trust. What do you mean, you don't eat breakfast?' he suddenly questioned her with a frown.

The lightning speed with which he changed subjects threw Imogen into total confusion. And distracted her from the shock of discovering that he intended to put the proposal he had made to her on a legal footing.

The proposal he had made to her? The blackmail he was forcing on her, she corrected herself fiercely as she heard him saying, 'No wonder you're so slender. Have some of these.'

Imogen's eyes widened as he reached out and picked up a packet of cereal from the table, shaking some into the bowl in front of her.

'Fruit Munchies with chocolate chips,' he told her humorously. 'You used to love them.'

'That was when I was thirteen,' Imogen reminded him, but Dracco wasn't paying any attention.

Instead he poured milk onto her cereal, before warning her, 'We don't leave this house until you have eaten, Imo.'

'Why? Are you afraid that people will think you're starving me as well as blackmailing me?' she demanded acerbically.

'Blackmailing you?' He gave her a sharply incisive look, but before he could continue the telephone started to ring. 'Excuse me,' he told her. 'This is probably a business call I was expecting. I'll take it in the study. I shan't be long.'

After he had gone Imogen stared at the bowl in front of her. She wasn't going to eat the cereal, of course she wasn't, but somehow she was dipping her spoon into it. In Rio she had eaten sparingly, knowing how little food the children they were dealing with had to eat.

She was over halfway through by the time Dracco returned, and, although she pushed the bowl away from her without finishing its contents, she had to admit that she had rather enjoyed the cereal.

Dracco's solicitor had an office in the same block that housed the offices which had originally been her father's and which were now, of course, exclusively Dracco's.

A sharp pang gripped Imogen as she remembered how often she had visited the office with her father. She still missed him, not with the savage intensity she had suffered

immediately after his death any longer, but with a sadness
that had become a small, familiar shadow in her life.

As he guided her towards the lift Dracco said quietly
to her, 'I've lost count of the number of times I've thought
about moving. I still expect to see your father here, coming
out of the lift, opening the office door. I still miss him and
I dare say I always will.'

His words were so in tune with her thoughts that Imogen
couldn't speak without betraying her emotions. Instead she
turned her face away from Dracco so that he couldn't see it.
How could he speak so about her father and yet at the same
time have betrayed him by falling in love with his wife?

Imogen continued to ignore Dracco as the lift bore them
upwards. When it stopped and the door opened he touched
her arm, and immediately Imogen flinched.

Despairingly she wondered how on earth she would be
able to keep her part of the bargain and provide him with a
child when she couldn't even bear him to touch her!

You managed to bear it very well when he kissed you last
night, a small inner voice told her, adding, And what about
that dream? Then you weren't just bearing it.

'No,' Imogen protested out loud, covering her ears with
her hands.

'What is it?' Dracco demanded sharply. 'Are you feeling ill again? I really do think you need to be checked out
by Dr Armstrong. You could have picked up something on
the flight.'

'I'm fine,' Imogen choked. She could see an office door
ahead of them.

There was still time for her to change her mind. Still time
for her to decide that she was not strong enough to make
such a sacrifice and to fly straight back to Rio. All it would
take was one sentence, but even whilst she longed to speak
it, to tell Dracco that she had changed her mind, Imogen's

pride refused to allow her to do so. Her pride and the deep inner knowledge that she would never forgive herself for her selfishness if she did.

Dracco pushed open the office door, ushering her inside ahead of him. A smiling receptionist greeted them. It was obvious that she knew Dracco well and was more than a touch in awe of him.

'David shouldn't be long,' she told Dracco, glancing at her watch. 'He was called out to a meeting with a client. He didn't want to go, really, knowing that you were coming in, but it was an urgent case.'

She seemed almost to be apologising, Imogen recognised as the other woman turned to smile a little uncertainly at her. She was about her own age, Imogen guessed, brunette with hazel eyes and very obviously pregnant.

Shakily Imogen averted her gaze from the other woman's body. She was still saying something to Dracco, but then she stopped as the office door opened and a slightly thick-set young man with an open, honest face came in.

'Oh, there you are, darling,' she said with obvious relief. 'I was just explaining to Dracco that you'd had to go out.'

As she reached up to kiss him briefly Imogen noticed the wedding ring she was wearing and guessed that they were husband and wife even before Dracco had introduced them to her as David and Charlotte Bryant.

'Mrs Barrington.' David Bryant smiled as he shook Imogen's hand. 'I've heard an awful lot about you. My uncle Henry was a great fan of yours and of course he and your father were very close friends. He often used to talk to my mother about you. She was his sister. I know how much it would have meant to him to learn that you and Dracco are…have decided… That you are reconciled.' He stopped, colouring up and looking slightly uncomfortable, whilst Imogen automatically asked him to call her by her Chris-

tian name. It irked her that Dracco had been so sure of her
reaction that he had already told David Bryant that they
were 'reconciled'.

She must not allow herself to forget that Dracco was
a master manipulator, she warned herself as she thanked
Charlotte Bryant for the cup of coffee she had just made her.

'Yes,' the other woman was confirming quietly, 'David's
mother often talks about her brother to us. I know she is
particularly grateful to you, Dracco, for everything you did
when he had his fatal heart attack, going with him to the
hospital, staying with him.'

'It was the least I could do,' Imogen heard Dracco saying curtly, almost as though he didn't want the subject to
be discussed.

Imogen shivered. If Henry had not had his heart attack,
would Dracco have come after her and stopped her from
leaving? She had believed he had let her go out of indiffer-
ence and relief, but now it seemed that she might have been
wrong. Had she been wrong about anything else?

David and Charlotte Bryant obviously thought a lot of
Dracco, but then they didn't know him the way she did!

'So what now? A celebratory glass of champagne? We aren't
too far from one of the city's new hotels, and, since it's time
for lunch…'

Imogen stared at Dracco in disbelief as they stepped out
of the office block and into the sunshine.

'You might feel you have something to celebrate,' she
told him wildly, 'but I most certainly don't.'

'No? I've just signed a legally binding document agreeing
to give your charity over one million pounds. I should have
thought that was sufficient cause for celebration,' Dracco
was telling her with deceptive mildness as he caught hold
of her arm and drew her against his side.

Immediately Imogen tried to pull away, but Dracco refused to let go of her.

'That might be—under different circumstances,' Imogen retaliated, 'but, since I've just sold the use of my body to you in return for it...'

She could see Dracco's mouth thinning and see too the warning glint in his rapidly darkening eyes.

'You loved your father, didn't you, Imo?' he asked her grimly.

'You know I did,' Imogen responded immediately.

'How do you think he would have reacted to being a grandfather, to knowing that his genes, your mother's and your own were being passed on to a new generation?'

For a moment Imogen was too shaken by his question to answer, but when she did her voice trembled with the intensity of her feelings.

'How dare you do this to me, Dracco?' she demanded. 'How dare you use my father to blackmail me?'

'You keep throwing that accusation in my face. Be very careful that I don't throw it back at you.'

'By doing what?' she challenged him recklessly.

But instead of answering her he said calmly, 'Since you don't want any lunch, we might as well head straight for Knightsbridge and get you kitted out with some new clothes.'

'I don't want any new clothes,' Imogen started to say, but Dracco wasn't listening to her, his attention concentrated on the taxi he was hailing.

He was still holding onto Imogen's arm, his fingers curling firmly around it, and as a group of passers-by jostled against her she automatically moved closer to him. The cool wool of his suit jacket brushed against her bare arm. As she looked up she could see the faint shadow on his jaw where he had shaved earlier. There was a maleness about Dracco, she acknowledged with a faint inner tremor, a strong, dangerous sense of power that was like an unseen aura. Unseen but not unfelt. She could feel it now as he urged her into the stationary taxi. She could feel it and she was afraid of it—and of herself.

'And just remember,' Dracco was warning her as the taxi lurched into motion, 'from tonight you and I will be sharing a bedroom. And a bed.'

Ignoring him, Imogen stared out of the taxi window, praying that she would get pregnant quickly—no, not just quickly but immediately, she amended hurriedly.

Straight away, the first time, so that it would be the only time. Would Dracco wait to see if…? Or would he…? Her mind shied away from the questions bubbling inside her head. She certainly had no fear of sex as such. These were not, after all, Victorian times, when a virgin bride was simply not told anything about what lay ahead of her. In Rio children well below the age of puberty sold themselves on the streets in order to eat and were shockingly graphic about what could be demanded of them. If providing Dracco with a child saved only one of those children…

Dracco's child. Her child. Unable to stop herself, Imogen turned to look at him. Just as she had been, he was gazing out of the taxi window, his face averted from her. Imogen cleared her throat to speak but did not get the chance. The taxi was drawing up outside a department store.

'No, that's enough—more than enough,' Imogen protested helplessly as she surveyed the full rail of clothes the store's senior personal shopper had produced.

They—Dracco, herself, the shopper and a hovering alterationist—were all in the store's elegant personal shopping suite, where Dracco and Imogen had been escorted following Dracco's production of a discreetly logoed charge card and request for a selection of clothes for Imogen to choose from.

Initially dizzy from the mouth-watering variety of outfits the personal shopper had produced, Imogen was now beginning to feel slightly nauseous in a way that reminded her of how her teenage self had sometimes felt after the consumption of a mega-sized knickerbocker glory.

Tempting though the clothes were, Imogen's conscience was causing her to experience a sense of disquiet. Just how many small stomachs would the cost of such luxurious clothes fill? And thinking of stomachs, small and otherwise, raised another consideration…

Yearningly Imogen looked at the trendy pair of designer jeans she had just tried on. The assistant had explained how they were cut to fit and flatter the female body, and they had hugged Imogen's hips and bottom in a way that had made her reluctant to come out of the cubicle until the shopper had insisted. When she had done, she'd felt acutely self-conscious standing in front of Dracco wearing them, guessing what he must be thinking—that they were far too sexy for a woman like her!

'They're not really me,' she said now, shaking her head, but Dracco, it seemed, had other ideas.

'Why not?' he asked her. 'I like them.' As he spoke Imogen was infuriatingly aware of the disparaging look he was giving the outfit she had put back on.

Lisa had always worn very fashionable, sexy clothes, and no doubt as he looked at her Dracco was mentally comparing her to his mistress.

Did he perhaps think that by dressing her in sexy clothes she would somehow become more desirable to him, more the kind of woman he wanted?

Imogen had never forgotten the disparaging comments Lisa had made to her on the morning of her marriage, and somehow since then she had favoured loose-fitting clothes that cloaked rather than emphasised her figure.

'They're very popular—and very sexy.' The shopper was smiling encouragingly.

Until he had decided that he wanted a child with her Dracco had shown no sexual interest in her whatsoever. Before their marriage he had never even kissed her properly, and yet now he apparently wanted to buy her the kind of clothes that subtly enhanced a woman's sexuality. Why? Because that would make her more acceptable to him in bed? More like Lisa?

'No,' she insisted, ignoring the jeans the shopper was still holding. 'They're very expensive and I wouldn't get much wear out of them.'

'We'll take them.' Dracco was smiling as he spoke to the assistant. 'If it's that social conscience of yours that's troubling you,' he told Imogen as he turned towards her, 'then let me remind you that it's my money you'll be spending, and…'

'Your money?' Immediately Imogen started to frown, anger taking the place of her earlier self-consciousness. 'I can afford to buy my own clothes, Dracco,' she told him fiercely. 'I did have a salary for my work for the charity, albeit a small one!'

Discreetly the personal shopper had moved out of earshot.

'I know you can,' Dracco agreed, 'but surely it's a husband's privilege to be allowed to indulge his wife?'

Thoroughly angry now, Imogen glared at him. 'If you really want to "indulge me", as you put it, there are other ways!'

To her disbelief, she could see that Dracco was actually starting to smile.

'You haven't really changed at all, have you, Imo?' he challenged her ruefully. 'I can remember how much it amused your father—and infuriated Lisa—when you insisted that you'd rather he bought some winter feed for the ponies tethered illegally on the village common than buy you a Christmas-party dress.'

To her own mortification, Imogen felt emotional tears start to prick the backs of her eyes.

Yes, she could remember that incident as well. Her father had been amused, and in the end she had not only got his agreement to provide winter feed for the ponies, but she had also, at Lisa's furious insistence, got a new party dress as well. She had hated that dress, it had been baby-ish, pink, with frills and a big full skirt, not suitable for a teenager at all.

Lisa—was Dracco thinking of her now? Was he wishing that Lisa was here with him; that she was the one he was buying a new wardrobe for that she would wear for his de-lectation—both in bed and out of it? Imogen forced herself to take a deep, calming breath.

'Anyway,' she told Dracco, 'there isn't much point in you buying me these kind of clothes.' When Dracco raised one eyebrow interrogatively she flushed a little as she was forced to explain huskily, 'They're all very fitted, and I won't... I shan't... I shall probably soon be needing things with more room in them,' she told him, unable to stop herself from giving him an indignant look when the enlightenment finally dawned in his eyes.

'If you're trying to say that you'll soon be needing ma-ternity outfits, then, yes, I agree,' he said in obvious amuse-ment. 'But I think our reconciliation alone is going to cause enough speculation without us adding to it by you appearing in public in maternity gear.' Giving her an oblique look, he added softly, 'I must say, you've surprised me, Imo; I hadn't realised you were so actively looking forward to the con-summation of our agreement!'

'That isn't what I meant. I'm not!' Imogen hissed in immediate denial. She couldn't believe his sudden and unexpected lightheartedness. It was almost as though he was teasing her, and enjoying doing so as well. 'I just don't want to see money being wasted on clothes that—'

'Will it make you feel better if I agree to match pound for pound everything I spend on you with an additional donation to the shelter?' Dracco asked.

Imogen opened her mouth and then closed it again. She didn't want to see him like this, to remember how wonderful and special she had once believed he was. To make up for her own foolish weakness she gave him a mutely hostile look before telling him frostily, 'That's bribery.'

'It's your decision,' Dracco replied. 'Just remember that the less you spend on yourself, the less I give to the shelter.'

The personal shopper was moving determinedly back towards them, obviously having decided that they had had enough time to sort out their differences. Was there anything Dracco would not do to get his own way? Imogen wondered helplessly.

Whether it was because of Dracco's comment, the personal shopper's skilled salesmanship, or her own unexpected pleasure in the clothes she tried on, Imogen didn't know, but when she finally left the suite she was the slightly guilty owner of a much larger new wardrobe than she had planned—and the shelter was in line to get a substantial extra 'bonus'.

'I take it that on this occasion you won't want to celebrate a successful conclusion to our activities at the Soda Fountain,' Dracco drawled as they left the store with half a dozen large carrier bags.

For some reason, his reference to a favourite rendezvous for her schoolgirl treats on her visits to her father's office filled her with a welling sense of emotion. So much so that she stopped dead in the street, causing Dracco's smile to change to a frown as he watched her.

Imogen felt as though she wanted to run and hide.

Just for one betraying millisecond of time she had caught herself actually wishing that things could be different, that she and Dracco were genuinely making an attempt to start afresh with one another and that the planned conception of their child, her father's grandchild, was an event they were undertaking in a mutual mood of love and joy.

What on earth was happening to her? Did it really only take the mention of the Soda Fountain to wipe away the betrayals that lay between them? Surely she wasn't really so foolish and so vulnerable?

Her head lifted, her pride responding to the challenge she had given it. Managing a valiant smile, she told Dracco coolly, 'Somehow I doubt that indulging in calorie-laden snacks and these clothes—' she swung her carrier bags meaningfully '—go together.'

'You could do with putting a bit of weight on,' Dracco informed her, still frowning.

Of course he would think that! Lisa was far more voluptuously shaped than she was. 'Well, if you have your way I expect I soon shall be,' Imogen returned, and then caught her bottom lip in her teeth, her face burning a hot, self-conscious pink.

For a moment Dracco said nothing, simply studying her with a hooded gaze whilst more than one woman passer-by paused to look interestedly at him.

'If that's meant to be an invitation—' he began.

Immediately Imogen stopped him, shaking her head vigorously as she denied any such intention. 'The day I invite you to take me to bed,' she told him furiously, 'is—'

'Be careful, Imo,' Dracco told her softly. 'I've already warned you about challenging me.'

CHAPTER FIVE

ALMOST CHILDISHLY IMOGEN kept her eyes tightly closed, even though she had been awake for well over ten minutes, knowing already what she would see the moment she opened them.

Outside the bedroom window she could hear a blackbird carolling noisily. Fighting to ignore the sensation of despair in the pit of her stomach, Imogen opened her eyes and stared across her pillow to the one that should have borne the imprint of Dracco's dark head. But, just like the huge double bed itself, it showed no evidence of Dracco's presence.

It was five days now since they had returned from London, almost a week, and still nothing had happened; still Dracco had not…they had not…

All right, so he had been away on business for three of those nights, but she had moved into the master suite the evening of their return from the shopping trip filled with trepidation. Dracco had never come anywhere near the room, or her, preferring instead to sleep downstairs on the sofa in his study, apparently because he was in the middle of a very important business deal which necessitated him making and receiving calls from other continents.

'There was no point in me coming upstairs and disturbing you, not when I knew I'd got these calls coming through,' he had explained carelessly to her the next day when she had eventually seen him. 'You weren't disappointed, I hope?'

Imogen had not known what to reply. And she had told herself that she was only too pleased to hear that he would be going away for a few days.

But in his absence, no doubt because she had had the unfamiliar luxury of time to think about such things, she had found herself questioning just why he had not as yet made any attempt to ensure that she gave him the child he wanted; the child that was, after all, the reason for them being here together.

Yesterday, when he had returned without warning late in the afternoon, she had been convinced that the event she was dreading was imminent, but once again Dracco had left her to sleep alone.

Because he didn't want her? Because he only wanted the child she could give him? Because in reality the woman he truly wanted was Lisa?

The pristine pillow next to her own began to blur. Wrathfully Imogen told herself that she didn't care and blinked away the tears. She was not going to cry!

No, instead of wanting to cry she ought to be asking herself why she was being so illogical. After all, by rights she should have been pleased.

Once she had showered and dressed, Imogen made her way downstairs. She had grown up in this house. Absently she ran her fingertips along the smooth rich wood of the carved banister rail. Hidden in its carving were tiny little animals; Imogen could remember her mother showing them to her. When her mother had been alive this house had been a home, the kind of home she would have wanted to give her own child, but her mother's death and her father's remarriage had changed that and had turned it into a place she had needed to seek refuge from.

And the person she had sought that refuge with most often had been Dracco! Dracco. Where was he? The study door was closed. Tentatively Imogen hovered outside it and then, taking a deep breath, she reached for the handle and turned it.

Inside the room the computer hummed softly, its screen illuminating the semi-darkness. Frowning, her housewifely instincts aroused, Imogen started to make her way towards the window to release the closed blind and let the sunlight in, but then, abruptly, she stopped as she saw Dracco's sleeping form sprawled uncomfortably on the narrow sofa.

He was still wearing the clothes he had arrived home in the previous afternoon—a lightweight suit, the jacket of which was lying on a chair. At some stage he had obviously started to unbutton his shirt, and as her eyes adjusted to the half-light of the room Imogen could see the deep dark 'V' of exposed flesh stretching from his throat all the way down to where his trousers lay low on his hips.

Her muscles contracted in helpless reaction, a silent, tortured contortion that sliced through her body. She made an involuntary movement towards him and then stopped. In the shuttered heat of the room his fine, silky body hair lay in damp whorls against his flesh; his chest rose and fell with his breathing. Even relaxed, his muscles had an imposing male tautness that drew and held her gaze. Once, as a girl, she had yearned to touch Dracco's body, her imagination, her senses, her deepest self driven crazy with excitement and longing.

In Rio, whenever she had fallen into the trap of thinking about Dracco, or remembering how she had felt about him, she had told herself sternly that her imaginings had been those of a hormone-fevered adolescent with no bearing whatsoever on reality. She had assured herself too that as an adult she would look scornfully on the reactions of the girl she had been, that she would be safely beyond such foolish feelings.

She had been wrong, Imogen recognised dizzily. Right now the effect the sight of Dracco was having on her was—

'Imo?'

Imogen jumped as though she had been stung as Dracco suddenly said her name. How long had he been awake, watching her watching him? Guilty heat stained her skin and she started to back towards the door.

'I…I wasn't sure if you were in here,' she began huskily.

'I had some work to do,' Dracco told her casually as he sat up and grimaced slightly as he flexed his body. 'I remember feeling tired.'

'It can't have been very comfortable for you, sleeping on the sofa,' Imogen told him.

She barely knew what she was saying; all she could think about was the extraordinary and very definitely unwanted surge of feeling that had filled her whilst she had been looking at him.

'Mmm…it could have been worse,' Dracco responded.

For some reason the way he was looking at her made her face burn even hotter. What exactly was he implying? That sleeping on the sofa was preferable to sleeping with her? He was the one who had insisted that he didn't want their marriage annulled! Imogen turned round and reached for the door handle.

She was opening the door when Dracco said abruptly from behind her, 'If you like we could go out later. Drive to the coast?'

Once such an invitation would have filled her with incandescent joy, and no power on earth would have prevented her from accepting it. Perhaps it was because she could remember that feeling so vividly that she felt she had to punish herself. Imogen didn't know, but she could hear the anger and the pain in her voice as she replied pointedly, shaking her head, 'No, I don't like. There's only one reason I'm here, Dracco, and it doesn't have anything to do with trips to the coast.'

She was gone before he could retaliate, closing the door behind her as she hurried into the kitchen.

A solitary morning followed by an afternoon deadheading roses had not done anything to improve her mood, Imogen recognised as she sucked irritably on her thorn-pricked thumb while hurrying upstairs.

'Imo.'

She froze as Dracco suddenly appeared at the top of the stairs. He was virtually naked, a towel wrapped casually around his hips whilst he rubbed absently at his wet hair with another.

'I saw you coming in from the garden from the bedroom window,' he began, 'and I thought—'

'That you ought to warn me that you were wandering around half-naked, just in case I got the wrong idea?' Imogen supplied grittily for him. 'You were the one who threatened to seduce me, Dracco, not the other way around,' she couldn't resist pointing out.

'Actually, what I wanted to discuss with you is the fact that you're going to need some form of transport. I was thinking perhaps of a small four-wheel drive. They seem very popular with mothers.' His voice dropped to a dangerous softness that brought up the hairs on the nape of Imogen's neck in sensual awareness as intensely as though he had physically reached out and touched her, when he added smoothly, 'However, since you have raised the subject...'

'I have not raised anything,' Imogen objected immediately, and then went bright red, whilst Dracco continued to look at her with that detached hooded gaze of his that was so unreadable.

'And am I to take that as an indication that you do want to raise…something?' Dracco queried dangerously gently.

'You're the one who insisted that our marriage was to continue and that…you wanted me to…that you wanted a child,' Imogen told him wildly.

'And if I remember correctly you were the one who said that there was no point in me attempting to seduce you,' Dracco pointed out. 'However, if you're trying to tell me that you've changed your mind…?'

Changed her mind? No! Never! She would die before she did that! But for some reason Imogen found it impossible to voice that fierce denial. Perhaps, she decided, it was because her attention was concentrated not on her own thoughts but on the precarious way in which Dracco had wrapped the towel around his hips, so loosely that…

Imogen discovered that she couldn't drag her fascinated gaze away from it. And nor, it seemed, could she resist allowing that same gaze to skim helplessly over the flat muscular plane of Dracco's belly with its dark arrowing of hair that disappeared beneath the soft whiteness of his towel. She found that, as badly as she wanted to swallow, for some reason she could not.

'Imo.'

There was a smooth, liquid sensuality in the way Dracco mouthed her name, a spellbinding dark magic that somehow paralysed her so that she couldn't move until his fingers curled round her wrist as he firmly tugged her towards him.

'You smell of fresh air and sunshine,' she heard him whisper against her hair. 'And roses.'

'You smell of…you,' Imogen whispered helplessly back. Her eyes, already huge in the delicate triangle of her face,

widened even further when she saw the look that leapt
fiercely to life in Dracco's own eyes. The look of a hunter, a
male animal, aroused, dangerous, silently waiting to pounce.

'Have you any idea just how provocative that remark
is?' he asked her with a soft savagery that made her whole
body shudder.

As she shook her head he mouthed her denial for her,
questioning, 'No?' His hand moved to hold the side of her
neck, tipping it back, his thumb rimming the shape of her
ear, sending a shower of pleasure darting over her skin.
The warmth of his breath as he bent his head towards her
scorched her senses. His fingers, stroking the delicate, sensitive flesh just beneath her hairline, made her tremble wildly
without knowing why she should do so.

'You don't know just what it does to a man when you tell
him that you can recognise his personal scent? Shall I tell
you? Show you?'

He had closed the distance between them, enclosing her
with his body, so that she could feel its heat—and more. Automatically she tensed against her awareness of his arousal,
a virgin's shocked reaction to a man's sexuality, but beneath
that reaction, running hot and wild, was a river of flooding sensation.

'No.' Her denial slid from her lips into the infinitesimal
space between them, and was lost for ever as Dracco's mouth
brushed hers—the briefest of touches, and yet somehow so
sensual and commanding that Imogen automatically felt her
toes starting to curl.

'More? You want more?' she heard Dracco murmuring,
even though she could have sworn she had said nothing.
Perhaps it was her body that had given her away, her lips?
'Like this, Imo?' Dracco was asking her, his voice so soft
and low that she had to strain to hear it, just as she was having to strain to reach out for the feel of his mouth against

her own. 'Your mouth should taste sweet and virginal and not all dark enchantment, the mouth of a sorceress no man can resist. Are you a sorceress, Imo?'

Dizzily Imogen tried to listen to what he was saying, but there was a sharp, fierce ache in her body. Beneath her thin top she could feel her breasts swelling, her nipples tight, hurting with the need to have Dracco touch them, stroke them, suck them.

She shuddered wildly, her eyes suddenly wantonly feral as her female instincts overwhelmed her. It was as though time had telescoped backwards, as though somehow she was feeling once again what she had felt as a teenager, only now she was feeling those desires and needs with all the authority and power of a truly mature woman.

Somehow, too, her body considered Dracco to be its mate, a mate from whom it had been parted for far too long! Denied far too long!

Urgently she wound her arms around Dracco's body, holding him to her, her gaze smouldering passionately into his.

'Do you want me?' he asked her softly. 'When, Imo?' he demanded when her body shuddered in response. 'Now?'

Imogen felt her body jolt against his as though it had received a charge of electricity. 'Yes,' she responded hoarsely. 'Yes, now,' she told him. 'Now, Dracco!' she repeated urgently, raising herself up on her tiptoes and pressing her mouth passionately against his.

For a second there was no response, and then Dracco opened his mouth on hers, the fierce drive of his tongue into the intimate sweetness she was willingly offering shattering all her teenage preconceptions about what such a kiss would be.

It was like drowning, dying, being turned inside-out, giving something of herself so intimate that she felt as though he was totally possessing her, and yet at the same time filling her with such an aching hunger that she felt as though she would die unless he satisfied it. And she knew only he, only Dracco alone, could satisfy her.

Beneath her hands she could feel the sleek, hard warmth of his bare skin, the breadth of his shoulders tapering down into the narrowness of his waist. The barrier of his towel frustrated her and beneath the increasingly demanding thrust of Dracco's seeking tongue she made a small, angry sound of protest.

Immediately he released her, staring down into the desire-hazed darkness of her eyes with a gaze so green and luminous that it made her heart turn over.

'What is it?' he asked her rawly. 'Too much—too soon?'

He was holding one of her hands in his own, and as she turned away, unable to answer his question, his fingers suddenly tightened almost painfully on hers, causing her to look quickly back at him.

'This doesn't say that you don't want me, Imo,' he told her, and her breath caught on a frantic gasp of mingled shock and pleasure as he ran his fingertip over the jutting outline of her breast, pausing deliberately to circle her nipple, erect and aroused beneath the fine fabric of her top.

Without waiting for her to answer him, he turned towards the master suite, firmly drawing her with him. Imogen didn't try to resist. She didn't want to resist.

The bedroom was dappled with evening sunlight; it shone through the voile curtaining, giving the peaceful cream comfort of the room a golden gleam.

As a new extension to the original house, this room did not share the air of sad shabbiness that had so struck at Imogen's emotions when she had first walked into her childhood home. In her parents' day this room had simply not existed, and Imogen acknowledged her sense of relief and release that this bedroom held no painful memories for her, and that she was coming to it as an adult woman.

'This room suits you, Imo,' Dracco was telling her quietly whilst his thumb ran lazily up and down the inside of her bare arm, the effect of his touch on her so devastatingly erotic that she found it almost impossible to focus on what he was saying.

'Cream is your colour. Cream and gold.' He leaned forward, his lips caressing the side of her neck, his fingers so swift and deft on the fastening of her top that she was barely aware of the fact that he had slid it off her shoulder until she felt the heat of his mouth caressing her there.

A hundred thousand fiery darts of pleasure thrilled over her skin. She heard the sound of her own low, aching moan filling the room; a counterpoint to the rapidly increasing rate of their breathing.

Dracco's hands were sliding beneath her top, easing it off her body. A delicious shivery sensation shimmered over her skin.

'Cream, and honey-gold,' Imogen heard Dracco saying thickly as he freed her breasts from the confines of her bra and gently kneaded them, playing tenderly with the stiff peaks of her nipples in a way that made her writhe hotly in his embrace. She closed her eyes and bit into her bottom lip as she fought to suppress the raw moan of appreciative delight she could feel building up inside her.

'Beautiful! You are so very beautiful, even more perfect than I knew. So perfect that I can hardly bear to look at you. Do you know what it does to me, Imo, seeing you like this?' she could hear Dracco demanding as he looked down at her naked breasts and then back up into her eyes.

The expression she could see in the depths of those eyes both shocked and thrilled her.

Dracco wanted her. She could see it; feel it in his body; hear it in his voice.

That knowledge was all she needed to loosen the last faint threads of inhibition binding her and set herself free to be the woman she had always known she could be—with Dracco.

As his hands came to her waist, so narrow that her trousers slid down from it to lie loosely on her hips, Imogen raised herself up on her tiptoes. She still wasn't quite brave enough to look down at Dracco's body. Miraculously his towel was still in place, but he had not made any attempt to disguise how aroused he was.

When she reached to wrap her arms around him Dracco held her slightly away from him. He whispered thickly, 'Let me see all of you, Imo.'

Although his words made her tremble, she didn't try to resist as he carefully removed her trousers, unzipping them to let them fall to the floor and then lifting her out of them, holding her right there against his own body. She was pressed deep into his hard masculinity, thigh to thigh, hip to hip, groin to groin, whilst he kissed her with a slow passion that burned and smouldered potently.

Imogen ached to open her legs and wrap them tightly around him, to lure and coax him by any means she could to take the gift she was so wantonly ready to give him. Just the thought of feeling him sliding powerfully into her was enough to make her shudder again wildly, her eyes stormily dark with longing.

How could she have lived so long without this, without him? It was a question she couldn't even begin to answer.

Mutely she let him slide her down to the floor, his hands smoothing the flesh of her back, her waist, her buttocks, cupping the soft feminine cheeks, his fingers splayed over them.

Imogen could hear the frantic high-pitched sound of her

sharp protest that he should arouse her so intensely and tormentingly without satisfying her, but it was something she heard from a distance, her whole being concentrated on the increasingly urgent necessity of feeling him, having him touch her with the full intimacy of a lover.

Her nails clawed his naked back, echoing the intensity of what she was feeling. Impatiently she tugged at the soft fabric of the towel covering his body.

Against her ear she could hear him asking, 'Imo, are you sure this is what you want? Because if it isn't and you don't tell me now…'

How could he even ask her such a question? Couldn't he tell? See? Feel?

'I want you, Dracco,' she told him. 'I want you now.'

It was like nothing she had ever imagined, and so much— so much more than everything she had ever dared to hope for. Tears of emotion stung her eyes at the look on Dracco's face as he studied her naked body, his gaze absorbed, hungry, fiercely hungry, in direct contrast to the tender touch of his hands.

When he kissed her breasts, each one in turn and then each nipple, slowly laving the aching peaks, she shivered in mute ecstasy. The slow trail of his tongue-tip down over her belly had the same effect on her skin as red wine might have had on her blood—a hot, sensual rush of pleasure that took control of her senses. To call the effect he was having on her mind-blowing fell so far short of the reality of what he was doing to her that it was almost an insult. When his tongue rimmed her navel, and dipped gently into it, she moaned out loud in bewildered pleasure.

Never in a thousand lifetimes had she imagined this kind of intimacy with him, and never had it even crossed her mind that she would be the one urging him on with her hands, with the hoarse cry of her voice and with the frantic writhing of her body. Through her half-closed eyes she could still see the full, powerful maleness of him. She ached to reach out and touch him, but the sensation of him gently parting the outer covering of her sex made her forget everything but her intense need for him.

Instincts she hadn't known she possessed were driving her, possessing her now, insisting that the mere touch of his fingers was not enough, not what her body really needed, even though their careful touch was making her shudder from head to foot.

'Dracco,' she whispered, pleading.

Immediately he was beside her, looking deep into her eyes as he demanded hoarsely, 'What is it? Do you want me to stop?'

'No, it isn't that,' Imogen denied immediately. Helplessly her gaze, hot and fevered with longing, jolted over his body. 'I want you, Dracco,' she told him fiercely. 'You… With me. Inside me.'

For a moment the triumphant blaze in his eyes shocked her. It was as though she had said something, given him something he had hungered for for a very long time. But it was too late to try to analyse what she thought she might have seen; Dracco was gathering her up in his arms, holding her, positioning her, moving over her and then finally and oh, so blissfully into her.

The high, wild sound of her cry of longing mingled with the harshly guttural groan of Dracco's male growl of possession. Their bodies moved together in an urgent harmony that felt so right, so natural that it seemed to Imogen she had finally found a vitally important missing piece of her life and herself.

And then there was no room for thought, no room for anything other than absorbing the feel of Dracco's body, the hot, musky scent of his skin, the physical reality of him here with her and within her as he drove them both to that place she knew she would die if she did not reach it.

But she did reach it, reached it and exploded in a million tiny pieces of piercingly intense release to lie exhausted in Dracco's protective arms. She was dazed with satisfaction and an awed disbelief that it was possible to experience something so spectacularly wonderful as sleep claimed her.

CHAPTER SIX

IMOGEN OPENED HER eyes and stretched luxuriously. Dracco might not still be in the bed beside her but she could still smell his scent, feel the warm place where his body had been, feel the secret, special, place within herself where he had been.

Rolling over, she looked towards the window. It was a wonderful day. How could it not be? The revelations of the previous night still clung to her, filling her emotions with the same golden glow the sun brought through the window, its brightness softened into a mellow gilding by the voile curtains.

And so it was with her own feelings; they too were softened, gilded by the wondrous power of love, the love she had rediscovered in the breathless passages of the night when Dracco had held her, touching not just her body and her senses but also the deepest and most precious part of her.

They might not have spoken of love, but they had breathed it, shared it, given and bequeathed it to one another, surely? There was no way she could be mistaken about that.

She turned her head and studied the pillow next to her own, the pillow that still bore the imprint of Dracco's head. It was a new and sweet thing for her, this soft heaviness within her body, this small ache of satisfaction and remembered pleasure.

She had so many plans for her future, their future; so many hopes. Joy trembled uncertainly within her. She didn't want to question what she was feeling, nor to analyse the past. She didn't, Imogen recognised, want anything to intrude on the special memories and pleasures she and Dracco had created together.

She and Dracco together...

And perhaps, just perhaps, memories weren't all they had created!

A fierce quickening sensation gripped her body. A child. 'I want your father's grandchild,' Dracco had told her. And now her body was telling her that it wanted Dracco's child.

Somewhere outside the warmth of the bed, beyond the sunlight of the bedroom, lay certain sharply informed realities, but Imogen was in no mood to acknowledge them. What did they matter now? she taunted in silent mental recklessness. What, after last night, could matter more than what she and Dracco had shared? What she had discovered?

The love he had denied her as a girl had been there for her last night. She was sure of it.

The muslin voile curtains moved in the breeze, throwing small shadows across the room that were as ephemeral and as easily despatched as her unwanted doubts.

She loved Dracco. She couldn't not love him and have shared with him, as she had done yesterday, that deepest and most intimate sense of herself. And he surely could not have touched her, aroused her, savoured and satisfied her in the way that he had if he had not cared about her? Loved her in return?

Love. It was such a small word to cover such an infinity of emotion. Did she even truthfully know what it was? She had gone from loving Dracco to hating him, and then last night... Imogen took a deep breath, willing herself to think logically and realistically, but it was no use. Every time she tried to do so all she could see was Dracco's face, all she could feel was his touch, all she could hear was the immeasurably sweet sound of his breathing.

She was twenty-two and a woman, she reminded herself fiercely, and, even though physically she might have been a virgin, she was mature enough to know that sex, however good it might be, wasn't love.

Her heart refused to acknowledge such unworthy thoughts. What she and Dracco had shared had gone way beyond mere sex. It wasn't just one another's bodies they had touched; they had touched one another's hearts, one another's souls. Whatever had happened to them individually in their lives before last night no longer mattered. Her whole body was quivering, singing in the sweet, intoxicating aftermath of love. All she really wanted was to be with Dracco! To drink in the reality of him, breathe in the scent of him.

Imogen smiled ruefully at her own giddiness. She and Dracco needed to talk, to face one another and their shared past.

She took another deep breath. Surely in the light of what had already happened between them they were both adult enough to discuss everything? Their future and their past?

It was time to get up, for her to face the day—and Dracco.

Her foot poised on the topmost stair, Imogen paused and looked down through the banister into the hallway towards the closed door to what had once been her father's study and was now her husband's. Her husband, Dracco! The melting, delicious warmth just thinking such a thought gave her was a revelation. Dracco. Her husband. The father of her child…their child. A sensation not unlike the delicate touch of a skilled musician on a treasured instrument trembled across her skin.

Suddenly she couldn't wait to see him, to be with him, to reach up and pull that dark head down toward her, to feel those male lips caressing hers.

Light-heartedly she quickened her footsteps.

The study door was closed and Imogen paused outside it, suddenly feeling slightly nervous. Her senses felt preternaturally heightened; she could almost smell and taste the dust motes dancing on the sun-warmed air. The enormity of the moment and what it might portend made her heart beat unsteadily. On the other side of that door lay not just Dracco, but also her future. Their future, and potentially the future of their child.

Instinctively she touched her stomach. It was too soon to know if yesterday…

She gave a small gasp as the study door opened. Dracco was standing within the opening watching her, frowning at her. Her own forehead automatically started to mimic the expression she could see on his, although, whilst his frown was one of impatience and distance, hers was one of questioning concern.

'Imo.'

Even the way he said her name had a certain harshness about it, Imogen recognised as her glance slid from his face to his body. He was wearing a formidably businesslike dark suit, the jacket unfastened over a crisp white shirt, and as she watched him he shot back his cuff to look at his watch.

One did not need to be an expert at interpreting body language to recognise his impatience.

'You look as though you're very busy. I had hoped that we might be able to talk,' she began.

'Talk? What about?'

It was not a promising start, Imogen acknowledged, but she was not a teenager gazing star-struck at an idol any more. She and Dracco were equals now.

'About us, and last night,' she responded calmly.

Imogen was proud of the way she managed to keep her gaze steady under the pressure of the look Dracco gave her.

'Last night?'

If anything his voice had become even more curt, carrying an edge to it that warned Imogen she was trespassing on a no-go area. But, as Imogen had discovered in the years she had been away, she possessed her own brand of strength and courage, and the issue that lay between them was not one she was going to allow to be ignored.

Moving closer to him, she reiterated softly, 'Yes, Dracco, last night. You do remember last night, don't you?' As she spoke the gentle mockery in her voice gave way to a soft liquid tenderness that shone in her eyes and curled her mouth. 'Last night, when you made love to me. You do remember that, don't you?' she teased.

'What I remember is that we had sex.'

The brutality of the cold words ripped into the shining delicate warmth of Imogen's hopes and dreams.

Now it was her turn to repeat Dracco's words.

'Sex.' She could hear the stammering anxiety in her voice, the desire to be reassured, but Dracco was already turning away from her, looking irritably towards the front door, as though he couldn't wait to escape.

'Dracco,' she protested, and she could hear the pain trembling through her voice. 'It wasn't just sex. It was…'

Helpless in the face of his remoteness, she couldn't bring herself to say the word 'love', to expose it and herself to the savage pain of his contemptuous dismissal. Instead her voice trailed away on an unsteady protest that held echoes of her childhood insecurity as she told him, 'It was more than that.'

'It was sex, Imo,' Dracco overrode her tersely. His head was turned away from her but she could see his profile, see the bleak downward turn of his mouth, the grimness in his expression, which warned her that he wanted the conversation brought to an end.

But there was a stubbornness in her that refused to allow her to let go, and, as though he sensed it, she heard him draw in his breath in open exasperation before he turned fully towards her. His gaze, clinical, cold, rejecting, swept her from head to toe.

'Sex, that's all,' he repeated. 'No more and no less.'

All the fiery passion that was so much a part of her nature rose up inside Imogen.

What she had felt with him, for him, last night was too important to be swept aside. She believed in her feelings and her instincts, even if Dracco didn't, and she was prepared to fight and fight hard if she had to to have them recognised.

'I'm twenty-two years old, Dracco; I've been independent for the last four years. You might remember me as a naïve teenager, but the woman you held in your arms last night, the woman you made love with—'

'Was a naïve virgin,' Dracco cut across her impassioned speech. He was watching her with almost clinical detachment to see how she reacted, how she recovered from the cutting edge of his blow. 'It's true that I do remember you as a child, Imogen. A very immature and romantic young teenager, who idealised the physical relationship between men and women, and who could only allow it into her life wrapped in the pretty packaging of "love". You claim to be mature. But a mature woman would never have clung to her virginity the way you have to yours.'

The cruelty of his clinical dissection of her took Imogen's breath away. It was as though he was determined to strip every last bit of emotion from what they had shared and turn it into something cold and meaningless.

'Psychologically for you,' he continued ruthlessly, 'the mere fact that you have had sex with me—and enjoyed it—

means that you have to convince yourself that the physical arousal and desire you felt had to be the product of "love". Loving someone, Imo, means knowing them, accepting them, valuing them as they are. You and I do not…'

Imogen was not prepared to listen to any more. Boldly she stepped up to him; so close to him in fact that she was virtually touching him. As she put her hand on his arm she felt his muscles lock against her touch.

'Imo, I've got an appointment I have to keep, and I'm already dangerously close to being late for it.'

Willing him to allow her through the barriers he had thrown up against her, Imogen leaned into him, whispering, 'Dracco, please… Last night must have meant something to you. I—'

'It meant a great deal.' Imogen felt tears begin to sting her eyes. But her relief was short-lived.

Instead of reassuring her as she longed for him to do, Dracco told her crisply, 'It meant that, if we are lucky, nine months from now we shall have a child—I shall have a son or daughter who carries your father's blood, which is, after all, what this is about.'

He couldn't have made it any plainer to her that she meant nothing to him, Imogen recognised, as he sidestepped her.

Her vision blurred as she stared towards the stairs she had come down less than half an hour ago, her hopes so high, her belief so sure!

Dracco had reached the front door.

Somehow she managed to make herself turn towards him. 'And if…if we aren't lucky?' she challenged him desperately.

There was a small pause before he told her quietly, 'Then in that case we shall just have to try again until we are.'

As he opened the door and walked through it Imogen felt a shudder tear through her body as though it and she were being ripped apart. How could she endure that? The cold lovelessness of the act of sex with a man who did not love her but whom she…

She didn't cry. She couldn't! The pain was like a wound inflicted so deep within her body that it destroyed internally without any outward evidence of the injury.

Dracco got down the drive and as far as the main road without giving in to his emotions, but once there he recognised that, feeling as he did right now, he was a danger to himself and to others.

Cursing sharply beneath his breath, he pulled off the road and stopped his car.

He had lied to Imo about the urgency of his appointment. He was on his way to see David Bryant to sign the new will he had had the other man draw up.

'You want to make Imogen and any child she might conceive the main beneficiaries of your estate?' David had commented when Dracco informed him of his wishes. 'We're talking about a very large inheritance, Dracco. You say you want Imogen to have full control of it?' He had paused uncertainly. 'It is customary where such a large amount is concerned to appoint trustees or set up a trust fund.'

'There is no one I trust more than Imogen,' Dracco had responded firmly.

Imogen would never know just what last night had done to him, the sheer unbearable immensity of the guilt and remorse it had brought him—and the pleasure! So much pleasure that it was impossible to quantify it. How could I measure something that had been so longed and hungered for? How could he estimate the breadth and depth of how he had felt when after a virtually sleepless night he had leaned over in the first minutes of the new day to look down into her sleeping face?

Even in her sleep she had been smiling, her lips curved in

soft, sensuous warmth. The tears of release and fulfilment she had cried in his arms had gone, but their salty trail had lain gently crystallised on her skin. Beneath the bedclothes she'd been naked, and the temptation to run his hand possessively down her body from the top of her head right the way to her toes, just for the luxurious pleasure of knowing she was there, had almost overwhelmed him.

He knew he had given her pleasure—would have known it even if she had not cried it out to him in a voice of shocked, delighted wonder—simply from the way her body had responded to him, fitted itself around him, accepted and embraced his touch upon it and within it.

But he had always known that there would be pleasure between them; had known it from the moment he had looked beyond the shy awkwardness of the girl she'd been and seen the woman she would become. She had desired him then with all the innocent hunger of a young girl's awakening sexuality and he had known it, and known too that he was equally drawn by longing to her as she was to him. The only difference had been that he'd been an adult and she had not. An adult male with an adult male's needs for a mate, a woman.

Dracco closed his eyes and breathed in, filling his lungs.

What he had told her about wanting her father's blood to run in the veins of his own child had been true, but it was only a small part of the truth.

John Atkins had been an astute and loving father. He had seen as clearly as Dracco had himself the growing intensity of Imogen's youthful crush on Dracco.

'She imagines herself in love with you,' John had told him in a no-holds-barred man-to-man conversation he had instituted shortly before Imogen's sixteenth birthday.

'I know,' Dracco had concurred. 'I love her, John,' he

had told his friend and mentor rawly, 'and I know too that she is far too young as yet—'

'Dracco,' John Atkins had interrupted him immediately, 'I don't dispute your feelings, but, as Imogen's father, I would ask you to give me your word that you will allow her to have time to grow up and experience life before you tell her of your love. If you love her you'll understand why I'm asking you this.'

And of course Dracco had, even though the thought of having to stand to one side and watch whilst the girl he loved grew into womanhood with someone else had torn him apart.

'If you and Imogen should eventually become a couple,' John Atkins had continued emotionally, 'and I can promise you that there is nothing that would give me more pleasure, Dracco, it has to be as two equals, adults, not now whilst Imogen, for all she thinks she is passionately in love with you, is still little more than a child. I know how hard what I'm asking of you is going to be but, for Imogen's own sake and for the sake of the love I hope you may one day share, will you promise to say nothing of your feelings to her until she is twenty-one?'

Twenty-one. Five years! But Dracco had known why John was demanding such a promise from him, and he had given it. Had Imogen been his daughter he would have done exactly the same thing.

He had told himself after her father's death that he owed it to his friend and mentor to protect his only daughter, if necessary against himself, but then circumstances had left him with no choice other than to marry Imogen, for her own sake.

How he had agonised over that decision, ultimately seeking the advice of Henry Fairburn, John's solicitor and oldest friend.

He had told himself that he would not break his word to John, that he would somehow find the strength to make sure that his marriage to Imogen was in name only and that she knew nothing of his feelings for her.

But then as they'd left the church she had asked him if there was someone he loved, and he had known that she knew the truth, had seen in her eyes that she already knew the answer to her own question. Her reaction to it had made it plain how she felt.

After all, there was no more obvious a way of stating that someone's love was not wanted than to run away from them.

Lisa had taunted him about it, saying that he should have left Imogen to play teenage sex games with someone of her own age, claiming that the thought of having sex with a real live man had probably terrified her.

'A real man needs a real woman, Dracco,' she had told him, her hand on his arm, stroking it suggestively. He had shrugged her off, barely able to conceal either his dislike or his pain at losing Imogen.

Out of guilt and remorse and pain he had managed to stop himself from going after Imogen and bringing her back.

How could he possibly have claimed to love her and then forced her to accept that love when she didn't want it?

And then David Bryant had told him about the letter he had received from her, and, almost as though he was watching himself from a distance, a part of Dracco had looked on in grim contempt whilst he set about making plans to…

To what? Couldn't he even admit to himself what he had done? Well, perhaps it was time he did. He had manoeuvred and manipulated Imogen into coming back to him. And the result had far exceeded even the most fevered scenarios conjured up by the long lonely nights of wanting her.

To hear that note of wonderment in her voice earlier when she had talked about last night, about them 'making love', had made him want to take hold of her right there and show her that last night had been a mere fraction of what they could share together. But what he wanted from her was a lot more than the orgasm-induced emotion of physical satisfaction. What he wanted was her love, a love that matched his own; a love that went way beyond the giving and taking of pleasure in bed. Yes, it was satisfying to know that physically Imo wanted him, but it was a bitter, tainted pleasure. It was her love he wanted, not her body, and how the hell could he ever win that after what he had done?

Even now Dracco found it hard to explain to himself why he had overreacted so uncharacteristically when Imogen had assumed that he wanted a divorce.

Yes, of course he wanted her to have his child, and, yes, he very much wanted to share a blood tie with the man who had meant so much to him, but to use that as an excuse to force Imo to consummate their marriage... There was no acceptable explanation for what he had done.

Dracco opened his eyes. He had kept track of Imogen all the time they had been apart, knowing that it was what her father would have expected him to do.

He had never for one moment intended... But somehow things had got out of hand; and he had found it far harder to control his feelings than he had expected. The reality of dealing with a fully grown woman and not a girl had brought it home to him how dangerously vulnerable he actually was.

He had tried to keep as much physical distance between them as he could, working away from home, sleeping downstairs in the study. But last night all those plans had been crushed out of existence, along with his self-control. Last night he had done the very thing he had promised himself he would never, ever do under any circumstances.

And now Imo was telling him that she loved him. Not because she did—dammit—but because he was her first lover, her only lover. For a woman as idealistic as Imogen, that meant she could not allow herself the physical pleasure they had shared without convincing herself that she must love him. But she hadn't loved him when she had run away from him on the day of their marriage.

He had seen the hurt in her eyes when she had turned away in the hallway just now, and he had ached to take her in his arms and tell her just how he felt about her, just what she did to him, had always done to him.

Right now he didn't know which was causing him the greater pain—his love for her or his guilt.

Dracco closed his eyes again. He had no idea how long he had been sitting here in his car, and neither did he care. He was back in the study of the house he had just left, Imo's father's study. It was the morning of Imo's seventeenth birthday, the morning she had run downstairs to him and begged him shyly for a birthday kiss, when he had known that he had to plead with his mentor and friend to release him from his promise.

'Yes, I know how hard it is, Dracco,' John Atkins had accepted gently when Dracco had finished his terse little speech. 'But Imogen is only seventeen.'

'Seventeen going on a thousand,' Dracco had groaned. 'She looks at me sometimes with all the knowledge of every woman that ever lived in her eyes, and then at other times...' He had paused and shaken his head. 'At other times she looks at me with the unknowing innocence of a child.'

'And it is the innocence and the future of that child I would ask you to protect and respect, Dracco,' Imogen's father had responded gently, getting to his feet and coming to Dracco's side, placing his hand on Dracco's arm in a benign, almost fatherly gesture.

He had paused before continuing in a sterner voice, 'If

you love her you will want her to give you her love as a woman, not take from her the naïve love of a child.'

His words had hit home, and Dracco had acknowledged their truth.

'Nothing will ever change the way I feel about her,' he had told the older man fiercely. 'But for her sake I will do as you ask, and I will wait.'

'It is nearly as hard for me as it for you, Dracco,' Imogen's father had told him gently. 'When I said I love you as a son that is exactly what I meant, and I can think of no greater pleasure than having you marry my daughter unless it is that of holding your children. But Imo is far too young yet to be burdened by a man's love. She needs time and space to grow up properly.'

Dracco hated himself for what he had done last night. He felt corrupted by his own emotions, his love, his desire, the constant, aching need for Imogen that had flared into a fiercely unstoppable conflagration the moment he had touched her.

He could feel it still now, knew he would feel it forever, just as he would love her forever.

It was over an hour since he had stopped his car. Reaching for his mobile, Dracco put a call through to David Bryant to explain that he was going to be late for their meeting.

Tugging viciously at the nettles growing in amongst the roses she could remember her mother planting, Imogen muttered an angry protest as she felt them stinging her through the thickness of the gardening gloves she had found in the old-fashioned potting shed.

Dracco's rejection of her love and the scorn with which he had reacted to it and to her, instead of making her question the validity of her feelings had somehow had totally the opposite effect and brought out in her a passionate strength she had not guessed she possessed.

How dared he try to tell her that she did not know what love was? She tugged furiously on another nettle, giving a small sound of triumph as she threw it into the wheelbarrow without getting stung.

How dared he imply that she was some kind of naïve ninny who thought that just because she had sex with a man she must be in love with him?

Another nettle joined its fellows.

And as for his comments about her virginity… Well, it just so happened that the reason she had not…that she was still…had been still…had nothing to do with naïveté or timidity; it was simply that she had never met a man she had wanted enough.

Imogen yelped in pain as her momentary loss of concentration, whilst she battled against the dangerous images her brain was sending, resulted in a sharp reminder that nettles, carelessly handled, could and did sting.

'Ouch,' she protested out loud, as she inspected the swiftly lifting rash on the palm of her hand.

Like Dracco, it had caught her off guard and the result was pain. Well, this time at least she could retaliate, she decided grimly as she bent towards the offending weed and very determinedly removed it from the soil.

'Now see how you like that!' she told the nettle triumphantly.

'Excuse me.'

The sound of a hesitant male voice behind her caused her to spin round, her face pink with confusion at being caught conversing with the vegetation.

'It stung me,' she said rather lamely to the young man who was standing several feet away from her.

'My wife hates nettles,' he responded easily. 'Her brothers hid her doll in a nettle patch when she was a little girl.'

'Oh, how unkind of them.'

'Well, I suspect she might have deserved it,' he told her, his voice ruefully candid. 'She had buried all their toy soldiers in a pile of builders' sand. The builder wasn't too pleased when it ruined his concrete. Her excuse was that they had been overwhelmed by a sandstorm in the desert.

'I was looking for Dracco,' he went on. 'I rang the bell but no one answered and then I saw you here in the garden. You must be his wife.'

'Yes, yes, I am,' Imogen responded. Who was this young man, and how did he know that Dracco was married?

As though he guessed what she was thinking, her unexpected visitor quickly explained, 'I'm Robert Bates—I work for Dracco. He left a message at the office, saying that... that he had got married, and asking me to bring him some papers he wanted.'

He was looking rather pleased with his deductive powers, and Imogen couldn't resist gently teasing him.

'And because of that you assumed that I must be Dracco's wife?'

'Not just because of that,' she was told sturdily. 'He has a photograph of you on his desk, and I recognised you from it straight away. Your father started the business, didn't he? Dracco told me about him.'

Now Imogen was surprised. Dracco had a photograph of her? She remembered that her father had had one taken on her seventeenth birthday; presumably Dracco must have inherited it. However, before she could reply her visitor was saying something she found even more surprising.

'I know that your father started the business, but Dracco is the one who made it the success it is today.' As he spoke Imogen could hear the admiration and respect in the younger man's voice. 'I couldn't believe my luck when he took me on. I didn't have the qualifications or the background.' He flushed a little whilst Imogen watched him in silence. 'I certainly didn't deserve the faith he's shown in me. The night we met I was sitting in a bar, full of self-pity and drinking myself into oblivion. Natasha, my wife now but my girlfriend as she was then, had just told me that her parents had threatened her that if she married me they were going to stop her trust fund.

'We met at university and I knew straight away that she was the one for me, and she said she felt the same, but what I didn't know then was that Natasha's family had money—and ambitions.' His voice grew slightly bitter. 'And those ambitions did not include a son-in-law with no family connections, no money and no prospects. Oh, Tasha said that it didn't matter, but of course it did. I couldn't give her the kind of life she'd grown up with, the kind of future she deserved; I couldn't even get a job. And then I met Dracco.

'He gave me a job, and time off so that I could get my Masters in business studies; he let me and Tasha live rent-free in a flat above the offices. He even went to see Tasha's parents, and God knows what he said to them but…' He broke off and gave Imogen an embarrassed look. 'I don't know why I'm telling you all this. After all, you already know exactly what kind of man Dracco is—you're married to him.'

He paused and then added hesitantly, 'Once when I asked him why he had helped me he said it was because I reminded him of what he himself had once been, and of everything that your father had done for him. He said that he wanted to pass on the good deed your father had done, to honour his memory and to show his gratitude for it. He said that your father had taught him the value of true generosity of spirit and the importance of self-respect.'

Imogen felt sharp tears sting her eyes in the small silence that followed. When she was sure she had full control of herself she offered, 'I'll give Dracco the papers if you want to leave them with me. But first let's go up to the house. I'm ready for a cup of tea; would you like one?'

'No, I'd better not. I promised Tasha I'd be home early. It's our wedding anniversary today, and her parents are taking us out to dinner!'

After her unexpected visitor had driven away Imogen couldn't help thinking about what he had said to her.

She had come out into the garden after Dracco's departure, ready to hate him all over again, but now she had been shown a compassionate side of him that made her feel uncertain.

Her hand felt acutely painful where the nettles had stung her. She had always been sensitive to their sting and an unpleasant tingling numbness now accompanied the raised rash, swelling the palm of her hand and her fingers.

She massaged it absently, thinking about her father. She had always known how much he had thought of Dracco, and he had been held in high esteem by his peers for his shrewd judgement. She wished that he were here now for her to turn to.

Dracco still hadn't come back. And when he did... She quickly calculated how long it might be before she would know if she was pregnant.

And if she wasn't? Her face burned with mortified colour as she recognised that the bumping of her heart against her ribs at the thought of a repetition of the previous night was quite definitely not caused by dread or revulsion. Far from it. But Dracco did not love her and, according to him, she could not love him.

Who had he been thinking of whilst he touched her body,

whilst he aroused it, entered it, possessed and filled it with
the gift of immortality?

Imogen willed the acid sting of the tears burning her
eyes not to fall.

As a child she had cried over her loss of her father's
love to Lisa. As a woman there was no way she was going
to cry over the loss of Dracco's love to her stepmother. No
way at all!

Imogen sighed as she heard someone pressing impatiently
and repeatedly on the front doorbell. Today was quite obviously her day for visitors.

Running lightly downstairs, she pulled open the front
door, to reveal the features of her uninvited guest.

'Lisa!' It was impossible for Imogen to keep the shock
out of her voice.

Her stepmother was wearing a pair of white Capri pants,
her face and body tanned from her Caribbean holiday. Glar-
ing at Imogen, she stepped into the hallway without waiting
for an invitation and demanded sharply, 'Where's Dracco? I
need to speak to him. Is he in the study?' She was walking
towards the door before Imogen could stop her.

'No, he isn't,' Imogen told her as calmly as she could.

Seeing her stepmother here in the house which her presence had made so unhappy would have been bad enough,
but knowing what Imogen now knew made that pain a thousand times worse.

'Then where is he?' Lisa was asking her angrily.

'He's out on business,' Imogen told her reluctantly. She
would have preferred not to have to answer her at all. She
would have preferred, in fact, to have enough belief in Dracco's support to insist that Lisa leave the house immediately.

'You mean he's sleeping at the apartment in London because he can't bear to have to sleep here with you?' Lisa

taunted aggressively. 'It's a pity you were always so patheti-
cally antagonistic towards me, Imogen. Had you not been
you might have learned one or two things of value. Such as
the fact that there is nothing that a man abhors more than
a woman who doesn't have the pride to accept it when he
makes it obvious he doesn't want her. And Dracco doesn't
want you, Imogen. He never has wanted you. On the other
hand, of course, he did want the business. And who can
blame him? I certainly don't. Miranda warned me that you
had come crawling back to him. Somehow I wasn't totally
surprised. But it won't do you any good.'

Imogen had heard enough. She wasn't a shy, grieving
teenager any more, who instinctively believed she had to be
polite to grown-ups no matter how offensive and rude they
were to her. It was high time that Lisa had a taste of her own
medicine and Imogen was in just the mood to hand it out to
her! After all, what had she got to lose? Dracco had already
told her that he didn't love her. That they had only had sex!

If in punishing Lisa she punished Dracco as well, so
much the better. He deserved it—they both did! Imogen
couldn't remember ever feeling so furiously, gloriously
angry!

She was a woman betrayed, a woman scorned, and those
who had done the betraying and the scorning had just better watch out. They were going to find out that she could
give as good as she got!

'As a matter of fact, it was Dracco who insisted on giving our marriage a second chance, not me,' she told Lisa
with pseudo-sweetness. If she hadn't been enjoying herself
so much she might almost have been shocked by the savage
sense of satisfaction it gave her to say the words that were
responsible for the brief look of fury she saw in Lisa's eyes.
'And it isn't just my share of the business he wants, Lisa,'
she continued recklessly, only distantly aware of just how

dangerous the surge of euphoria sweeping her up into its enticing embrace might be.

'Well, it can't possibly be your body!' Lisa retaliated nastily. 'If it was he'd be here with you now.'

'Perhaps I should leave it to him to tell you just what he wants from our marriage,' Imogen suggested serenely. She was almost enjoying the effect her words were having on her stepmother, who was staring at her as though she was seeing her properly for the first time. 'Unless, of course, he has already told you?'

Lisa gave a dismissive shrug. 'Dracco and I don't discuss you, Imogen, we have far more important things to talk about.'

Imogen could feel her self-control cracking as the euphoria left her as suddenly as it had swept her up, leaving in its wake a wash of anguished pain. 'Yes,' she agreed bitterly. 'Such as the way the pair of you deceived my father.'

She could see from the smirk the other woman was giving that she had allowed her emotions to betray her.

'You're making assumptions, accusations that you simply can't prove, Imogen.'

'I don't have to prove them,' Imogen retorted. 'Both you and Dracco have already shown me how true they are. Your affair—'

'Dracco told you we had an affair?' Lisa stopped her. For some reason she was frowning, as though she didn't believe what Imogen was telling her. But then unexpectedly she smiled, as though she was actually pleased to be revealed as a woman who had broken her marriage vows.

'He didn't need to tell me. You did that…on my wedding day,' Imogen reminded her grimly.

Lisa's smile widened. 'Yes, so I did. Poor little Imogen; you were so naïve, so stupid… Umm… Well, if Dracco is at the office I suppose I'd better go and see him there. I'm sure he'll appreciate the privacy for our reunion,' she purred tauntingly. 'It's been almost a month since he last saw me, and a month for a man of Dracco's sexual appetite is a very long time. Don't expect him home too soon, will you, Mrs Barrington?'

She was walking through the door before Imogen could frame any kind of suitably cutting retort.

So it was true. Dracco was still seeing Lisa. He still loved her.

She wasn't going to cry, Imogen told herself with fierce pride. She wasn't!

CHAPTER SEVEN

'Imo, are you all right?'

'I'm fine, thank you,' Imogen responded, her voice as carefully devoid of any emotion as she could make it.

'Then why aren't you eating your dinner?' Dracco demanded sharply.

They had been living together as man and wife for just over a month, and Imogen had used the vast oasis of time Dracco's absences in London on business gave her. He had put his bank account at her disposal to set about restoring and refurbishing the house—it helped to keep her surface busy, during the day at least. At night, those long, lonely, aching nights when her thoughts and feelings couldn't be kept at bay, she felt as though she had entered a painful form of purgatory.

Not once since she had called at the house demanding to see him had he mentioned Lisa, and Imogen was stubbornly, bitterly determined not to be the one to bring up her name. Because she was afraid that if she did she would not be able to conceal what she really felt?

Lisa's cruel taunts had hit home. Had Dracco told Lisa just what he wanted from their marriage? There was no way Imogen could have borne to know that the man she loved was contemplating having a child with another woman, even a woman he did not love, but then Lisa had never been in the least bit maternal.

'Because I'm not hungry.' Imogen answered Dracco's question coolly, lifting her gaze to meet his down the length of the pretty table she had seen in an antique shop and bought for a sum that had given her a vicious slam of guilt that was only slightly appeased by the pleasure it gave her to run her fingertips over the old satiny polished wood.

A little to her own surprise, she had slipped back into life here in their small market town with unexpected ease. It was true that she had not made any close friends in Rio for her to miss. Her past had made it difficult for her to talk openly with her co-workers, and Dracco's rejection of her had left painful scars that had damaged her self-confidence.

She still thought about Rio, of course, and the children. After all, it was because of her determination to help them that she was trapped in this unbearable nightmare situation. One day she would go back, but right now there were issues closer to hand that were absorbing her time and attention!

'What is it, Dracco?' she challenged him. 'Were you hoping I was going to say I wasn't eating it because I felt sick? Because I'm pregnant?' She shook her head and gave him an unkind smile. 'I'm sorry to disappoint you, but I'm afraid that I'm not. Poor you, you're going to have to force yourself to have sex with me all over again.' She gave a small, brittle laugh as fragile as the crystal in the wine glasses they were drinking out of.

She scarcely recognised herself in the embittered woman she felt she was becoming. Was this what sex did to you when it was denied to you? When you were given a taste of what it could be and then not allowed to taste it again?

Imogen had no way of knowing; after all, as Dracco had said himself, what did she know about sex? She had been a naïve virgin when he had taken her to bed, a fool who confused sex with love and who believed that love mattered.

'Perhaps we should be more scientific and work out exactly when there is the optimum chance of me conceiving. After all, neither of us wants to have sex unnecessarily.' Somehow she managed to produce a sweetly disdainful little smile as she made this suggestion.

'You're lying to me, Imo!'

For a moment she was so caught off guard that she looked at him in shock. He was only guessing. He couldn't possibly know... She wasn't even properly sure herself... That unfamiliar bout of dizziness and the fact that she could not bear her normal cup of strong coffee in the morning was all the evidence she had to go on as yet.

'You want sex, and right now you want it so badly that I could take you right here, and, believe me, I'm sorely tempted to do just that, if only to prove it to you.'

Imogen went limp with relief. He didn't know. He hadn't meant what she had thought he meant at all. And then the reality of what he was saying pierced the blanket of her relief in tiny shocking darts of electric expectancy.

'You're wrong. I don't want you.'

What on earth was she doing, pushing him to the point where he would have no choice but to...?

Imogen gave a small gasp as Dracco got up from his seat and started to walk purposefully towards her.

'I've warned you before about challenging me, Imo,' he reminded her.

He had reached her now and pulled her easily to her feet and up against his body, holding her there as he looked down into her eyes, his mouth curling with insolence whilst his gaze lingered with deliberate intent on her mouth and then her throat, where her pulse was beating frantically fast, before dropping to her breasts.

It had been a hot day and she was wearing a thin top, against which her nipples had suddenly started to push with impatient eagerness.

Very carefully Dracco flattened the fabric against one of them, studying the openly erect outline in a way that made the heat flaming her face nothing to the heat burning inside her body.

'But then, this is exactly what you wanted me to do, isn't it?' he asked her softly.

Her denial never got beyond her throat, because suddenly Dracco was covering her mouth with his, kissing her with a fierce, smothering passion that her own senses leapt to meet.

It was almost as though they were fighting a battle that each was determined to win, anger searing and sizzling through both of them.

As his mouth possessed hers Imogen made an attempt to bite at it, forestalled by the fierce thrust of his tongue between her parted lips. She could feel its smooth roughness against the edge of her teeth and then its hot, dominating slide against her own tongue.

Something inside her started to melt. She gave a keening moan, her fingers curling into the thin cotton shirt he was wearing. As though she had crushed a flower in her fingers, she could smell the hot scent of him her grip had released. It dizzied her, sending a wave of longing melting through her, a slow, sweet melt of butter-soft pleasure.

'Dracco!'

She felt his mouth take his name from her as her lips formed it; knew he had absorbed and recognised the need that pierced her with such shocking sweetness.

Behind her closed eyelids she could see his naked body already, remember it in intimate and erotic detail, every bone, every muscle, every heart-wrenchingly perfect inch of him.

'I want you so much.'

The words were drawn from her as painfully as tears. She was powerless to suppress them and even more powerless to suppress her love for him. But it wasn't love. Dracco had told her that. It was just sex!

Her whole body shuddered.

Did Lisa make him react like this? Did he make her want him like this?

The savagery of her feelings lacerated her pride, but somehow she couldn't withstand the pressure of her need.

'Take me to bed, Dracco,' she urged him.

Because she wanted him or because she wanted to prove to herself that she was woman enough to overpower his resistance? That what Lisa had done she too could do?

She felt him hesitate.

'You were the one who wanted this,' she reminded him. 'You're the one who wants me to have your child.'

She knew, of course, that when she returned to sanity, when the madness of her longing and misery left her, she would despise herself for using such a weapon, for demeaning herself. But right now, what did such things matter? Right now she wanted him so much…too much.

This time it was different. This time she was anticipating every touch, every sensation, savagely hungry for him, her body rising up to meet him and demanding more. More!

But then abruptly, like someone who had fed themselves on rich confectionery, she suddenly felt nauseated by what she was doing, appalled and disgusted by her own greed and lack of self-control.

This was sex, she reminded herself. Sex, not love. Was she really so lacking in self-control, in self-respect, that she could be satisfied with a physical act given without any kind of emotional grace?

'What is it?'

She could feel Dracco's hands holding her stiffening body as he leaned over her in the summer darkness.

'I've changed my mind.'

She could feel the sharpness of his indrawn breath.

'Am I allowed to ask why?'

She could hear the tension underlying the outwardly silky words.

'You wouldn't understand.' Any minute now she was going to cry. Defensively she turned her head away from him.

'Try me.'

Was it her imagination or was his voice softer, gentler? His hands on her arms certainly were. She could feel him rubbing her skin, soothing it, stroking it as though in some way he was trying to reassure and comfort her. A touch could say so much more than words. A touch couldn't lie… could it? Or was it more that her lack of experience was making her read too much into it?

She felt drained, defeated, overwhelmed by her emotions.

'I don't want it to be just sex between us, Dracco.'

There was a long silence whilst she waited for him to answer, during which Imogen asked herself furiously why on earth she had made such an admission.

'No? Then what do you want it to be?'

His hands were on her shoulders now, cupping them, working up delicately towards her throat, gently massaging away her tension.

Imogen gave a small gasp as she felt the tiny quivers of sensation darting over her skin. The pulse at the base of her throat had started to beat fast again. Dracco placed his thumb on it, measuring it, and then lifted his hand to her lips, rubbing against her bottom lip very slowly.

'Tell me, Imogen,' he demanded huskily, his voice a soft, sensual enticement. 'What is it you want from me?'

Her whole body was trembling now. It was those two little words 'from me' that had done it.

'I want you, Dracco!' she told him helplessly. 'I want you.'

And then she was reaching for his mouth with her own, devouring it with tiny, longing-filled little kisses interspersed with soft, whispery moans.

It wasn't the way it had been before. It was sharper, sweeter, deeper, with her not merely responding but actively drawing her own response from him! Touching him with fingers that trembled slightly and then grew more confident as she saw the naked agony of wanting delineating every aspect of his expression. He wanted her touch, needed it, yearned for it so much that he was prepared to walk across burning coals to get to it and her. It gave Imogen a wave of shockingly savage pleasure to see it.

She rode that pleasure like a surfer, telling herself that she was the one controlling it and Dracco, until suddenly it crested, splintering her into a thousand diamond darts of tormentingly hot need which only the sure thrust of Dracco's body within her own could satisfy.

Only when it was over and she was sure that Dracco was asleep did she allow herself to cry, to grieve for what Dracco had not given her—his love.

It didn't matter what Dracco said, what male logic he tried to superimpose on her feelings to validate his own lack of love for her and force an emotional distance between them, Imogen knew she loved him. She didn't want to and it galled and lacerated her sensitive pride to know that she did.

She had lost count of the time she had wasted trying to rationalise her emotions, trying to list mentally all the reasons she had for not loving him. Her heart just wasn't prepared to listen to them. Not even when she tormented it with the strongest antidote of all—not even when she reminded it about Lisa!

Imogen hesitated as she stopped her car outside the house, next to Dracco's. He had told her only the previous evening that he intended to work as much as he could in future from home.

'With modern technology I don't really need a London base any more, and, besides…' He had glanced with deliberate emphasis at her stomach as he spoke. Imogen had felt a now familiar fluttering of guilty panic invade her body.

Sometimes it was almost as though he already knew and he was deliberately directing the conversation down an avenue that would give her no choice but to tell him of her own growing conviction that she had conceived their child.

But she didn't want to do so. Not yet. And, anyway, she had nothing official to go on. Only her own awed belief that she was carrying a new life. She could quite easily have found out one way or the other, but she didn't want to do so, and she didn't want to question just why not either.

Was it because she wanted to punish him? Or was it because a part of her hoped that his desire to father their child would keep him close to her and away from Lisa?

She was beginning to hate what her love for him was making her do, the kind of woman it was turning her into. What had happened to her moral beliefs, her pride?

They were having a truly golden summer weather-wise, and in their local town this morning she had bumped into a friend from her schooldays. They had had coffee together, exchanging recent histories. Lulu, her friend, had been living with her partner since they had left university. She had recently been headhunted for a job, which would mean her relocating to New York.

'I envy you,' she had confessed to Imogen. 'You've done things the right way around, explored the world and then settled down. I can't bear the thought of losing Mac, but I want to do something with my life. I want to see something of the world, to explore it and my own talents.'

'Won't Mac go with you?' Imogen had asked her sympathetically.

'Not a chance,' Lulu had told her ruefully. 'He wants us to get married, have babies.' She had pulled a wry face. 'I've got three brothers and five step-siblings, the youngest of whom is still in nappies... Right now the thought of a baby...'

'Do you love him?' Imogen had asked her quietly.

The look Lulu had given her in response to her question had spoken volumes.

'You're right,' Lulu had agreed ruefully. 'I'm just going to have to accustom myself to the thought of frequent transatlantic travel—and finding a good nanny.'

They had parted, agreeing that they must make a regular date to meet up, and Imogen had driven back to the house reflecting on how good it felt to have started to develop a network of supportive friends.

A new interior-design business had opened in the town, and Imogen had arranged for the young women who ran it to call at the house one day so that they could discuss some ideas Imogen had for redecorating.

As she walked through the back door Dracco came into the kitchen. As always when she saw him Imogen's feelings were mixed and very emotional. She loved and wanted him so much, and yet at the same time she dreaded being with him because of the pain it gave her to know that he did not return her feelings.

'I thought we might have lunch out today,' Dracco announced, casually removing the supermarket bags she was carrying and starting to put away their contents for her.

'I…I thought you were working?' she responded uncertainly.

Dracco paused in the act of opening the fridge door.

'I am, but I can take a couple of hours off. You mentioned that you'd like to do something with the garden; there's a particularly good garden centre with its own design team, a specialist outfit that has an excellent reputation, about ten miles away.'

Imogen chewed on her bottom lip. It was true that she did want to redesign the garden. With the needs of an active toddler to consider, the notion of a safe enclosed play area close to the house quite naturally appealed to her.

She and Dracco hadn't been out together as a couple since the early days of their reunion, nearly two months ago now. She chewed harder on her lip. He was spending more time at home, though.

'There's a very good restaurant where we could have lunch down by the river,' Dracco was saying.

If she was to refuse to go with him he might be tempted to ask Lisa. The sheer savagery of the jealousy that gored her made her catch her breath. What was the matter? She ought to hate and despise him for what he was doing, for what he was, instead of… What she was feeling was totally illogical! But then, when had love ever been anything else?

Helplessly Imogen watched him. She could feel the sheer intensity of her love melting her resistance.

'When were you thinking of leaving?' she asked him.

'Now,' Dracco told her promptly, putting the last of the groceries away and then coming towards her. 'Ready?'

His hand was beneath her elbow, guiding her back towards the door. What was the point of denying herself the opportunity of being with him when she wanted it so much? When she wanted him so much, she acknowledged with a small, sensual shudder of pleasure at his touch.

'No, not a pond.'

Imogen could feel the sharp look Dracco gave her as she shook her head in rejection of the garden designer's suggestion for a water feature in the patio area proposed for the garden.

'But you love the garden's existing formal fish pond,' Dracco reminded her with a small frown.

'Yes, I do,' Imogen agreed. She could feel her face starting to burn self-consciously as both men looked at her, waiting for her to explain her rejection. 'I was thinking that a pond so close to the house might not be a good idea,' she began hesitantly, pausing before continuing, 'Small children can drown so easily and quickly in even a few inches of water.'

The young garden designer gave a small, approving nod.

'Of course. I should have realised. And there are some totally child-safe alternatives that we could discuss—water bubbling over pebbles; that sort of thing.'

As she listened to him Imogen was conscious of Dracco's silence and his concentrated gaze, although he waited until she had thanked the designer for his suggestions and moved out of his earshot before bending his head to murmur speculatively in her ear, 'There isn't anything you want to tell me, is there, Imo?'

'No.' Imogen knew she sounded both defensive and flustered. 'When there is something…anything…to tell you then I will.'

'I'm sure that you will,' Dracco agreed urbanely. 'After all, there's no way you're going to put yourself in the position of having to have sex again with me—unnecessarily—is there? Mmm?'

Imogen gave him a seethingly angry look. How dared he torment her like this, mocking her for her vulnerability to him, for her desire for him?

He had taken to coming to bed later, so late, in fact, that by the time he eventually did so she had fallen into an exhausted sleep.

And she knew why, of course. He didn't want to sleep with her because he really wanted Lisa. How could he be so cruel, so uncaring of her feelings? Surely he must know just how much he was hurting her?

Their lunch, followed by a walk along the river, and then well over an hour here at the garden centre had left her feeling unusually tired. She had noticed increasingly over the last few days a lassitude which tended to overwhelm her during the afternoons, sometimes to such an extent that she had actually fallen asleep. Luckily the hot, sunny spell of weather they were having meant that she could lie in the garden on a sun lounger and doze off to sleep under the pretext of sunbathing.

Now, as they walked back to Dracco's car, Imogen could feel her footsteps lagging, and despite her frantic attempts to do so she couldn't quite manage to smother a sleepy yawn.

Dracco, of course, saw it and stopped in mid-stride to frown down at her and demand, 'Tired?'

'It disturbs my sleep when you come to bed so late,' Imogen parried.

'If that's meant to be a hint that you'd like me to come to bed earlier...?'

'It isn't,' Imogen denied immediately. 'Why should I want you to? I'm not the one who forced this marriage on you, Dracco.'

Before he could retaliate she hurried ahead of him, and then ignored him when he caught up with her just as she reached the car.

A young family of three small children and their father were playing with a ball, and as she watched them Imogen was suddenly reminded of the street children in Rio. Not that these well-fed and obviously very much loved children in front of her were anything like Rio's unwanted orphans, but seeing them made her think about her old life and the people she had shared it with.

Unexpectedly she suddenly ached for the stalwart comfort of Sister Maria's calm wisdom.

Imogen woke up with a start. She had actually gone to bed after their return from the garden centre, claiming not totally untruthfully that she had a headache. Having showered and re-dressed, she headed lethargically for the stairs. Soon now she was going to have to put her suspicions to the test, not that she really had any doubts that she was pregnant, but once that knowledge was 'official' then she was honour-bound to make it known to Dracco.

Normally a couple looked forward to the arrival of a child, especially a wanted child, as an event that would bring them closer together, but in their case Imogen was certain that it would have totally the opposite effect. Once she had given him the child he wanted there would be no room in Dracco's life for her.

Halfway down the stairs, where they turned at a right angle to themselves, there was a small half-landing with a tall, deep window that overlooked the driveway. The stained glass in it had a soft-hued richness which had always delighted Imogen. She stopped automatically to look through it and then froze as she recognised the familiar figure of her

stepmother picking her way from her car to the front door
on spindly high-heeled sandals.

So far as she knew, Lisa had not visited the house since
their confrontation.

Instinctively Imogen stepped back out of sight as Lisa
rang the front-doorbell. She heard the study door open and
held her breath as she listened to Dracco's strong masculine
footsteps and felt the small surge of early-evening air waft
into the hallway as he opened the door.

'Lisa.' His voice was expressionless, but in a way that
dragged sharp, poisoned nails of anguish across Imogen's
heart.

Since Lisa's previous visit to the house Imogen had not
confronted the role she knew her stepmother had played and
she suspected continued to play in Dracco's life. But her
awareness of it shadowed every aspect of their life together.
Lying awake on her own in their bed at night she had tormented herself with the knowledge that Dracco was staying
away from her because he really wanted to be with Lisa.

She had known exactly why Dracco had not wanted her
love, and why he had been so insistent that all they had done
together was to have sex, a physical coupling devoid of emotion. He kept his love only for Lisa. And yet, knowing that,
she had still wanted him, responded to him, stupidly allowed
herself to believe in the impossible fantasy that she, Imogen,
had to mean something to him, that he couldn't possibly be
with her if she didn't. She had even been so desperate for
his love that she had allowed him to mock her for her own
helpless desire for him.

Every time he taunted her about it she sensed some deep,
hidden, ambivalent feeling behind his words. Because he
resented her for taking what should only be given to the
woman he loved?

Imogen could feel herself starting to shiver and then to

shudder, deep, racking manifestations of her traumatic emotional pain. She could hear Lisa saying with soft seductiveness, 'I knew you'd be expecting me.'

And then the study door was closing, shutting her out, enclosing both of them in their own private world.

If she closed her eyes Imogen could see them in it... could see the way the late-afternoon sun would illuminate dust motes of gold through the long sash windows either side of the traditional fireplace her father had insisted on keeping. The desk, an antique partners' desk at which she could vividly remember both her father and Dracco sitting, working amicably together, was in one corner of the room. Behind it were floor-to-ceiling bookcases. To one side of the fireplace was a large leather chair, and in front of it a narrow sofa, long enough for her to lie down on at full stretch, something which she had done often in the early days after her mother's death.

Was Dracco laying Lisa down on that sofa now, slowly, lovingly, longingly undressing her whilst she...?

Imogen gave a low, tortured moan of pure anguish.

She wanted to scream, to cry, to claw at her very flesh for so foolishly and wantonly betraying her, to tear her treacherous heart out of her body, to sear and seal her emotions so she would never feel again, but most of all she wanted to run as far and as fast away from Dracco as she could. Just as she had done once before.

But she wasn't a mere girl any more and answerable only to herself. She was a woman now, with responsibilities. Briefly, her hand brushed her stomach. A single tear rolled down her cheek. Imogen lifted her head.

She was Dracco's wife. He had married her of his own free will. She was carrying his child, their child. This house held so many precious happy memories for her of her life with her own parents. Her mother and her father. She fully intended that her child would enjoy the security of being loved by both its parents. No matter what the personal cost to herself.

And if that meant outfacing Lisa, standing her ground and claiming her rights as Dracco's wife, then that was exactly what she was going to do.

Lisa might have his love, but she was the one who would have his child!

CHAPTER EIGHT

'YOU'RE VERY QUIET; is something wrong?'

'I was just thinking about the past and my father—and Lisa,' Imogen responded with deliberate emphasis, shaking her head as Dracco indicated the bottle of wine he had just opened.

She had visited her doctor earlier in the day and had had her pregnancy confirmed.

Whilst she suspected that the odd glass of red wine would not do her baby any harm, she was not prepared to take any risks. Already he or she was infinitely precious to her, and part of the reason she had been thinking about her father. He would have so loved being a grandfather, especially when Dracco, whom he had valued so much, was that baby's father.

But then, unlike her, her father had not known the truth about the man he had treated as a son. He had not known how Dracco had betrayed him with his own wife.

'Lisa never really loved my father. She only married him for his money.'

It must be the confirmation of her pregnancy that was making her feel so emotional, Imogen decided, that and the fact that her baby's father didn't love her. There had been another woman in the surgery at the same time as Imogen, very heavily pregnant and accompanied by her partner, who had watched her with such a look of tenderness and adoration that Imogen had felt her eyes sting. When the woman's hand had rested against her stomach he had lifted it to his lips, kissing it before replacing it on her belly and then covering it with his own.

'Lisa was a lot younger than your father, Imo.'

'Oh, of course you would take her side, wouldn't you?' Imogen stormed.

Dracco had been about to raise the glass of wine he had just poured himself to his lips, but now he put it down, frowning as he did so.

'I have no idea what all this is about, Imo,' he began austerely. 'You know—'

'I know that I saw Lisa here in this house and that you haven't said one word about her visit to me,' Imogen told him trenchantly.

'You saw her?' Dracco's frown deepened, his voice sharpening.

'Yes. What did you do, Dracco? Ring her up and tell her that it was safe to come over? That I was asleep? That you were tired of making love—oh, I'm sorry, having *sex*—with a woman you didn't really want and certainly didn't love? A woman who wasn't her? Well, this is my home, Dracco, and just so long as it is there is no way I intend to tolerate you entertaining your…your mistress in it…'

Imogen broke off and took a deep breath to steady her voice, but before she could continue Dracco was demanding tersely, 'What on earth are you talking about?'

Imogen couldn't believe his gall. It left her breathless, mute with a fury that visibly shook her body.

'You know perfectly well what I'm talking about,' she threw at him when she could finally speak. 'I'm talking about the affair you are having with Lisa, the affair you were having with her when she was married to my father and which you have continued to have with her even though both of you have married elsewhere.'

She could see the muscles clenching in Dracco's jaw. He didn't like what she was saying—well, tough! How did he think she felt? How did he think her father would have felt?

'You think I'm having an affair with Lisa?'

He had to be working very hard to project such a convincing air of stunned disbelief, Imogen acknowledged, which just showed how important it was for him to keep his relationship with Lisa a secret.

'No, Dracco,' she told him calmly, 'I don't think you are having an affair with my stepmother; I know you are. Lisa told me so herself, on the morning of our wedding.'

There was a long, tense pause before Dracco asked grimly, 'Is that why you ran away?'

'What do *you* think?' Imogen responded bitterly, shaking her head before he could say anything else and telling him, 'That's it, Dracco. I'm not prepared to discuss it any further.' She felt amazed and awed by her own unexpected self-control—and the way she had taken charge of the whole situation. 'What's past is past, and it's the future that concerns me now. A future which you have forced on us both. I want to make it clear that I will not tolerate Lisa's presence here in this house. Not whilst I am expected to live here!'

Now she was going to tell him about the baby, their baby. And she was going to beg him, no, demand that he think about the effect his continued relationship with Lisa would have on the child he claimed he wanted so much! But before she could begin to speak the telephone suddenly rang.

Dracco turned away from her as he picked up the receiver, quite patently not wanting Imogen to overhear anything of the call. Because it was from Lisa? Suppressing her instinctive urge to wrench the phone from him and break the connection between them, Imogen turned instead and hurried into the hallway.

Where was her bravery now? she derided herself as she battled against her own emotions. Why wasn't she challenging Dracco? Was it because she was desperately afraid that she would lose, that he would choose Lisa above their baby?

There was no way she could allow herself to become the pathetic, unwanted, cheated-on wife of a man who found his pleasure with and gave his love to another woman, she reminded herself determinedly.

And if Dracco chose to ignore the demands she intended to make, the battle lines she intended to draw? Imogen could feel herself start to tremble. Her earlier buoyant surge of exhilaration had drained away, leaving her feeling afraid and vulnerable, not for herself but for her baby, who deserved surely to be loved by both its parents.

'Imo.'

She froze as Dracco came out into the hall and called her name.

'I've got to go to London, but when I come back there are things that you and I need to discuss, certain misconceptions you appear to have that need to be addressed and corrected.'

'I see. When will you be back?' She held her breath, even though she suspected she already knew the answer.

'I'm not sure.' Dracco's tone was cautious. 'I may have to stay overnight.'

May? Imogen only just managed to stop herself from laughing bitterly out loud. Even if the formality of his language hadn't been enough to tell her how furiously angry he was, the look on his face did, but Imogen had far more to concern her than Dracco's anger. Like, for instance, the source of that telephone call he had been so anxious for her not to overhear. It had to have been from Lisa! And now he was going to London to see her and no doubt spend the night with her!

She hated herself for not having the courage to challenge him. Was this what love did to you? Made you vulnerable? Afraid? Being unable to put her suspicions into words made her feel humiliated and ashamed.

Now, more than at any other time, surely, she ought to be able to turn to Dracco for his support and protection.

But she didn't seem to matter to him!

The sight of his own grim-faced expression as he glanced in his driving mirror only reinforced what Dracco already felt. It had stunned him to hear Imogen accusing him of having an affair with Lisa. Lisa might consider herself to be beautiful and desirable, but so far as Dracco was concerned she was ugly, ugly inside with malice, greed and selfishness. He had always suspected that Imogen's father had regretted marrying her, although he had been far too loyal to say so. His mouth tightened on the memory of the accusation Imogen had flung at him that he had been having an affair with Lisa whilst she was married to her father. Did Imogen really believe he was capable of that kind of disloyalty?

On the morning of their marriage when Imo had demanded to know if there was a woman in his life whom he loved he had assumed that she had been talking about herself. The horror and rejection in her voice and her eyes when he'd told her of his feelings had made him curse himself under his breath for what he had done to her.

The youthful infatuation she had had for him had quite plainly been destroyed by the unwanted reality of his love for her, a love which he had already been guiltily conscious she was really too young to be burdened with.

When she had run away from him that belief had been compounded. Dracco's eyes darkened with remembered pain. He had been on the verge of running after her when Henry had collapsed, and in the panic which had ensued everyone had automatically looked to him to take charge.

By the time he had been free to go after Imo it had been too late. She had already left the country.

He had tracked her down, of course, his concern for her as great as his searing anguish at losing her.

He had kept track of her ever since—for her sake and for what he owed her father. And it was for Imogen's sake that he was driving to London now, when he would far rather have been at home with her, explaining to her, reassuring her that Lisa was the last woman he would ever be interested in. Because there was and could only ever be one woman he loved and that woman was Imo herself.

However, his telephone call had been from the same agency he had used to keep track of Imogen during her absence, and they had rung to inform him as a matter of urgency that it looked as though the shelter was going to be closed down.

It seemed that the man who owned the building and the land on which the shelter stood wanted to sell the land on, and he was using strong-arms tactics to try to frighten the sisters into giving up their lease on the property.

Dracco knew just how much the shelter meant to Imogen, and he wanted to do everything he could to help save it, even if that meant helping to find and finance new premises for it.

He was driving to London so that he could, without Imogen discovering what was happening, negotiate some way of keeping the shelter open. No matter what it cost him.

Despairingly Imogen stood in the empty silence of the hallway. Dracco had left her to go to Lisa. What was she going to do?

She felt weak, defeated, frightened and alone. Her earlier confidence and bravado had completely left her. She desperately wanted to be with people who cared about her, people she felt secure with. Suddenly she missed Rio, and the sisters, the people she had known there—desperately.

What was going to happen to her and, more important, what was going to happen to her baby?

He or she needed to be loved. To be with people who cared—and for the right reasons!

Imogen knew exactly what she had to do!

This time there was no urgency, no sense of flight or desperation, just a chilling, calm acceptance of what had to be.

She packed carefully, and even managed to be controlled enough to ring ahead to Heathrow to book her seat on the first available flight to Rio.

It was leaving just before midnight, and she had plenty of time to get there.

Midnight. No doubt by then Dracco would be with Lisa in London at his apartment. In bed with her, no doubt, swearing eternal love to her.

Clutching her body, Imogen raced to the bathroom, her stomach churning with nausea.

'She has that effect on me too,' she comforted her still flat stomach sadly. 'He doesn't deserve you, my darling, no matter how much he wants you. I'm going to take us both somewhere we can be happy together without him.'

Even as she whispered the words to the new life growing inside her Imogen was aware of a small inner voice she couldn't quite silence that was objecting to what she was saying. It reminded her that although Dracco might not love her, that did not mean that he would not love his child, and that she had no real right to make decisions that would separate that child from Dracco forever.

She did not want to listen to that kind of criticism and she wasn't going to.

The taxi she had ordered arrived. She was travelling light—everything Dracco had bought for her, except this time her rings, she was leaving behind.

One small tear glittered in her eye as she closed the front door behind her. Refusing to look back, she got in the taxi.

Dracco grimaced, rubbing his hand over his tired eyes as he replaced the telephone receiver and switched on the computer on his desk.

He had managed, he hoped, to avert the crisis with the shelter—Dracco had managed to persuade the landowner to sell the shelter and the land to him, at a vastly inflated price, of course, but he didn't regret having to pay for it, not knowing how happy it would make Imogen. However, there were still certain ends he had to tie up, e-mails he had to send, people he had to contact—lawyers, accountants, bankers—but first...

He checked his watch; Imogen should still be up, and suddenly he desperately needed to hear her voice. He had hated having to leave her without talking through the whole ridiculous misunderstanding about Lisa, but he had felt that he needed time to explain everything properly to her. However, right now his need to speak to her was overwhelming everything else. He could at least tell her how much he loved her.

Dracco frowned. He had made three attempts to telephone Imogen without success. She could, of course, be asleep, or simply refusing to answer the telephone, but instinctively he knew that there was a more serious reason for her silence.

Without wasting time analysing his feelings, he reached for his car keys and headed for the door.

Heathrow was busy. Imogen had plenty of time before she needed to check in.

To distract herself from the pain of what she was having

to do, she tried to make mental plans for the practicalities she would need to address once she arrived in Rio. Initially she would have to book into a hotel. Someone had now taken over her old apartment but even if they hadn't with a baby to consider she would have had to find somewhere more suitable to live, preferably a small house with its own garden.

She would also, no doubt, have to make arrangements to retain enough of the income from her share of the business to support herself and the baby, and perhaps even go back to teaching as well, instead of working full-time for the shelter.

At least there would be one advantage to her returning to Rio: her son or daughter would be bilingual. And yet for some reason, instead of making her smile, this recognition made her eyes fill with hot, acid tears.

It was nearly time to check in. Automatically she picked up her bag, and then realised that she needed to visit the ladies' cloakroom—a small side-effect of her pregnancy.

There was a little girl leaving the cloakroom at the same time as Imogen; blonde-haired and dressed in trendy denims, she appeared to be on her own, and instinctively Imogen kept a protective eye on her.

As they emerged onto the concourse the little girl ran towards a man who was standing several yards away.

Imogen could hear the love in her voice as she exclaimed, 'Daddy!' And she could see too the answering love in the man's eyes as he held tightly on to her, swinging her up into his arms.

'Come on, we'd better get you on your flight. If you miss it your mother will never let you come and see me again.'

Now Imogen could hear pain and anger in his voice and, transfixed, she stood where she was watching them anxiously.

'I don't want to go back. I want to stay here with you,' the little girl was saying, and Imogen could hear the tears

in her voice and see more in her father's eyes as he shook
his head and started to carry her towards the departure gate.

Imogen felt as though she had been struck a mortal blow.
One day would her child be like that little girl? Less than
half a dozen yards away from her she could see another
small family group, two adults—a man and a woman—and
two children this time, two children with parents who loved
them. Did she really want any less than that for her child?

If she went back to Rio now, and brought her child up
alone, denying him or her to Dracco and denying him to
them in return, what would her child ultimately think of
her? Would he or she understand or would they blame her?
Or, even worse in Imogen's eyes, would they simply suffer
in silence, longing for the father they did not have?

She thought about the relationship she had had with her
own parents, especially with her father. There was no way
she could deny her child the right to have that magical, wonderful bond, to experience the love she had experienced.
Dracco would love their child, his child; Imogen knew that
instinctively. She took one step and then another, slowly at
first, and then more quickly until she was almost running.
She stopped only when the stitch in her side commanded
her to, and her lungs were full of the sharp, acrid smell of
the diesel fumes of the taxis outside the airport building.

It normally took two hours for Dracco to drive home from
London—less when he did so late at night, but on this occasion he was unlucky. On this particular night an extra-
wide load of dangerous chemicals was travelling along the
motorway ahead of him at a speed which meant that it took
Dracco over three hours to reach home.

When he did so he found the house in darkness and Imogen gone. Gone without any kind of explanation, any note.
Her hairbrush and a bottle of the perfume she always

wore were still on her dressing-table. The perfume bottle
had fallen over and Dracco could smell Imogen's familiar
scent all around him.

He closed his eyes, his throat tight with emotion, raw
with helpless anguish and fear. He could still see the look
in her eyes when she had accused him of loving Lisa. Dear
God, how could any woman be so blind? And how could
any man be so stupid?

Why? Why hadn't he stopped to tell her the truth? Why
the hell had he gone off like that, leaving her alone and
vulnerable?

She believed him to be guilty of the worst kind of disloyalty, to her and to her father. And there were other issues at
stake, such as the way he had treated her, the things he had
said to her—and the things he hadn't said.

CHAPTER NINE

IMOGEN FELT HER heart starting to thump nervously as her taxi pulled into the drive. It was one in the morning, but all the house lights were on and Dracco's car was parked outside.

He had come back. He wasn't spending the night in London with Lisa!

As she got out of the taxi she had to fight against the feeling of dizziness filling her.

She was becoming used now to that disconcerting feeling of giddiness she sometimes experienced, especially when she first got up. But at least she wasn't actually being sick.

'You're a very good baby,' she whispered unsteadily to her stomach as she paid off the taxi and fought to hold on to her courage, 'a very good baby, and your mummy and your daddy are going to love you so very much.'

Had she been a fool to come back? From her own point of view, probably, she acknowledged as she opened the front door. But if Dracco dared to think that he could supplant her in her baby's life with Lisa then she was going to make sure he soon learned otherwise. She and the baby came as a package...a twosome, and if he wanted to make that a three-some then he had to take the pair of them together.

It was amazing, the strength and determination that being a mother could give you, she acknowledged wryly as she came to an unsteady halt in the hallway, her heart pounding.

The study door started to open and Dracco came out. He looked as though he had undergone the most soul-destroying trauma. Dracco, whom she had never seen looking less than totally in control. His shirt was crumpled, and he needed a shave. His eyes were even slightly bloodshot!

Refusing to give in to the longing weakening her body, Imogen reminded herself of the decision she had just made and, drawing herself up, she fixed him with a look of angry distaste before demanding accusingly, 'I don't suppose I need to ask who you went to London to see?'

Dracco was looking at her with the kind of blank-eyed shock more appropriate, surely, to a man who had seen a ghost than one who had returned home from a rendezvous with his lover.

'Imo! You've come back. Oh, thank God, thank God!'

His voice sounded cracked, hoarse, and the look in his eyes as he strode towards her suddenly made her heart flip over inside her chest. Instinctively she backed away from him.

'I'm tired, Dracco,' she told him. 'I want to go to bed.'

'We need to talk.' He was insistent but Imogen shook her head. She knew she was far closer to emotional exhaustion than she dared to admit. If they started to talk now, to argue, she knew she wouldn't have the strength to say the things she wanted to say.

'No, not now,' she refused sharply. 'Not now, Dracco. Tomorrow.'

As much as he ached to beg her to listen to him, to find out where she had gone and why she had returned, to tell her how much he loved her and plead with her never, ever to leave him again, Dracco could see how vulnerable she was, and he wanted to protect her, to put her needs before his own.

'Very well,' he agreed heavily. 'But,' he told her, and,

even though he gave her a wry smile, Imogen sensed that he meant it, 'I shall be locking all the doors and keeping the keys, Imo. So no more running away. I want you to promise me that.'

'I promise,' Imogen conceded tiredly as she headed for the stairs, praying that Dracco wouldn't make any attempt to follow her.

When he didn't, and when she finally closed the door of her old childhood bedroom behind her a part of her was weakly disappointed that he hadn't followed her. That he hadn't taken her in his arms and…and what? Face facts, she told herself wearily as she prepared for bed. Grow up, Imo. He doesn't love you. He loves Lisa.

'Can you answer that?' Imogen asked Dracco. 'I'm going to put the kettle on.'

Imogen had just arrived downstairs in the kitchen, having overslept, to find Dracco already there.

As he had said himself, they needed to talk, and the most important thing they had to talk about was the fact that she was carrying his child. Their baby!

Did she have the strength to concentrate on that all-important fact and to negotiate an acknowledgement from Dracco that their child had to come first—with both of them?

As he answered the phone Dracco kept on looking at Imogen, greedily, hungrily, absorbing the reality of her presence. He loved her so much!

What had happened? Why had she come back? Absorbed in his own thoughts, he took several seconds to realise what the caller on the other end of the telephone line was saying to him.

'Yes, I'll pass that message on to her,' he agreed quietly,

his gaze still fixed on Imogen, who had turned away from the kettle to look at him.

He was watching her as though he had never seen her before, as though he was... Dizzy with the implausibility, the impossibility, surely, of what she seemed to be seeing in his eyes, Imogen stood still.

Silently Dracco replaced the receiver.

'What is it?' Imogen asked him uncertainly.

'That was the doctor's surgery,' Dracco announced with heavy quietness. 'They wanted to tell you that they've made an appointment for you at the hospital for your first ante-natal clinic. You're pregnant with my child, and you didn't tell me!'

For the first time in her life Imogen did something she didn't think women did except in novels—she fainted!

When she came round she was lying on the sofa in the study, with Dracco leaning over her.

In the few seconds it had taken him to assimilate the information that Imogen was pregnant he had come from hope to despair as he recognised the reason why she had decided not to leave him. Imogen had her father's old-fashioned morals. She would not be able to leave him and take from him the child he had bargained with her to have. He had known that all along, and believed too that it would be impossible for her to leave her child either, which would mean that she would have to stay with him.

But now suddenly the realisation that she was here because she had conceived his child, rather than because she wanted to be, left a sour taste in his mouth.

Imogen shivered slightly, nervously aware of the way that Dracco was watching her and of the brooding, almost despairing look in his eyes. Because he had changed his mind? He didn't want a child by her any more?

'You're pregnant.' Dracco's voice was flat and empty of any expression for her to read.

'Yes,' she acknowledged. Please, God, don't let her cry, but this wasn't how such news should be broken—or received. So what had she expected, she challenged herself as her senses started to clear, a fanfare of trumpets proclaiming an ode to joy? Dracco gathering her up in his arms, his eyes full of tender worship and adoration?

Maybe that was unrealistic, but some expression of pleasure wouldn't have gone amiss, for their baby's sake if not for her own.

'Is that why you didn't leave—why you came back?'

'Yes,' she conceded as she swung her feet to the floor and then stood up. There was no way she intended to have this discussion with Dracco whilst in the disadvantageous position of lying down as he stood over her.

She intended to ensure that from now on whenever they met in the arena of conflict that she suspected wearily was going to be their marriage it was going to be on equal terms.

'I wanted to leave you, Dracco. You're having an affair with...with Lisa.' She stopped, her voice unsteady. 'But there was this little girl with her father, and suddenly I couldn't!'

Imogen turned away, but not before Dracco had seen the sheen of her tears in her eyes.

'Imo.'

Imogen tensed as Dracco grasped her hands in his, refusing to let her go, even though she tried desperately to pull away from him. She could feel his thumbs caressing the vulnerable undersides of her wrists in a way that sent hot shivers of pleasure racing up her arms.

'I don't know where you've got the idea that I'm having an affair with Lisa, but I can assure you that nothing could be further from the truth.'

That he could lie to her so uncaringly infuriated Imogen. Did he really think she was that much of a fool?

'No?' she challenged him. 'Then why did you go to London last night?'

Dracco shook his head, mentally cursing beneath his breath. Until everything was finally legalised, every 'i' dotted, every 't' crossed, he didn't want to tell her what had been going on, just in case something should go wrong.

'I can't tell you that, I'm afraid, Imo, but I can promise you that it wasn't to see Lisa.'

Imogen curled her lip in acid contempt as she pulled herself free of him.

'I don't believe you. Lisa told me on the morning of our wedding that you loved her. She challenged me to ask you about it. And she's confirmed her relationship with you to me since. I don't know which of you I despise the most. I suppose it must be you, if only because I never liked Lisa, whilst you…'

Imogen paused and then swallowed. What did it matter what she admitted to Dracco now about her past feelings for him? After all, she was pretty sure he must have known all about her foolish teenage crush on him.

Determinedly she looked up into his eyes and told him as calmly as she could, 'I adored you, Dracco. I put you up on a pedestal. I believed in you and I…' She stopped, appalled to discover how emotional she was becoming. 'After losing my parents, discovering how wrong I was about you was the most hurtful and traumatic thing I have ever experienced.'

She wasn't being totally honest with him, Imogen acknowledged as she looked away from him. The deaths of her mother and father had hurt, but after the immediacy of her shock and loss had worn off she had been left with the comforting knowledge that they had loved her.

In recognising Dracco's treachery she had been left with no such comfort whatsoever!

Dracco surveyed Imogen's downbent head for several seconds whilst he struggled to control the urgency of his longing to take her in his arms and hold her there until he had convinced her just how wrong she was.

'Do you really think I would have betrayed your father's trust like that?' he asked Imogen quietly.

'When love is involved other loyalties can sometimes cease to matter,' Imogen responded emptily.

Talking like this was stirring up so many painful memories inside her; too many.

'What I can't understand or forgive, Dracco, is that you were willing to marry me just for the sake of the business, even though you loved Lisa. And the way you lied to me about it… You did lie to me, didn't you?' she challenged him.

Dracco turned to stare out of the study window.

'Yes,' he admitted. 'I did. But not in the way that you think, Imo.' He heard her gasp and turned round just in time to see her almost running out of the room.

Oh, she was such a fool, Imogen derided herself as she hurried into the garden. She had to be to allow herself to still feel so much hurt over Dracco's behaviour towards her.

Instinctively she headed for her mother's rose garden, seeking its solace and comfort.

How could she possibly love a man who could so easily lie, and not just to her? Look at the way he had denied Lisa! Her hand stilled on the rose she had been touching.

What did she mean, love? She did not love Dracco.

Liar, a knowing inner voice taunted her. Of course you do; you've never stopped loving him and you never will!

'No!' A sharp pain slid through her heart. No, it couldn't be true. But of course she knew that it was.

* * *

Dracco frowned. Should he go after Imogen, make her listen whilst he tried to explain just how wrong she was and why? If he did, would she listen? He might have got what he had wanted for so long, Dracco acknowledged, but there was no real satisfaction in knowing that he was forcing Imogen to stay with him. Her presence in his life through force was not what he wanted; not in his life, or his bed. No, what he wanted was for her to be with him because she wanted to be, because she loved him.

His telephone rang and he went automatically to answer it, forcing himself to concentrate on what the client on the other end of the line was saying to him.

An unfamiliar car was coming up the drive, and Imogen shaded her eyes from the sun as it stopped and the driver got out. She smiled as she recognised David Bryant, Dracco's solicitor.

He was smiling back at her.

'How is your wife?' she asked him.

'Very pregnant and very hot.' He laughed. 'She hasn't got very long to go now, though. She wants Dracco to be one of the baby's godparents: she thinks the story of his love for you is very romantic.'

Imogen looked at him.

'I hope you don't mind me telling her,' he added uncertainly. 'My mother told me about it; she had heard it from my uncle. He thought a lot of Dracco, and of course Dracco consulted him after your father's death about what he should do. My uncle knew that your father made Dracco promise not to tell you about his feelings for you until you were over twenty-one. But he could see that your father's untimely death had changed things, and that you desperately needed someone in your life to protect you. According to my mother, my uncle fully endorsed Dracco's decision to ask you to marry him so that he could protect you and your inheritance.'

He avoided looking at Imogen as he continued, looking embarrassed, 'Of course, I don't know the whole situation—my mother has always maintained that you ran away because you were young and afraid, and suffering from young girl's wedding nerves—but it must have been hard for Dracco to lose you like that when he loved you so much.'

There was just the faintest hint of a gentle accusation in his voice.

'Still, at least it's all worked out well for you both now. My mother claims that she always knew that you'd be reconciled. Is Dracco in, by the way? I've got some papers for him to sign.' He was looking a bit self-conscious now, as though aware he'd said too much.

Her head was spinning with the shock of his revelations. Automatically she nodded and then watched as he walked towards the house. Then, very slowly and thoughtfully, she followed him.

Wearily Dracco got up from behind his desk. The house felt still and silent. Dracco had spent the hours since David Bryant had left thinking about the past—and the future—and questioning the role he had played in Imogen's life. Meanwhile he had mentally drawn up two tables, one listing the reasons why they should stay married and the other listing those why they shouldn't.

And from Imogen's point of view that list weighed heavily in favour of him setting her free, giving back to her the right to make her own decisions and choices.

He and Imogen needed to talk and there was no point in putting off what had to be said.

He found her upstairs in her old bedroom. She was sitting

on the window seat with her knees drawn up into her body
and her arms wrapped around them, a pose he remembered
from her childhood.

Silently Imogen watched as Dracco came into her bedroom. She had come here after she had left the rose garden,
moving like someone in a dream, needing somewhere safe
to retreat to, somewhere she could examine and analyse her
chaotic thoughts in peace.

David Bryant's comments had given her a tantalising
glimpse into a situation she had never known existed; a
situation, moreover, which totally changed her own inter-
pretation of past events.

It wasn't hard for her to accept that her father would
have guessed how she had felt about Dracco; after all, she
had never tried to keep it a secret. But David's inference
that Dracco had loved her and that her father had made him
promise to keep that love a secret...

Ask him if there is a woman whom he loves, Lisa had
challenged her on her wedding day, and she had done just
that, and Dracco...

Could she have got it wrong, made a huge misjudge-
ment and been encouraged to make it by Lisa? What if she
had? What if the someone Dracco had loved had been not
Lisa but her?

Her heart somersaulted and thudded so heavily against
her chest wall that her whole body shook with the agitation
of her emotions.

'Imogen.'

The sound of her full name on Dracco's lips when he
nearly always called her 'Imo' seemed somehow portentous.

She took a deep breath, her gaze searching his face, looking for some clue as to what he might be feeling, something
to guide her, show her, but there was nothing. She would
have to rely on her own intuition, her own need.

'Why did you marry me, Dracco?'

She could see that it wasn't the question he had been expecting. Even so, she noticed how he turned slightly away from her before he answered it, almost as though he didn't want her to be able to see his expression.

'You know why,' was his careful response.

'I certainly thought I knew why,' Imogen agreed quietly, getting off the window seat and coming to stand in front of him so that she could see his face. 'I was in the garden when David Bryant arrived. He told me...' She paused, wondering if she had the courage to go on. And then she thought of her baby, their baby, and knew that what she was doing wasn't just for herself, that it wasn't just her own future that was at stake, or her own happiness.

'Is it true that my father made you promise not to tell me you loved me until I was over twenty-one?' she challenged him.

At first she thought that he wasn't going to reply, and that alone was enough to make her heart start to hammer with fierce pleasure. After all, if what David had told her wasn't true then Dracco would have denied it immediately, wouldn't he?

'Is it, Dracco?' she persisted.

'Yes,' Dracco admitted tersely.

Dracco had loved her... Joy sang through her whole body, a glorious, empowering surge of deep female wonderment.

'Your father knew how I felt about you,' he told her. 'I couldn't have hidden it from him; it was hard enough hiding it from you, especially when...' He paused, his eyes dark and bleak, as though he was looking into a secret place that haunted him. 'He said that even though you had a teenage crush on me you were far too young to commit yourself to any kind of relationship with me, any kind of future. He said that such a relationship would be unfair to you, unbalanced, untenable, and that you needed time to grow up, to learn something of life and yourself.

'He knew that my feelings wouldn't change, but he was concerned that you should have the opportunity to change yours, and I agreed with him. Not that it was easy, not with you.' He broke off and shook his head. 'I ached for you so badly that sometimes…' He stopped. 'And then your father died.

'I didn't want to break my promise to him, but I had no choice. I talked to Henry about it, and he urged me to go ahead. He said that under the circumstances your father would have understood. You were only eighteen and so damned innocent; I knew that.' He stopped again. 'As it was, I hardly dared trust myself around you, but I had to honour at least part of my promise to your father. And so…'

'And so you planned for our marriage to be in name only,' Imogen supplied softly for him.

'Yes. I told myself that somehow I would find a way of waiting until you were twenty-one. You wanted to go to university. But then when we came out of the church you told me that you knew how I felt about you, and then…' he paused and looked directly at her '…then you ran away, leaving me in no doubt as to what you felt about being loved by me.'

'I didn't run away because you loved me, Dracco,' Imogen told him shakily. 'I ran away because I thought you loved someone else—Lisa. That was what she'd implied to me. She said there was someone in your life. She challenged me to ask you. If I had thought for one minute that you loved me then…'

'Then what?' Dracco asked her softly.

'Then.' Betrayingly Imogen's hand strayed towards her stomach as she tried to draw air into her lungs. 'Then right now this baby would probably be our third and not our first.

Why didn't you tell me?' she demanded emotionally. 'You must have known how I felt about you.'

She ached for the years they had lost, the love she had gone without, the pain she had endured.

'You know why. I had promised your father, and I agreed with everything he had said. You were too young. I knew for your own sake I had to let you go. Not that I ever really did,' he admitted. 'I kept tabs on you the whole time you were in Rio, and when you came back—'

'You rejected me when I tried to tell you I loved you,' Imogen interrupted him sadly.

'Imo, I hated myself for the way I'd forced you into my bed, and because I wanted so much more from you than just sex. Too much more,' he groaned. 'Everything, all of you, just as I wanted you to accept and love all of me.'

She trembled wildly as he reached for her, allowing him to draw her into his arms, against his body.

'Kiss me, Dracco,' she demanded, lifting her face towards him, 'just to prove to me that this is really happening.'

Tenderly his lips brushed hers, but it wasn't enough for Imogen. She placed her hand on his jaw, maintaining the kiss, prolonging it, running her tongue-tip along the firm outline of his lips, tormenting and teasing them until Dracco gave a raw groan and gathered her even closer, close enough for her to feel his arousal.

'I felt so guilty about what I was doing,' Dracco admitted. 'I had forced you into a situation where you had no option other than to go to bed with me.' He stopped as he saw that Imogen was shaking her head.

'I could have refused if I'd really wanted to. Deep down inside it was what I wanted, you were what I wanted, even though initially I wouldn't admit it even to myself. That first morning after we'd made love…' she paused and shook her head in bemusement '…I felt as though finally my life was complete, Dracco, as though finally I was complete. But when I tried to tell you you rejected me, and then I remembered about Lisa.'

'Lisa never meant anything to me. I detested her both for the way she treated you and the way she abused your father's love.'

'She wanted you, though,' Imogen told him.

Dracco grimaced. 'Yes.'

Imogen waited. She knew that if he had tried to deny Lisa's desire for him she would have felt reluctant to trust him completely.

'She came on to me both during her marriage to your father and afterwards, and I suspect that in implying to you that she and I...well, I suspect it was her way of hurting you and getting back at me. She knew how I felt about you. Although how on earth you could believe that I could ever be remotely interested in her...!'

One arm was holding her close to his side whilst his free hand lazily caressed her throat.

'She came here to see you,' Imogen pointed out.

'She gets biannual payments from your father's estate, and she wanted to try to persuade me to increase them. I told her that she was wasting her time. Just as we're wasting time now,' he whispered to her, adding, 'You don't know just how much I want to take you to bed.'

'Don't I?' Imogen teased him, moving closer to him with a small, blissful sigh as his hand cupped her breast, slowly kneading it whilst he started to kiss the soft, vulnerable flesh of her throat.

Tiny, delicious darts of pleasure rushed over her skin, making her shiver visibly and moan his name into the thick darkness of his hair. She could feel him drawing her towards her bedroom door.

'Right now, what I want more than anything I've ever

wanted in the whole of my life is to lay you down on my bed, our bed, and…'

'There's a bed in here,' Imogen reminded him, gesturing towards the narrow bed of her girlhood.

Immediately his eyes darkened. Shaking his head, he told her steadily, 'No…this room was yours as a child, Imo…a girl…and it isn't that child or that girl that I want to make love with now, much as I loved them both. It's you, the woman, my woman, I want to hold in my arms.'

As he very gently drew her through the bedroom door and closed it behind them Imogen felt her eyes smart slightly with tears.

Blinking them away, she touched his mouth with her fingertips. Soon now she would be kissing it, kissing him, touching him every way and being touched by him. As her breathing started to quicken with loving longing she suddenly remembered something.

'Well, if you weren't with Lisa last night, where exactly were you?'

The sombreness of his expression sent a tiny prickle of anxiety tingling down her spine.

Dracco took a deep breath. Now that David had brought the papers to him the future of the shelter was secure, and he could tell Imogen what had been happening without subjecting her to any anxiety. Very slowly he did so.

When he had finished she went quiet, and then Dracco saw the tears burning her eyes.

With a low groan he wrapped her in his arms, rocking her protectively.

'I shouldn't have told you. I've upset you and that's the last thing I wanted to do.'

'No, no, it isn't that,' Imogen reassured him shakily.

'Then what is it?' Dracco demanded.

'It's just knowing that you would do something like that

for me, to make me happy. Me… You didn't know then about the baby.'

'Imo, there isn't anything I wouldn't do for you,' Dracco told her seriously, 'any sacrifice I wouldn't make.'

'Well, was it as good as you were expecting?' Dracco asked softly.

They had just woken up and Dracco was propped up on one elbow as he looked down at her.

Stretching luxuriously, revelling in the sensuality of his naked body next to her own, Imogen told him truthfully, 'No. It was even better…but just to make sure…'

As she traced the line of his jaw and reached up to kiss him Dracco groaned against her mouth.

'Come here, you wonderfully wanton woman,' he demanded as he wrapped his arms around her, 'my wonderfully wanton woman, my wife…my love…my life!'

EPILOGUE

'SHUSH…' TENDERLY IMOGEN rocked her three-month-old son in her arms before turning proudly to listen to Dracco's short speech.

They had flown out to Rio early in the week, especially for the ceremony. Several of the sisters were crying openly as Dracco presented them with his cheque, and Imogen felt rather emotional herself, remembering just what he had done.

Alexander John had been less than three hours old when Dracco had come into her room at the hospital—the room that he had only left an hour earlier, having stayed with her throughout her labour—holding out to her an envelope, plus a small jeweller's box.

She had opened the box first, assuming that the envelope simply held a card, her eyes shining with shocked delight when she had seen the beautiful antique diamond ring Dracco had given her.

Whilst he'd slid it onto her finger he had told her, 'Before you open the envelope, let me tell you that it is not a gift from me to you, or even on account of you, infinitely beloved and precious though you are to me.'

Bemused, Imogen had waited.

'This is a gift on behalf of Alexander to those children who may not receive the love he is guaranteed.'

Imogen had been conscious of Dracco watching her as she opened the envelope and removed the cheque inside it.

It had been made out to the shelter in Rio, and when Imogen had seen the amount of it her hand had trembled.

'Dracco…I know we made a bargain,' she had begun, 'but my feelings for you, our love…'

'You weren't listening properly to me,' he chided her gently. 'This has nothing to do with that, Imo. This is not so much payment of a debt but recognition of a gift. Your gift of love to me, mine to you, ours to our son, your father's to both of us.'

She had cried then, tears of joy and love and gratitude for everything she had been given, but most of all for Dracco himself and for their child.

And now here she was, watching as Dracco formally handed over his cheque to Sister Maria.

She had been talking to one of her old colleagues, who had informed her that it was only thanks to Dracco's timely intervention that the shelter had been saved. They all thought that he was wonderful and that she was very lucky to be married to him, and Imogen fully agreed! In her arms, Alexander gurgled and smiled up at her. Hugging him, she kissed him. He was the image of Dracco, apart from the fact that he had her father's nose.

Dracco, his speech over, was walking towards her. Imogen smiled lovingly at him. Suddenly she couldn't wait for them to be alone together.

As though he had guessed what she was thinking as he reached her, Dracco drew her into his side, bending his head to kiss her. The love in his eyes as he looked at her made her heart flood with joy. He was everything she had ever wanted and everything she would ever want.

'I love you,' she whispered emotionally to him as he released her mouth.

'I love you too, Imo,' he responded tenderly. 'I always have and I always will.'

* * * * *

REQUEST YOUR FREE BOOKS!

 HARLEQUIN *Presents*

 PASSION GUARANTEED SEDUCTION

2 FREE NOVELS PLUS
2 FREE GIFTS!

YES! Please send me 2 FREE Harlequin Presents® novels and my 2 FREE gifts (gifts are worth about $10). After receiving them, if I don't wish to receive any more books, I can return the shipping statement marked "cancel." If I don't cancel, I will receive 6 brand-new novels every month and be billed just $4.30 per book in the U.S. or $4.99 per book in Canada. That's a saving of at least 14% off the cover price! It's quite a bargain! Shipping and handling is just 50¢ per book in the U.S. and 75¢ per book in Canada.* I understand that accepting the 2 free books and gifts places me under no obligation to buy anything. I can always return a shipment and cancel at any time. Even if I never buy another book, the two free books and gifts are mine to keep forever.

106/306 HDN FVRK

Name _____ (PLEASE PRINT) _____

Address _____ Apt. # _____

City _____ State/Prov. _____ Zip/Postal Code _____

Signature (if under 18, a parent or guardian must sign)

Mail to the **Harlequin® Reader Service:**
IN U.S.A.: P.O. Box 1867, Buffalo, NY 14240-1867
IN CANADA: P.O. Box 609, Fort Erie, Ontario L2A 5X3

Are you a current subscriber to Harlequin Presents books and want to receive the larger-print edition?
Call 1-800-873-8635 or visit www.ReaderService.com.

* Terms and prices subject to change without notice. Prices do not include applicable taxes. Sales tax applicable in N.Y. Canadian residents will be charged applicable taxes. Offer not valid in Quebec. This offer is limited to one order per household. Not valid for current subscribers to Harlequin Presents books. All orders subject to credit approval. Credit or debit balances in a customer's account(s) may be offset by any other outstanding balance owed by or to the customer. Please allow 4 to 6 weeks for delivery. Offer available while quantities last.

Your Privacy—The Harlequin® Reader Service is committed to protecting your privacy. Our Privacy Policy is available online at www.ReaderService.com or upon request from the Harlequin Reader Service.

We make a portion of our mailing list available to reputable third parties that offer products we believe may interest you. If you prefer that we not exchange your name with third parties, or if you wish to clarify or modify your communication preferences, please visit us at www.ReaderService.com/consumerschoice or write to us at Harlequin Reader Service Preference Service, P.O. Box 9062, Buffalo, NY 14269. Include your complete name and address.

In Buckshot Hills, Texas, a sexy doctor meets his match in the least likely woman—a beautiful cowgirl looking to reinvent herself....

Enjoy a sneak peek from USA TODAY *bestselling author Judy Duarte's new Harlequin® Special Edition® story,* TAMMY AND THE DOCTOR *,the first book in Byrds of a Feather, a brand-new miniseries launching in March 2013!*

***

Before she could comment or press Tex for more details, a couple of light knocks sounded at the door.

Her grandfather shifted in his bed, then grimaced. "Who is it?"

"Mike Sanchez."

Doc? Tammy's heart dropped to the pit of her stomach with a thud, then thumped and pumped its way back up where it belonged.

"Come on in," Tex said.

Thank goodness her grandfather had issued the invitation, because she couldn't have squawked out a single word.

As Doc entered the room, looking even more handsome than he had yesterday, Tammy struggled to remain cool and calm.

And it wasn't just her heartbeat going wacky. Her feminine hormones had begun to pump in a way they'd never pumped before.

"Good morning," Doc said, his gaze landing first on Tex, then on Tammy.

As he approached the bed, he continued to look at Tammy,

his head cocked slightly.

"What's the matter?" she asked.

"I'm sorry. It's just that your eyes are an interesting shade of blue. I'm sure you hear that all the time."

"Not really." And not from anyone who'd ever mattered. In truth, they were a fairly common color—like the sky or bluebonnets or whatever. "I've always thought of them as run-of-the-mill blue."

"There's nothing ordinary about it. In fact, it's a pretty shade."

The compliment set her heart on end. But before she could think of just the perfect response, he said, "If you don't mind stepping out of the room, I'd like to examine your grandfather."

Of course she minded leaving. She wanted to stay in the same room with Doc for the rest of her natural-born days. But she understood her grandfather's need for privacy.

"Of course." Apparently it was going to take more than simply batting her eyes to woo him, but there was no way Tammy would be able to pull off a makeover by herself. Maybe she could ask her beautiful cousins for help?

She had no idea what to say the next time she ran into them. But somehow, by hook or by crook, she'd have to think of something.

Because she was going to risk untold humiliation and embarrassment by begging them to turn a cowgirl into a lady!

***

Look for TAMMY AND THE DOCTOR from Harlequin® Special Edition® available March 2013

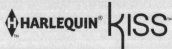